SPIES & HEROES

An International Anthology of Stories

Edited by Dixiane Hallaj and
Marjorie Rommel

S & H Publishing, Inc.
Purcellville, VA

Dixiane Hallaj/S & H Publishing, Inc.
P O Box 456
Purcellville, VA 20134
www.sandhpublishing.com

Publisher's Note: This is a work of fiction. Names, characters, places, and incidents are a product of the individual author's imagination. Locales and public names are sometimes used for atmospheric purposes. Any resemblance to actual people, living or dead, or to businesses, companies, events, institutions, or locales is completely coincidental.

Ordering Information:
Quantity sales. Special discounts are available on quantity purchases by corporations, associations, and others. For details, contact the "Special Sales Department" at the address above.

Spies & Heroes/Dixiane Hallaj and Marjorie Rommel, ed. – 1st ed.
ISBN 978-1-63320-028-9
Ebook ISBN 978-1-63320-029-6

SPIES & HEROES

An International Anthology of Stories

Table of Contents

(NOTE: Spelling and punctuation vary by country of origin)

SUPERMAN CAN FIND ANOTHER GIRL ... 1
Liz Fyne

RUSSELL FEHMER'S WAR 16
Lenora Rain-Lee Good

TESTAMENT OF COURAGE 27
J. J. Knights

THE HERO OF STOLEN TIME 57
Ian Lahey

SPYING ON THE SPY 86
Lisa Cox

THE DORK 112
Diane Hall

HONORING DEBTS 123
Jess Barry

IF I SHOULD DIE BEFORE I WAKE 143
J. D. Kipfer

MURDER ON THE THAMES 154
P. M. Pevato

SILENT NIGHT, STILLE NACHT 185
Maria Elizabeth McVoy

BEST FRIENDS FOREVER 208
Terry Korth Fischer

ALL DOORS OPEN TO A BARD 220
Michelle Markey Butler

LONGEVITY UNDER COVER 248
Margaret Pearce

SPYING ISN'T EASY 260
George G. Moore

DANCING DUTCH COMES HOME...............274
Olympia George

FORGET ME NOT 294
S. M. Kraftchak

YOU ARE A GARDEN...........................316
Jane Buchan

A short story is a précis: an essential essence,
a sharp quality distilled from quantitative narrative.

— *Richard Bunning*

SUPERMAN CAN FIND ANOTHER GIRL

Liz Fyne

My hero was the person I never met.

I stood at the doorstep and waited for him, but he never came, so I invented him from those other people who filled my life but failed to step up.

His name was John, Evan, Matt. Simon. Settle on Simon.

A high school girl like me wasn't so picky about names.

One night I was at home and Simon came to the house and offered to take me for a drive. I was desperate to leave because the voice of my mother droned on in the background, crushing me, and I had fantasies of making her gone and dead. When I opened the door to find Simon on the step the knots in my brain untied and I realized the air was light enough to pass through my lungs.

Breathing. It was a simple thing. It was something you missed.

In the hot summer night we drove from the heat of the valley to the cool of the mountains. In the desert the sky is clear and the stars are bright. The roads wind through darkness, people are sparse, and their home lights are more so.

Simon laughed at the names of towns as we passed them. He imagined them as their own lewd derivatives, and because he thought they were funny, I did too.

Socorro.

"Do you think Orro likes to be sucked?" he asked.

Such is the way a man's mind works.

His left hand was on the steering wheel. His right hand was on my leg.

Simon had a big mouth and a big laugh. He carried a money clip and licked his fingers before he pulled fifty-dollar bills from a great wad of cash and used them to pay the dinner bill.

Simon liked to lie, but he called it acting.

Why I liked him, why I needed him so badly, I didn't quite know. Maybe it was from the things he said to me when we sat in his car, in the restaurants, in his big old house with the hot tub he claimed he never used and the bathroom where the tiled floor was only partly finished. It had been in that same unfinished state for months.

"It was bad at home," I said to him as we drove through the night.

"No," he said. "Actually it was worse."

Worse. Was it worse? Better? No, it was worse. He was right.

The external validation of your condition, it's like your MasterCard. Maybe even more so. A greater great than priceless. More like spooning milk from God's own hand.

"Are we going to your house?" I asked.

"We're going wherever you like."

In your fantasy, you can drive for hours and end up only yards from where you started.

At his house we got out of the car and passed through the yard, up the walk to a doorway I would lie in bed at night and cry for. But now, in a miracle of imagination, I could follow him through it and be far, far away from the lonely bedpost I hugged when I was sad.

He ordered late dinner delivered and then licked fifty-dollar bills when it came.

We ate on the big bed he shared with other dreamers when I wasn't hogging him for myself.

"You know," he said, "I'm leaving tomorrow."

I turned to look at him.

"No. Why, where are you going?"

"I'm going to—"

Asia, Africa, India. I realized the details didn't matter.

"Tonight," he said, "you can stay all night. But tomorrow I'm gone until—"

That also didn't matter. Any amount of time was more eternity than I could stand in his absence.

"What will I do? When night comes and I need you?"

He looked at me, kissed me.

"Wish for me," he said.

Such were the trials of having an imperfect hero. I had tried. I thought maybe next time I could do better. But truth was, I was out of material—too many heroes already imagined then lost. Now I would lose again, all of it: the big bed and his big body that I required but somehow wasn't fond of.

But if he was gone then he was gone and that was it.

***

The next night I stood at the doorstep at my own house and waited. I sat on the porch, with the door closed behind me, and breathed the dry night air. But no one came. Not Simon, not anyone. Just that morning he'd dropped me back here, back home, and the journey from his place to mine had been short, not at all like the dreamy trip out, those hours of pleasure, from my place to his the night before.

Time swells and contracts in inverse proportion to misery and joy.

Now the days passed in a slow motion stutter. I walked

in circles around the block. I took my own car and drove in circles around the city where I lived. Like a slave on the galley I was always pulled back to the sinking ship that was my life.

I rang Simon's number but he didn't pick up.

I grew bolder and walked for hours through the night, arriving home to early morning birdsong. I read *Crime and Punishment* and developed a fast kinship with Rodion Romanovich Raskolnikov as he roamed endlessly through the streets of St. Petersburg. It startled me that other people in my class described this behavior as silliness. I wondered what lives they had that they didn't understand.

On the weekends I drove my car far from the city limits, past Socorro and up winding mountain roads. In the mountains, where there's rain, trees and grass grow freely, without being coaxed and mollycoddled with drips of water from the spout. It's a miracle that will always give me moments of appreciation.

I slid out of my car at the scenic overlook and leaned over the rail, catching flashes of birds. Leaves rustled underfoot from the passage of deer.

Jumping would be easy.

My fingers gripped the wooden rail, and I thought of Simon, how at this point in the day he would ask about dinner. I closed my eyes and put myself back in his big black car, his hand on the steering wheel, the road spread out behind us. I thought how I could live at his house because it was surely big enough for five people, certainly big enough for two. People would visit and I would be there. So easily I'd pass from misery to bliss. His smile would be my smile. His things would be my things. His lies would be my lies.

Lies were better than nothing.

Except if I was living it, then it wouldn't be a lie, right?

Simon, if he were here, would dismiss such deep concerns. He might pull out his big money clip and recommend a restaurant.

"My car," he'd say, "it's parked over there." He would give me the keys. "Go inside and wait for me. I'll be there in a second and then we'll eat."

In his car the reality of my situation would intrude, and when he joined me I would ask him: "Why do you leave me? You're not supposed to leave me. You're my dream."

"Your dream isn't very good then, is it?"

He would drive past Socorro and then past it again and he would ask.

"Do you think Orro—"

"No, I don't think he does."

I pulled out my phone and dialed Simon's number, but he didn't pick up.

***

My phone rang. It was him. As always, I'd had to return home from the mountains. Simon was back from his own adventures in Europe, Europa, Greenland.

We sat outside on a rooftop restaurant eating Italian under the stars. A warm summer breeze ruffled the tablecloth. I was happy again, content to escape in the moment.

After dinner we ordered chocolate martinis in a shop down the street. Simon sat next to me, touching me, sharing the warm lifelike sensation I struggled to draw from the bedpost. My mother had insisted on giving me a four-poster bed because she thought it was quaint. She probably hadn't considered the possibility that those posts would later become my most dependable substitutes for her own startling lack of maternal affection.

Simon's bed, unlike mine, had no bedposts, but it had

Simon and often featured a cat named Uranus. Back from dinner, we three occupied the bed. I was still fuzzy from the martini. Simon was fuzzy. Uranus was fuzzy.

"You can't leave me anymore," I told Simon. "I've made up my mind."

"No?" asked Simon. "You think you can tell me what to do?"

"I do, actually. I thought about it while you were gone."

It was true. During the long hours I'd suffered in his absence, I reached the conclusion that I had no resources to replace him. The solution was to keep whatever of him I had.

Simon gave me *the eye* and then turned away.

"We're going to leave this place once and for all, " I said. "I've decided we're moving to New York."

***

Since I had nothing to bring, the move was easy. We got a penthouse suite in lower Manhattan. Uranus would be indoors now, so we got a second cat named Moneypenny. Simon found a job at Sotheby's where his acting lessons came in handy and he spoke with great elocution. For me he arranged a job at a small gallery. I showed pieces that were supposedly art but mostly resembled aluminum cans.

Now the nights were warm, but thick with city. Every one of them included Simon in my bed, his bed, our bed. I was far from bedposts, from my mother's droning insults. Evenings, we dressed up, went out. Sometimes to movies, sometimes to parties.

We encountered Daniel Craig at a rooftop gathering where people held specialty drinks in chilled glasses and posed for their own egos.

"So," said Simon, speaking to Daniel, "that parkour scene in *Casino Royale*, that was impressive. Did you hurt yourself?"

"I had a stunt double."

"I think you're the sexiest 007," I said. "Aside from Sean Connery."

Daniel slid his blue, blue Hollywood eyes in my direction.

"OK, maybe even more than Sean Connery." Then I reconsidered. "Or not."

Daniel moved on.

"I really do think he's sexy," I said, speaking now only to Simon. "Not just as 007. I guess I wasn't clear on that."

"And me? Do you think I'm sexy?"

I looked at Simon. It seemed like a silly question, but then I wondered: Did I?

"If you had a choice between me or Daniel Craig," he said, "who would you sleep with?"

I gave his query consideration, which was more than I should have done, because the delay implied there was a contest.

"I would suck Orro," I said.

Simon used a straw to stir his custom drink. He didn't reply.

Of course I *did* find Simon sexy, I always had. But it was in the fashion one finds a tree sexy, which would generally mean not sexy at all. Except that a tree can be appealing when it stands above you and keeps you dry from the rain. It's the living precursor to the bedpost, which makes it worth hugging. Maybe even worth loving.

But Simon lied. He called it acting. He was the best I could do for a hero. Even so, the rain was fierce and one way or the other, I required a safe place for retreat. I turned my head to locate Daniel, Danny, the Dan Meister, and I wondered if I could actually like him. Because even though

Simon's departure from my life would leave me too weak to stand, I wasn't sure I *liked* him. At one point, though, I was sure I had.

But should you *like* your hero? Or was it just a matter of being grateful for the relocation?

Would Lois Lane have been satisfied if Superman switched out with Spiderman? If he traded her for Mary Jane Watson?

If he's interchangeable, is he really *your* hero?

I watched Simon, and all I knew was that he was better than the alternative. In other words, the alternative of living at home. But prostitution, I thought, would be better than living at home. Now I had a penthouse and an enviable lifestyle. It was more than I could ever have hoped for.

"Really," I said, "I do think you're sexy. I would pick you over Daniel Craig."

I asked myself if I'd adopted Simon's propensity for acting. I wondered if Simon would notice.

***

Winter came. Snow fell and I would sit inside the penthouse, drinking hot chocolate and watching the flakes land soundlessly on the freshly made cotton ball world. Simon spiked his own chocolate with Baileys. Sometimes I took Baileys, too. It warmed me on the inside and filled me with a soft sleepiness.

Uranus and Moneypenny snuggled to resemble a single multicolored stole.

In the bedroom there was a big window across from our big bed. At night we would sit next to each other, propped against the headboard and covered with blankets, silent, watching the snow. I would close my eyes and feel the tender weight of sleep come to me in its leisure, beginning in my feet, giving them comfort, causing them to lose the border that separated them physically from the mattress. I lost awareness of them as they drifted from my mind, followed by my ankles, then my calves, thighs.

This act of giving my self to sleep was a gift to myself. The descent to deep unconscious was a process of surrender, restful as the endless, dreamless slumber Briar Rose slept within for a hundred years.

Let me sleep without dreams.

Let Simon keep watch in the silence of the snow.

In the early mornings I rose from the peace of sleep and took the subway to SoHo. At the gallery I started the hot cider we served in paper cups. Customers were less frequent now and random couples rushed inside more to escape the winter wind than to admire the art-inspired cannery. I would give them cider, and as they huddled for warmth it would make me think of Simon as I'd seen him that morning, still next to me in bed, sleeping with a mild snore. I was grateful for him, for his good sleep, and mine, for everything that filled my now-so-much-better life. Still, something was lacking. I could sink into sleep but not into Simon. He blocked me, in some fashion that escaped definition. Watching these other couples in the gallery, I ached for that missing component and wondered what it was, exactly, that eluded my grasp.

So one night after closing the gallery I didn't go straight home, choosing instead the familiar milieu of a local Starbucks. I sat across from the central gas fireplace, drank hot tea, and let the flames warm my feet. I loosened my jacket but kept my scarf still wrapped at my throat, just because I liked the feel of a scarf, an experience so new and special to me. Despite two months now of scarf weather, the concept struck me as stylish and spectacular.

The luscious cold, it was glorious and unlike the barren

desert winters I'd endured so long.

When my phone rang, Simon's name showed on the screen.

"Love," I said, just because the snow and a filthy Starbucks floor made me happy.

My greeting took him by surprise. There was a delay before he spoke.

"I'm calling," he said, "to let you know I'll be home late tonight. I have meetings."

Meetings so late? Simon didn't usually have late meetings.

I closed my eyes and tuned out the sounds of Starbucks, focused instead on background noises on his end of the line. Was he at work? At Starbucks?

At a pay-by-the hour motel?

So many times I'd heard him speak those same words to other people when really he was in the car with me, driving through a scalding harsh wind and using his free hand to rub my thigh.

"So what about me?" I asked. "Should I make do with Orro?"

"You could invite him for dinner, but it would be a long commute."

"Really," I said, "what time do you think you'll be home?"

"Not sure. Two maybe? Don't be lonely. You can get a drink at the bar downstairs."

Downstairs from our penthouse were a restaurant and bar — the arrangement was a perk of renting in a Manhattan skyscraper. The unfortunate truth, however, was that this same establishment, in the absence of male companionship, was the domain of *friends* who slunk like zombies from the woodwork. They didn't want your brains; they did want everything else.

To avoid new friends, among other reasons, drinking at the bar downstairs by myself was an unwelcome proposition.

"It's so cold," I said, speaking to Simon. "You're going to stay out even though it's so cold?"

"I'll get a cab home. Don't worry about me."

Simon rang off and in the silence that followed I thought it wasn't him I was worried about. At least not like that.

In the absence of a better plan, I stared into the blue and orange flames of the gas fire. Then I got a latte, served in a white ceramic cup, yin and yang swirled unrequested in the coffee and cream. Back in my seat the delicate pattern shivered from the unsteadiness of my grip.

In a moment I should have foreseen, Simon would not be home that night when I went to bed. The cats would come to me for dinner, but Simon wouldn't be there to laugh at Uranus and his big appetite.

It was only a matter of time—I knew Simon too well—when I'd get the other call. The one where Simon told me he didn't plan to come home at all.

He'd affect sympathy and then let fall that he'd booked that flight to Paris, London, Monte Carlo. He'd made such big sales at Sotheby's. He would be flush with rewards.

"You can stay," he'd say, "until the rent runs out. It's paid through February."

"But you're my dream," I'd say.

"You keep saying that. But what can I do? Other people dream, too."

Other people dream better than you, that's what he meant. I was trouble for him and when my concentration waned he could slip from view and find someone better. If he were a genie, then I could keep him locked in the lamp.

11

But Simon, his bonding to me was less straightforward. He struggled to escape and I knew it.

I pulled my chair nearer the flame, but still felt a chill.

***

March. The new lease started and Simon showed himself at home, erratically. As his delays became more frequent I braved the restaurant downstairs and ate at the bar. The food was good. The blueberry pork chop was outstanding. If I brought something to read and stared pointedly, it was easier to ward off the zombies.

I did my best impression of a stranger to the New York area who'd stopped in at random. Like there was a good reason I ate alone at a bar on a Saturday night.

Sometimes, when it wasn't so busy, the chef would emerge from the kitchen and spend time making conversation. He'd appear wearing his token toque blanche and that silly white shirt that resembles a double-breasted suit.

The chef, Bob, seemed like a decent person and didn't fall into my definition of zombie.

"So why do cooks wear that uniform?" I asked, indicating the button-down component of his shirt which, in his case, used knots instead of buttons.

"It's better for dueling," he said. "I can disrobe one-handed."

"Dueling?"

"While still holding the skillet."

I had a mental image of a shirtless man using one hand to wield his rapier while flipping an omelette with the other.

"That happens a lot?"

He shrugged.

"When I'm *not* dueling, it's useful because I can turn my jacket inside out and instantly look like I've changed into fresh clothes. That's the real reason. One of them, at least."

"Ah," I said. "The pork chop is extra good tonight."

Bob crossed his arms and leaned against the drink counter behind the bar. He was an attractive man, not as good looking as Daniel Craig, but less tree-like than Simon. Like if you touched him, his skin might pucker.

If you hugged Bob, it wouldn't be like hugging a giant sequoia.

"What's with that guy you used to eat with?" he asked.

I'd resumed eating, but now I looked up from my plate. It hadn't occurred to me that Bob would notice something like that.

"He's busy," I said.

He's leaving me. Slowly. When he's gone I'm going to die.

I wasn't sure I should actually say that part.

"You used to be with him all the time," said Bob.

"You could tell?"

"I'm here at all hours. And not always just locked in the kitchen." I bought myself time by cutting extra pieces of pork chop, more than I needed at that very moment, and considered my response. On the one hand, Bob was basically a stranger. On the other hand, there are times when talking with strangers can be easier than talking with people you actually know.

"He's leaving me," I said. "But he's taking his time about it."

"And then what will you do?"

"I'll be homeless, I think."

"Homeless? That seems extreme. You can't just get your own place?"

My income from the SoHo gallery was a pittance. Especially for New York. It was the sort of job held primarily by young bohemians living large off their parents' trust funds.

"No," I said. "I can't get my own place."

"No one to stay with?"

"No." I looked at Bob, and it seemed strange I'd elected to share so much. But the empty nights of my life had an effect that was more exponential than additive. I was back to the point where, if I'd had a bed post, I'd have hugged it.

Bob watched me and I noticed that his eyes were soft, crinkled at the edges, but crinkled because he would close them just a bit to see a thing carefully. I'd spoken with him many times at this point, but I hadn't noticed his eyes, or even the rest of him. I'd been distracted first by Simon, then by my own despair. All that time, however, Bob had seen me for the person I was. He took the time, in his own life, to see the truth.

"Don't be homeless," he said. "Stay at my place."

***

Bob was the man I married.

But I didn't really meet him at the bar from the luxury building I shared with Simon. I didn't meet him there because I never had a penthouse in lower Manhattan, and because Simon never existed, except in the fearful nooks of my brain, at night or in the early morning, when I was alone and terrified I'd lose my mind.

I met Bob later, when I was attending NYU, after escaping home with some sanity although not much. I was at a party one night, sitting on the bathroom floor and crying in such a way that no one would hear. Bob came in and nearly tripped over me. Then he took a seat across from me, on the floor, watching me with his soft crinkled eyes.

He said he was studying at the Institute of Culinary Education. He offered to cook a late dinner.

He offered me his hand, his love, his life. One following

the other, in a timeframe that blurs because it all merged into a single memory of joy.

His kindness was understated. If I hadn't made an effort to let it reach me, I would have missed it. And that was something new, something I'd gained. In the past, I'd required a kindness that was thrown upon me and wrapped tight, even if it was a pseudo-kindness like what was offered by Simon.

Thus, unlike Simon, Bob was the real hero in my life. I thought back to the long-ago past when I'd believed that my hero was a person I'd never met, and I realized now that statement had become untrue. It was the sort of untruth that was actually good for you.

In the years that comprised our lives together, Bob never left me for Dresden, Barcelona, or Rome. He never traded me for Mary Jane Watson and I never traded him for another man.

I found no reason to hug either bed posts or trees.

Sometimes when we watched TV together we would laugh at the silliness of X-Men and Aquaman and the sadness of the Beast. And during those hours and others, in the comfort of a regular apartment with no penthouse luxuries, I would know that I was happy, and that superheroes could use their powers on others.

I don't need them.

Superman and his varied ilk, they can find another girl.

———

Liz Fyne has an M.S. in neuroscience, and over a decade post-graduate work experience in biomedical research. She enjoys deeply beautiful writing that explores issues of psychology. Ms. Fyne lives in Sewickley, PA, with her husband and cat. Learn more on: linkedin.com/in/elizabethfyne or find her on goodreads: goodreads.com/author/show/14244663.Liz_Fyne.

RUSSELL FEHMER'S WAR

Lenora Rain-Lee Good

Russell Fehmer — tall, sinewy, well-tanned — tossed his backpack to the dock and awkwardly stepped from the small boat to stand beside it. His movements would have been the fluid movements of an athlete, had he not worn a brace on his left leg.

He spoke English. He could speak fluent Spanish but saw no reason to let the locals know that. He turned to the boatman and asked, "When will you return?"

"Return? Oh, señor, I have no regular run. José, who runs the cantina, he comes downriver every so often. Ask him."

Before Russell could say thank you, the boat was well out into the river, the little motor making its rat-a-tat-tat like so many misfiring firecrackers.

Russell turned toward the village. No noise came from it. No little children ran or screamed or played. The village seemed pulled in on itself under the heat of the siesta sun. Had there been sidewalks, he speculated, they would have been rolled up and put away during the midday heat. Sidewalks had not yet become available, let alone necessary, to this tiny village carved from the steamy jungle in this forgotten corner of Latin America.

It did not take long to find the village square. A short walk up the trail from the river, past a few shacks with fishing paraphernalia scattered about the weedy yards and then he entered the village. Typical of small towns, one side of the square was the Catholic Church, balanced by the cantina across from it, with sundry dilapidated buildings making the other sides of the square. If any of the buildings had ever been painted, Russell couldn't tell; they were the color of mud, now. In fact, thought Russell, it was hard to tell where the dirt ended and the buildings began. The only clues were the weeds and flowers growing next to the buildings.

Odd, he thought. There are no children. Perhaps their parents hid them because a stranger, a gringo, comes? The older ones would be in school, but there should be youngsters about. And no inn in which to rest my weary head.

Russell limped to the cantina, well aware of curtains being discreetly pulled aside by unseen hands so unseen eyes could watch his movements. Russell smiled as he entered the cantina, which was also the general store. Bags of what smelled like fertilizer were stacked along one wall. The opposite wall held bags of rice and beans. The bar, with the cashbox, was at the front where José could see all who came in and went out — and collect whatever payment was due. Plugs and sacks of tobacco resided in boxes on top of the bar. Russell assumed the beer was kept up front under the bar.

Along the back wall were shelves stacked with sundry canned, dried, and bottled goods. Old metal tables, chipped and rusted, stood in the center of the room, surrounded by chairs and stools. Smells of stale beer, spices, and fertilizers assailed Russell's nose — a not entirely unpleasant cacophony of odors. The ever-pervasive smell of jungle mud and mold rode the odors as an unwanted guest. Dirty, old calendars and beer posters covered any bare places on the walls and door. The posters, most of suggestively posed women, were smudged where grubby fingers had groped the photos.

"Sir?" An old man, heavy with too many of his own beers, looked up from the yellowed newspaper he read behind the bar.

"Are you José?"

"Sí, señor."

"Do you speak English?"

"Sí. Yes. A little."

"I will be here for a few weeks. I need a room to rent. Is there a hotel or an inn?"

José studied the gringo before speaking, "Señor, there is no inn. Rosa has a back room she sometimes rents. It is small, but clean. It has an outside door. And a window."

"Does it have a bed?" Russell smiled while he blatantly studied the old man.

"Sí, señor, it has a bed." José chuckled. "Come, I will show you Rosa's. You tell her I sent you, she will rent you the room." José waddled from behind the bar to the door of the cantina to point to Rosa's. Her place stood next to the church. "She cleans for the padre. He is an old man. Been here since the Flood."

"Oh? What is his name, Father Methuselah?"

José thought a minute, caught the joke, and laughed. "No, señor. His name is Augusto. Padre Augusto. He is very old."

"That is good to know, José. Thank you." Russell picked up his pack and limped across the square to Rosa's, again aware of all the unseen eyes as they followed his every move.

The room was small and relatively clean, though it smelled of must. Everything in the jungle smelled of must. A washbasin stood outside his door beside the rain barrel. The bed reminded Russell of the army surplus cot he slept on as a child. He paid for two weeks, took his clothes out of the pack, and hung them on the nails provided for such purposes. He then placed his pack so he would know if it was moved or searched and limped back to the cantina. He wasn't worried about Rosa finding the hidden pockets.

Russell worked on his second beer, sitting in the back of the cantina where he could watch those people who went by and any who came in. A few men did come in, more to check Russell out than to buy a beer. A stranger was an oddity in this out-of-the-way place. He knew oddities were not always welcome. Especially here.

When it again became just the two of them, Russell asked, "So, José, where did you learn English?"

"Many years ago, señor, when I was a boy. Padre Augusto saw I had a head for the numbers, and sent me to school downriver at Punta Gorda. I think he wanted me to become a priest like him. But," José shrugged and smiled, "I like the girls too much."

Russell smiled too, and they lapsed into a long, companionable silence.

"José, where are the little children? I expected to see and hear children, but there are none. Do the very young attend school, or am I that frightening?" Again, Russell smiled, to show it was a joke.

"Oh, señor, long time ago," José stopped and collected his thoughts, "it was maybe thirty years ago, I think. Yes, yes it was. It was just before I went away to school. There was a terrible thing happened here. And we were cursed. Since then, once our young are old enough to leave, they move downriver to the towns and cities to find work. They have their families there. Sometimes they come to visit, but never do they stay, señor." José sighed. "My Rafael is the last. I expect him to make the journey any day now. My wife and I—well, we hope he will stay. But the curse...."

"A curse, you say? Come now, can't Padre Augusto remove the curse?"

"Perhaps, señor, had he not been the cause of it."

"But, if he is the cause of the curse, why not get a new priest and absolution for the village?"

"Because, señor, Padre Augusto's presence is our penance."

José clamped his mouth shut, turned, and busied himself with other business, a clear sign the conversation was over. José did not see the smile flit across Russell Fehmer's face, nor hear Russell softly hum the *kyrie eleison* as he found his way back to his room at Rosa's and his bed.

***

Russell Fehmer leaned back in his chair, rocking it to the back legs. He'd chosen the chair at the back under the slow, somnolent fan. José had electricity to operate the fan during siesta and the lights at night, when the village wakened to conduct its business. That is, he had electricity as long as his son, Rafael, rode the stationery bicycle in the small and cramped back room to charge the generator and battery next to him. Today, Rafael rode the bike. Today, the fan turned, though not, Russell noted, with enough speed to keep the flies away. Tomorrow, Rafael might join the other youngsters in the downriver towns. The last youngster in the village, Russell noticed, looked with longing at the river. Russell hoped the boy would head out soon.

"José," Russell quietly spoke the name. José looked up from the same old and yellowed newspaper; Fehmer raised a finger. José nodded and slowly made his way to Fehmer's table with a bottle of warm beer; the label stated its brand, but Fehmer doubted it truly came from the Dos Equis brewery in Mexico. He didn't care. It was wet and tasted passably like beer, albeit warm beer.

"Señor," said José as he placed the beer on the table and collected the money. José did not look at the money; he knew what it would be and how many warm beers it would buy. There would be no change, but two more bottles would follow when Fehmer spoke and raised his finger.

"Señor?"

Fehmer looked into the sad eyes of José.

"The padre, he and some men came last night. They asked questions about you. The padre, Father Augusto, threatened to send Rafael downriver if I lied."

"What did you tell them?"

"Señor, I told them what I know. That you are a gringo from Norte America; that you came with nothing but a pack and some money; that you ask no questions. I told them you rent the back room at Rosa's. I told them, señor, that I could tell by your eyes and your limp that you have suffered a great hurt and are trying to find peace in our little village. That is what I told them, señor."

"You did well, José. Always tell the truth as you know it, my friend." Fehmer gave one of his brilliant smiles; his white teeth glowed in the dark of the cantina.

"You are not angry, señor?"

"Of course not. Why would I be angry? The truth should never cause anger."

"Thank you, señor." José smiled, nodded, and returned to his station behind the bar.

Russell Fehmer reached down and massaged his leg under the brace. He did not like wearing the brace and inwardly sighed at the prospect of removing it and walking normally again. He stretched his leg then carefully placed the foot on the chair across from him. José watched from the corner of his eye.

***

Two nights later, Russell Fehmer woke to quiet, insistent voices coming from Rosa's part of the house. He rolled over, as if still asleep, and put the high tech listening device in his ear with a movement that, should anyone be watching him, would seem as if he had swatted a fly in his sleep. He was sure someone watched through the window.

"He rents a room from me. That is all." With the device in his ear, Russell had no problem hearing through the wall as Rosa spoke.

"What does he do with his time?" The man spoke with a tone that said if she didn't answer — and answer honestly — she would live to regret it.

"I do not know, Augusto. He sleeps in his room at night, and in the morning I give him beans and rice for breakfast, with an egg, if I have one. Then he washes and goes to the cantina where he sits all day. You will have to ask José what he does there. I do not know. I do not go into the cantina."

"What time does he come back?"

"Late. I don't always know. The back room where he sleeps has its own door and...."

"Does he come to your room? Answer! Under the seal of confession, daughter."

"Augusto! How can you say such a thing?" Russell smiled at the shock in her voice. Rosa was neither young nor beautiful, and from her smell, he judged she seldom bathed and even less often used soap.

"Look at me, Augusto. Do you think me a whore? I am Rosa, the woman who cleans for you, who cooks for you. I am Rosa, the woman who has held you and loved you all these years. I am Rosa, *who listens to your confessions and dries your tears!"*

"Do not speak of that! The walls may have ears. Does the gringo ever ask questions?"

Russell smiled. So the priest, too, likes the girls. He wondered if José knew that. Of course he does. Hard to keep a secret like that in a tiny village like this.

"No. He asks nothing. I don't think he speaks Spanish."

Russell smiled. "Rosa, does he not look..." The priest paused as if collecting his thoughts and choosing the right words, "familiar?"

"No. Should he?"

The man outside the room who watched through the window moved a bit. Grinding out his cigarette. If he's going to smoke while he spies, he should remain downwind of the open window. He heard the sound of leather on gravel, the sound of change in a pocket. A sleeping man would not have heard, but Russell did not sleep. He stretched then curled as a sleeping man might and held his weapon in his hand, trained on the door.

The conversation in the next room ceased, and at a soft call from the priest, the guard outside Russell's room walked away, unaware that he had been but a door's opening away from death.

The next day found Russell in his usual spot in the cantina, his back close to the far wall where he could watch the comings and goings, such as they were, both inside the cantina and outside in the square. His braced leg bothered him, and he spent some time rubbing it. José, with his sympathetic eyes, tried not to stare.

"Señor, perhaps you have been to our little village before? That is how you know it?"

"No, José. I've never been here before. Why do you ask?"

"If you will pardon, señor, something about you. You look, how you say, family? No, that is not right, but like I have seen you before, many years ago."

"Familiar. I look familiar."

"Sí. Yes, that is the word. Thank you."

"You're welcome, José. Perhaps we met years ago when I spent some time in Mexico City? That is the only place south of the border I've been until I came here."

"No, señor. I have never been out of my village, except to Punta Gorda for school. It is your eyes, señor. They remind me of someone. The men who came in yesterday, they said it, too."

Russell sipped his warm beer, massaged his braced leg, and let his memories wander back to happier days when he and his brother had been in college. Russell, dark, sinewy even then, studied mine engineering while Raymond, pale and shorter, softer, studied anthropology. He smiled. The older villagers *were* beginning to remember, beginning to place him. Or at least his eyes. The older villagers took on a wariness when they saw him, as if Russell Fehmer might be a ghost from a past they preferred not to remember.

Good. Be wary. Better yet, be afraid. Russell continued to smile as he drank his beer and watched.

Traffic in the square picked up a bit. Russell watched with interest.

"Tomorrow is market. Those who live out, away from our village, will bring their goods. Some come from upriver, some through the trails. There will be many people here. You will be able to buy many nice things, señor. And then tomorrow night will be a fiesta with dancing and pretty young women. Sunday, everyone who did not return home will sober up and go to mass. You will come to the fiesta, señor. And to mass?"

"I wouldn't miss them for the world, José. Especially mass. It has been a long time since I've been to mass."

"Ah, you are Catholic, señor? Perhaps you need to go to confession first?"

"I'll think about it, José. Thanks for the reminder."

Russell almost laughed out loud, thinking of his confession. The confession he had no intention of making for a future sin he had every intention of committing. Forgive me Father, for I am about to sin....

He sat outside the cantina on Saturday night, watched the fiesta, drank warm beer with the men. When introduced to Padre Augusto and their eyes met, Russell noticed the shock of being recognized, and heard Augusto's barely audible gasp. Augusto remembered. Russell was sure Augusto at least remembered the eyes.

Once the other men made eye contact with Russell, they began to find excuses to wander off, to be with their women, to be anywhere but near the man who reminded them of a past nightmare, and the curse Padre Augusto had brought down upon this poorest of poor villages.

***

Before the birds started their early morning screeches, before the dogs in the village woke, Russell Fehmer placed the last charge of the explosives. There would be survivors, there was nothing he could do about that, but he would take out the Padre and as many of the murdering bastards as he could. Those who survived, if they were old enough, would finally know why he looked familiar....

And they would understand. They would know why Russell looked familiar when they looked into his eyes. They would understand why Raymond's brother came to the place the young man died thirty years ago. They would understand that Raymond, the college kid, really only wanted to learn. Raymond, the boy whom the village priest, the same Father Augusto, convinced everyone was a communist spy, and whom all the men in the village then tortured to death.

In case the survivors did not understand, Russell left a photo of his brother tacked to a tree next to the jungle trail. A photo of Raymond. The one taken by the Army when they found his mutilated body three days after his death, tossed like last week's garbage into the jungle.

Russell removed the fake brace from his leg, unwrapped and strung the detonation cord concealed inside it and, when he was far enough from the church, attached the detonator.

Russell stood at the edge of the jungle and watched the church fill with the faithful. He smiled when he saw Rafael slink away to the river. He still smiled when the *kyrie eleison* began—then he pressed the button, turned, and walked down the trail into the jungle.

Those who survived would know their penance was complete.

He never looked back.

————

Lenora lives in the high desert of Washington State where she writes poems, novels, and radio plays. When not writing, she reads, quilts, makes jam, and takes road trips. Her novel, Madame Dorion: Her Journey to the Oregon Country, *is published by S & H Publishing, Inc.*
See https://www.facebook.com/MadameDorion

TESTAMENT OF COURAGE

J. J. Knights

Twenty-three year old Jeremy Kyner sat in the parlor of the small apartment he shared with his wife, Betty, in Wilmerding, Pennsylvania, just southeast of Pittsburgh.

It was mid-afternoon on a weekday. He should have been at work, but his supervisor at the Westinghouse Airbrake Works—known as "the Brake" to the locals—let Jeremy have the day off so he could report for his pre-induction physical exam. Since the Japanese attack on Pearl Harbor a few months earlier, the Brake as well as every other company in the country was losing workers to the military.

Jeremy, a civilian pilot, had volunteered for the Army Air Corps. When he produced his pilot's certificate and held it up for the recruiting sergeant to read, the man snatched it from his hand and became so excited Jeremy thought he might pass out from hyperventilation.

"Hey, wait a minute," the sergeant said waving the certificate. "Are you 1-A? Do you have any physical problems?"

"Heck, sergeant," answered Jeremy, "I've never been healthier."

Jeremy hadn't actually *lied*. Not technically.

Now he sat alone in the small, darkened apartment and stared at his newly stamped draft card: 4-F. Unfit for military duty.

Jeremy looked at the bottle of bourbon on the side table.

Then he once again read the stamp on his draft card: 4-F. An orthopaedic surgeon had been on duty that day, of all the rotten luck.

He could still hear the doctor's order to the medic after he finished twisting and probing Jeremy's foot and watching him walk across the cold tile floor of the sparse white examination room.

"Sergeant, label him 4-F."

Then he'd said to Jeremy, "I hope your wife likes you son, because she's stuck with you."

Jeremy heaved a sigh and reached for the bottle.

***

Betty was surprised to find the apartment dark when she returned from work at the usual time.

That's strange, Jeremy should be home by now.

She was disappointed. She was anxious to learn the results of his induction physical examination, though she had no reason to doubt Jeremy would pass without a problem.

"Jeremy?"

There was no answer. She walked across the darkened parlor toward the bedroom to change into something more comfortable.

Clink.

She froze. It sounded like an ice cube being dropped into a glass.

"Who— Who's there?" Her voice trembled.

The only answer was another *clink*. She saw someone sitting in the easy chair. A man had broken into the apartment and was waiting for her! She was about to scream when she heard a voice.

"What s'matter?"

"Jeremy! Is that you?"

"Yesh, who d'ya think it was?"

"You scared me half to death! I thought someone had broken in! Why are you sitting here in the dark? Why is your speech slurred? Are you all right?"

She turned on a table lamp. Jeremy was slumped in the easy chair. An ice bucket sat on the table next to him. He held a glass in one hand and a bottle of sour mash Tennessee whiskey in the other. The bottle was half empty. It had been almost full the last time Betty saw it.

"I dunno. Is my speech shlured?"

"Jeremy, you're drunk!"

"You are very observant. No one can trick *you*." He lifted the glass to his lips and sipped.

"What's going on? Why are you sitting alone in the dark getting drunk?"

"Which is it? I'm either already drunk or I'm g-getting drunk. C-Can't be both. I *am* an engineer, you know. You can't trick me, either."

She walked to the chair and stood in front of him.

"How long have you been sitting here drinking?"

"As long as I've b-been home."

"How long has that been?"

"I dunno. Forgot to check the clock. Maybe an hour and a half?"

"That bottle was almost full. You drank that much whiskey in an hour and a half? I'm surprised you're not on the floor."

"Yep. I guess. Are ya proud o' me?"

"Tell me what happened."

"Betty?"

"Yes?"

"Do you like me?"

"What?"

"Do you like me?"

"Of course I like you. What are you talking about?"

"That stiff-assed Army doctor wanted to know if you like me."

"An Army doctor? What Army doctor? Why would an Army doctor want to know if I like you?"

"Well, because if you do, then he sends his c-congratulations."

"Why, because I like you? Jeremy, you're not making any sense."

"No, because, Mrs. Kyner, your husband has been officially classified by the United States Army as a c-cripple. The Army doctor thought that would make you very happy, but only if you like me, he said, because now you're stuck with me. No $10,000 life insurance policy for *you!*"

Betty focused on only one word in Jeremy's slurred sentence.

"He said you're a cripple?"

"4-F, honey. You're ol' hubby is 4-F. It's official. I'm as u-useless as a g-glass hammer."

Betty knelt down beside Jeremy.

"Jeremy, tell me why you're 4-F."

Jeremy held up his left foot and wagged it left and right. "See that?"

"Yes, I see it." She gave him a quizzical look. "So?"

He put his left foot down and lifted his right foot into the air and held it there—motionless except for some swaying owing to his inebriation.

"Now," he said, "do you see *that?*"

"See what? It's not doing anything."

"Preshishley, my dear. It's not doing anything. It d-doesn't move sideways. The Army says I can't march on a shtupid foot like this so they shlapped a big fat red label on my file that shays I'm 4-F." He lowered his foot and took another sip of whiskey.

"But you had surgery for your clubfoot when you were fourteen, Jeremy. They fixed it. I don't...."

"Did you hear what I just said? The guy was a goddamned ortho...orthopaedic surgeon. What luck, huh? They had to have a damned orthopaedic surgeon on duty the day little crippled Jeremy Kyner had his physical examination. I should have had plastic surgery to hide these lousy scars on my foot. He's as shmart as you, Bettsy-wetsy. Couldn't get nothin' past him, either."

He took another sip.

"Oh, Jeremy! Now I understand! I'd forgotten your foot was fused and you can't move it side to side. Now the Army says that disqualifies you. Oh, honey. I'm so sorry."

"N-No you're not. You're happy. You didn't want me to go an' now you got your wish."

"You're right. I don't want you to go. You're staying here with me and it's not my fault so you can't hold it against me for the rest of our lives, but I'm not happy you're disappointed."

Jeremy didn't hear her. "D'ya remember the first day of eighth grade?"

"Eighth grade? Of course I remember. I also remember our horrid teacher, Miss Vilis. What about it?"

"Remember the argument my mom and Miss Vilis g-got into over my d-damned clubfoot? Mom sent us out into the schoolyard, but we listened through the window. Remember?"

"Yes, Jeremy. What are you getting at?"

"I c-can still hear that ol' crow's voice. She said, 'With his deformity, Jeremy is really only half a person.' D'ya remember she said that?"

"Oh, Jeremy. Yes, I do, and I also remember your mother's reaction. Miss Vilis is lucky she didn't skin her alive then and there. But darling, that was years ago. You walk normally now. The operation fixed it"

"Well, shweetie, I'm back there again. '4-F Kyner.' That's what they'll call me at work. Ole' 'Crippled Kyner.'"

"No one will say that about you, Jeremy. Besides, will staying home with me really be so bad?"

"Shweetie, I love ya, but yeah, it'll be pretty bad, actually."

Betty drew back wearing a pained expression.

"Oh, no, honey," Jeremy said, "not being with you. That's not what I m-meant."

"What, then?"

"Oh, c'mon. You know; sitting here on my ass while everyone else I know is in the Army, or Navy, or wherever, but ya know what else?"

"No, Jeremy, what else could there be?"

Jeremy took another drink before answering. "It's all the crap I put you through since the Japs bombed Pearl Harbor. All I c-cared about was joinin' the Air Corps and flyin' while you w-worried about b-bein' left alone after I got myself killed, like my dad did in the first war. All for nothin'. I p-put you through Hell for nothin'. How could I'a been so shtupid? I should'a realized this damned foot would keep me outta the Army. I wanted to go so bad that I wasn't thinkin' straight. G-Goddamn, I'm a shelfish ass!" He upended the glass into his mouth.

"Oh, honey," said Betty as she moved the bottle of whiskey out of Jeremy's sight, "it's all over, now. You were torn, I understand. You felt you had to volunteer; that was the right thing to do. What's important is that it's all settled now. We love each other and we'll get through this together. Everything will be all right."

"You're a wonderful woman, Bettsy-wetsy," Jeremy drawled. "I d-don't d-deserve you."

Betty smiled. "Someday all of this will be far behind us. The war won't last forever, darling."

"Oh, some parts of it will," said Jeremy.

"Whatever do you mean? It can't last forever, Jeremy."

"Ask my grandpa and my mom. Go ahead. My dad was killed in the last war and he's still dead. The war is still goin' on for them."

"Oh, Jeremy."

"And for some people, like my dad, the war will be their only forever—all the future they'll have. I never knew my dad, dammit."

Betty sobbed as she buried her face in his chest. "I love you and I'm glad you're not going. I know I'm selfish, but I can't help it!"

"But there's somethin' else that's b-been b-botherin' me."

"What's that, darling?" said Betty without moving.

"That b-bottle of whiskey you just tried to hide from me. It's really b-bourbon. Why do the people who make it call it whiskey?"

Betty's tears turned to anger. After everything she'd just said to Jeremy, he was thinking about bourbon and whiskey? Before she could think of a biting response, he was snoring.

***

At that moment, a small freighter on course for England was 144 miles southeast of Cape Sable, Nova Scotia. Several hundred yards away, a periscope broke through the waves of the Atlantic Ocean.

Less than a quarter-hour later the U-boat was on the surface. Having completed its task, the gun crew was securing the 105-mm deck gun before retreating into the bowels of the boat. Kapitänleutnant Hans Richter, the U-boat's commander, took particular note of the bright red Canadian merchant flag against the deep blue sky as it fluttered in the stiff breeze from the masthead of the old freighter. He smiled as the flag followed the ship silently into the deep.

Turning to his first officer, Oberleutnant zur See Dieter Jäger, he said, "Number One, resume course to the coast of New Jersey. We'll find more worthy prey there."

"*Jawohl, Kapitan.*"

***

"Grandpa, have you ever considered buying a tractor?" said Jeremy as he unhitched the team of horses from the combine. He'd spent this weekend as he'd spent every weekend in the months since learning he was 4-F, helping his grandfather and Hiram, the hired hand, around the farm in Mars, Pennsylvania, twenty-five miles north of Pittsburgh. The work helped him keep his mind off the feeling that he had been set back in life by ten years.

"If we had a tractor, we'd be able to finish the harvest in a third or maybe even a quarter of the time it takes with horses."

"Why do you want so much free time?" asked his grandfather, Benjamin Kyner. "What do you wanna' to do, sit around readin' flyin' magazines? Besides, gasoline is rationed because of the war."

"Sure it is, Grandpa, but as a farmer, you'd get extra ration cards and...."

Hiram pulled Jeremy aside. "Jeremy, what're ya doin'? Ya got to know you're just wastin' your breath."

Jeremy heard himself sigh. "Yeah, you're right, Hiram."

"Sorry, Grandpa." shouted Jeremy. "I forgot about the ration cards. Horses are better."

"Damned right. Besides, we're almost done for the year." Benjamin turned and walked into the barn.

"Ben's been drivin' me hard," Hiram said to Jeremy. "Just like every harvest time for the past thirty years. I'm sure glad you've been around to help. We couldn't 'a gotten this far without ya."

"Thanks, Hiram," Jeremy said warmly as he put his arm around Hiram's shoulders. He'd known Hiram his entire life. "You're a talented liar. You and Grandpa managed to get the harvest done at least four years in a row while I was in college."

"I am not lyin', young man," Hiram said with indignation. "I said we need you around here and I meant it."

"I think you're really trying to make me feel better about still being home while my classmates from high school and college are in the service. I'm getting along just fine, but thanks for worrying about me."

Hiram faced Jeremy. "Now listen, Jeremy. You're needed around here just as much as in the Army or Navy or wherever. Maybe more. They're passin' out those draft deferments for agricultural workers, just like they are for you people in defense work. The way I see it, you got yourself two important jobs: one as an engineer and one as a farmer. That ought to tell ya somethin'."

"You're right, Hiram, but I just can't get past it, that's all. I feel I've been left behind. I know it's not my fault, but somehow I feel it is, especially when people look at me and wonder why a guy my age isn't in a uniform when their husband or brother or son is. The guilt is eating at me, and it's frustrating knowing there's nothing I can do about it."

"Well," said Hiram, "forget the Army. Try the Navy."

"I did, Hiram. And the Marines and the Coast Guard. I didn't get very far with a '4-F' already on my record."

"Then you did all you could. Jeremy, if the good Lord wants you in a uniform, He'll put you in a uniform. Just trust Him to run things." Hiram slapped Jeremy on the shoulder, and they headed to the barn to help Benjamin clean up.

A movement caught Hiram's eye. "Hey look," he said, pointing at his approaching nephew, "Here comes Luce just when the work's all done!"

Friends since childhood, Jeremy and Luce sat side-by-side watching the late-summer sun dipping low amongst puffy white clouds.

Luce asked, "Jeremy, how've you been doing?"

"You mean since the Army showed me the door?"

"Yeah. I suppose that's what I mean."

"Crappy, actually. Thanks for asking," said Jeremy.

"Jeremy, look...."

"I'm sorry, Luce. I'm an ass, but like I said, I'm doing rather crappy. I feel pretty miserable. Sometimes I'm not fit company."

"Forget it, man. I understand."

The two friends sat in silence. Luce became pensive and fiddled with a blade of grass.

"Is something bothering you, Luce?"

"I can't hide anything from you, can I?"

Jeremy shook his head. "What's going on? Don't tell me your number finally came up in the draft lottery."

"Nah, that hasn't happened. Jeremy, this might not be the right time to tell you, because, you know, because of the way you're feelin' right now, but there's not a lot of time."

"Not a lot of time? What do you mean?"

"Do you remember a while ago I told you about a school in Alabama where the Army is training negro pilots?"

"Yeah," said Jeremy, "I remember. It's called Tusk something or other."

"Tuskegee," said Luce. "Tuskegee Institute. Well, I applied and they accepted me, Jeremy. First, I have to get through basic training, and then I go to Tuskegee. After that, it'll be regular military flight training, if I make it that far. I leave in a few weeks. You're the first person I've told. Uncle Hiram doesn't even know, yet."

Feeling as though he'd been stabbed in the heart, Jeremy instantly felt ashamed. Hoping Luce didn't notice, he got a grip on himself.

"Luce! That's incredible. You'll make it for certain," said Jeremy, feigning happiness for his friend.

Jeremy was still reeling from Luce's news when they heard approaching footsteps.

"Hey, you guys," said Betty as she came bounding down the hill. "Have you been talking about me?"

They both turned at the sound of her voice. Luce was smiling, but Betty froze when she saw the look in her husband's eyes.

"What's happened?" she asked.

***

Kapitänleutnant Hans Richter leaned over the railing of the conning tower and took in the lights of Atlantic City, New Jersey, only a few miles from the bow of his U-boat. It was a cool moonless night. The U-boat's crew had been breathing stale air all day while they hid on the bottom. There was little danger that they would be discovered owing to the darkness and the U-boat's low profile amidst the waves.

Richter waved toward the shoreline. "Look at it, Number One. The whole shore is lit up like a Christmas tree. The fools. All we have to do is sit here and wait for the silhouette of a nice fat freighter or tanker to pass between those beautiful lights and us. It's not a very challenging way to fight a war, but I'll take it."

"I must admit, Herr Kapitan," said Jäger, "I'm surprised at their carelessness. Why are those lights ashore not extinguished? And most of their ships run at night with navigation lights. They make such easy targets. Don't the Americans realize the advantage they're giving us?"

"The reason is simple, Number One. That place in front of us is a huge tourist attraction. Shutting off the lights would cut down on tourism and cost money. It's the same in the big eastern cities. What do they care if their ships are lost to our U-boats as long as their businesses stay afloat? Do you think they'd willingly lose even a pfennig to save the life of a common seaman? Don't forget these people are actually proud of having a population made up of polluted bloodlines. They boast about what is written on the Statue of Liberty in New York harbor: 'Give me your tired, your poor; Your huddled masses yearning to breathe free; The wretched refuse of your teeming shores.' I saw it in a newsreel. With those words the Americans proudly proclaim to the entire world who and what they are, the pious, ignorant fools. They asked for 'wretched refuse' and that's what they got. That's what they are."

Both Richter and Jäger laughed aloud. The sailors on watch turned around to look at their two officers. They couldn't imagine what was so funny, given their immediate circumstances.

Jäger suddenly stiffened. "*Herr Kapitan!*"

"I see it, Number One," said Richter. "She's long and low in the water." He put the binoculars to his eyes. "She's running without lights. I don't see any silhouettes of deck cranes or rigging. She must be a tanker—at least 10,000 tons, maybe more. She's riding so low, she must be loaded to the gills! We'll use a torpedo."

***

The next afternoon found Jeremy sitting alone in a booth at his and Betty's favorite diner. It was lunchtime, but Betty was held up at work and sent Jeremy ahead to get a table because the diner was usually crowded. The war had pulled Pittsburgh out of more than ten years of economic depression and brought prosperity to the entire region. Factories and mills were expanding with many hiring to staff shifts around the clock. Restaurants and bars were usually packed to overflowing.

All around him he could hear the other diners talking about the war. He tried to ignore the chatter as he sipped a cup of coffee and read the newspaper. His eyes took in the headline: "U-Boat Sinks Tanker Off New Jersey Coast." The *Alexandra Summer*, a 10,000 ton tanker, had been carrying aviation fuel bound for England.

Jeremy heaved a heavy sigh of exasperation. Jesus Christ, some U-boat captain probably thinks he's due for a promotion.

He read on. All 37 men on the tanker died when it exploded.

Poor bastards. They never had a chance, sitting on top of all that aviation gas.

"Hey, handsome, care to buy a girl lunch?"

Jeremy looked up to see Betty standing next to him smiling. She slid into the opposite seat.

"Why so glum?" she asked.

He showed her the headline and said, "The Nazis will keep at it until somebody stops them. They have the run of the entire coast. Why the hell can't the Army or Navy do something?" His voice dripped venom.

"Oh, my God," said Betty. "I'd actually forgotten about the war for a few minutes. Look at this place. Listen to what they're saying: 'war, war, war.' Can't I even have lunch with my husband in peace? When will this stop?"

"When the war stops, Betty."

"And you, Jeremy. You're just as bad as they are."

"Betty, what's gotten into you?"

"What's gotten into me? How can you ask me that? If the Army hadn't rejected you because of your old operation, you'd be off fighting right now. I might already be a widow!" She put her face in her hands and began to cry.

"But that didn't happen, Betty," said Jeremy as he looked around the diner hoping no one had noticed Betty's outburst, "so there's no reason for you to be upset."

"Isn't there?" she said through her tears. "Jeremy, I know you haven't said anything, but I can see you're miserable. The fact you're not in uniform is eating away at you."

Suddenly startled, they both looked up to see the waitress looming over them, pad in hand, gum in mouth.

"What can I get 'cha?" Noticing that Betty was crying, she added, "Hey, honey, are you okay?"

"Yes, thanks," said Betty, "I'm fine. Just a Cobb salad and hot tea, please."

Jotting the order down, the waitress gave Jeremy a suspicious look then wheeled away toward the kitchen.

When she was out of earshot, Jeremy said, "Am I that bad of an actor?" As he spoke, he looked into his coffee cup as though expecting to find something valuable hidden at the bottom.

"Yes, you are," answered Betty, " and I'm worried."

"Why? Like that Army doc said, you're stuck with me. I'm not going anyplace."

"But you would if you could. Jeremy, I'm hurt because you'd rather be off risking your life than staying home with me. I know I shouldn't feel that way, but I can't help it."

Jeremy's eyes stayed glued to his cup. "Dammit, Betty. Of course I want to stay with you, but it seems almost every day somebody at work leaves for the service. I'm a pilot, but the Army won't let me fly. I could contribute to the fight, but I'm not allowed to because of my damned foot. Christ!"

"Jeremy, you *are* contributing to the fight. Your job at Westinghouse is 'essential to the war effort.' Even if you weren't 4-F, you couldn't be drafted."

"Honey, it's not the same and you know it. Listen, this is torture for you, but it is for me, too. I know it's crazy of me to want to go and leave you alone, but I can't help it."

"Jeremy..."

"And there's not a damn thing either one of us can do about it, Betty."

Betty wiped her eyes with a tissue. "But if you could find a way to go, you would."

Jeremy only nodded.

The gum-chewing waitress arrived with Betty's salad and tea and a withering look for Jeremy at no extra charge.

***

"Go around, Cadet, and try it again."

Luce was afraid this would be his final flight in the PT-17 Boeing Stearman, the Army's workhorse training aircraft. It was a 'phase check.' If he passed, he'd be allowed to solo and go on to Basic Flight Training. If he didn't pass, he'd be washed out and sent to the infantry. There was a stiff crosswind and he'd messed up the first landing. He couldn't afford to let it happen again. Luce did not want to be in the infantry.

Luce shoved the throttle forward and the Stearman's big propeller clawed at the air, lifting the machine back into the sky.

"Okay," said the instructor, a captain, "stay in the pattern and go back around."

The next time, Luce did a perfect three-point landing.

"Good," said the instructor. "Now do it again."

Luce did it two more times. After the third landing, the instructor told Luce to taxi to the apron. As they cleared the taxiway and Luce headed toward a vacant spot to park, he heard him say, "Don't bother. Stop here. Shut it down."

Luce was confused.

After climbing out of the Stearman, the officer said to Luce, "Get in the rear cockpit and go solo, Cadet."

"Solo, sir?"

"Solo, Cadet. That's what I said."

Luce beamed. "Yes, sir! Thank you, sir."

"Do three stop-and-go landings and then park this thing."

***

After landing for the third time, Luce handed over his logbook to the instructor who signed off his solo flight. While the officer took care of the paperwork that would ensure Luce's graduation from primary flight training, Luce noticed a bright yellow Stinson Voyager land, taxi in, and park. Instead of the U.S. "star and bar insignia," it bore a white triangle within a black circle. Two pilots emerged wearing khaki uniforms similar to his but with crimson shoulder straps instead of khaki. They began tying down the Voyager.

"Excuse me, sir. Who are they?" Luce said pointing to the newcomers. "Canadians?"

The instructor looked up. "Them? Nah, they're not Canadians. They're Civil Air Patrol, a new volunteer group assigned to Army Air Forces. Believe it or not, CAP is flying anti-submarine patrols along the east coast. I think they're recruiting if you know any civilian pilots."

"Really?" replied Luce. He looked at the two CAP pilots who were now walking toward the hangar. "Actually, I think I do know someone who'd be interested."

The instructor handed Luce his logbook. "Congratulations on soloing, Cadet, and good luck. Now, you'd better hurry if you want to talk to those guys from CAP."

***

"What did Luce say?" asked Betty after Jeremy hung up the telephone.

"Well," replied Jeremy, "Let me tell you...."

After Jeremy told Betty Luce's news, she almost shouted, "Luce soloed? Oh, that's so wonderful! But what's CAP?"

"Civil Air Patrol. They landed just after Luce soloed and he was able to talk to them. They're a new organization of volunteer civilian pilots flying anti-submarine patrols."

"Why?" asked Betty, "Don't we already have an air force?"

"Well, considering that the German subs can do whatever they want, we obviously don't have much of an air force. CAP started patrolling along the east coast a little while ago. Apparently they're pretty good at it. They found a few U-boats. In fact, the President has ordered them to be armed."

"Civilians?"

"Right. Civilians. At least for the time being until the Army and Navy can get up to speed. They do other things too, like search and rescue missions, courier flights, transporting military personnel and equipment. Stuff like that."

"And Luce thinks you should join?"

"He suggested CAP might be a good option for me. Since there are no military physical exams to take, CAP offers a way to serve for people who are 4-F, too old, or can't join the military for some other reason. There are no enlistments. They have 90-day contracts. Pilots just need a license and a civilian medical certificate, which I already have. It seems like a reasonable alternative for, well, for people like me."

"I suppose Luce told you they'd love to have you?"

"The CAP guys told him they need pilots pretty badly. So, yeah, they're recruiting."

"But it has to be dangerous," said Betty. "Flying over the ocean looking for enemy submarines? Don't those submarines have guns? They won't just sit there and let you fly circles around them."

"I suppose you're right, Betty, but I can't let this opportunity go by without considering it."

"No, I don't suppose you can."

"Luce gave me an address. I'm going to write to them to see what they have to say."

"Uh huh," said Betty, "Just to see what they have to say. Sure."

Betty's sarcasm wasn't lost on Jeremy. "I need you on my side, Betty. I want to do more for the war effort than push a pencil across a drafting board. This is my chance. It's better than being an air raid warden, especially when we all know damn well neither the Germans nor the Japanese can bomb Pittsburgh."

"Well," she said not at all happily, "at least you wouldn't be overseas, and missing you for three months is better than missing you for years."

***

Two months later, Betty stood in a stiff breeze at Allegheny County Airport and waved to Jeremy as he taxied past in a single-engine Fairchild 24 with the Civil Air Patrol insignia painted on the fuselage. When she saw the airplane lift into the sky and disappear into the east, she turned and walked to the bus station alone.

***

On a sunny August day, Second Lieutenant Jeremy Kyner stood at a table in the CAP operations room at Wildwood Naval Air Station, New Jersey, with Captain Phil Anders and two CAP observers preparing for the day's anti-submarine patrol. They were to shadow northbound merchant vessels headed to the mouth of New York Harbor where a convoy was assembling.

The telephone on the radio operator's desk began to ring. Jeremy and the others ignored it. The radio operator picked up the telephone receiver and exchanged a few words with the caller. Holding the receiver in her right hand and covering the mouthpiece with her left so the caller couldn't hear her, she turned in her chair.

"Jeremy, it's your wife. She sounds upset."

Jeremy took the telephone receiver and put it to his ear. He could hear Betty's sobs. "Betty? What's wrong? Are Mom and Grandpa all right?"

"Oh, Jeremy," Betty said in a tearful, broken voice, "Luce is dead."

Time stopped. Jeremy felt as though he had stepped out

of his body and was watching himself from a distance. It was all like a dream. But it wasn't a dream. He listened as, sobbing, Betty told him what little she knew.

Finally, he replaced the telephone receiver in its cradle

"Jeremy?" asked Anders. "Are you all right?"

Anders' voice sounded far away. Long seconds later, Jeremy understood the words. Was he all right? No, of course not. It was as though he had just witnessed every memory of his childhood murdered before his eyes.

Jeremy looked at Anders. "My best friend was killed a few days ago over Sicily."

No one spoke. Finally, Anders said, "Was it your buddy in the Air Force? The guy you grew up with?"

Jeremy nodded and said, "Yeah, it was. His name is— was—Luce."

"Jeremy," continued Anders, "everyone here understands and feels for you, but you can't fly today."

"What?" said Jeremy, glaring at Anders. "Why the hell not?"

"Because you just lost your best friend and you'd be too distracted. It wouldn't be safe. I'll call the C.O. and explain. He won't have any problem with sending out another pilot."

"No, Phil," said Jeremy. "The Germans killed my best friend. I'm not going anywhere but out over that ocean to find those bastards."

"Jeremy, look," said Anders, "the people out there in that U-boat didn't kill Luce. Maybe in a few days...."

Jeremy's eyes flared. "Phil, the people out there in that U-boat have killed other Americans. They've killed other best friends and fathers and sons and brothers. They're just as responsible as the German who killed Luce. Would you want to take a few days off if you knew the people who had just killed your best friend were within striking distance? Would you?"

"Jeremy," said one of the observers, "Phil's right. The C.O. would never allow you...."

"To hell with C.O.," shouted Jeremy. "He won't know, not till later! I'm not staying on the ground with Luce lying dead."

"Jeremy," said Phil in an even but determined tone. "You just can't go."

"Phil, try and stop me."

***

The captain of the SS *Angel of Liberty* stood outside the bridge of the 10,000-ton tanker scanning the horizon toward the open sea. The big ship had sailed out of Delaware Bay without incident on its way to join the convoy assembling near the mouth of New York Harbor. The ship's tanks were laden with aviation gasoline destined for Liverpool.

The captain lowered his binoculars, but continued to stare out to sea. The wind ruffled his shirt collar. The first officer left the bridge and joined him.

"Next stop, Liverpool," said the first officer.

"I hope you're right, Dave," said the captain. "I hope our destination really is Liverpool and not a blazing funeral pyre somewhere between New Jersey and England."

The first officer looked at the captain and then out to sea, toward England. His hands were on the railing. His knuckles were white.

"I don't know, Dave," said the Captain. "I don't have a good feeling. If you're a praying man, I'd say you should start now."

"I've already started, Captain."

A droning noise in the distance caught the Captain's

attention. "Do you hear that?"

"Yeah, I do."

Both men put their binoculars to their eyes and looked skyward.

"There!" said the Captain, pointing.

"Civil Air Patrol," said the first officer. "Two of them,"

"Well," said the Captain, "you said you were praying. It looks like someone was listening."

***

Jeremy flew his Fairchild 24 and its single 100-pound bomb in a wide circle around the *Angel of Liberty* as he scanned the ocean for some clue that would give away the U-boat's location. Jeremy squinted into the distance and saw Anders' Fairchild as a speck a mile away on the opposite side of the ship.

That U-boat could be anywhere along the coast but according to the Navy it's been in this area for some time, so why wouldn't it come after this fat tanker?

Anders and the others were right. He was distracted. Luce was gone and never coming back. He knew what he needed—to grieve, but he couldn't afford that luxury right now. It would have to wait. This is what it had to be like for men in combat in every branch of service. You lose a friend but you keep going on. You have to. Grieving is for later.

The minutes dragged on, eventually becoming half an hour. Then an hour. Jeremy listened to the relentless drone of the engine and fought to keep his fatigued and over-stressed mind from wandering.

He remembered when Hiram first brought Luce to the farm. All three of them—Jeremy, Betty and Luce—went down to the pond. They began tossing stones into the water. Kids having fun. In his mind's eye, he could see each stone splash as it hit the water, causing a small geyser of white foam to erupt....

Jeremy caught himself. He could actually see the same small geysers bursting amidst the ocean waves below. He closed his eyes and shook his head to clear it. He re-focused his eyes. It was real! He saw a white, foamy wake cutting through the waves. A periscope! Every time it struck a wave, it sent an explosion of foam high into the air like a white flare! Jeremy grabbed the microphone.

"I see a periscope! We're just passing over it, but at the wrong angle to drop the bomb. If I miss, he'll dive deeper and that'll be the last we'll see of him. Phil, it's up to you."

"Roger," replied Anders. "We're on the way."

Then Jeremy caught his breath. He couldn't believe his eyes. "Holy Christ!" he shouted into the microphone. "Forget the periscope. He's surfacing!"

Jeremy watched the U-boat emerge from the waves, seawater cascading from the conning tower and deck.

As soon as the sleek hull of the U-boat surfaced, men emerged and took up positions at the gun emplacements.

***

"Gun crew!" shouted Richter, "as soon as you can, fire for effect into the hull below her funnels! Hit the engine room!"

"*Herr Kapitan!*" Jäger shouted. "Look!"

Richter spun around to see Jäger pointing into the sky. He lifted the binoculars to his eyes and saw Anders' aircraft heading straight for the U-boat. Richter turned to the anti-aircraft machine gun crew who were still loading their weapon with a drum of 20-millimeter ammunition.

"Hurry, you fools!"

The seaman manning the machine gun chambered the first round, flexed his knees to elevate the barrel, put the CAP aircraft in his sights, and squeezed the trigger.

***

Jeremy couldn't believe what he saw. Tracer rounds reached out from the U-boat toward Anders' Fairchild.

"Phil!" he shouted into the microphone. "Get outta' there!"

"Why would I do that?" answered Anders. "This is what we signed up for. I have a chance to get this guy, and I'm gonna do it."

In the background, Jeremy could hear Anders' observer shout, "Oh, my God!" Anders had just begun to level off and was reaching for the bomb release when the Fairchild's cabin exploded. A screaming wind tore through the cabin and red ooze covered everything, including most of the windscreen. A single 20-millimeter round had punched through the floor between the observer's rudder pedals. The observer had a hole in his chest the size of a softball. His eyes were open, staring at nothing.

"Goddamn it!" screamed Anders.

Anders looked down. He wiped the blood off the windscreen as best he could. He couldn't see the U-boat. He'd flown past it.

"Jesus Christ!" he shouted in frustration. He began to turn the Fairchild for another pass.

The machine gunner on the U-boat followed the yellow airplane as it passed overhead and continued to spray 20-millimeter rounds at it.

Concentrating on the immediate threat posed by Anders' aircraft, no one on the submarine noticed the other small airplane in the distance.

***

Jeremy saw Anders fly past the U-boat. Why hadn't Phil dropped the bomb? Something had to be wrong. Jeremy headed toward the Germans.

***

As Anders banked the Fairchild, he felt it vibrate as more 20-millimeter rounds tore through it. Two rounds pummeled the observer's corpse and flung it forward into the instrument panel. Anders was spattered with bits of warm flesh and blood. At the same time, another round passed through the bottom of the aircraft, struck part of the steel frame behind Anders and shattered, sending splinters of hot metal into his lower back and legs. Blood began to drain from his lower body onto the seat and floor.

***

Richter scanned the sky. "*Gottverdammte!* There are two!" He turned to the machine gun crew. "Fire on that second target! Now!"

***

Jeremy saw tracers erupt from the U-boat and fly toward him. He was still too far away to release the bomb. He had to maintain his course.

"Dear God," he muttered, "I'm playing chicken with a German U-boat."

As Jeremy concentrated on lining up on the U-boat, he heard his observer shout, "Jesus! What's Anders doing?"

Jeremy looked up just in time to see Anders cut in front of him, just missing clipping his Fairchild with his left wingtip. The fabric skin of Ander's airplane had been shredded.

Jeremy screamed into the microphone, "Phil! What are you doing?"

"You know," replied Anders, "they shouldn't p-paint these things yellow." His voice was labored. He was having trouble speaking. "They m-make too good a target."

"Phil, you've been hit. Break it off and get home."

"My observer's dead," said Anders in a calm voice "I'm hit and losing blood fast."

"Phil, get back to base while you can!"

"Jeremy, I c-can't get back. I c-can't make it. I've still got this bomb strapped to my ass and I'm gonna use it before it's too late."

"No, Phil! You'll be killed! Go home!"

"It's not your time, yet. You've got yourself a beautiful wife, Jeremy. Go home to her."

"Phil!"

No answer.

"Phil!"

***

Richter pointed at the CAP aircraft and screamed at the machine gun crew, "Fire! Fire on that target!"

The gunner shifted his aim and pressed the trigger.

***

Jeremy watched as the wings and fuselage of Anders' Fairchild, now far ahead of him, flew apart as countless 20-millimeter rounds struck the once proud machine. The propeller shattered and one blade flew away. The force of the resulting imbalance began tearing the engine from its mounts. With smoke pouring from its cowling, the Fairchild shuddered, rolled inverted, and slid into a dive. Not believing his eyes, Jeremy watched it slam into the Atlantic Ocean.

"Phil!" screamed Jeremy. No, this was too much. The bastards can't do this-not two friends in one day.

***

"Hah!" shouted Richter, delighted at the sight of the yellow airplane plummeting into the sea. "The fools! I told you, Number One, I told you! Wretched refuse!"

Jäger stared at Richter in disbelief. The man was endangering his boat and crew simply to make a point!

"Keep firing!" shouted Richter. "Knock that second

target out of the sky!"

He needn't have wasted his words. The machine gunner had already shifted his aim and was pressing the trigger.

***

Jeremy had only seconds to act. He leveled off and put his hand on the bomb-release cable.

***

Richter heard the bolt of the machine gun slam forward. Clank. That was all. The gun was silent.

"Fire! I said!" screamed Richter, "I told you to fire!"

"The gun is out of ammunition, sir!" said one of the seamen as they scrambled to remove the empty ammunition drum.

"You imbeciles!" Richter shouted at the top of his lungs. "Hurry, or we'll all be killed!"

***

Jeremy's observer yelled, "Why aren't they firing at us?"

With blind determination, Jeremy pushed the nose of the Fairchild down and dropped to within a hundred feet of the waves.

"What the hell are you doing!" the observer shouted, terrified.

Jeremy shouted back without taking his eyes off the U-boat, "They're not shooting at us! I'm going in while I can. I'm not gonna miss!"

In desperation, Jeremy aimed the airplane at the U-boat. The U-boat grew larger and larger in the windscreen.

Almost there.

Suddenly, the faces of Luce and Phil filled Jeremy's vision. He shook his head to clear it.

He was mere seconds from slamming into the U-boat. He saw the German sailors diving for cover.

Now!

He tugged the bomb release cable and yanked the control wheel back. The Fairchild hurtled upward.

***

Richter stared as the bomb detached itself from beneath the Fairchild and tumbled downward. The airplane seemed about to graze the U-boat's radio antennae before it pulled up and away.

Jäger, too, watched the bullet-shaped weapon fall toward them.

"Now it's too late, Herr Kapitan," whispered Jäger.

Richter didn't hear him. Everyone on deck watched as the bomb continued its inexorable track. There was nothing else they could do.

For a moment it seemed the bomb would sail past its target and fall harmlessly into the ocean, but it didn't. Instead, with a loud clank the bomb struck the steel plating of U-boat's bow.

Then there was nothing. Only silence.

The men stared. The bomb had partially penetrated the steel plating of the bow. Only its tail fins were visible.

"A dud!" cried Richter. "Hah!" He laughed with relief and looked at Jäger. What can you expect from mongrel refuse? The fool probably forgot to arm...."

Jäger finally had enough. He opened his mouth to tell Richter to shut the hell up when the delayed blast from the diminutive aerial bomb ignited the remaining torpedoes nestled in the submarine's bow tubes.

A thunderous explosion ended Kapitänleutnant Hans Richter's smug diatribe as well as his life. The bow of the U-boat rose for just a moment, then dropped back into the gray sea. The crew of the SS Angel of Liberty cheered as the U-boat slid bow first into the depths.

* * *

The young Air Force captain turned to face his guest. "Well, Mister Kyner, that about does it. You've seen the whole base. All that's left is CAP headquarters. They're expecting you."

Standing with his family outside of the cream-colored two-story building, the old man bent down to lift his great-grandson for a better view of the little airplane on permanent display. Their tour of Maxwell Air Force Base in Alabama now finished, he and his wife and assorted children, grandchildren and great-grandchildren had this one last stop to make.

"Why's the airplane on that rock, Grandpa?"

"That's called a 'static display,' Bobby. It's a memorial to everyone who served in the Civil Air Patrol."

"Did you fly it?"

The old man shook his head. "No. I flew one like it, but that was a long time ago."

"Is that why the man gave you that big coin?"

The boy's mother reached out to smooth his wind-swept hair and said, "Bobby, that's not a big coin. The general awarded your great-granddad the Congressional Gold Medal because he was in the Civil Air Patrol during World War Two. Your great-granddad sank a German submarine and saved a lot of sailors on a ship."

The little boy appeared to be deep in concentration for a moment.

"Grandpa, are you a hero?"

The old man breathed deeply and his eyes misted over. "No, Bobby. I don't think I'm a hero, but two of my best friends were."

———

A retired FBI Special Agent, J. J. Knights authored several published articles on law-enforcement recruiting and flew as a volunteer Civil Air Patrol pilot and flight instructor. "Testament of Courage" was excerpted and condensed from his fictional trilogy, Benjamin's Field. To read more about it, please visit www.jjknights.com.

THE HERO OF STOLEN TIME

Ian Lahey

Crime does not pay, the saying goes. Or at least it doesn't pay as much as it did before the Vynns raided the coast.

Raids belong to that category of events which sensibly unhinge the habits and customs of peaceful folk. Take a medium-sized town, Bleakham for instance, shake it up with a few thorough plunders and let it rest a while. After a couple of years you will notice the overall feeling of the town has gone from warm hospitality to mild distrust, and those few who do not bar their doors fall into two broad categories: Those who are too poor or too dead to care about intruders, and those who are certain no burglar in his right mind would ever *dare* to muck with their property.

Five minutes in the dark abode, and Ratscrap knew he shouldn't have mucked with a necromancer's property. Shelves of dusty books and bottles, turbid jars with contents which, in some cases, stared back at him in defiance, and smelly boxes with labels like "dehydrated eye jellies" took up half the space of the small cottage.

The recognizable half, anyway. Here and there, hung on the walls, dangling from the ceiling and lurking between rows of books were the *other things*, which would have given convulsions to the most stalwart taxidermist. He could barely look at them, let alone touch them. A big birdlike creature with bony-fingered wings and withered skin was perched on top of a dusty cupboard. Its head and chest—Ratscrap knew the image would haunt his dreams for months—were the desiccated head and corrugated breasts of a woman, her expression frozen in a horrible screaming grimace.

It was impossible not to notice how different this cottage was from the other wizard's place, the tower built on the beach, which Ratscrap had burglarized years before. Now *that* had been a real looting, he thought. Brazzo the Magnificent had kept beautiful bejeweled bottles, silver knives, and rare magic scrolls just waiting for him to creep inside one night and make off with two large bags of the more valuable stuff. Even better, Brazzo had not used his powers to locate and punish the perpetrator, possibly because his head had been the first to roll when the Vynn raiders landed their longships right next to his tower the following morning.

It was quite clear to Ratscrap that this time he wasn't going to leave with much loot at all.

The snoring from the far end of the room reassured him that the old man was asleep. Ratscrap would be sure to put a few miles between him and this place by the time the necromancer woke up. He hoped a quick getaway would be enough to protect him from becoming a new specimen on one of the wizard's shelves. That uneasy thought, added to his nervousness, made him wish he was elsewhere. But first he had to check under the bed. Old people often had the strange notion that their precious belongings were safer if they slept over them. That was how he'd once relieved an old merchant's wife of her jewels, and there was a good chance the old mage might have chosen a similar hideout. He hoped it wasn't *exactly* the same—he'd found those gems in the merchant's chamber pot.

Careful not to make the slightest noise, Ratscrap went down on all fours and began to inspect the dark space between the floor and the bed itself. The moonlight filtering between the shutters was barely enough for him to see, but he needed to move near the window to get a better view. Slowly, in time with the necromancer's snoring, he moved on his hands and knees, like a gangly cat.

He was rounding the short end of the bed and getting ready to tackle the longer side when the front door flew open with a loud, smashing noise. Two large, aggressive-looking men barged in, shoving the furniture aside while jars fell to the floor crashing or, depending on some of the contents, cursing loudly in strange languages. The wizard was wearing a night mask with little golden stars and moons embroidered on it. He jerked up, right next to Ratscrap's face.

"The Vynns have returned!" he yelped as he removed the mask and rubbed his eyes. Ratscrap scuttled under the bed.

"You wish," one of the men answered the wizard. His voice sounded like dragging boulders.

"It's us. Master wants the potion. Now," the other added. His voice was the sound of boulders dragged over a cat.

The bed creaked over Ratscrap as the old man stirred nervously. "It...It's not ready. Come back tomorrow night. Knock, if you can manage."

"Master said you'd lie. Give it to us." There was a loud smash, then a creaking sound like felled timber and a thunderous crash. A few long feathers fluttered around the floor and landed near the bed.

"My harpy!" the old man wailed. "I cannot give you the potion as it is! It's too powerful, too concentrated! I will dilute it and bring it to your master myself when it's safe! I won't even ask to be paid—er, the full amount." Ratscrap saw two bare feet descend in front of him as the wizard got up from his bed. "Please don't break anything else! You have no idea how difficult it is to find some of those... *ingyenth-ael tharrrt, Mael thryorn Dah! Urush!*"

The wizard was casting a spell! Ratscrap felt an odd, scalding sensation in his chest while little bursts of energy bolted through his body.

One of the two men rushed forward. The old necromancer's voice hesitated. "I said *Mael thryorn D—*"

There was a crunching noise. The wizard crumpled to the floor and Ratscrap jerked back in terror when the bloody, broken face landed right in front of him. He felt something sharp pierce his left buttock and bit his tongue not to scream, holding his breath until his eyes watered.

"Master said he would try magic," one of the men said.

"He ain't moving. You hit him too hard, Hort."

"That's so he won't try more magic, Murd."

"But now he can't give us the potion for Master!"

"Maybe we can find it. Let's look around."

The two men's idea of "looking around" involved turning over furniture and breaking more things.

"I dunno, Hort. It's too damn dark to see anything," the one called Murd said a bit later.

"Wait. I think I have an idea."

Ratscrap blinked at the sudden silence and realized the two thugs were actually waiting for Hort's idea to surface.

Hort spoke again. "Hmm. We could go get a drink and wait for morning, it's only an hour away, then come back when we can see."

"I like your idea, especially the drink part," the other agreed, and the two trunched their way out through the broken glass and furniture. The door slammed shut.

From under the bed Ratscrap stared at the old man's bloody face. The old man stared back.

"Futhp," the wizard suddenly spat through broken teeth.

"What?" Ratscrap said, startled.

"Feethf."

"I really don't-"

"Theef!"

"Who, me?" He crawled out from under the bed and stood, genuinely offended. "I assure you there's nothing in here I'd want to steal."

The necromancer sat up, groaning in pain, and pointed a knobby finger at Ratscrap's chest. "My wand."

Ratscrap looked where the finger was pointing and saw a gnarly wooden stick clinging to his roughspun wool shirt. "This? Your wand?" He plucked it gingerly. It left a charred trace on the wool. "I was lying over it by mistake. Maybe that's why I felt so warm." He looked at the wand, then at the burned shirt and finally at the wizard. "Er... Did I prevent it from answering your magic summons just a minute ago?"

"Yef."

"Would it have saved you from getting mauled?"

"Yef."

Ratscrap moved closer to return the object, then changed his mind and pulled back. "Will you use it against me if I give it back now?"

"No."

Still holding the wand like a dead snake, he placed it in the wizard's waiting hand. The old man muttered something with his bloodstained lips and touched the wand to them as it glowed purple.

Ratscrap watched as the light engulfed the necromancer's face and then faded again. "It didn't do much for your broken jaw. You're still a bloody mess," he said helpfully.

"That waf for pain. Healing will call for a potion."

"Will it fix the lisp too?"

"What lifp?"

"Never mind. Was that the potion those two sons of a landslide were looking for? A healing potion?"

"No, no. Much more powerful, expensive and dangerous, none of your bufnef." the wizard said as he stood up and dusted his nightgown.

"Oh," said Ratscrap, "I just realized that you're perfectly right: none of this is my business, and I certainly don't want to become their business when those two demolition fanatics come back."

"Wait. I must punish you, thief."

"Punish me? But you said you wouldn't use the wand against me."

"I won't." The old wizard pulled a dried frog out of his sleeve. "Tranfmutation." He grinned a bloody broken toothed grin, which made the ugly bird woman look like a fairy queen.

Ratscrap didn't know whether to be more horrified by the fact that he was going to become a toad or that the old man slept with dead, dried animals in his clothes. As he turned to flee he heard the necromancer catch his breath. This is it, I'll be feasting on flies from now on. "Wait! Wait!" was what the man shouted instead.

"Why? So you can aim better?" Ratscrap dared a glance and saw the wizard had lowered his arm and was staring at him, with his mouth open at a crooked angle.

He stopped.

"You, Thief, found the potion I was hiding." He pointed at Ratscrap's rear.

"How much stuff do you keep in that bed old man? Did the bottle cling to me too?" He spun round a couple of times as he tried to grasp the glass object he could barely see hanging from the seat of his pants. "Rest assured I didn't drink it."

"It wasn't for drinking." The wizard rubbed his wrinkled forehead. "None of my elixirs are, the reagents I use are too ftrong. It was an injection."

Ratscrap finally got hold of the glass tube and held it up before his eyes. He could see the needle, which was slightly bent, and remembered the pain he'd felt when he was under the bed. "It's empty," he said in a squeaky voice.

"Yef, it is." The necromancer was slowly stepping away.

"Well, what does the potion do?" Turning into a toad now almost seemed like a pleasant alternative.

"I'm not too certain, the title of the fcroll was all muddled, but we can approach this fientifically. Do you feel any fymptoms? Perhaps a demon from the nether dimenfionf about to erupt from your body?" He seemed almost eager.

"Er...No. I honestly don't."

"That's odd, I never fcrewed up a potion in my entire life." The old necromancer scratched the bald spot at the top of his head. "Try to open a portal."

"A what?"

"A breach in the fabric of fpace. You know, a wormhole."

Ratscrap nodded and concentrated for a few seconds. "A what?" he repeated.

The wizard shook his head. "Here, hold thif. Make the fand go up again."

Ratscrap looked at the hourglass he'd been given. "Without turning it?"

"Concentrate, I will measure your magic aura. You don't happen to be pregnant, do you?"

Ratscrap almost dropped the hourglass. "Of course not!"

"Are you *certain*?"

"Are you blind? I'm a man!"

"You have no idea how bad fome demonic liaisons can turn out to be. Now ftand ftill!"

The necromancer waved strange devices in the air around Ratscrap, took measurements of his skull circumference and even a sample of his toenails. When he finally finished he stared at Ratscrap in silence for a long time. "Well, you muft be fo completely unmagical that maybe the potion can't have an immediate effect on you. I ftill may be able to extract it and give it to my cuftomer."

"Splendid! You can remove this stuff from my body then. Will you have to collect my sweat? Leech me?"

"You must be chopped, boiled and diftilled," the wizard said.

"Uh… I'll be going now, wouldn't want to be in the way when your guests come back." Ratscrap started backing away.

"Don't worry, I have my wand now. And I ftill want to have a little chat with you about your burglary attempt. Before I chop you up."

"No, really, let's meet some other time, for eyeball tea, perhaps?"

"I faid ftay!" The wizard raised his wand.

The door flew open again. Literally. It broke off its hinges and pirouetted in the air before smashing into a bookcase and ending its fall on the floor. "Knock knock," the thug said. "Look, he ain't run away," he added.

"He ain't dead neither," the other one said. He sounded disappointed.

"*Deyaelln afthp... aftth...* crap... *asthap yoggoth pfhang!*" the wizard sputtered. An angry purple bolt of lightning leapt from the wand in the wrong direction, narrowly missed Ratscrap's nose, and bounced off the broken door, which burst into flames. After several right-angle turns it embedded itself in the broken remains of the stuffed bird-woman.

Speech-impeded wizards should avoid casting spells.

Ratscrap felt his stomach contract when the cracked head of the creature moved in agony and started emitting a loud screeching noise. He sprinted towards the open doorway, hoping to dodge the two men blocking it, and knowing there was no way he'd be able to do it. Hort swung a huge metal-tipped mace at his head—

—He blinked—

The door flew open again. Literally. It broke off its hinges and pirouetted in the air. Ratscrap barely avoided being hit by it, and dropped flat on the ground as it smashed into the bookcase above him and ended its fall over him. There was a loud, whistling noise between his ears.

"Knock knock," the thug said. "Look, he ain't run away."

"He ain't dead neither," the other one said. He sounded disappointed.

The wizard raised his wand: "*Deyaelln afthp... aftth...* crap..."

"Oh no!" said Ratscrap. He struggled desperately to wriggle away.

The door burst into flames.

—Blink—

Suddenly, Ratscrap was free. Without thinking, he opened the front door and sprinted out of the wizard's cottage.

He'd been running on the narrow backwoods trail for two full minutes before he realized both his eyebrows had been singed off. Also, he had just opened a door he'd seen fly off its hinges, twice. Still running, he turned his head to see if anyone was chasing him.

That's when he slammed into the two men and fell on his back.

"Running without looking can be dangerous, you know," one said. "You could break your bones. Let me show you exactly what I mean..."

"Murd! Hort!" Ratscrap shrieked, "You were in the wizard's house!" His head was starting to hurt now.

"No," the one called Hort said. "We was just getting' back now to finish... Hey! How do you know?" Hort's forehead creased as the puzzled thug tried to sort the question out.

"No, no, I know nothing! But the wizard's trying to escape! You'd better hurry!" Ratscrap spoke quickly to take advantage of their momentary confusion, and darted away. He zig-zagged past some bushes and hid behind a tree, straining to listen for footsteps above the noise of his pounding heart and ringing headache. He began to relax a little as he glanced at the footpath and saw nobody had come looking for him.

"Ah, there you are, *Thief!*" the tree said.

Ratscrap shrieked, leapt into the air, and was already running when he landed, but a tree root coiled around his ankle and he fell flat on his stomach.

"Don't flee again! Remote Seeker potions are expensive to prepare."

Ratscrap turned and faced the tree, which faced him back...with the necromancer's wrinkled face.

"I refuse to be chopped and distilled!" Ratscrap cried.

"Bugger that. The potion has had its effect."

"What effect?"

"Don't tell me you haven't noticed any unusual happenings recently." The tree scowled.

"Yes," Ratscrap replied, "your lisp's gone."

"Not that, you doorknob! I'm communicating with my mind. I meant strange things like events repeating."

"Oh, those. Your door has the unnerving habit of getting knocked down and catching fire, and then doing it all over again."

"My door hasn't been knocked down... yet. You went backwards."

"I what?"

"You can take time and move it around, but apparently not at a conscious level." The wizard's face on the tree looked pensive. "I was measuring your worthless skull and you disappeared. I only saw you for an instant as you reappeared next to the door with your eyebrows aflame and left."

"You're telling me the two thugs came back and nearly bashed my nose in, your misfired fireball spell burned my face, and I escaped before it all happened?" Ratscrap's headache was singing war chants between his ears.

"I suppose so. None of that happened for me. You stole that time."

"So I ran away before they knocked the door down, and met them on the road as they were coming back..." Ratscrap was beginning to understand.

"Yes, which means I don't have much time, they've destroyed nearly all of my magic stock and from what you tell me I can't even cast spells straight. Listen. Go back in time and stop those two from breaking into my home."

"Stop them? You're out of your tree!"

"Here is something to help you get them into a cooperative mood." The tree spat out three small red vials. "It's all I've got left."

"What's this? More injections?" He held up one of the vials by its needle.

"Obedience potions, the dumber the victim, the longer the effect. I reckon it'll be permanent on those swine and there's an extra one in case you mess up, as you probably will."

"I'll be mincemeat before I can manage to give even one of those two an injection. Let's say I refuse..."

"I'll find you again and process you to recover at least some of the ingredients. *Painfully.*" The wizard looked away, as if he'd heard a noise. "Here they are. Save me and save yourself!" The face disappeared from the tree and Ratscrap was alone again.

The outskirts of Bleakham were not too far. Ratscrap knew the town well—the narrow alleyways and slippery rooftops, the musty, easily unlockable cellars, and all the nooks, crannies and other hideouts that had saved his hide many, many times, especially during the Vynn invasion. He'd snuck up in one of the deeper holes with blankets and food and waited until news came that someone had driven them away.

He was headed for one such place, just behind the Cog Tooth Inn. That meant entering the inn itself and leaving through the back door. To be more precise, that meant entering the inn, drinking a couple tankards of ale, and wobbling out through the back door. The ale Burren the innkeeper sold was dark, lovely, and nearly as thick as Burren himself. He was looking forward to a couple pints of that, and also to seeing Tika, Burren's daughter. Tika was dark and lovely too, and the thought of her made Ratscrap's headache begin to recede.

The inn came into view, and his eager strut stumbled to an abrupt halt. Hort and Murd had come here for their drink and had left a nice vertical crack in the door to mark their passing.

Ratscrap tried to relax. There was nothing to fear. Hort and Murd were in that crazed old man's cottage now. Still...he slowly made his way towards the inn while keeping his eyes on the door, defying it to do anything even remotely magical.

He took one final step. From here he could see light seeping through the break in the door, which chose that precise moment to burst open.

Ratscrap shrieked.

"Come back you louts!" the man cried. "Ratscrap, what happened to your eyebrows?"

"Burren! You owe me a pair of clean breeches," he gasped. "Those two are long gone. You should've chased after them earlier."

"What? And actually have them coming back? Come see what they did to my inn!"

Brawls at the Cog Tooth Inn were more frequent than beer stains on the furniture, but everyone involved usually had an equal share of the fun. This last one had been clearly unilateral, and harder on the furniture. Ratscrap was relieved to see Tika walking around, tending to the hurt, and painstakingly picking up the mess. She had a serious, concentrated expression on her face and, when she brushed her curls to the side, Ratscrap looked at her eyes and realized the girl was making a valiant effort not to cry.

"One o' them two criminals had me grabbed by me collar," Burren said, "and me child Tika pushed him away.

Then they were all about them not paying because of rude service and dumb customers. Some patrons got pissed off, and it got real violent after that. They never went near Tika though. Funny, maybe they was afraid of her, she gets this look when she's upset."

Ratscrap could feel his headache lurking somewhere beneath his conscious level, ready to pounce on him at any moment. He needed ale and a good rest. He also wanted to comfort Tika, but he was too shy to attempt anything more audacious than "A pint, please. When you can."

"Right away," Tika replied, and managed to smile at him.

There was a soft rumble. Ratscrap instinctively put a hand over his stomach, where rumbles usually came from, though this time it had felt like it was coming from the ground. "And some spiced potatoes, if there's any left."

"I'll see to that," Burren said. "But you'll have to pay up front. I'll be needin' money to fix all the mess."

Ratscrap dug into his many pockets. "This should cover the rent and pay for my meals for the next couple of months." It was a good-sized ruby, all he had left from the merchant's wife. He knew he was overdoing it, but he was rather fond of the hideout made possible by the presence of the inn, and seeing Tika like that... He'd pay tenfold to wipe those tears away.

Burren's eyes went wide as he held the ruby between his stubby fingers. "Well, you're certainly gettin' a generous portion of my spicy taters!" he said as he rushed towards the kitchen. Moments later Tika returned with his pint, brimming with foam. As she laid the tray down, she placed a quick kiss on his cheek.

"Thank you, you're my hero. Like the Unseen Avenger"

Ratscrap could feel his face flushing crimson. "No really... I'm no hero. I can scarcely confront myself in a mirror, let alone an army of Vynns. I'm no avenger, though I do try very hard to remain unseen."

"Too bad, I sure wish you were as daunting and mysterious as the man who sent the Vynns packing and then disappeared. But you're not unseen to me, you're my good friend Ratscrap." Tika patted his shoulder affectionately.

"Er, yes, I suppose so... To friendship..." Ratscrap drowned his already sinking spirits in his tankard.

Later that evening he retired to his hideout, with the knowledge it would give him no protection from the wizard. He made a mental note to exclude the entire category of wizards from his future targets. He'd been lucky once, with Brazzo the Magnificent, but he shouldn't have tested his luck again. The jeweled bottles from that burglary had been sold long ago, but some of the scrolls were still poking out of a vase in a corner of the small room. He picked one from the pile and inspected it, hoping it would provide some means to ward off that crazed necromancer.

"Elixir of Prolonged Love-Makinge" it said in bright blue letters. He couldn't think of any way he could defend himself with that. He tossed the scroll aside and took a second one. This one looked more promising. The magic letters glowed golden and red:

Casimir's Essence of Time Travelle, in convenient intra muſcular shottes.

Being a powerfull ſynergie of diverſe magicks, including Black ſorcerie, to guarantee permanent efficacy well unto and beyond the Death.

Caution, do not injekte in women bearing child, riſke of infinitely recursive parenthoode.

*May cause headde-achef, drynefe of the mouthe and mi-
nor earthe-quakef.*

Ratscrap stared at the spidery text for a long time. Could
this be what had been injected in him? He scanned the
parchment, trying hard to skip the disgusting details on
how to prepare (and sometimes kill) the ingredients, until
he found what he was looking for:

*Inftructions: The potion shall work its effekte whenever
the bearer's life faces a violent ende, or upon the verbal
command "Culdesac".*

*In either cafe the bearer shall travelle to the nearefte paft
when his fate might be avoided.*

There was only one way for Ratscrap to be sure this was
the recipe to the concoction which was now swilling in his
blood. He shut his eyes.

"Cool day sack," he said.

There was only one way for Ratscrap to be sure this was
the recipe to the concoction which was now swilling in his
blood. He shut his eyes.

"Cool day sack," he said.

There was only one way for Ratscrap to be sure this was
the recipe to the concoction which was now swilling in his
blood. He shut his eyes.

"Co… shit!" he said.

A high-pitched scream came up from the inn. Ratscrap
rolled up the scroll and slid it up his sleeve. He normally
would have fled in the opposite direction from the source
of the scream, but knowing he now had the option to check
out the situation before rewinding time and opting for the
cowardly alternative gave him unusual courage.

The inn's main room looked as it usually did. That is,
there were the usual people lying on the floor and the usual
people going around holding large weapons. The unusual

thing was that half of them were as transparent as morning fog.

"Ratscrap!" Burren laughed, "The Vynns have returned... more or less."

The transparent ones with weapons were evidently Vynns. They were tall and red-haired, with horned helmets and heavy swords they used to attack the patrons, but when the ghost weapon went through a body, only a ghost copy of the patron fell, horribly wounded, to the floor. Some of the guests were clearly enjoying the situation.

Tika was standing near the counter. Ratscrap walked up to her, shyly. "I... Uh, I heard a scream."

"Yes," Tika replied embarrassedly, "that was Dad when they got him." She pointed at the transparent copy of Burren's fallen body, open from shoulder to navel.

"I nearly wet meself!" Burren said as he continued tending the bar. "But it ain't so bad, and they only attack you once. Look! Here comes one for you, Tika!"

One of the hefty, long-haired ghosts was stomping towards them. The large iron chandelier in the center of the room shook slightly.

"I vill challenge to fightan," the giant said in his thick accent, looking at Tika. "You refusan, you be a craven *argr*," he said, slowly, almost enunciating, then he stared at her intently.

"I'm not a fighter. Go challenge someone else," Tika replied.

"Nyarrrr!" the ghost shouted and swung his axe. Tika's headless and transparent body crumpled to the floor while the head bounced behind the counter.

"That tickled!" Tika said, still standing and touching her intact neck.

The Vynn turned to Ratscrap. "I vill challenge to fightan, you be craven argr also?" he said.

"Maybe accepting the challenge will make him happy." Tika suggested.

"Oh… all right, I be no argr as you say, and I accept your challenge," Ratscrap said, hoping to sound heroic.

"Gut!" the red-haired ghost said and nodded in satisfaction, "Defendan!" The longsword came down vertically. Ratscrap felt as if someone had blown cold air down his spine. Then he saw the two transparent halves of his body topple forward and land over each other awkwardly.

"I think I'll need a drink after that," Ratscrap said as he stared at the bleeding copy of himself. He went to one of the stools lined up along the wooden counter.

"Me, too," Tika replied and went behind the counter. The ground trembled again and the chandelier bobbed a bit. "I'll go see if anyone else wants a drink." She placed the tankard in front of him.

Ratscrap nodded. That had been the longest conversation he'd ever had with her. Pity for the "friends" business though. He lifted his ale to toast to that.

"What the hell are you doing, you idiot?" the tankard shouted. Ratscrap toppled from his stool, showering himself with froth. Some of the patrons laughed. None of the ghosts seemed to notice.

"Stop doing this!" Ratscrap told the wizard's face.

"No! You stop! You and your powers are altering reality. My magic probes are off scale. Didn't you notice anything strange?"

"Yes," Ratscrap said, "my ale is insulting me and my ghost is dead. But I didn't do anything."

"Your ghost is dead?" the wizard asked, "You mean you were killed in the other reality?"

"Not sure what you mean by that, but I suppose so. Don't worry, it's just a shadow. I didn't feel anything."

"Those shadows, as you call them, are gradually replacing the real world with a different one. In that world the Vynns never left and you just died, probably stupidly. Look at your hands."

Ratscrap raised one of his hands which, when held up against the light, looked vaguely transparent. "Well, I suppose that when I die I'll just jump back to a safer moment."

"No you won't. You're already dead in the other reality, and you didn't jump, which means you don't have any powers there."

Ratscrap was beginning to worry. Was it his impression or was his corpse beginning to look more material? "What can I do?"

"Jump! Use your power now before it's too late!"

"I tried before. It only brought me back a few seconds."

"Then was then, now it's different. Now your fate is to fade into oblivion. To avoid it you will jump to the moment before all this became inevitable."

"When was that?"

"Beats me, I'm all poured out."

"Ratscrap, look!" Tika gasped. She was standing behind the counter and holding up her own severed head. "I can touch it now!"

"Don't worry, everything's fine," he said to reassure her. "My mug thinks all I have to do is say the magic word."

The ground shook again, Ratscrap stood and almost slipped on his own blood. The corpse on the ground seemed as real as he was. No, he looked at his hands and realized *he* was the one looking more like a ghost now. He stepped away.

"Go back now! Use the..." the wizard said. "Wait, how did you discover the magic word?"

"I found a copy of that scroll you used for the potion."

"Don't be silly. Each scroll is uni—"

The ground shook once more, violently enough to make him drop the tankard, which shattered on the floor with a strange "Ooh shi-crash!" sound. There was a grinding noise from the ceiling. Ratscrap looked up just in time to see the large iron chandelier fall on him.

"Cool day sack!"

***

Burren was waving his hands in front of his eyes and moving his lips, but Ratscrap couldn't hear him because of the shrill whistling noise that accompanied his splitting headache. He tried to shut it out by covering his ears, but that just made it worse.

"WHAT?" Ratscrap shouted above the noise, and immediately wished he hadn't. His headache reared and sparked angrily.

"I said I didn't see you come in, do you want a drink, and WHY ARE YOU SHOUTING?" Burren shouted back into his ear. His headache went into a frenzy of motley pain and excruciating colors.

Headaches are awful things indeed; even normal ones sometimes seem to have a life of their own. Magical headaches raise the paradigm to entirely new levels, and so when Ratscrap passed out again from the pain his headache simply decided to go romp somewhere else. It tried Burren's head on for size but realized there wasn't much room for romping, so it hovered around until it spotted a drunkard outside the inn who was just beginning to get the first symptoms of a mild hangover and embedded itself in his skull with a soft "sssnyuk!"

"Gnnnh," Ratscrap said. His head felt light and airy, like the charred frame of a large house after everything else had burned to ashes.

"Ouch," Burren said. He massaged his own sore forehead. "You're so stoned it's catching. I hope you paid for whatever you've been drinking."

Ratscrap looked around the room to see if he could spot any details that might help him get his bearings. One of the patrons waved at him. It was Split Ankle Pete, though the way the old man was standing made it look like he hadn't yet split anything. He'd fallen from his peach tree a couple of weeks ago, so Ratscrap reckoned he'd traveled to some time before that. No wonder his ears were whistling hymns to the gods. Stealing two weeks back in time had been quite a jump.

He saw Tika behind the counter and waved.

"Hi Ratscrap, welcome to the Cogwheel Inn," Tika called back.

Ratscrap froze in mid-wave. The Cog Tooth Inn hadn't been the Cogwheel Inn for at least— "Two *years*?" Ratscrap shouted. That was before Bleakham had been half demolished by—

"The Vynns!" A man in leather armor stormed in. A long shaft stuck out at an angle from where the arrow had perforated his shoulder blade.

"That's the third this month!" Burren cursed.

Ratscrap's natural instinct took control and he darted for the back door.

Which wasn't there. Fool, the door and hideout were part of the new, rebuilt inn. Like a trout in a vat of brandy he zigzagged aimlessly for a few moments before sprinting towards the main entrance, dodging Not-Yet-Split-Ankle Pete and clearing the snoring bodies of two drunk patrons in a single bound. It was dark outside, the darkest hours before morning, when the Vynns attacked.

A wild-eyed man desperately tugged at his sleeve. "Help! I promise I'll never touch alcohol again! Arrrrgh! My head!"

Ratscrap shook free and glanced down the dark street, trying to get his bearings. This was a different Bleakham, before the last, terrible raid. Mediating between his rabbit instinct to hide in the first hole and his good sense, he ran down streets and alleys he seemed to remember, all the way to a dead end blocked with a pile of old, abandoned carts. He slipped between the splintered planks, flexing his thin body this way and that, and reached the small door he knew he'd find behind the pile. It led to a forgotten storage room. He put his hand on the rusty doorknob.

"Go away! Find your own hideout!" a squeaky, terrified voice said from within.

Ratscrap stopped, wide-eyed. That had been his own voice! This was where he'd hidden during the invasion, like the fear-stricken coward he'd been, back then. He still was fear-stricken, but hearing his own trembling voice made him feel twice the coward.

He slowly crawled out of the piled up scrapwood and into the street again. Aimlessly, he wandered through the town, which had already sped through the defensive phase, hastened along with the retreat part and settled in a final and sullen take-the-beating-while-burning-down stage. Half dazed he walked, avoiding the raiders by sidling through dark alleys, flattening himself against doors, time-stealing out of danger when a horned Vynn spotted him and attacked.

It became such a routine that his mind began to wander. How—

Another Vynn. He ducked, and the arrow embedded itself in a door behind him.

—was he supposed to put the future back in its tracks?

Vynn approaching. He hid behind a woodpile.

All he knew about the events of the night of the invasion...

Vynn attacking. "Cool day sack."

All he knew was what they'd told him after he'd crawled out of that hole.

Duck again.

All he had to do was hide somewhere else, maybe outside the city—

"Cool day sack."

—maybe outside the city, and wait for the Unseen Avenger to show up and get rid of the Vynns.

He kept on walking without a precise destination while he pondered that last thought. The Unseen Avenger *had* to show up. If he didn't, the Vynns would never leave, and instead raid the coast and Bleakham again and again. Ratscrap frowned. In his present time, the Vynns were attacking again, as ghosts of a possible reality. Maybe the Avenger hadn't shown up. Maybe his job was to find the Unseen Avenger and get him to...

"Oh no!" Ratscrap looked up and saw where he was.

"Vot?" The Vynn guard outside the invaders' campsite raised his sword.

"I'm the Unseen Avenger!" he sobbed as the shock of realization hit him.

"Vot is dat? Messenger?"

"No, sorry. Wrong address." Ratscrap smiled reassuringly and turned to run.

The sword came down behind him.

—Blink—

"Messenger?"

"Yes, that's me. Important war message." Ratscrap's voice indicated resignation..

"Oh, gut! Ve speakan treaty, just like big wars, ya? Unt then ve refusan and burn more houses. Come, ve speakan to the hilmir, the chief."

The tall Vynn guard led him through the encampment, between large tents made of animal hides. Other warriors who crossed their path growled at him, and occasionally drew their swords. His guide motioned for them to let them pass and repeated the word "*Sendimaðr*."

They finally stopped before the largest tent, placed on piled-up ground resting on an artificial hill overlooking the seashore and the large dragon ships at anchor off the coast. It was made from skins of wolves and bears, and had a stunning assortment of horns over the entrance.

"Now what do we do?" Ratscrap asked.

"Now vait." The guard stomped his foot three times.

A small flap opened near the entrance and immediately folded shut again. It opened once more a few minutes later, as if to be absolutely sure of the situation. It shut again, and all was silent.

Somewhere, in the town, the headache stopped hovering in circles over the decapitated corpse of its former host. All the fun had ended abruptly and too soon. Where was that first head, the cozy one he'd been born in? It sniffed the air until it caught a scent. Ah, home, it thought, and made a beeline.

"Well," Ratscrap said, "looks like it isn't a good day for a house—er... tent call. I'll be back tomorrow."

"No. Listen."

A low horn blowing could now be heard, coming from within the large tent. The entrance flew open and the sound came braying through, followed by rows of Vynn warriors in full armor. They formed a circle around Ratscrap, and when they knelt to jab their large, sharp-edged shields into the ground, he found himself completely surrounded except for an opening that faced the tent.

With the sound of ripping seams, the Vynn leader pulled himself out of the tent. He was a giant among giants, standing a full head above his warriors and at least three above poor Ratscrap. His hair, unlike the others, was so fair it almost looked white.

"*Sendimaðr*," the guard repeated with a bow and pushed Ratscrap towards the leader, before heading to the only gap left in the circle of warriors and blocking it with his shield.

"So," the Vynn chief grinned. "You vill givan message to me or directly to Odin after I kill you?" The other warriors laughed.

Ratscrap looked around at the wall of shields. He was in an arena. He knew he couldn't be killed, but he suspected the experience of not being killed was going to be very painful. He summed up what little courage he could find and tried to remember the Vynn challenge he'd heard in the inn.

"You," he said. "I challenge you to fight. If you refuse, you are a craven argr."

"Gut! Now I must kill you." He drew a longsword which was taller than Ratscrap himself. He looked around Ratscrap with a puzzled expression. "Vot is weapon you bringan?"

"All I need are my hands for one like you." He hoped his voice didn't sound too shaky.

"You speakan too much. Enough *pappekakka*. Now die!" The long sword came down like a flash. Quick reflexes built over a lifetime of avoiding blows kept his head from being split like a ripe melon, but the blow cleaved a path from his shoulder to his navel.

—Blink—

—The long sword came down like a flash, but Ratscrap sidestepped it just in time. Still flinching from remembered pain, he charged with his shoulder against the Vynn's side, and almost broke his own arm. Roaring, the Vynn chief brought his blade in a wide, low arc. Ratscrap jumped back to avoid it, but bumped into the warriors on the side. They shoved him forward, making him fall face first. He turned just in time to see the sword come down towards his chest.

"Cool day sack!"

—The sword came round in a low arc again. This time he jumped the blade and kicked the Vynn's ankle as the momentum kept him turning. The Vynn roared as he completed the circle, his gloved hand came round and caught Ratscrap by the throat.

"Ool day ack!" Ratscrap coughed.

Nothing happened.

The chief held him up close to his eyes. "You twistan like veasel!" he said. "I keep you for sword practice, ya? Or maybe I kill slow!"

There was a soft "sssnyuk!" sound, like that of a dart embedding itself in a pumpkin. Ratscrap's vision exploded with stars. "ARRRRRGH!" he shouted as his body twisted in pain. The Vynn chief dropped him, startled.

"Look!" a warrior said from the circle of shields. "He's becoman berserker!"

"Dat is impossible!" the chief said. "The Gods givan bloodlust only to great warriors!"

"OOOOOW my head!" Ratscrap wailed.

The ground shook.

In a red haze he tried to stand and look at his huge opponent. Was the giant shaking or was it the ground under his feet? He looked around at the wall of Vynn warriors. Some hid their faces behind their shields when he turned towards them. The great broadsword moved. Ratscrap saw the chief charging towards him but the slow-motion attack looked almost half-hearted. Still fighting the pain in his head, Ratscrap dodged the charge and, with pickpocket speed, took one of the red obedience potions and stabbed the Vynn's backside with the syringe.

Ratscrap fell to his knees, so drained he wasn't sure he'd even be able to make a time jump now.

The cold steel of the broadsword slid up to his throat.

"Stop!" he said.

"Ya." The sword stopped.

He had the chief, but needed to put on a show to fool the others too. He pulled the scroll from his sleeve. The first part had been stained with mud and was unreadable. He held it up for all to see the glowing letters.

"I am a *Sendimaðr*, a messenger yes, but from your gods." Ratscrap knew he was trying to get away with so much bullshit even his headache was momentarily shocked into submission.

"A *Sendimaðr* from the gods, ya," the chief said. Some of his men repeated his words.

"They want you to leave the peoples of the coast alone, for many of them have been granted the bloodlust, and it would be ill to anger them."

"Ve must leavan at once, ya." More heads in the circle nodded.

"That's right. And don't forget to tell everybody in Vynnville or Vynnland or whatever to never touch these shores again, or they shall face my er... anger."

"And vot is your name, o *Sendimaðr* of the gods?" said one of the wide-eyed warriors in the circle.

"Er, we'd better keep my name low key." There was much oohing and aahing at this.

"Ya. Dat is good. The Vynns shall never land here or they will face Loki's anger."

"No, that's not exactly what I– ARRRGH!" Ratscrap doubled in pain again as his headache kicked back into action.

There was a loud, stampede-like sound and, when Ratscrap finally managed to open his eyes, he saw that he'd been left alone in a deserted encampment, and the Vynns were frantically rowing their longboats towards the dragon ships.

Oh, no, I'm a hero. Ratscrap thought. Now people would hail him and expect him to save damsels and slay dragons and such. He knew what had to be done...

EPILOGUE

Hiding for two years hadn't been a problem. Ratscrap had used the time to organize himself and his plan.

Now was the crucial moment; finding those two brutes had taken some time and considerable effort, especially giving them their injections while always remaining unseen. He was wearing a dark hood now as they stood, dazed, in front of him.

"Now repeat my instructions."

"We must give this scroll for your potion to the necromancer in the woods near Bleakham," they replied in unison. "And when we are to collect it, he will lie and say it's not ready, and he will resist us with magic."

"Perfect. And when you go to the inn, don't you *dare* lay your hands on the girl. Now go."

Murd and Hort nodded in unison. "Yes, Master."

———

Ian Lahey was born in Milan, Italy, to an American father and an Italian mother. He teaches English Literature and Aviation English in Udine, Italy, and leads a quiet and ordinary life with his wife, his two children and his invisible cat, Laurelin. To learn more about Ian, visit him at his Facebook page: http://www.facebook.com/lovewritingstuff

SPYING ON THE SPY

Lisa Cox

**SENATOR JOHN WHITMAN VANDENBERG'S
BALLROOM, WASHINGTON CITY
JULY 28, 1814, 8:00 PM**

It was a night like any other summer night. Sticky, sweet, and slow. The windows and doors were open in the hope that a breeze might trickle in off the Potomac River. The ballroom was teeming with people and heavy with air. Malodorous perfume assaulted the nostrils and closed the throat, but did nothing to mask the stench of the perspiring bodies.

Time itself was suspended on a pinpoint. Movements were as slow as the night, speech was thick and heavy as the night. The dancers moved past me as if I were the ballerina on top of a dying music box.

It was a party like any other. Music, dancing, drinks, debutantes nervously tittering near their chaperones, politicians' wives whispering their judgments in tight circles. The politicians themselves laughed boisterously at their own jokes and drank entirely too much champagne, then retired to some room forbidden to ladies to drink hard liquor, tell bawdy jokes, and smoke expensive cigars.

I was a debutant, like any other. Trussed up, nervous, and eager to please.

Except I wasn't. I am not.

I am not pretty or graceful or charming, I cannot dance or flirt or even curtsey very well, and I do not possess the qualities a man finds attractive in a potential wife. I am young and well bred, but I am too tall, too chubby, and too smart to appeal to a potential husband.

I was taught all the social graces, but I forget them the moment I step into a crowded room. People make me nervous. Actually, they terrify me. I find it hard to defend myself when people whisper about me, because I lack quick wit and courage. It is only well after I have pondered the incident for a while that I think of a snappy retort, and by that time it's too late.

I do not enjoy light-hearted novels written especially for young ladies of my station. I do enjoy Shakespeare, Homer, and Dante, classic Greek and Roman literature, art, religion, languages and music.

But the greatest passion of my life is numbers. They fascinate me.

I had a governess, growing up, and she and my mother taught me everything I needed to know to be a good wife and run a household well. Not once did geometry, algebra, or any other advanced mathematical theory fit into the equation. Pardon the pun, but math seeps into even my most ordinary thoughts.

I read everything I can about math. I practice adding large sums in my head whenever I am nervous, which seems most of the time. I look at a room or an object, and calculate its area or circumference. This is my own secret.

I hate social events and I am almost always required to be in attendance. Right now I am hugging the wall and praying for a very large and very cold snow storm. In Washington City. In July. The odds are not in my favor. I know, I calculated them.

My older sister, Rose, is now dancing with a congressman from Virginia. Her blue ball gown moves with her, as if part of her body. The sky blue was carefully chosen to bring out her eyes, the beautiful eyes she inherited from our father.

Her husband is a very prosperous lawyer, also from Virginia. To say this marriage was beneficial to all parties would be a gross understatement. Augustus Carter, her husband, is the son of a judge. August, as we call him, will be a judge, too, one day.

Rose has always been graceful and charming, everything I am not and have never been. I was still in the nursery when she left home, so I have few memories of her before her coming out. Since then, she has had little to do with me. I do not know if it is my shortcomings or hers that prevent a closeness between us. I am hoping it is hers.

Just for something to do, I go to the refreshment table and get a lemonade. The buzzing conversation around me is, inevitably, about the war. The slaughter has been going on for two years now and I do not see a positive outcome for America.

England has done some very bad things to us, and I am just as patriotic as any other American. However, we are a foundling nation. How are we to defeat the Empire again? Do we really believe the English will not learn from their mistakes?

Robust laughter draws my attention to a group of politicians in the corner. My father, the Senator, is among them. He, like most men here, is a War Hawk. He started his career as a Federalist and is now a Democratic-Republican. He follows the power.

My father is a very tall, broad-shouldered man. Over the years, his love of rich food and brandy has expanded his paunch and slowed his gait, but he is still an impressive man. His crystal blue eyes are sharp, and what is left of his blond hair has not lost its color.

Father swears his mother is a Whitman (of the Boston Whitmans), descended from one of the families on the *Mayflower*. I seriously doubt the validity of this claim. I think Grandmother was the daughter of an Irish house-maid. The closest they came to being Whitmans was polish-ing their silver.

Grandfather Vandenberg fought in the Revolution, as did Father. They were at Fort Ticonderoga and never fail to recount their glorious victory for America. One of only a handful, I might add.

After the war, Grandfather returned to the mill he owns, but Father had no desire to run the mill and entered local politics. That is where his talent truly lies, he says. I am proud of all my father has accomplished. I just wish when he is at home he were more my father and less the politi-cian.

Father spoke from the Senate floor in support of Presi-dent Madison in his quest to declare war. I did not hear the speech, as young ladies are not allowed to have independ-ent thoughts on politics; however, I am told it was most stirring. My older brother, Ethan, could not stop talking about it.

At this moment, Ethan is flirting with Kathleen Murphy, the granddaughter of an Irish diplomat. Looking handsome in his dress uniform, he is no doubt doing his best to impress her by recounting his heroics in the battle of York. I am sure she is awed by his tales, most of which are true. I suspect their engagement will be announced later this summer.

Ethan volunteered for the Army in June 1812, when the war began. He was wounded rather severely at the Battle of

York last year, was promoted to the rank of captain, and sent home. I do not know if he will return to battle, but I suspect Father is doing his best to keep Ethan home. He has been urging Ethan to run for political office for years, and I think he will finally heed Father's advice.

My parents are good people who care a great deal about their two children. The only problem is that they have three. They have never been very attentive to me. For instance, my mother, Claudine, is currently holding court with her friends, telling them all about our dinner with President Madison and his wife, Dolley. Not once has she even looked around to see what I am doing. She's my chaperone.

Mother is from Quebec. Her father, a French soldier, fought in the War of Austrian Succession. Grandmother was an Austrian battlefield nurse during the war. Grandfather's father forbade him from marrying her, so they ran away to settle in Quebec. Grandfather made a fortune in fur trading and moved his family to New York, where he introduced his three daughters to society. My father was a New York congressman at the time.

That leaves me, Georgina Violet Vandenberg, standing in a corner all by myself at a party adding large numbers in my head and estimating the distance between me and every possible escape.

The buzz around me shifts slowly, then faster, until the drone assails my ears. I may be tall, but I am standing in the back of the room and I cannot see the reason for this sudden frenzy. Then, a strange golden blond head pops out from the sea of familiar faces.

Wending his way through the crowd, the stranger appears oblivious to the stares around him. If he does not know they are talking about him, he is an idiot. On the other hand, if he knows and is pretending not to care, he is my new hero. All right, I may be stretching my esteem a bit.

He makes his way to the refreshment table with a grace I silently envy. His long, elegant fingers reach for a champagne glass. In the candlelight, he is startlingly handsome. Strong jaw, clean-shaven, high cheekbones. His dress clothes are silk. Black jacket, white waistcoat, black breeches tucked into sturdy boots. A lacy white cravat tied neatly at his collar completes the outfit. So far, he is perfect.

Then he turns to me and smiles and I see he has the most beautiful chocolate eyes.

I wait for my knees to weaken and my stomach to flip over itself at such sculpted male beauty. I listen for my heart to race and carefully measure my breaths for the inevitable loss thereof.

Nope. This handsome, graceful, angel-on-earth gives me none of the classic love-at-first-sight symptoms. However, he is potentially the most interesting person at this party.

Of course, I cannot speak. I am terrified of saying something utterly idiotic. Just as I am trying to force a welcoming smile on my face, he leans close to me and whispers in a thick southern accent, "This room is so stifling, I think I would prefer to be in York."

The reference to the American burning of the British Canadian capital sends me laughing, and miraculously, my tongue and mouth become unglued.

"Preston Beaumont, at your service miss." He sweeps a bow over my outstretched hand and brushes my gloved knuckles with his full lips. The name is the most pretentious I have ever heard, but I keep this to myself. I attempt a curtsey and introduce myself to Mr. Beaumont.

"Tell me, Miss Vandenberg, do you dance?"

"Not very well," I mumble.

"Would you honor me with a turn about the floor?"

He smiles and bats his long eyelashes so prettily that I giggle, and agree to accompany him in a country dance. As he puts his gloves on, I note a scar on his dimpled chin and another just above his left eye. Poor man. But for those scars, that face is the model of perfection.

I almost trip over my new ball gown, which is a pastel purple that looks horrid on me. I much prefer earthy tones to pastels, but Mother insisted, and I cannot argue, because I did not pay for my wardrobe. My embarrassment over the color only adds to my self-consciousness, but I try to put it out of my mind as the dance begins.

There is little time for conversation, as the music plays and the couples are parted and reunited in quick succession. His warm eyes never leave mine and, although I know there is no romantic interest, I am flattered by his attention.

The music dies as the dance ends, and Mr. Beaumont holds out his gloved hand in front of him, urging me to take it. I lay my hand on his and he guides me to the refreshment table. I feel perspiration glisten on my brow so I dab my forehead with my handkerchief. Mr. Beaumont offers me a lemonade, and I happily accept. I am certain he will beg his leave of me now and, when he does not, the silence lies awkwardly between us. I search my brain for something to talk about.

"The weather really has been unbearably hot of late, has it not?" I ask lamely. Taking a large sip of lemonade keeps me from talking, so I finish my drink in quick order.

"Indeed it has, Miss Vandenberg. May I refill your drink?"

Nodding, I hand him my glass and he is not gone long enough for my taste. He stands in front of me, but every so often I see him scan the room. I assume he is looking for someone, but to ask would be rude, so I continue the inane questions I overhear my mother ask at parties. The conversation is so stilted I can feel his boredom matches my own, so it is a great surprise to me when he asks softly, "May I escort you to a cooler place? Perhaps to the terrace?"

I am baffled by this abrupt change in conversation but nod in assent.

"My mother..." I blurt, looking around for her. "She is my chaperone and will need to follow."

"Of course," he smiles politely. I am again captivated by his charming good looks. Still, I feel no romantic spark. I then wonder if I am obliged to feel grateful that such a handsome man should not only dance with me but pay me any mind at all. My back stiffens and I hold my head a little higher. I refuse to feel anything at all. I do not owe him or anyone anything.

My mother is immersed in conversation with another senator's wife, so Mr. Beaumont and I go in search of Rose. He seems a bit impatient and continually looks over his shoulder toward the terraces and garden. I am now certain he is setting me up for a trick of some sort. It is a relief when I cannot locate my sister.

"I am sorry, Mr. Beaumont, but I cannot go to the terrace with you."

"I promise to be a gentleman," he says, one hand over his heart.

While I hesitate, he whispers "please" several times.

"If this is a trick, Mr. Beaumont, I will be certain you are tossed out on your ear," I threaten just as softly.

His eyes widen and sincerity washes over his face.

"No, of course not! Why ever would you think this a jest?"

I almost state the obvious, but instead, shrug.

"I will ask someone to accompany us," I say simply and lead him to the hall where I see one of our maids, Angela, loitering about. Preston seems anxious, so I quickly usher the three of us to the terrace. Once there, he manages to find a private corner for us and asks again why I thought he was tricking me.

"Never mind," I answer with a shake of my head.

"You did not look like you were having a very good time at the party. Is everything all right?" He asks.

"Mr. Beaumont, I do not know you well enough to answer that. For that matter, you do not know me well enough to ask such an intimate question."

"I am sorry, Miss Vandenberg. I meant no offense. You just look so sad."

I am immediately taken aback by his accuracy. It hits me right in the heart and travels up to my tear ducts and threatens to spill over onto my cheeks. Instead, I take a deep breath and change the subject.

"Pray, where are you from Mr. Beaumont?"

He smiles that impish smile again and, lit from behind by the ballroom, looks like a devil sent to tempt me.

"Avoiding the subject? All right, I will play along. I am from Charleston, South Carolina. Ever been there?"

When I shake my head, he continues.

"Oh, Charleston is the most beautiful town you ever saw. Palm trees everywhere. Bright sunshine. I often ride my horse, Pythagoras, down the Ashley River to Middleton Place. My friend Henry Middleton lives there," he explains while his eyes roam over my shoulder to the gardens.

"It sounds lovely," I murmur. Then something he said catches my attention.

"You said your horse's name is Pythagoras? As in the Pythagorean Theorem?" I ask excitedly and he smiles distractedly. When he does not return his attention to me, I turn in curiosity.

Two figures stand in the garden. I cannot discern who they are or, indeed, much of anything about them. I blink, trying to adjust my eyes to the darkness. After a moment, I am able to identify the silhouettes as men. I do not recognize either man. One hands what appears to be a parcel to the other gentleman. The man takes it, looks around, then disappears into the darkness.

"That was odd," I blurt. Mr. Beaumont nods in apparent agreement.

"Did you recognize them?" he asks.

"No. It is much too dark. Could you discern their features in the darkness?"

"No. I wish my brother were here. He has excellent night vision." He sighs and runs a hand over the back of his perfect blond hair.

"Your brother?" I ask politely, but Preston does not seem to hear me. After several silent heartbeats, I try a different tack.

"I wonder what those men were doing?" I ask in what I hope is a casual manner and not a lifeline to ease this awkward conversation.

He smiles and says he really does not want to waste the lovely evening talking of clandestine meetings when we could share one. After all, he says, I am such a beautiful and interesting lady.

At this, I openly scoff. Really, this flirtation has gone too far. "Mr. Beaumont, flattered as I am, you cannot possibly be interested in me romantically. For that matter, I have yet to say anything so interesting as to warrant that compliment. What is your game?"

His eyes widen again and he smiles, not in that charming way he has employed all evening, but a simple, sweet smile. I get the feeling he does not smile in such a manner often. His other smile is obviously practiced; polished to a bright glow. This one is natural and a little crooked. This is a smile I can work with.

"There is no game, Miss Vandenberg. Why do you think of yourself so meanly?"

"I am a realist, Mr. Beaumont. I have heard the whispering for years now."

"The whispering? About what?"

"About me. The matrons and the debutantes have been talking behind my back for years. You cannot pretend you do not know why."

"I honestly do not know why they would gossip about you. Do you have a secret?" he asks, the mask firmly back in place.

"No, of course not. I am the most boring person in America." I laugh without humor.

"I doubt that. In my experience, gossip is just petty people spreading lies out of jealousy or just plain cruelty. Do not take their words to heart," he urges.

"Their words are extremely hurtful. They say I am 'pretty for a chubby girl.' That my height is 'not my most unfortunate attribute.' They think me a snob because I read too much and socialize too little. They do not even like the books I read. The girls called me names when we were younger, and now they whisper them in their little circles. I am a black sheep, Mr. Beaumont. An anomaly. An equation without a result."

I have no idea why I have confided in a total stranger, but I probably will never see him again, which is a comfort. My confession will surely drive him away for good.

"Then they are all fools," he says simply.

My mouth opens and I try to close it quickly, but my jaw feels too heavy.

"If I may be so bold, you are beautiful. Everything about your appearance is enviable and worthy of praise. If I had to pick one flaw it would be your eyes for they are the saddest eyes I have ever seen. Stormy, desolate gray. There is so much hurt in their depths."

"That is a mighty pretty speech. Do you practice that in front of the mirror?" I let slip before I catch myself. I rush to apologize, but he bursts into laughter.

"You are a treasure, Miss Vandenberg. And too clever for your age."

"I will take that as a compliment," I nod in appreciation.

Our laughter continues for a moment then he sobers.

"You should never let others take away your happiness. That comes from inside you. You are much too intelligent to pay the gossips any mind at all."

Even though I am having a good time with this man, I find him much too forward by half, and nosy to boot. And, if I am honest, he is the only person who has ever truly understood me.

I sigh, stuck in the middle of my inner conflict and not knowing what to do. I suppose it would do no harm to continue this discourse with Mr. Beaumont, and it would make the evening go by quickly to converse with a person of moderate intelligence and amusing charm instead of calculating the square footage of the ballroom again.

I quickly decide to give myself more time to warm up to him.

"Thank you, Mr. Beaumont. You are a very kind man, though I must confess I know so little about you. Other than that you are from Charleston. You were telling me about your horse, I believe."

I find most men like to talk about their horses or something else about themselves I find terribly boring, so I am surprised when he responds, reading my mind.

"Pythagoras? Yes, I have a fine horse. I must confess I do not know much about horseflesh, so you will have to forgive me if I cannot keep up my end of that conversation."

"No, no, no," I stammer, then mentally kick myself for stuttering. "That is, whatever you want to discuss is my pleasure." *Nice recovery*, I silently congratulate myself.

He smiles that natural smile and I wonder if he even knows it. This man is practiced, polished, and utterly false. However, there is something about him so sincere that I cannot help but be drawn to him. Even though he seems to be playing a character for my amusement. Or maybe for his own amusement. Now, this thought sets off a challenge in my mind. By the time this party is over, I will find out which is the real Mr. Beaumont, and what are his real intentions.

THE TERRACE – 9:45 PM

Mr. Beaumont and I have been on the terrace for at least twenty minutes. Entirely too long, and completely inappropriate, to my mother's thinking. Angela is hovering near, there are other people around us, and we are the proper amount of distance from each other, but I am unwilling to break *all* the rules of propriety. Bend them, perhaps, but if I break them I could be forced to marry this stranger. That would never do.

"Will you escort me back to the party, please?" I ask him, not really wanting to leave the peace of the terrace but sensible enough to return to the party.

"Of course," he replies, offering me his arm.

When we are back in the ballroom, he looks around again. I note his distracted demeanor and try to guess possible solutions. One, he is looking for a woman with whom he shares an affection. Two, he is looking for a man with whom to ingratiate himself for the possibility of beginning a career in politics, or he is simply looking to further his business contacts. Three, he is a lunatic.

I eliminate the third possibility right away. We have had a couple of very lucid conversations. If he were insane, I would know it.

I remember the terrace, how important it was that we go out there at that particular moment. The two gentlemen in the garden were also of particular interest to him. That leads to another possibility. Four, he is a government agent.

Unlikely, but possible. I laugh it off as flight of fancy, but remember we are at war. Spies could be anywhere. Again, I laugh at myself for my wild imagination, hiding a smile behind my fan.

The second possibility is most credible. Beaumont Shipping must have contacts in Congress. Most likely, he is there by invitation from one of the South Carolina senators. Disappointed, I say nothing as he escorts me back to the refreshment table. He picks up two champagne flutes and we begin to walk the perimeter of the room. We talk a bit, leaving just enough space between us to maintain propriety but not so much that we cannot hear each other over the music and accumulated conversation.

We dance once more but are not allowed another turn about the floor. Since I have no other prospective partners, I find this silly. However, I do notice the tongues wagging in our direction and cannot help a bit of a thrill run up my spine. After all, how many times has my name been mentioned in connection with a handsome stranger? Yes, I am relishing my sudden fame. I suppose it would not hurt to have a little fun while I am conducting my investigation of my new friend. I am hoping he has a secret. If he is really here for the reason I think he is, my game is up. And wouldn't that be a pity!

Just as we are coming from the dance floor, my mother approaches with drawn eyebrows, pinched mouth and sharp gray eyes. Yes, I am in trouble now. I assume she will toss him out of the party. I do not remember seeing his name on the guest list, after all.

Her short brown hair is loose, with ringlets framing her face. They sway as she approaches. Miraculously, the pearls adorning the crown of her head stay in place. She holds her pink silk ball gown in one hand, just lifting the hem so as not to step on it with her matching slippers. The neckline of her gown is as daring as fashion allows.

"Mother," I manage as she approaches us. Ignoring me, she holds out her hand to Mr. Beaumont.

"I am Mrs. John Vandenberg."

"It is a true pleasure to make your acquaintance, Mrs. Vandenberg. I am Mr. Preston Beaumont of Charleston, South Carolina."

Studying my mother, I see her mouth is still pinched in that lemon-sucking way.

"Are you a member of Congress, Mr. Beaumont?" I stifle a nervous laugh. That is Mother's polite way of saying Mr. Beaumont was not invited to her party.

"No, madam. My family owns a shipping company."

"My deepest regrets on the blockade, Mr. Beaumont."

He laughs and I smile, but I cannot relax with Mother's piercing gaze aimed at my companion. Her assessment of him is making me squirm, and I pray that she does not throw him out. I have three theories that need further examination. Well, two that are the most plausible.

"Beaumont Shipping Company?" she asks, her eyes assessing him.

"Yes," he confirms.

I have never seen my mother's face light up so quickly.

"Well, Mr. Beaumont, we are exceedingly pleased to welcome you to our little party. I will inform the staff to set one more place at dinner. Mrs. Madison has personally shared her recipes with me."

I roll my eyes at Preston and he grins but gives nothing away. The gleam in Mother's eyes tells me I will be sitting next to Preston tonight. Her obvious attempt at matchmaking is laughable, but there is no way to discourage her. Besides, I am on a mission.

Mother excuses herself, presumably to see to the seating arrangement but whispers to me before she takes her leave. "Senator Girard must have invited him," she says, referring to Francis Girard, one of the senators from South Carolina. He and my father have been political rivals for years. While they have voted similarly of late, they have competed with one other since they were both state representatives.

Preston and I resume our walk about the ballroom. While he tells me about his family's business, his attention is focused somewhere over my right shoulder. I turn quickly so Preston does not catch me spying. Senator Girard is across the room talking to my father's clerk, David Thompson. David is Father's protégé. I have known

David since I was twelve. He has a lot of ambition. That is why my father likes him so much. I, however, have always found him to be slimier than a snake.

Something clicks in my brain and I smile. Time to move my chess piece. I tilt my head ever so slightly to a point across the room.

"Mr. Beaumont, I hate to interrupt, but the man standing next to Senator Girard is David Thompson. I recognize his profile as the man who was in the garden earlier."

Preston's eyes grow big as he looks in the direction I indicated.

"Senator Girard is here? He wasn't supposed to be," he blurts. An impatient sigh escapes his lips and he fingers a button on his black silk dress coat.

"Well, he is. And I am certain the senator could introduce you to Mr. Thompson. If you were interested in meeting him, that is."

He smiles that fake smile and I know he is up to something.

"You must know everyone at this party, Miss Vandenberg. *You* could introduce me."

"I could. Surely it would be better coming from a friend as close as Senator Girard," I persist.

"Possibly." He strokes his chin in thought. He moves in closer to whisper conspiratorially in my ear. "Truthfully, I would rather not speak with Frank. I lost quite a bit of money to him over cards and I am rather embarrassed by my behavior afterward." His familiar use of the Senator's nickname is clever, and his excuse is plausible but does not throw off my suspicions. There is the possibility he is a party crasher. This also opens up more questions. Who is he really if not the person he says he is? Why lie and tell everyone he is Preston Beaumont when there is a credible witness to contradict that fact? Or, is my imagination running away with me again? But isn't this the point of the game?

Time to move another piece.

"I might be able to provide an introduction," I concede, "if you tell me what you want with David."

"Just to talk, of course."

"Just to talk? I doubt that. Your interest in him rose tenfold when I told you I recognized him from the garden. So, I repeat, what do you want from him?"

"Are you always this forward?"

"Do you always avoid personal questions?"

The pawns move about the board and we square off, plotting our next moves.

"What do you care about my interest in Mr. Thompson?"

"Why should I answer any of your questions when you will not answer mine?"

"Touché. So, will you introduce me or not?"

I sigh, because I know he won't directly answer any of my questions. Not yet, anyway. I need to gain his trust.

"Are you convinced I won't be able to keep up with matters of business? You told me I was clever; was that a lie? You spoke earlier of my beauty. Do you think that the sum of my attributes?" I challenge him. Yes, it is bold but we are past the pretense of respectable conversation.

Preston's eyes light up in admiration.

"I think you all that is worthy, Miss Vandenberg." He smiles crookedly and a softness touches his eyes.

"Then let me help you," I persuade.

For a moment, he doesn't move and time itself seems suspended on his ruminations. The conversations around me cease, the music grows silent, and the champagne lays untasted on many tongues. Then he moves, and the room follows.

"May I request a private conversation, Miss Georgina?"

If Preston wants a private word, I know it's important. More to the point, I know he means *private*.

I nod and he offers his arm.

"It is stifling in here, shall we walk out again?"

I smile at his double-meaning but say nothing as we leave the oppressive heat of the ballroom with its mindless conversations. It is late enough now to catch the breeze off the river. I dab at my forehead as my body cools down.

Preston takes me in his arms and smiles lovingly at me. I struggle a bit, but he shakes his head.

"Come now, love, just one kiss," he says and I now believe it is for the benefit of those around us.

His lips brush mine, move to my cheek, then quickly find my ear.

"I believe I can trust you, Miss Georgina," he whispers, "Please do not make me regret that."

I pull him closer and stroke his hair.

"I am the model of discretion," I assure him softly.

"Good girl. I sought you out tonight as my entreé into this party. You know everyone here and are observant enough to assist me. You are clever, to boot. An invaluable asset."

I stammer a question in reply but he cuts me off quickly.

"No time to explain that. I have been investigating Senator Girard for some time now. To come to the point, he is innocent of any wrongdoing. David Thompson has been passing information to Admiral Cockburn and fabricating evidence to implicate Senator Girard. He has used his position in your father's office not only to attempt to disgrace both Senators but he has also committed treason."

His words tumble out in a rushed murmur. My heart races at the accusations and implications.

"I need your help. Just introduce me to David Thompson for now. I will do the rest. Please do not worry. I will protect you and your family," he assures me.

"Who are you really, Preston Beaumont?" This is all happening so quickly, my head is beginning to spin.

"Tonight I am Preston Beaumont. If you know me only as Preston, there will be no need for you to lie or worry about two names."

"You are a spy," I sigh happily.

"Yes," he admits and I am taken aback at his honesty. This is definitely not the evening I had envisioned. Huzzah for that.

We stare at each other for a heartbeat, his eyes pleading for help. I nod mutely and wait for him to offer escort back to the party.

Dinner is announced as we are just slipping back into the ballroom. Mother forces me to enter the dinning room on David's arm, but I manage a covert look at Preston. At least, I hope it was covert.

My heart has not slowed its hectic pace.

THE DINING ROOM — 11:00 PM

I am seated between Preston and David. To help Preston, I have made proper introductions. My part seems to be over, however, and they seem content to ignore me. Now I have no choice but to sit quietly and pick at my food.

The turtle soup is served and the conversation slows as everyone samples the fare. I wait for the conversation to pick up again. There is much to be gained listening to others' conversations.

"Mr. Thompson, are you enjoying the party?" Preston finally asks.

"Indeed, sir, I am. And you?"

"Very much so. Miss Georgina has been charming company," Preston smiles with a pointed look at me. Too pointed. Is he trying to make David jealous? If so, he is completely off target.

David coughs and I automatically swivel around to inquire after his well-being. Once the fit passes, Preston resumes his interrogation.

"I understand you work for Senator Vandenberg. That must be an exciting position." Preston steers the conversation to where he wishes it to be. I marvel at his ability.

"Yes, I enjoy politics. Might I say, without sounding too boastful, that I seem to have a knack for it?"

I nod and can only assume Preston does too because David continues.

"Yes, our young country is on the verge of greatness. We will open westward and stretch to the Pacific Ocean some day. The rivers are plentiful and the land is vast. It is an exciting time to be in politics. Once we win this war, the world will be convinced of our superiority, that we are not afraid of England or her Empire. Your father and I will have a great hand in that." He nods toward me.

The soup is removed and I realize I had barely touched it. No matter, there is much more to eat. Roasted lamb and beef, boiled French green beans, pickled cucumbers, roasted potatoes, green peas, and rockfish topped with a creamed crab sauce are divided amongst the guests. The fish is fresh from the Potomac River and absolutely delicious. Preston slathers mushroom ketchup over his beef while David continues to expound on his vision of America's future between bites of his own meal.

"Our cities will expand, each one to rival London in culture and opulence. Indeed, there will be several cities in the West to compliment those here on the East Coast."

"Hear, hear!" Preston raises his wine glass in a small toast.

Buoyed by this show of solidarity, David continues his boasting.

"As this great nation of ours expands, we must build a navy and army to protect our shores. I believe Commodore Barney has laid the very foundation on which we can successfully accomplish this action," David mercifully finishes. His speech is pretty, but I can only assume false, given Preston's accusations.

"I cannot imagine a better future for our country, Mr. Thompson. I am hoping that Beaumont Shipping will be a part of your vision," Preston smiles and I turn to see David smiling proudly.

Dessert arrives and everyone stuffs themselves with fresh lemon tart, pound cake topped with strawberries, and almond cream pudding.

Conversation slows around me, and the murmurs of appreciation tell me everyone is enjoying their dessert as much as I am. Soon the women will leave the table and I will be relegated to the parlor while Preston continues to have fun without me.

THE PARLOR — 12:30 AM

There is a small gathering of ladies in the parlor enjoying sherry and exchanging pleasantries. A few have decided to play cards at the table near the empty fireplace. I try counting the cards but do not have a good vantage point to see every hand, so I resign myself to calculating the volume of my mother's Chinese vases. After another ten minutes, I excuse myself to the ladies' retiring room. Preston appears in the parlor doorway like the sunrise, and my relief is palpable.

"It's time," he whispers to me.

"What do you want me to do?" I ask eagerly.

"Find David and ask to speak to him privately. I will be hiding in the library. When you get him in there, tell him you saw him in the garden earlier and ask him what he was doing. No doubt he will try to explain away his actions but you must persist in your accusations. He will become defensive and verbally attack you. Do not falter. He will break. And if you should absolutely need to, flirt with him a little to get him alone."

I snort at the suggestion but follow him to the billiard room where the gentlemen are congregated.

I tell the butler I need to speak with David in the library, and he dutifully leaves to fetch him for me.

I pace for a good ten minutes, then down a bit of whiskey and feel it burn all the way down into my stomach. I have tried it once before but it did not settle well and, embarrassingly, came back up. No one, thankfully, was around. This time the whiskey rests comfortably in my body and fuels my veins with courage. Preston has been silent the entire time, but I feel his presence through the curtain on the right wall window.

I hear footfalls nearing the door, and David enters the room on the heels of the butler. He nods to me and, suddenly distracted by a piece of thread on his coat sleeve, picks it off cleanly. Once we are alone, I shift from foot to foot. His bored expression quickly turns to agitation.

"What is it, Georgina?" He sighs.

"I just thought I would tell you that my father thinks very highly of you."

"That is a welcome thought but hardly one that warrants pulling me from a card game."

"Well, I just would not want my father to be hurt in any way."

"You needn't worry about him," David says, rolling his eyes. I know I do not have much time before he leaves, and I need a confession.

"Well, um, David, I wanted to tell you I saw you, um, in the gardens earlier."

"What of it?"

"I saw you hand a package to a man." There, I said it.

"What business is it of yours?" He replies lazily.

"It is my business because...well..." I stammer.

He laughs.

"Go back to the nursery, Georgina."

"I am eighteen. Hardly a child," I reply, stiffening my back.

"You are very much a child. Hardly old enough to understand politics," he replies distractedly while checking the watch at his waist. His booted foot taps the carpet.

"I understand more than you suppose."

"Since this appears to be some sort of diversion for your own amusement, I shall take my leave."

David bows mockingly and starts toward the door.

"Traitor," I accuse softly.

He turns, and his smile is as slippery as snake oil.

"That depends. To which country?" he asks. I cannot believe he did not even attempt a denial.

"Your big speech at dinner was nothing but a big lie," I continue.

"No, I meant every word. England will once again rule our country and it will be her coffers that fund our new cities. This country is bankrupt, my dear. It cannot possibly stand on its own."

"My father trusts you. He supports President Madison. What will happen to you when he finds out?"

"His Majesty will rule the country by then. I will be above reproach in the seats of power in Parliament."

As he is speaking, I feel myself curl into a ball of rage. He is such a vile, contemptible snake. I almost shout these words at him when Preston appears from behind the curtain and punches David square in the jaw. David crumples instantly.

"Thank you, Preston," I nod to him just as two uniformed and armed men appear in the doorway. They pull David up, shackle him, and haul him away.

"The pleasure was entirely mine. Now, Miss Georgina, shall we go back to the party?" He asks, offering me his arm.

"Well, now I don't have to dance with him tonight," I say, and Preston chuckles.

"Sir, we need to ask you a few questions," one of the uniformed men says to Preston.

"Go," he tells me softly and kisses my knuckles.

Back at the party, the buzz around me is quite different. News of David's arrest is spreading quickly, and my part in it is being greatly exaggerated as the story spreads. I beam with pride, as I am now the talk of the party. And my parents could not be more proud that I was able to assist in removing a traitor from our midst. I am still a novelty, but something of a hero, too. Finally.

I spend the next hour fielding questions from all in attendance. The party should be over by now, but the night's events have everyone much too excited to seek their beds. After a time, I go in search of Mr. Beaumont. Surely, he is done with the authorities by now?

"Have you seen Mr. Beaumont?" I ask about two dozen times as dawn breaks. No one has seen him in hours and I begin to worry about my friend. Then I remember that he is a spy. And spies never stick around to share in the glory. They simply disappear to resurface as someone else; in another time, in another place.

———

Lisa Cox loves little known stories from any era and finds the War of 1812 particularly interesting. She lives in Leesburg, Virginia, and has written two historical novels, Behind Your Eyes *and* Unbridled, *under the name Susannah Woods. https://www.facebook.com/profile.php?id=100003197841514*

THE DORK

Diane Hall

Dork fiddled with the combination dial and hoped the locker's owner wouldn't show up too soon. And if he did, Dork prayed there wouldn't be a jock with him. Encounters with jocks were always painful. Nevertheless, it was worth the risk. This was the perfect locker, with the perfect view of perfect Ernestine's locker.

His name wasn't Dork, of course, it was Wayne, but he'd grown so used to Dork that he answered to it. He even *thought* of himself as Dork. Most people around school, including the phys ed teacher, called him Dork, as in "the loser has to play Dork in the next round" or "shape up or you'll get Dork on your team." Yeah, he was a real threat in phys ed class.

Uh-oh, Ernestine just closed her locker and moved down the hall, going the wrong way. Oh, she was headed for the restroom. Dork leaned against the wall and rummaged through his backpack so he wouldn't seem to be loitering outside the girls' bathroom. Ernestine was taking a long time. Girls kept coming and going, but she hadn't shown up yet. Maybe she was trying to tame her glorious red hair. He couldn't understand how anyone could think Ernestine's hair looked like a haystack dipped in orange paint, but he'd seen it on snapchat, and it went viral, at least within the school. He'd downloaded the picture, which was now hanging in his room, along with the ones he'd managed to shoot himself. He'd ordered one of those little spy cameras from the internet, and now had some great shots and a couple of little videos starring his beloved Ernestine.

She came out the door—this was his chance. He grabbed his best felt-tipped pen and slung his backpack over his shoulder. "Ern...Ernestine...I think you dropped this." She looked at him! Right straight in the eye, she looked at him! The brown flecks in her green eyes were mesmerizing.

Music of a thousand violins began to play, and Ernestine, now surrounded by sparkling lights, turned her radiant smile in his direction. A breathy voice that floated above the violins asked, "How can I *ever* thank you?"

Her eyes dropped to his outstretched hand holding the pen, and the moment was gone. The violins were replaced by the usual cacophony of between-class noise.

"I dropped that? Really?" She frowned and one adorable freckle disappeared in the fold of her forehead. "Thanks." She reached out and took the pen. Her fingers brushed his, and the touch weakened his knees. The violins returned. Ernestine hurried on, but he was paralyzed, standing in the middle of the almost empty corridor with a grin he couldn't control. He moved toward his next class in a haze, remembering her soft, light touch.

***

"Wayne." The name clanged through his head like a fire alarm. "Wayne, I asked you a question."

Dork jerked up in his seat, searching for any memory of the class discussion. What were they studying? "Uh...Slovenia?" It was a wild guess, and the guffaws of his classmates were ample proof of just how wild. His cheeks burned what he knew was a flaming shade of red.

"Good one, Dork." A voice from across the room caused a new wave of laughter.

The teacher's ruler rapped on a desk. "In spite of the reaction of the class, that was *not* funny. I am very disappointed in you, Wayne."

He looked down at his desk and willed the blush to recede. The teacher repeated the question, but Dork couldn't get his tongue unstuck from the roof of his mouth. He knew the answer, of course, but all he could manage was a shrug. His breathing was uneven. Humiliation was usually confined to the lunchroom or the gym. It didn't belong in social studies. Was he having a panic attack, or was it asthma? He reached into his backpack for the rescue inhaler. He hated using it, especially in public, but he had to breathe.

The teacher rapped the ruler on her desk to restore order, and announced a pop quiz. Great. Now everyone hated him even more. The room got unnaturally quiet, and he was able to take a deep breath in the silence. He didn't look up as he slipped the inhaler back in his pack. It could have been worse. Marginally. If he'd had to use the inhaler, he might have been sent to the nurse—with an escort to make sure he was all right. Another humiliation.

By the end of the day, he managed to focus on the main objective once again. He decided to follow Ernestine home. Once he knew where she lived, he could find ways to see her on weekends, too, and maybe get some more pictures.

He hurried to the exit nearest Ernestine's last class, and waited until he saw her attach herself to a little knot of girls. He trailed the group from what he hoped was a safe distance as one by one the girls dropped off, waving and calling their good-byes. Finally there was only Ernestine and one other.

The two stopped and talked for a few minutes, causing Dork to duck behind a bush. He couldn't get a clear line of sight, but by bobbing his head every few seconds, he kept his eye on them. The conversation was lively, and Ernestine threw one hand in the air to emphasize a point. Rose petals cascaded from her hand, and he heard her voice over the sound of a string quartet. "He is chivalrous and gallant. He noticed when I dropped my pen, and returned it to me. Our hands brushed, and sparks of electricity..." Dork bobbed again as they resumed walking, and caught a glimpse of them turning to the left. The music stopped abruptly with the slam of the door to the house behind him.

"Hey! You there! What do you think you're doing, trespassing in my yard?"

Oh, no! Dork glanced over his shoulder and took in the size of the irate housewife wielding a broom in his direction. "Sorry, ma'am," he shouted as his feet propelled him back to the street. He stopped at the corner where the girls had turned, and paused to catch his breath. Peeking around the corner, he could see they were not very far away, and the street was almost deserted. He would have to use all the tricks he'd learned reading pulp fiction mysteries to keep out of sight.

He was lucky. The two girls were so engrossed in their conversation that they never once looked in his direction while he was in the open. At least, he never saw them look over their shoulders. After a few more turns, he figured out they were headed for the park. Once inside, there would be plenty of trees for cover. He could get closer and maybe even hear them talking. He almost lost them as the string quartet appeared again, and he was entranced by a vision of the girls sitting under a tree. He was standing on the other side listening to Ernestine say, "Isn't Wayne dreamy?"

The girls stopped and, just as in the vision, sat down

under a tree. Dork ducked behind another large tree a few yards away and examined his surroundings. Might he actually get to the other side of their tree? No, there was too much open space between his tree and theirs. They would see him.

He watched every move Ernestine made. He sighed over the dappled sunlight that filtered through the leaves to dance in her hair. He groaned over the exquisite beauty of her freckles. The violins, now accompanied by a flute, wove a background to Ernestine's words. "My fondest wish is for Wayne to invite me to the big Spring Dance, but alas, I am surely destined to pine away that night...alone and forgotten."

***

Again, fortune smiled on him. Ernestine took what looked like a sandwich from her book bag. The two girls raced to the pond, apparently intent on feeding the ducks, or geese, or whatever they were. They left their bags under the tree! Bonus! Snagging a memento of something that actually belonged to Ernestine would add substance to his collection of photos. Too bad no one carried handkerchiefs anymore. Tissues just didn't make the grade as mementos.

His head jerked up at the sound of girlish screams. The girls were running toward him, with frequent looks over their shoulders. Geese (or ducks or whatever) were squawking and flapping behind them. He had to hide quickly. He was yards from the nearest tree. The only way to go was up. Panic lent wings to his feet and strength to his hands as he scrambled up the tree. Precariously balanced on the lowest limb, he froze as the girls appeared beneath him.

Unexpectedly, the geese, ducks or whatever continued past the tree—their flapping and squawking unabated.

Racing along behind came another source of noise and commotion — a large black dog. His lips were curled and his teeth looked sharp and menacing. The incessant barking increased in volume as the distance between the dog and the tree decreased.

"He'll follow the geese, won't he?" Ernestine's voice quivered with fear.

"We can hide behind the tree." The other girl grabbed Ernestine's hand and they circled to the other side of the tree.

What if the girls decided to climb? Dork grabbed the next limb up and began to go higher. He didn't worry about the girls hearing him. The geese, if indeed they were geese, were making far too much noise, not to mention the girls were keeping their eyes on the dog. Still feeling vulnerable, he climbed another level, and then another. No one looking up from the ground could see him now.

The agitated birds squawked and flapped right past the tree and kept going. The dog, however, made a sharp turn toward the tree. Why had he abandoned the birds? Perhaps the sweet scent of Ernestine herself had distracted him. Dork's heart pounded so hard he thought it might shake the tree. What if the dog was after Ernestine?

No, the dog was sniffing and snuffling around the book bags. He must have caught the lingering scent of the sandwich the girls were feeding to the birds.

"It's quiet." The whisper drifted up to Dork. "Maybe the dog went away. Look, the birds are coming back." The girl was right. The geese, ducks or whatever were making their way back toward the pond. Maybe the dog would start chasing them again and leave the girls alone. Dork wanted to tell the girls to stay still, but he couldn't get any words out. He managed a small squeak that even he could barely hear.

The girl who wasn't Ernestine peeked around the tree and ducked back. "The dog hasn't left," she whispered. "I'm going to run away and come back later for my bag, if it's still here."

"Who would want a book bag?" asked Ernestine.

"The dog with the big teeth for one. It looks like he's trying to eat yours."

Ernestine looked around the tree. "NOOOO! Not my new book bag!"

Dork watched as the other girl took off like a track star toward the nearest street, deserting her bag and her friend.

The dog, startled out of his search for food by Ernestine's screech, planted his front feet solidly on the bag and growled at her. The growl seemed to come from deep within his savage chest as the animal showed its teeth, and its muscles bunched, prepared to attack.

Dork spied a man running in their direction brandishing what was either a whip or a dog leash. Whichever it was didn't really matter — either would do the job. The question was, would he get there in time? Or would the dog get to Ernestine first?

Fortunately, Ernestine had the good sense to freeze in her tracks and not snatch her bag. That would surely have been suicide. Now it was not only his racing heart that worried Dork, his whole body shook with fear. This was worse than the time he'd bumped into the captain of the football team in the hallway and made him drop his books. At least he'd been fairly certain the jock wouldn't actually kill him. There were no such certainties with the dog.

The man was still running and brandishing the whip or leash — and there was another monster dog loping after him. Dork thought he heard the man shout, "Sic! Sic! Sic the girl!" The faint, distant words raised Dork's terror level to a new high. He felt the limb he clutched vibrate with his own fear. His breathing came in gasps, but his inhaler was yards away under a different tree. Suddenly there was a sound like a gunshot. The dog looked up, momentarily distracted. Ernestine grabbed her book bag and took two steps backward, not taking her eyes off the dog. She took another step, and the dog's attention returned to her. He barked once and growled again, sounding more menacing than before.

Another shot sounded, louder than the first. Dork realized the shots he was hearing were actually coming from the tree limb beneath him as it gave way. Dork managed to find his voice. His scream seemed to hang in the air as the limb broke away entirely and dropped toward the ground in what felt like slow motion. As the ground rushed toward him, he saw the world in excruciating detail. His scream, which now sounded very far away, blended with Ernestine's scream as she rushed backward, out of the way of the falling branch. The dog moved toward the man, taking him farther from the trunk of the tree, but still under the falling branch.

Dork closed his eyes as tight as he could and prepared to die. His ears were filled with the rushing wind of his downward flight, the sound of tortured leaves and breaking twigs, all soon drowned out by the dog's shrill yelp as the branch crashed down. The loud thump of his own body hitting the ground obliterated all else, and blackness enveloped him.

When he opened his eyes, it was to see Ernestine kneeling beside him. "Are you all right, Dork? I mean Wayne?" He didn't have enough breath to answer. Maybe the fall had knocked the wind out of him, or maybe it was just seeing the concern in Ernestine's beautiful brown-flecked green eyes that took his breath away.

"I say there, young man, are you quite all right?" It was the man with the whip or leash. Ah, it *was* a leash, with the attack dog sitting innocently at its other end. "Sorry about that," the man said. "I'm just training her. She got distracted by the geese, or maybe they're ducks. I yelled at her to sit, but she didn't hear me." The dog got up and started toward Dork with its tongue lolling out one side of its mouth. "Sit, girl." The man spoke the command, and pointed down. The dog sat. So that was what he'd been saying. It wasn't "Sic the girl" at all.

Dork gave a weak smile. The man reached his hand down and helped him up. Ernestine took his other hand, and she didn't let go, even when Dork got his balance.

"You saved me," she cooed, "and you saved my new book bag from that dog. You're my hero, Wayne."

As Wayne relived his daring rescue, a full orchestra began to play. He saw himself sitting on the branch, waiting until the dog was directly under him before shaking the branch enough to crack. He screamed to warn Ernestine to move aside as, heedless of his own safety, he caused the branch to break. He took a deep breath and smiled at Ernestine. Yes, everything had worked out just perfectly.

"Ernestine." The orchestra made a smooth transition to a faster tempo.

"Yes, Wayne?"

"Will you go to the Spring Dance with me?"

"Oh, Wayne, I'd love to."

***

"Young lady, I apologize for any inconvenience my dog may have caused. If you and the young man are quite sure no harm has been done, I will take my dogs away before they cause any more trouble." The man gave an old-world bow and started back the way he came, with both dogs at his heels.

Where were the violins? The warmth of Ernestine's hand spread through his body like an elixir. He had never felt so good. He knew exactly what he had to do, and he had already gone through a dress rehearsal. "Ernestine?"

"Yes, Wayne?"

"Will...will you go to the S-s-spring D-dance with me?"

"Oh, Wayne, I'd love to." Exactly on cue. Wayne breathed a sigh of relief and happiness. It was even better without the orchestra.

***

When Wayne arrived at school the next morning, Ernestine detached herself from a group of girls and walked toward him. Yes, it *was* true. Wayne threw back his shoulders, held his head high, and walked toward the love of his life.

As he reached for Ernestine's hand, someone bumped him from behind. "Sorry," the person said as Wayne stumbled, dropping the book he'd been holding.

"Hey! Watch it!"

"I said sorry." A hand reached down and picked up the book.

"Thanks." Wayne took the offered book, his eyes still fixed on Ernestine. The expression on her face made his chest swell with pride. He didn't need the violins now. He had Ernestine.

"Oh, Wayne, you really are a hero. The way you stood up to that jock was so brave. I mean, considering how..." Her voice trailed off.

Wayne's confidence wavered. He could finish that sentence. Considering how the jocks went out of their way to make fun of him. "That was a jock?"

"Yes, it was the captain of the football team. I guess he didn't recognize you, now that you're a hero."

A full brass band struck up a march. Confetti drifted down from the sky. Wayne squeezed Ernestine's hand and they strode off into the sunset together. Well, maybe it was just homeroom, and sunset was still hours away, but it felt just as good.

———

Diane Hall used to write nasty collection letters as the CFO of a small IT company. She has since kicked off the traces of accountancy and taxation and begun writing short stories. Who knows what the future holds? Diane lives quietly in Northern Virginia with no internet presence whatsoever and is rather proud of being a quasi-Luddite.

HONORING DEBTS

Jess Barry

Rona shivered as the Norwegian winter's frigid air fled in the face of the crackling blazes in the five fire pits evenly spaced in the sprawling bench-lined room. The smell of roasting boar, faint outside the longhouse's earthen walls, now filled her nostrils and made her stomach growl with hunger. That morning's hunt had gone well, but she expected no less of the king's attendants.

She brushed away the snowflakes clinging to her heavy fur cloak and stomped on the longhouse's earthen floor to dislodge the clumps of snow from her boots. Casting a sidelong glance at her new husband Vidar, she grinned as the big man closed the door behind them to shut out the howling winter gale, then mirrored her actions to get rid of the snow.

Her grin broadened of its own accord, and she smiled up at Vidar as his sparkling gray eyes met and held her gaze. Her father teased — affectionately — that she liked Vidar only because his red hair matched her own, but Rona didn't care. She considered her towering red-headed husband quite handsome, the embodiment of kindness and gentleness that belied his impressive skill with a sword and spear.

Thank Odin and the rest of the gods that her parents had decided in favor of Vidar instead of the king's youngest son. Her smile wavered as she spotted the prince at the far end of the long rectangular room. His bellowing laughter —

matching his size as one of the few men larger than Vidar—made it impossible for anyone to miss him. He and the twenty or so young men surrounding him hoisted their clay mugs high between drinks. No fine glassware for them. Only the king drank from the elegant cone-shaped beaker of green glass with its beautifully wrought silver holder sitting atop a nearby table.

No surprise that the prince and his cohorts didn't. So much of the mead ran down their bearded chins that Rona wondered how they'd gotten so drunk to begin with. They'd undoubtedly smash anything easily breakable.

Vidar leaned close. "We don't need to stay long," he whispered.

She beamed up at him. "I am grateful to be invited." Although cordial enough, her family had no close ties with the king. Vidar's brother, however, was married to the king's daughter. He had invited Vidar and, naturally, his new wife to the feast.

They circulated among the boisterous revelers who ostensibly were celebrating the birth of the king's new grandson. At least that's what had brought the bulk of the guests.

Rona wiped a smirk from her face before anyone noticed. She knew the young prince and his churls required no special event to celebrate. Instead of gaining maturity as he aged, she thought derisively, the prince seemed to be imbuing his family with more rowdiness.

Ah well, not her concern. She finished gnawing the succulent meat off the bone, then tossed the rib into the pile. The noise level in the room rose and fell in waves, although with nearly two hundred people present, the word "quiet" never applied.

A gust of wind swept through the longhouse as several of the young men slipped outside.

Rona gave Vidar's arm a squeeze, then stood and set her mug on the bench. "Be right back." She threaded her way through the crowd to a small room in the back near the end section of the longhouse, where the livestock was housed.

Raucous laughter stopped her as she finished readjusting her clothing. The prince's voice rang out loud and clear among the bleating sheep. "Those fools will sail with no idea they won't have a home to return to!" A guffaw followed the spite-filled words. "I'll make sure I'm there when Leif tells them!" Another roar of mirth emphasized the proclamation, getting louder as several others joined in the merriment. "It will be a tragic day for Hamar and that sea-captain wife of his." The words reeked with contempt.

Rona froze in the act of smoothing down her smock. She held her breath and stood still as an ice carving, afraid the slightest motion or sound would betray her.

Leif, head of a jarl family like her own, wealthy and noble-born, had detested her paternal grandfather since long before Rona was born—perhaps even before her father was born. She could never get any details, but she did wonder what could possibly have transpired with Leif to threaten the estate.

The answer hit her, horrible and inevitable.

Her grandfather loved games beyond all reason. Her parents tried to hide it, but Rona was no longer a child, and people talked. Some—especially Leif's progeny—boasted. Everyone knew how much silver her grandfather had lost—and to whom.

But this?

Rona fought the desire to bolt from the lavatory. People shuffled by outside, and she feared what they'd do to her if they knew she'd overheard.

She had to get to her parents, to make sure they knew, so

they could fix it. Rona had faith in them. She had no idea how, but she was sure they could solve this. They had to. She couldn't conceive of any other outcome.

After a of couple minutes, she heard the volume level spike again but nothing in the immediate vicinity of the little chamber.

She raised the latch on the door, hesitating, then risked opening it just far enough to let her peek out into the main room. Only Vidar saw, a perplexed frown on his face as he cast a questioning look in her direction, no doubt wondering what was taking her so long.

No one else paid any attention. She barely paused to catch her husband's eye as she darted for the door and out of the longhouse. Vidar appeared seconds later, wearing his fur cloak and carrying hers.

"What's wrong?" He easily matched his stride to hers as she rushed up the road running between the longhouses comprising the village. Her boots crunched in the ankle-deep freshly fallen snow, but she didn't let it slow her down. Huge flakes swirled around her, driven by the wind and cutting visibility.

But Rona didn't have far to go.

"Hurry!" she couldn't catch her breath to say more. Not that she needed to, as Vidar had absolutely no difficulty in keeping up with her pell-mell sprint. She prayed to Odin she'd find her parents at home. Otherwise, the only other place she could think of to search would be aboard *Seedrache*, their ship.

The ship wouldn't sail without her, she knew. Her Grandmother Aaricia was training Rona to be a healer. Still, she needed to tell her parents now. The sooner they knew about the problem, the sooner they could solve it.

"Mother!" She banged into the door as she shoved it

aside and burst into the house, stumbling down the steps. "Father! Mother!" Her chest heaved from the exertion.

Her parents and her mother's mother sat eating their own dinner. A deep crease between her brows, Rona's grandmother Aaricia looked up from the fire pit. Hamar kept chewing, but his eyebrows arched high on his forehead. Mariel tilted her head in silent question.

Rona bent double, sucking in several deep breaths before she could straighten.

"I overheard the prince." She gasped for air, the words coming between ragged breaths. "Grandfather gamed against Leif, who is claiming that Grandfather lost the entire estate to him! Leif is going to wait until we sail and then collect the debt."

Mariel made a strangled sound deep in her throat. Aaricia sat, slack-jawed and wide-eyed, her food held partway to her mouth as if forgotten.

"What!" Hamar bellowed, the only time in her whole life Rona ever recalled him showing all-out rage. Now, red-faced and trembling with fury, he looked ready to tear someone limb from limb with his bare hands.

"Could you have misheard?" Mariel asked, without much hope in her voice. "Could the youths have been telling tales? Are you certain they were talking about Jens?"

"I did not mishear," Rona stated flatly. "As to the rest, they mentioned Father *by name*..." her words trailed off.

"We need to find my father." Hamar didn't so much speak, as growl.

"We didn't see him at the king's longhouse," Vidar spoke with uncharacteristic timidity. "But I'll go back and check again. He may have been..." Vidar bit off what he'd been about to say, and strode out to match his actions to his words. He hadn't wanted to say that her grandfather may have been outside around back, still gaming.

"Bring him here," her father called after Vidar as the heavy oaken door swung back into place across the doorway.

"I'll see if he's on *Seedrache*." Heart still pounding from the last sprint, Rona dashed outside again. Her grandfather even now fancied himself connected to the sea, although his sailing days had long since ended.

She loved the majestic longship with the fierce dragon carved into its prow, but today she took no pleasure at the sight of the ship bobbing peacefully on the choppy river that emptied out into the fjord.

Here, they kept a dock instead of pulling the ship onto the unforgiving rocky riverbank. She vaulted the rail and landed deftly on the polished wood deck, startling the two sailors on watch. Her mother never left the ship unattended.

Her cousin Kelda and the man looked up from the wooden hurstwic game board they'd been hunched over.

Kelda's blue eyes narrowed to a steely glare. "What happened?" she demanded.

"We need Grandfather. You haven't seen him, have you?"

"Not since this morning." The long-limbed blonde rose smoothly to her feet as Rona turned to go. By the time Kelda said, "I'll send someone else out," to the man still sitting at their game, Rona was already back on shore and moving fast. In moments, her cousin caught up to her.

A few yards from their home, Rona stopped short and Kelda slid to a stop beside her in the snow. Rona had no idea where else to look. Grandfather had some friends outside the village, but he'd never venture forth with a storm rolling in. Vidar and her parents were already looking in all the likely nearby spots.

"What's he lost now?" Kelda snarled.

Rona looked at her helplessly, eyes welling up from the anger she'd been trying to stifle. She spread her hands and shook her head as she let them fall back to her sides. "Everything."

Kelda caught her breath then mouthed the word, as if certain she'd heard wrong. "You mean...everything? The estate? The ship?" She flushed red from wrath rather than from the blustery cold air.

Rona hadn't thought of that. The ship belonged to her mother. Technically her husband's father had no right to stake it in any bet. "I'm not sure about *Seedrache*, but he lost the entire estate to Leif. He plans to claim it after we leave tomorrow."

Kelda spat out a string of curses. "Now what?"

"I don't know." Rona turned her head one way and then the other, searching their surroundings as if she'd spot something that would magically eliminate the problem.

A figure appeared through the dancing snowflakes. As it trudged toward them, Rona recognized Vidar.

"I think they found him." He huffed some from the exertion, nodding briefly to acknowledge Kelda before continuing to address Rona. "Someone just came into the lodge and said they'd heard shouting, they thought from our place." He scowled. "They were laughing."

A heavy silence hung over the street. Certainly no shouting now. Fearful of what she'd find, Rona rushed to their longhouse, the other two on her heels.

Inside, Mariel and Aaricia had taken a few steps back, leaving the matter between father and son, who stood glowering at each other.

What recourse did they have? Legally, the estate still

belonged to her grandfather. Yet after a point, the community *would* acknowledge when a person had completely lost his senses.

Leif would certainly *not* accept that as an excuse to void the debt, but perhaps in the future people would take heed, refuse to take advantage of an addled old man, and quit gambling with him.

A huge wave of sadness washed over her that her grandfather had come to this, but it did nothing to dispel her anger or anxiety. What would they do without a home? Where would they go? How would they live?

Shame burned in her, but also fear. Never in her young life had she imagined that their status and comfortable life could simply vanish in an instant.

At least they still had *Seedrache*.

She believed.

She hoped.

If they'd lost that as well.... The ship was fully provisioned to sail, and heavily laden with silver and textiles for trade. If it were lost, the blow might well be insurmountable. They wouldn't end up as *bræll*—indentured and serving some master's every whim—but close to it.

"I *might* have an idea," Hamar rasped through clenched teeth, his normal good humor nowhere in evidence. He shot his wife and Vidar a beseeching look. "I need to see the king. Just make sure Father stays here. Please." Then, to his father, "Just. Stay. Here."

The old man harrumphed and flung himself on one of the sleeping benches as Hamar stomped toward the door. Mariel gave her daughter a quick nod, indicating she wanted Rona to follow. Rona and Kelda ran after him.

Only the king had enough money to pay off the debt. Rona knew that. But what could her father possibly offer with the whole estate already gone? What arrangements could he make?

Rona feared she didn't want to know the answer.

The moment they entered the lodge, all heads turned toward them and everyone fell silent. Eerily silent, for such a large group of people.

As if no one else were present, Hamar approached the king and greeted him, not with his usual merriment, but naturally enough. Rona and Kelda flanked him, offering their support.

The king's throne raised him above the rest of the hall. A keen, speculative look filled his eyes as he regarded Hamar. "Eventful day, is it not?" the king asked mildly.

"That it is," Hamar admitted, "as the whole town no doubt already knows." He paused a beat. "I have a proposal that might interest you, Lord."

"Really? Explain how that is possible, considering the day's happenings." The king leaned forward, his long golden beard covering the elbow that rested on his knee.

Back straight and chin up, Hamar didn't falter. "We're about to set sail, everyone knows that. Our voyage will be an immensely profitable one. I offer a wager. If I win, you pay Leif now, and allow us to repay you in full, plus one hundred silver, upon our return. If you win, the estate is yours, as is the cargo we return with."

"Hmmmm." The king leaned back and rested his hands on the chair's arms, unconsciously massaging the beautifully carved wood. "And if you don't return with anything of value?"

"Then our hold will still be full of cloth and silver," Hamar responded without a pause. "We'll give you the cargo as well."

Anything but the ship itself, Rona found herself thinking. Anything but the ship. As long as the family still had *Seedrache*, they could always rebuild their fortunes.

The king pondered that, the glint in his eyes growing harder and colder. "And what would this wager be?"

"Skiing. A race against your choice of champion. Starting and ending at the bridge."

What? Only shock stilled Rona's tongue long enough for Kelda to clamp a cautioning hand on her arm and prevent her outcry of objection. What was her father thinking? Hamar had said "king's choice" but there was no question as to the selection.

The entire village knew the king's youngest son rarely lost any sporting contest. The prince lacked grace but not speed, and had plenty of power in his big frame, and good balance as well.

Rona risked a quick sidelong glance. Kelda looked stone-faced, as always, not alarmed. Her cousin must have gleaned something from the exchange that Rona had missed. So—with great difficulty—she held her peace

The king cocked his head and raised a single brow, clearly suspecting that Hamar must have some plan, but unable to discern what. The bet Hamar suggested was a common one. The next closest bridge, the only route to the opposite shore, lay three miles upriver. No assistance by boat was allowed. The racers were required to ski; anyone who didn't, automatically lost.

"I require more incentive to cover such a huge debt," the king said slowly. "If I win, your family becomes my bræll. For five years."

Kelda's already-viselike grip tightened, shooting pain through Rona's arm. Rona couldn't believe what she was hearing. Surely her father wouldn't even consider such a thing? The payment offered was already substantial.

"No," Hamar said. But the relief flooding through Rona turned to horror as her father added, "No, not my family. But I will."

Rona cried out in inarticulate protest, and Kelda said, "Hamar, no!" They started forward but the king's attendants blocked their way.

Hamar ignored them, as did the king. The king regarded the other man for a long, long moment, then said, "Agreed. The bargain is made. Thirty minutes at the bridge."

Hamar turned and marched out. The two women hurried in his wake. "Father, what have you done?" Rona stumbled a moment as she followed him into their longhouse.

He turned and held up a hand, and she swallowed the rest of her words. Swiftly and quietly, he told Mariel what had transpired.

Rona had never seen her mother so pale, white as the falling snow. Rona could barely believe her mother's voice sounded so steady when she asked, "And why did you do this?"

After a hesitation, Hamar said, "I can win. I can beat him if I cross the ice. It's been cold enough for weeks. The surface should be frozen solid a ways upriver, far before the bridge."

Rona could hear the doubt in his voice no matter that he tried desperately to conceal it. Her mother undoubtedly could too. Mariel folded her arms across her chest, her lips a tight line of apprehension.

"I'm a better skier..." Kelda started to say.

"No." Rona interrupted so forcefully that everyone else jumped from surprise. "No," she repeated, even more emphatically. "You're the better fighter; *I'm* the better skier. I'm faster. I'm smaller. *Much* smaller. It's safer for me to cross the ice."

Neither of her parents looked convinced. Hamar opened his mouth to protest, but Kelda spoke first. "If you thought *you* could make it, Rona definitely can."

Rona could see them wavering. Not *liking* the idea any better, but perhaps thinking of accepting it, however reluctantly.

"Hamar, if you get yourself killed, we lose the estate *and* we lose you," Kelda said sharply. "I still think you should let me go, but she's right. She's the better skier. And she's a good fifty pounds lighter than I am. The king's son weighs twice as much. He won't try to follow unless *he* has a death wish."

Rona waited, knowing there was nothing more to say. She knew she was right. The only question would be whether her parents took the logical course or not. Her father seethed, every bit as mad as before. Her mother's mouth twisted in disgust at the whole situation. Aaricia stood by, watching, but having no better solution to offer.

Jens sat up from where he'd lain, listening, on the sleeping bench. Rona spared him barely a glance, then did a double-take. A deep sadness in his eyes, something she'd never, ever seen there before, led her to believe he might finally be cognizant of the enormity of what he'd done.

She went and sat beside him, taking his hand in her own. "It's all right, Grandfather. I can do this. And you'll quit betting, right?" she added softly, but intractably.

"Yes, you can." He kissed her forehead. "And yes, I will. No more."

The entire village gathered at the wooden plank bridge, one of very few in the land. They normally forded or ferried across rivers. But the king had wanted a bridge after seeing them in the south. Another jarl, in competition, had built the other bridge upriver.

So they had a course they often raced.

The wind and snow picked up even more as the crowd assembled, as if the weather itself were feeding on the tension and excitement. Sunlight barely penetrated the falling snow, turning the day a bleary gray. The crowd parted to let Rona and her family approach the bridge where the king waited with his son. The prince already wore his skis.

Rona carried hers slung over her shoulder.

"What's this?" the prince exclaimed contemptuously. "A slip of a girl?"

But the king wasn't nearly so disdainful—just suspicious. "What is this, Hamar? You stand behind a girl-child?" Mistrust filled his tone.

Hamar shrugged. "You chose your champion. I chose mine."

Noting how careful her father was *not* to provoke, Rona bit back taunting remarks as she knelt to strap on her skis. The king wouldn't renege on the contest, but he could always claim the bet was with Hamar and Hamar alone.

Rona *needed* to ensure *she* competed.

The crowd grew rowdier and rowdier, cheering loudly as individuals chose sides. This, the king seemed to accept good-naturedly. The prince, not so much. His expression grew darker and darker.

"Very well," the king said. "The first person back across this bridge is the victor." He took a deep breath. "Go."

Rona half-coughed, half-choked. She didn't even have her second ski on.

But a person doesn't sprint the whole distance in a six-mile race. Endurance and strategy matter more. The king was trying to rattle her at the very start.

She didn't let him.

As swiftly as safety permitted, she strapped on the second ski. Her competitor had already vanished into the wall of white.

That didn't matter, she reminded herself.

In fact...

It benefitted her if he didn't see her leave the trail. So much the better if he thought himself securely in the lead. Or, possible but less likely, if he kept looking over his shoulder for her. Either way, she couldn't think of one good reason why she would want him to know her strategy.

She stood up, ski pole in hand, suddenly energized. She flashed her parents a wicked grin. "I'll see you soon." She lifted her feet as she carefully turned to face the right direction. Snow was already filling in the parallel tracks the prince left.

Good that Rona already knew the way.

After a few steps, she settled into a gliding rhythm, unconcerned with speed. The prince would traverse more than six miles. She'd go a quarter a mile, cross the river, then come back the quarter mile on the other side.

One mile to his six. She wasn't *that* much slower than him. She harbored no illusions that she could beat him in a straight-line race. Confident as she was in her abilities, she knew that they didn't include winning footraces (even on skis). But a course one-sixth of the length, no problem. Even she could manage that. Easily.

Her skin tingled from the cold, but the constant movement kept her warm. She matched her breathing to the pattern of her glide as her skis cut through the powdery snow. Wind whipped by, cutting visibility even more. She could only see a few feet ahead. But she knew the course well, so the lack of a view posed no problem. Her father had taught her to ski on this trail. She still had those child-sized skis.

Left. Right. Left. Right. She swayed with each stride, picking up speed and gauging how far she'd gone. She could barely make out the white-coated pine trees on either side of the path. When she got to a gap in the trees, she veered to the left and slowed as the degree of the slope increased.

She knew she'd hit the ice when the surface beneath her evened out and turned almost perfectly flat.

A swirl of white surrounded her. She could barely see yards ahead on her side of the river, let alone anything on the far shore. All she had to do now was ensure she ended up over there, instead of going in so much of a curve that she ended up back on the wrong riverbank.

She glanced behind her.

Her own tracks stretched back the way she'd come, still visible. Snow was filling them in quickly, but they'd last at least for five or ten minutes. Long enough for her to use them as a point of reference so as not to travel in a circle. Even with some deviation, all she needed to do was wind up across the river. Didn't matter if she hit the opposite bank directly across or not. Just so she hit it.

Just so the ice supported her.

She believed it would.

Without a doubt.

But she'd have been a total idiot if she didn't acknowledge for at least a fraction of a second that her conviction could be wrong.

She pushed those traitorous thoughts aside. The deep freeze had descended on the land weeks ago. This section of river—deep but not too wide—froze over before any other.

She was about to turn back to the river, then she blinked and squinted. Was something moving among the trees? Village dogs following? Or a bear disturbed from hibernating? No, more likely a deer or a wolf.

Just so they were smarter than her and didn't venture out on the ice, she snickered to herself.

The shadows gradually resolved into two-legged people. Two-legged *sword-wielding* people, young men who'd been busy laughing and joking with the prince earlier. Rona knew them by name, but not much more. She avoided them as much as she possibly could. They tormented everyone, from other jarl to the *bræll* to the sled dogs to the livestock. Not just tormented. One or two *bræll* hadn't survived their attention.

Now the pair closed in on her, moving apart from each other to come at her from both sides at the same time. They leered maliciously and clutched their swords in front of them, unmistakably ready to strike.

They wore skis as well, which explained how they'd followed so swiftly. The shorter wooden planks gave them better maneuverability than she had.

Confidence in her plan notwithstanding, she didn't want to rush out onto the untested ice and do their work for them by falling through. Yet she could not stand still. Mindful of not tripping herself, she took a step backward. Then another.

Someone whistled.

Whistled? But not one of the men about to attack her. They both turned to look back at the tree line.

Even as Rona puzzled over the unexpected sound, Vidar and Kelda emerged from the forest behind the threatening men. Kelda wasted no time. She simply ran one of the men through as he turned, sword raised, to engage her.

Vidar waited long enough for his opponent to face him. "You can walk away."

The man lunged; Vidar finished him off almost as swiftly.

Rona could scarcely comprehend what she'd seen. The prince had sent men to *kill* her? Low as her opinion of him had always been, she still would have questioned such an act if she hadn't seen with her own eyes.

"Go on," Kelda prodded, cleaning the blood off her sword with handfuls of snow.

Shaking off the murder attempt, Rona gave the ice her full attention.

Moving slowly, step by step, she counted on the skis to distribute her weight over a bigger area than her booted feet alone. She listened for any cracking or snapping sounds, difficult as they would be to hear over the raging gale. She slid each ski slowly, alert for the slightest give beneath her feet.

Every few yards, she cast a glance over her shoulder to confirm her direction. The storm quickly swallowed the lines behind her, but enough remained to reassure her she wasn't doubling back.

After ten interminable minutes, the ground beneath her feet began sloping upward.

Rona gave a huge sigh of relief, feeling the tension ebb from her body as she let her muscles relax.

She'd done it!

She'd made it across the ice!

But she hadn't yet won the race.

She clambered up the gentle slope, hampered slightly by her skis, and made her way between more fir trees. In five minutes, she found the trail.

The snow was now halfway to her knees, heavy and

wet. Without the sun to melt the surface so the cold wind could crystalize it to ice, her skis sank in and made the going hard.

After a few moments, she was able to work up enough speed to allow her to skim along on top. Laughter bubbled up inside her. She could barely imagine the trouble the deep snowfall was giving the much heavier prince.

She watched the trail closely, careful not to launch herself into any of the trees or miss any bend and take the wrong path.

Several minutes later, through the wall of white, she could barely make out the bridge ahead.

Finally!

She redoubled her efforts, suddenly afraid the prince would appear out of nowhere behind her.

Twenty yards.

Ten.

Five.

No shadowy figure erupted from the blizzard behind her.

The bridge spanned the narrowest section of the river before its mouth broadened and opened into the fjord. The wooden structure was wide enough to let five people walk it abreast.

Rona started across without any company.

She heard the low rumble of the crowd. But when she reached the halfway point, the volume gradually rose with cries of, "Look!" and "Someone's there!"

Her parents and king stood at the front of the throng. Right behind them, Aaricia and Jens waited along with Kelda and Vidar. Rona also spotted a stout older man bedecked in fine firs and silver jewelry: Leif.

Rona skied the final half of the span and turned her skis

to stop.

She quickly bit her lip so as not to laugh out loud at the expression of pure bafflement on the king's face.

"But...how?"

Before she could answer, Vidar surged forward and swept her up in a huge embrace, heedless of her skis as her feet dangled a foot off the ground. When he set her down, she found herself caught in a bone-crushing embrace from both her parents.

The reunion finished, Rona turned to face the king. Her father stepped forward with her, his arm around her shoulders. "Are you satisfied that Rona won?"

The king's expression flickered with annoyance before chagrin settled over his features. "Nicely done, young Rona. Yes, I acknowledge your victory." The king raised his voice. "Leif, I shall deliver the appropriate silver to you. You now have no claim on their family estate. Hamar, you shall repay me when you return from this voyage."

The king lowered his voice again. "Where did you cross the ice?" he asked conspiratorially. "Half a mile up where it narrows?"

She nodded.

He winked. "Nicely done," he said again.

A rush of satisfaction threatened to overwhelm her. Rona hadn't solved their problem, but she'd bought the time they needed to save the estate. She had every confidence her parents would come through.

Her grandfather said as much back in the longhouse when he echoed everyone else's praise of her.

Kelda snorted. "It's good we're leaving. We'll have a little break before the constant need to look over our shoulders."

"Kelda?" Hamar asked.

Vidar replied first. "The prince — we assume the prince — sent people after Rona to stop her."

"Vidar and I killed them," Kelda said flatly.

"Before they could kill Rona," Vidar added quickly. "We should probably tell the king, so he can let the families know where the bodies are."

Rona's feeling of triumph dimmed but didn't fade completely. She felt no happiness at the deaths, but nor did she let them mar her victory. They had no honor, being willing to kill over a gambling debt. Vidar and Kelda had saved her life.

Nevertheless, Kelda had spoken the truth. The men's families would not forget.

Nor would the prince.

She and her parents would have to deal with that eventually.

Later.

She'd won the race. The estate was safe — *for now* — and her family was together.

And they had a voyage of adventure awaiting them.

———

Jess Barry loves old architecture, live theater, and astronomy and aerospace news. Her works include a mystery/romance Masquerade, *and two Civil War-era pirate tales. A co-authored novel,* The Last Abbot of Linn Duachaill, *is with S & H Publishing, Inc. Learn more at* BluetrixBooks.wordpress.com.

IF I SHOULD DIE BEFORE I WAKE

J. D. Kipfer

Her eyelids slowly closed, and a wonderful peace slipped over her. The book started to slide away, and sleep, like a warm blanket, began to take over her body.

Oh hell! She had to go to the bathroom.

She tried not to open her eyes—so she'd be halfway to winning her nightly battle for sleep when she got back in bed. It didn't work.

It happened that way every night. Try as she might, sleep kept eluding her, allowing her mind to resurrect old injuries and insults she felt she just couldn't forgive, or things she had done to others that she couldn't forgive herself for doing. Some of them were pretty ridiculous, causing a great deal of fuss and bother at the time, but now they were just good for conversation. And there was always Jim—always there was Jim. Damn Jim. She rolled over on her side into a fetal position and proceeded to count sheep.

Her mind began to slip into oblivion, unaware of the storm gathering outside. Thunder rumbled on the far side of the mountains, and distant lightning flashed in the valley. She snuggled more deeply into her pillow, refusing to be disturbed. But when the storm broke right above her bedroom, she was immediately brought back from the brink. She quickly came to her senses and crawled out of bed to check the windows. It was an ancient house and the windows were all old and hard to operate. Many of them were crank-outs, difficult to get completely shut.

She stuffed her feet into her slippers and started down the back hallway toward her studio where the most damage could be done by intruding rain. She'd left one of the high windows half open and had to climb on the bookcase to get it shut, which was probably why it was left open in the first place.

After what seemed a futile struggle, she finally succeeded but at the expense of getting her nightshirt soaked. Shivering, she crawled off the bookcase, grabbed a rag from the pile she kept for cleaning brushes, and began to rub vigorously at her face and hair. A chance glance at her reflection in the studio window showed that, in her haste, she'd grabbed a rag from the wrong pile and had smeared her face with Alizarin Crimson and Ultramarine Blue.

"Hell!" she said aloud, threw the rag down and grabbed a fresh one, which did nothing but smear the paint more. She had just begun to apply turpentine when another streak of lightning, accompanied by thunder, exploded above the house. The lights went out, leaving her in total darkness. She shed her wet nightshirt and fumbled around until she found her studio work clothes draped on the chair where she was sure she'd left them. Another bolt of lightning, bright as stage lights, lit up the room. And there she was, naked as a jaybird, for all the world to see—at least anyone who happened to be looking. She grabbed the paint-smeared jeans and sweatshirt, pulled them on, and rushed from the overexposed room to the back stairway and down to the kitchen, to check the fuse box if she could remember where it was.

She'd only lived in the house a few months, since she'd decided to hide out from her life as she had allowed it to become. As an artist, she was a good copyist, but wasn't very inspired when it came to her own art. Then Jim got involved, and he'd led her into very profitable work as a copy artist. Only, unbeknownst to her, he had sold her copies of originals as if they *were* originals. When a few came back to haunt her, the man deserted her, and she took to the hills.

She'd found this ancient house in the valley through notice of an estate sale in a small town newspaper. The studio was the immediate draw, created from a maid's room at the top of the back stairway. She couldn't afford to buy the house, but when it didn't sell, the bank let her rent it, furnished, until such time as it did. She moved in immediately, without giving any thought to how isolated the valley was. During the day she was happy not to be bothered by neighbors, but once the sun went down, she wasn't so sure.

Right now, she would like to have a burly man with one of those belts around his waist that held tools that would fix anything. Since one of those was not readily available, she opened the basement door to go fix it herself. But when she was confronted by the absolute blackness at the bottom of the stairs — it seemed a bottomless pit where all manner of things could be lurking, she quickly closed the door and leaned against it. Taking a few deep breaths, she gritted her teeth and shrugged her shoulders.

"What the hell, this place didn't even have lights when it was built. People went to bed when it got dark and didn't get up until God turned the lights back on." Her voice sounded hollow when she spoke out loud, but she continued to talk, as the sound of any voice, even her own, made her feel better about being all alone. "As a matter of fact, the power is probably out everywhere, and it'll take a man with a truck to fix it."

She decided to get a glass of milk, go back upstairs, crawl into bed, find out what's wrong in the morning, and deal with it accordingly.

When she opened the refrigerator, she was momentarily surprised to find that light was out, too. She stood staring into the depths of the refrigerator's black hole until panic rose in her throat. To the empty room she said, "Get your act together. You've been in storms before. What makes this one different?" She grabbed the half-full gallon of milk, sloshed some into a tumbler she retrieved from the kitchen sink, and turned to put the milk back where it belonged.

The swinging door beside the refrigerator was standing open. A brief flash revealed the antique dining room filled to the brim with heavy, ancient furniture that smelled of the grave. Another flash of lightning lit up the interior of the house and she clearly could see the living room beyond the dining room and the front door, which was standing wide open.

"Oh dear," she whispered softly as she started across the dining room, leaving the milk on the table. She slammed the door shut, then stood there braced against it till it dawned on her that someone could've come in the open door and gone up the front stairway while she was coming down the back. Reflexively, she grabbed for her pocket, where she usually carried her cell phone, only to remember she'd left it charging in the bedroom. Her car was parked just outside the house, but the keys were parked upstairs by her phone.

"Oh dear, oh dear, oh dear." She moved to the bottom of the stairs and looked up. She had visions of someone wandering around from room to room through the upstairs of the house, looking for — she couldn't imagine who, or for what. Maybe whoever it was didn't expect to find anyone here. Maybe they were looking for someplace to sit out the storm, and thought the house was still vacant. But if they'd come in the front door, they'd have seen her car.

Or maybe they knew exactly who was in the house. What if Jim or one of his customers had tracked her to this place?

She had been so careful, covering her trail, coming here, stopping along the way in more than one place, acting as if she were making arrangements to stay. Getting farther and farther away from him, and the life he'd drawn her into. *Drawn* her into? What a choice of words, she had *drawn* — and *drawn* herself into — a real mess. Jim had just sold her down the river.

First, he had wanted her to do something in the style of the Spanish painter Joan Miró. He said some people wanted to decorate their home in a very modern fashion, and would pay well for a painting that carried out one of Miró's themes. They didn't want a print, even one replicated on a computer. She knew that copies could be very valuable in their own right if they were any good. So she was happy to do it, especially for the $2,000 she was paid, supposedly, by the customer.

Next, he wanted a Paul Klee, then an R.B. Kitaj. For each, he came through with a very nice little stipend. Over the next few years she collected quite a bit of money. But she hadn't known that Jim was selling her copies as the real thing! He'd collected quite a lot more money. The truth came out when someone who knew what they were looking at objected to a Rouault being called what it definitely was not.

The real problem came about when one of his best customers hadn't come into his wealth quite legally. And like all thieves, he didn't like to be stolen from any more than anyone else. He wanted his money back and a little extra for being made a fool of. If he wanted it from her, he'd be grossly mistaken about her split, because the difference between her pittance and the price of the real paintings was a lot of zeros.

She stood looking up the stairs and shuddered violently, not from the cold, but from sheer unadulterated fear. If it were Jim in the house, she didn't think she had anything to be afraid of, just a lot of things to be angry about. If it was one of his customers—well, that was another thing altogether. But why would they go to all the trouble to track her down—and in a storm like this one? Jim was the one they wanted, he'd got the biggest piece of the pie. Why would they track her down for the little bit she got out of the scheme?

There didn't seem to be any wind. The rain was coming straight down so hard that it filled the house with a terrible racket, so loud it covered any other sound. Was there actually someone rummaging around up there, and she couldn't hear them because of the rain, or was she just imagining the whole thing? Was she letting the guilt she felt for her part in that dreadful art scam fiasco guide her imagination? There was only one way to find out. She took a deep breath and started up the stairs.

A loud noise stopped her on the landing. It sounded like the entire upper floor had collapsed. She stood there with one foot already on the next step while her mind flew from her studio to her bedroom, trying to figure out what could have made such a noise.

Then, just as suddenly, it was quiet. The rain seemed to

have abated, as if it, too, had been frightened by the noise.

She sneaked to the wall and sidled up the stairs very slowly, listening to every creak and crack the house made. At the top, she peeked around the corner into the bedroom over the front porch. She felt fresh air coming from the large bay window and breathed a deep sigh of relief when she discovered a limb off of the huge oak in the front lawn, lying on the roof of the porch. It had broken one of the windows, but otherwise the room seemed intact. She wondered briefly if the bank was going to hold her responsible for the damages.

I'm going back to bed. This cat and mouse game with my imagination has worn me out, she told herself, and turned to cross the hall to her bed, pulling her sweatshirt over her head as she went. As her head popped through the neck of the sweatshirt, she looked straight into two large gleaming eyes.

"Jesus!" She screamed and would have fallen down, but for the wall. "What in the hell are you doing in here? And how did you get in?" She swatted at the cat, who jumped down from the dresser and went scurrying down the hall.

She'd seen the big yellow tomcat around the house for days. She hadn't even tried to make friends with it—she was not a cat person. It probably sneaked in through the front door. Right now, she could use a little company, but that cat did not satisfy her need. She slipped her arms back into the sweatshirt, and started after the cat, enumerating, in her sweetest voice, all the dreadful sorts of things she was going to do to it when she caught it.

The cat ran down the hallway into the studio, then made a rapid retreat back into the hallway with every hair on its back standing straight up. She stumbled and fell flat on her face just in time to see the terrified cat escape down the steps to the kitchen. The blackness in the hallway closed in around her, and she began to cry. Maybe it was just the dark and being lost in it. She had read about how a person could become disoriented in the dark or even in the snow, in any situation that trapped them in a world where they couldn't see.

She sat there for a little while, feeling sorry for herself, and then she turned over and crawled on her hands and knees until she got to the other hallway. She rolled over on her back and lay there thinking. What difference would it make if the cat stayed in the house all night, or every night, for that matter? She was getting out of here. Tomorrow. She was moving out.

She found her way back to her bedroom and collapsed on the bed. The jeans and sweatshirt she left in a pile on the floor, and crawled under the covers, naked as she was born. I'll put everything back the way it belongs tomorrow, when there's some light, she thought, as she snuggled down under the blankets. I can't imagine what had me so spooked. Thank God nobody else will ever know. As sleep began to overcome her, she gave a fleeting thought to what might have frightened the cat.

***

A flashlight came on in the studio. "Turn that damn thing off," the big man demanded softly.

"Who's gonna see?" His companion asked.

"Maybe that guy in the service truck."

The man turned quickly to look out the window and flipped off the flashlight. "What's he doing out there?"

"What d'ya think? The power's out. He's looking for why. We'll wait till he moves on," the big man explained. He looked over his shoulder at a large bundle lying on the floor. "He won't mind waiting."

They watched as the lineman stopped in the lane and got out of his vehicle. He couldn't possibly do anything as long as there was thunder in the area, but by the time it stopped, he hoped to have the problem located.

They watched as he got back in the truck and lit a cigarette. After talking on his radio for several minutes, he moved out of the area.

"He must get paid for all the time he wastes. Why don't he wait for it to stop raining before he comes out here?"

"Who knows, maybe he had an argument with his wife and wanted to get away," the big man surmised. "Let's get our work done and get home."

***

Hard as she tried to block out all the noise of the storm and her frantic, almost hysterical, journey through the house, looking for imaginary predators, she still couldn't go to sleep.

Suddenly she grew very quiet, but her eyes were wide open, and her mind on full alert. She heard something that sounded almost like a man's voice.

When she first moved in, she discovered her closet must have been added after the house was built. Someone had taken the bedroom closet and the closet in the studio, and made one long closet that extended the length of studio.

Thinking of that, she dressed and slipped into the closet. She began to listen at different spots along the wall until she came to the spot where the door had been. Here, there were only two flimsy sheets of drywall, and she could hear two men discussing the presence of a power lineman quite distinctly.

She dashed back to the bedroom, snatched up her phone and car keys, and fled from the room. She sneaked quickly past the door to the other room, and hid at the top of the stairs. Seconds later, two men came out of the studio, carrying a heavy burden. The thought went flying through her head that it might be Jim, but she didn't dwell on it. Instead as soon as they went into her bedroom, she dashed down the steps and out the front door.

She flung open the car door and jumped in, fumbling for the ignition. The engine came to life. Before she could get the door closed, something jumped into her lap. Her heart almost stopped, and she choked on her own scream before that awful cat meowed his greeting. She slammed the door, turned the car toward the lane and raced away from the house.

Trying desperately to miss the mud holes in the lane and dial her cell phone at the same time, she almost hit the power lineman. She had dialed 911, and the operator had just answered, when the lineman walked up the car window, an angry expletive ready on his lips. She hit the button to open the window and held up a hand to caution him to be quiet.

"No! It isn't my imagination," she said indignantly into the phone. "And I'm not a kid playing games. I sneaked out of the house with my cat. We were stopped on the road by a lineman. You can ask him if I'm just a kid playing games."

The lineman took the phone and identified himself, listened for a minute, and then said, "Okay, Fred, I'll keep the lady and her cat here until you have time to investigate. I did see an abandoned car parked back at the head of the lane. Maybe I'll go back and wait for you there."

He listened a moment longer. "I'm not gonna start anything. I have every business to be out here." There was a long pause: "Okay, I'll keep the lady with me."

He handed her the cell phone and opened the car door.

She assumed he meant for her to get out and follow him.

"I'm gonna move your car out of the way," he said, as reached back into the car, grabbed the cat and put him under his jacket. He helped her into the big truck and then handed her the cat: "Can't separate a lady from her cat."

While he was gone, she looked around the truck and then at the cat, busily cleaning himself on her lap. "I guess I'm stuck with you," she said. "What'll I call you? You've got a chewed up ear and bitten off tail, so I guess Tabby is out of the question."

The truck leaned slightly to one side as the big man climbed back in the front seat. "You and Garfield all right," he asked.

She laughed hysterically, "How did you know he's named 'Garfield'?"

"Same way I know yours is Pocahontas."

"Pocahontas?"

"You've got paint all over your face."

––––––

Jean (J.D) Kipfer studied at the Dayton Art Institute. While she raised her son, she began to write. Her latest novel, Indian Blood, *is part of S & H Publishing's catalogue. Jean lives in Zebulon, NC, where she writes stories and paints pictures.*

MURDER ON THE THAMES

P. M. Pevato

A nd to us sinners, eternal life." Professor Prufrock Holmes adjusted his flowing black robe and sat down next to Master Gladstone.

"Well done," the Master said.

Grace before Sunday evening's Formal Hall was a centuries old tradition at University College. Prufrock sighed. With his week-long duty over, he looked forward to quiet dinners at Beaufort Manor with Lady Penelope, his wife of forty years. Quiet, indeed, but not for long. Prufrock and Lady Penelope awaited the imminent arrival of their two beloved grandsons, on a short break for Michaelmas term from their boarding school on the outskirts of Oxford. On these special occasions, Prufrock and his grandsons invariably found mischief of various kinds. Or perhaps, mischief found them. No matter. It was all great fun, really, and in the end, things worked out rather well. Most of the time. There was that one time, for instance, involving Prufrock's hunting dogs and Lady Penelope's Persian cat, Hafiz, and the unfortunate incident of Lady Penelope's Oxford Flower Show award-winning delphiniums...

Prufrock found a note on his plate. "One of your Medieval History students left it for you," whispered Master Gladstone.

The note read, "Might I have a word with you after pudding?" Prufrock did not have to search for the writer. Harry Horbury's anxious face glowed in the candlelight. At

Prufock's nod, the light reflected upon Harry's head, giving Prufrock the impression that his student's dark ginger hair was on fire.

Master Gladstone lifted his fork and knife above his dinner plate and began to cut steamed buttered carrots. Within seconds, the somber Hall filled with clicking glasses and high-pitched scraping of knives on fine bone china. Oil lamps lined the dining tables at even intervals, casting shadows upon the boys' sallow faces, an accurate reflection of the evening's moody silence. Candlelight from wrought iron sconces fixed along the dining hall's walls shed gloom rather than the usual warm glow. The hall's enormous stone fireplace struggled to maintain an even flame. This ominous atmosphere added to the absence of laughter and deafening chatter that normally bounced off the stained glass windows and cathedral ceiling.

Try as he might, Prufrock could not keep his eyes off the empty seat, untouched cutlery, and unfilled water glass that marked Drake Barclay's place. Whilst Drake's colleagues dined on buttered carrots, roasted rosemary potatoes, Herefordshire filet mignon, and Yorkshire pudding, Drake was likely being served a pitiful meal of bubble and squeak with a side of mushy peas. Prufrock pushed his plate away, closed his eyes, and shook his head.

Within a fortnight, Drake had gone from popular, well-liked student to accused murderer of fifteen-year-old Philippa Percevel who, at the time of her murder, attended St. Mary's Hall, an all girls finishing school in Oxford.

The main facts seemed straightforward. Pippa, as she was known to her friends, died two weeks ago, from blunt trauma to the head. Ligature marks of unknown origin appeared around her neck, and a button was found clutched in her hand. A member of the Oxford Crew discovered her body in early morning, on the Thames embankment nearest the boathouse. Full accounts were published in the *Oxford Times* based upon the coroner and police-court reports. However, Prufrock knew from experience that seemingly straightforward cases were often quite complicated, and one could never be too careful when investigating any crime, especially a murder.

From the vest pocket beneath his robe, Prufrock drew his pocket watch and Albert chain, a gift from Lady Penelope on the occasion of his sixtieth birthday a few years ago. "So fashionable ever since Queen Victoria gave one to the Prince Consort," Lady Penelope had said. "Has Her Majesty been seen in public yet? The death of Prince Albert has taken a toll on her."

Prufrock checked his watch several times during dinnertime, convinced it was in need of repair. His curiosity mounted. Why did Harry want to see him?

II

Prufrock had hardly sat down and lit his oil lamp before Harry opened the heavy oak office door and closed it quietly behind him, looking over his shoulder as he did so.

"Professor," Harry said. "I am eternally grateful."

"No trouble, Horbury." Prufrock waved Harry to one of the chairs in front of his sizeable wooden desk, from which papers overflowed onto every available surface.

Harry picked up the stack of papers from the nearest of the weathered leather armchairs, and finding nowhere to put them, he placed the stack on the dark worn carpet and sat. Harry leaned closer to Prufrock, and the oil lamp accentuated the gaunt lines of his face—a marked contrast to his athletic physique. "It's Drake, Professor. He's innocent! I swear it upon my life! I would give mine for his, if need be. I would...would..."

"Horbury, I quite understand your loyalty to Barclay. But you must accept the verdict returned at today's inquest."

"A verdict of 'Wilful Murder'? Never! Drake is no more a murderer than you or I."

"Barclay will be brought before the Magistrates tomorrow, and if the Crown makes its case, his will be referred to the next Assizes. It is quite out of our hands at this point."

"Is it? Do you accept that nothing can be done to prove Drake's innocence?"

"How do you know Drake did not kill Miss Percevel?"

"I've known Drake since childhood. He has never hurt anyone, and never would. His temperament is calm. And he loved Pippa with all his heart."

Prufrock considered Horbury's plea. "Drake never demonstrated a bad temper? Was he the jealous type? Did Pippa lose interest, perhaps gave her heart to another?"

Harry shook his head. "I swear, Professor Holmes. There was nothing out of the ordinary. Drake was beyond happy. He was in love and never expressed any apprehensions or doubt pertaining to his relationship with Pippa."

"Were there witnesses? I do not recall the *Oxford Times* reporting any."

"No, none."

"Does anyone else believe Drake to be innocent?"

"Two of Pippa's closest friends insist Drake is not the murderer, Sybil Lloyd and Kathryn Maplethorpe, boarders at St. Mary's Hall. Pippa and Sybil were inseparable as twins."

Prufrock paused a few moments to fetch his Calabash pipe and tobacco. He took great care preparing and lighting his pipe.

Harry reached inside his robe and withdrew a cigarette

case. "Do you mind, Professor?"

Wispy clouds of smoke swirled above Prufrock's head. "Not at all." He puffed on his Calabash. "Does anyone believe Drake is guilty?"

"Jane Forbes and Thierry de Chavannes."

"Why?"

Harry took a long drag on his cigarette. "Jane Forbes, a student at St. Mary's, was constantly telling Pippa that Drake wasn't good enough for her. I also overheard Jane and Drake arguing about Pippa. Thierry pursued Pippa from the moment he enrolled at Oxford, turning on the charm as only a Frenchman can. Thierry told Chief Inspector Morris that Drake's clothes were soiled with mud the night of Pippa's murder. Acting on an anonymous tip, Chief Inspector Morris later found clothes covered with mud stuffed in a rubbish bin behind The King's Arms pub, clothes that belonged to Drake."

Prufrock chewed the tip of the Calabash. "The same clothes Drake wore the night of Pippa's murder?" Harry nodded. "Drake's coat button was found in Pippa's dead hand, was it not?"

Harry stood up and paced back and forth in front of Prufrock's desk. "Circumstantial evidence, Professor Holmes, is never reliable. You said so yourself in class, when we studied crimes in Medieval England."

"Well, yes, that is true. Interpretation often depends on point of view, an extremely subjective process. But we live not in Medieval Ages, my boy, but in this age of Queen Victoria, and we discuss a modern case, with modern methods of investigation, not based solely upon the word of a barmaid or a charlatan."

Harry stopped pacing, held his cigarette in one hand, tapped the tips of the fingers on his other, and counted.

"First, no witnesses. Second, no motive. Third, no definitive murder weapon. Fourth, no scratches or bruises on Drake's person. Fifth, no criminal past or pattern of criminal behaviour."

Prufrock looked up at Harry's tortured face. "You have no doubt?"

"None whatsoever. I would do anything to clear Drake's name. Anything. In fact," Harry hesitated before continuing, lowered his voice and said, "in fact, that is precisely why I came to see you. Because I have evidence that casts doubt upon Drake's guilt."

Prufrock raised his eyebrows. "Evidence?"

"Yes, evidence."

"What? Where?" Prufrock was stunned.

"In my lock box beneath my bed, here on the college grounds. I found it odd at the time, and thought it a joke." Harry ran one hand through his auburn hair. "How wrong I was."

"Yes? Pray, do continue," encouraged Prufrock.

"Drake asked me to keep a sealed envelope in my lock box, in case, he said, a tragedy should befall him. Truly, I did not take the matter seriously, but Drake and I were as close as brothers, and I assured him I would keep the envelope in a safe place. It was not until his arrest that I recalled the envelope and Drake's ominous words. I came to you immediately."

"Drake did not ask you to fetch this so-called evidence?"

Harry shook his head. "Only immediate family members may visit Drake. I appealed to Chief Inspector Morris's sympathies, but he would not bend. 'Rules are rules,' he said."

"And Drake's parents? Have you not spoken to them in regards to this mysterious envelope? Could they not request visitation on your behalf?"

Harry stopped pacing. "Drake's parents are abroad at their ranch in Argentina and only recently received word of Drake's predicament. It will take weeks for their ship to reach Portsmouth."

Prufrock frowned. "How utterly unfortunate. Indeed, truly disconcerting."

Harry took a seat again, leaned forward and dropped his head into his hands for a long moment. Then he sat up and looked directly at Prufrock. "Now do you see my sense of urgency? This envelope's contents might turn the tables, so to speak, in Drake's favour."

Prufrock drew on the Calabash. "I could not say for certain, until the contents of the envelope are examined. What did you make of them?"

"I did not open the envelope, so as not to contaminate the evidence, thus rendering it inadmissible."

"Well done, Horbury! Astute, I dare say." Prufrock paused, and the embers in his Calabash glowed brighter. "This envelope, it is still locked away?"

"No, Professor." Harry lowered his voice again. "I moved the envelope to a more secure location. Where no one will find it," replied Harry.

"No one? Are you certain?"

Harry smiled for the first time that evening. "No one, except perhaps the devil himself."

Prufrock felt reassured. It was unlikely the devil would find the envelope, thus it had to be safely hidden. "We must notify Chief Inspector Morris forthwith."

"No! Please do not, until we know for certain what the envelope contains, in the event that—"

"That the contents prove to be damning. The final nail in the coffin. The *coup de grâce*. Ah, yes, I quite agree,"

Prufrock said.

"I knew you would understand, Professor. And there is a request I wish to make of you, one that has taken all of my courage to bring to you this evening. Would you ask your son to review the case? I would pay his fees out of my trust fund," Harry said.

"You refer to Maddock, no doubt," Prufrock replied. "I could try, but make no promises. Maddock's current caseload at Marple Chambers is extensive. So much so, in fact, that his two sons, my grandsons, shall holiday with me and Lady Penelope at Beaufort Hall for a fortnight, but yes, I shall try, do not doubt that for one moment, Horbury."

"Professor, I do not know what to say. Truly, you have given me hope in a hopeless situation," replied Harry.

Prufrock took another drag on his pipe. "As regards any barrister's fees, let us first determine whether or not Maddock is willing to clear his schedule to travel from London for a few days. Perhaps he could use his sons' visit as an excuse, though I dare say he needs no excuse to visit them as both are dear to him."

"Thank you, Professor! How can I ever repay you for your kindness?"

Prufrock put his pipe down and pressed his fingertips together. "Let us not get ahead of ourselves, Horbury. First we must determine beyond a reasonable doubt whether Barclay can be exonerated. A rather difficult task in such criminal cases. When shall we meet to examine the envelope?"

"I would propose as soon as Maddock confirms he is willing, at least, to discuss the case with us, Professor."

"Ah, quite right you are. I'll have my butler send a telegram immediately. Then, shall we leave it at that?"

"Yes, Professor. Thank you, and a good night to you."

"Good night to you, Horbury. We shall nonetheless see you on the morrow in my Medieval History seminar? We are discussing, if I recall correctly, the devastating effects of the Black Death upon European commerce."

Harry and Prufrock shook hands. "Yes, Professor. On the morrow, then."

Harry exited Prufrock's office, and turned back momentarily. "Have you ever seen your best friend taken away in bracelets?"

"No, Horbury, fortunately I have not. Derbies cut not only the skin, but leave scars on one's emotions, do they not?"

Horbury did not reply, but mumbled something under his breath. Prufrock's heart sank as he watched the poor lad close the office door and sighed, hoping he was not too quick in promising Maddock's participation, in the event his son was unwilling or unavailable. Prufrock removed his robe, filled his Gladstone bag with several papers, shrugged on his Inverness cape, and locked his office door.

The porter waited for Prufrock at the main college entrance. "Yer landau, Perfessa." With a tip of his hat, the porter opened the carriage door.

"Good night, Dundas." Prufrock exchanged the gesture with the porter, touching the brim of his deerstalker.

"G'night, Perfessa," the porter replied, and called up to the coachman, who clicked twice, encouraging the four horses forward into the gloomy night.

The carriage rattled upon the uneven gravel road, and Prufrock fell into a brown study. When the coachman led the horses into the carriage sweep, Prufrock was unable to shake the feeling that Horbury might be correct. A young man was bound for the gallows, unless his innocence was proven. Prufrock decided he could not turn back. There was only one choice: to save an innocent boy from certain death by hanging.

III

The next morning, Prufrock recounted his conversation with Harry Horbury to his wife in Beaufort Manor's centuries old breakfast room.

"Oh my," Lady Penelope said. "How utterly dreadful. Poor dear boy."

Lady Penelope's counsel was invaluable to Prufrock. Before taking further steps, he sought her advice. "What are your thoughts, my dear, on summoning Maddock?"

Lady Penelope put her toast down on her plate and looked up at Prufrock. "We haven't a choice, have we, darling? A young man stands accused of murder, and his innocence is vouched for by his best friend. Horbury, I believe you said? We must act at once."

"It is settled then." Prufrock turned to Beaufort Manor's butler. "Tressilian, send a telegram immediately to Maddock, addressed both to Marple Chambers and the Diogenes Club." Prufrock scribbled several lines on a notepad. "That should do."

Tressilian accepted the note, bowed, and exited the breakfast room.

***

By midday, Prufrock had completed all but the Medieval History seminar, the last before the Michaelmas break. Prufrock was not terribly surprised at Harry's absence, given the subject matter of the seminar—the Black Death. Certainly, Horbury'd had enough of death and doom of late. Prufrock hoped the boy was keeping a stiff upper lip, although quite understandably a difficult task under the dire circumstances.

Prufrock left University College in the afternoon with his Gladstone stuffed with term papers, and walked to the main entrance. "Good afternoon, Perfessa Prufrock," Dundas said. "Not the landau today?"

"Not today, Dundas. Lady Penelope has sent our coachman to fetch our grandsons at Oxford station."

"Up from Abingdon again?" Prufrock nodded. "And 'ere's your trap, Perfessa. A fine day for an open carriage ride, ain't it?"

"Indeed, Dundas. A fine day, but not for everyone..."

Dundas looked around and lowered his voice. "It's 'bout that boy, ain't it? Barclay? A dreadful business, Perfessa. Dreadful indeed. The wife says she don't believe he's done it, but do we really know people, Perfessa?"

"I quite agree with your wife, and also with you, in that we do not always know what darkness lurks in the minds of others." Suddenly, Prufrock had an idea. "I say, Dundas, were you interviewed by Chief Inspector Morris?"

"Yeah, I gave me statement," Dundas replied.

Prufrock wrinkled his forehead. "So you were on duty?"

"Always on duty, Perfessa. The poor girl that was killed, she came round 'ere that same afternoon, before she was found dead in the evening. Saw 'er riding 'er bicycle. I only caught a glimpse of 'er, mind, but I'd swear it was 'er. Dropped off a note right 'ere, at the Porter's Lodge. I'd stepped out for only a minute, see. Turned around an' only saw 'er from behind. Wore that same red pea coat an' black 'at like them ladies do in Paris. Seen me wife's magazines, you see. In such a 'urry, she was."

"A note? Really?"

"Yeah, an' addressed to Mr D Barclay, it was," said Dundas. "I told them coppers but they said there wasn't no note found in Barclay's room or on 'is person."

Prufrock could not recall any mention of a note in the newspaper articles he had filed away in his cluttered mind. "Strange, Dundas. Very strange."

"If you ask me, Perfessa, I'd never bet a sovereign that the boy 'ad it in 'im to do murder."

Prufrock and Dundas shook hands. "Thank you for this information. Most interesting."

"Me mum always said the peaceful countryside ain't no different than the dark alleys in London. Both is full of crimes."

"Clever woman, your mother, Dundas. Clever indeed."

"She was, may God rest 'er soul," Dundas said.

Prufrock looked over Dundas's shoulder and caught a glimpse of *The Sporting Times*. He could not miss the distinctive pink newsprint. "Any tips for Ascot?"

Dundas turned pinker than the newspaper. "Er, uh, nah, Perfessa, just, eh, ya know doing a bit of reading now that things are gonna slow down round here. A buddy o' mine gave me the pink 'un, brought me Ploughman's lunch. I'd forgot it at 'ome. Good man, he is. Forgetful, I am," replied Dundas.

Prufrock raised one eyebrow. "Are you now?"

Dundas changed the subject quickly. "Your trap is ready, Perfessa."

The trap slowly pulled away from University College. Prufrock found himself thinking about Pippa's note and Drake's sealed envelope, and concluded that there was surely more to uncover.

IV

"Grandpapa!"

"What wonderful gifts the magic winds carried all the way from Radley College," Prufrock said. The boys ran to their grandfather and hugged his long legs. "Mycroft, how you have grown since I last saw you. And Sherlock, my boy, what a fine suit you have on. All grown up, are we? Splendid, splendid!"

Sherlock tugged on his grandfather's Inverness cape. "Can we go for a walk, Grandpapa?"

"I would rather study what is inside Grandpapa's Gladstone," Mycroft said. "Papa has one almost exactly the same and when he returns home, there are so many cases inside. But Papa will not let me read anything. One day I shall have my own Gladstone."

"I am very glad to be away from Radley," Sherlock said. "It's so *boring*."

"It is *not*," said Mycroft.

"It is *so!*"

Prufrock did his best to keep a straight face. "That will be enough, boys. I am certain you will not be bored at Beaufort Manor."

"Grandpapa, Sherlock despises Radley because Headmaster Rhodes assigned lines. 'I am an incorrigible boy' one hundred times on foolscap."

Prufrock suppressed the urge to chuckle. "Incorrigible is not always such a bad characteristic, in my opinion. In the sense of unrelenting, that could be quite useful in certain situations."

Sherlock's face lit up. "In what cases might that be, Grandpapa?"

"Let me think. Perhaps in the course of meticulous research, such as investigating a crime," replied Prufrock.

"A crime! Oh Grandpapa, might we investigate a crime?"

Mycroft moaned. "Splendid. Sherlock and his crimes. Grandpapa, please I beg you not to encourage him. Sherlock goes on and on and *on* about crimes and dead bodies and he's never seen either."

"I have *so*," Sherlock insisted.

"You have *not*."

"I saw Mama's Uncle Edward in the wooden casket at the funeral home in Kensington," Sherlock announced.

"Uncle Edward wasn't murdered," Mycroft said.

"How do you know that? I overheard the coroner tell Papa that the cause of death was 'inconclusive'. So there."

Mycroft laughed. "That means nothing, you numbskull."

Sherlock raised his voice. "I am *not* a numbskull. You are!"

"Boys! Manners!" Lady Penelope entered the foyer. "I heard you arguing all the way from the drawing room." Lady Penelope led the way inside, talking with Mycroft.

Prufrock lowered his voice and inclined his head toward Sherlock. "What say you about a walk along the Thames? I'll show you the scene of a crime, but you must promise you won't inform Grandmama."

Sherlock pretended to sew his lips together, and then whispered, "You mean the one about the girl found dead upon the Thames embankment?"

"Why yes, Sherlock. How did you learn about that? Surely Abingdon village has no interest in an Oxford case?"

"I finished writing lines quickly, using the headmaster's blotter and ink to create a stamp of the lines, and had so much time on my hands. Then I happened upon his *Oxford Times*. I have some thoughts about the case, Grandpapa," Sherlock whispered.

Prufrock smirked. "Do you, now? We must conceal the true nature of our little adventure."

"I promise. Otherwise Grandmama will send me to bed without my supper."

"Truth be told, Grandmama will send *me* to bed without my supper." Sherlock smiled. Prufrock raised his voice and clapped his hands. "Come, come! Let us take tea and Mrs Dobb's freshly baked scones with clotted cream in the drawing room, shall we?"

After high tea, Sherlock skipped up the stairs to Beaufort Manor's nursery. Within minutes he returned wearing his walking attire: a tweed coat in olive green that matched his eyes and set off his dark hair, a brown cashmere jumper, tan cotton trousers, and green Wellies.

Tressilian cleared his throat. "Does Master Sherlock not recall the rule pertaining to Wellington boots indoors?"

Lady Beaufort chuckled. "And where are you off to, dearest Sherlock?"

"A walk with Grandpapa, Grandmama."

"I would prefer to stay with Grandmama, if that is all right," Mycroft said. Lady Penelope beamed.

Prufrock and Sherlock exchanged a quick glance.

"Splendid, Mycroft. We shall catch up on Radley College and discuss activities for Christmas vacation," Lady Penelope said.

"*And* when Sherlock dared Michael Simmons to a boxing match, *and* hid George Hartwell's violin, *and* the visit by Constable Farr from Abingdon Constabulary, *and* the fire in the chemistry laboratory, where Sherlock was not allowed *and...*"

Tressilian grinned. Sherlock's face turned red. "Shut it, Mycroft!"

Lady Penelope gasped. "Sherlock! Manners! What *do* they teach you at Abingdon? Your Papa pays quite a sum in tuition. I shall have a word or two with Headmaster Rhodes."

Prufrock said, "Sherlock, apologize to Grandmama."

"I'm ever so sorry, Grandmama," Sherlock mumbled.

Lady Penelope sighed. "Do *not* be late for dinner. And that goes for you too, Prufrock. Try to stay out of trouble, will you?"

"I promise, my darling. And we shall be back well before the gong, won't we, Sherlock?"

"Yes, Grandpapa," said Sherlock, who shared a private wink with Prufrock.

"Until dinner, then," Prufrock said. But a nagging sense that something was amiss raised doubts that he would be able to keep his promise.

***

The River Thames and its surroundings were lovely in autumn. Fallen leaves floated on the blue-green water that carried yellow and orange and red foliage downstream. "I like your hat, Grandpapa."

"This old thing? It's a deerstalker, my boy, and some day it shall be yours. Would you like that?"

"Oh, I should be so delighted," Sherlock replied. "Where are we headed, Grandpapa?"

Prufrock pointed his walking stick. "Straight on, toward Oxford University's boathouse."

"Is that where she...where the girl..."

"Yes, Sherlock."

Grandfather and grandson walked quietly for the next mile or so until they reached the boathouse. Prufrock noticed how Sherlock became more and more serious, observing every inch of the area the closer they neared the scene of the crime. He crouched down, waved his hands above the ground, sniffed the air.

A squelching sound caught Prufrock's attention. "Don't get too close to the edge, Sherlock. You know how upset Grandmama would be if you came home covered in mud."

"It's all right, Grandpapa. My Wellies keep my feet dry."

"It's not just your feet that could get wet."

"Oh! Grandpapa!" Sherlock's voice went up at least an octave. Prufrock ran to intercept an imminent watery disaster, sending out a silent apology to the footman who would have to clean his boots that evening.

Prufrock stopped suddenly. "What is this? Oh dear me. Dear, dear me." What appeared to be a figure lay shrouded in a black robe face down upon the muddy shoreline. A figure with short ginger-coloured hair.

"Grandpapa, is he dead?"

Cautiously, Prufrock gently poked one leg with his walking stick. "I am afraid so."

"He was murdered, Grandpapa." Sherlock did not pose the question—he drew the conclusion. Prufrock nodded. "Do you know who he is?"

Prufrock nodded again, and sunk his head upon his chest. He was only vaguely aware of Sherlock walking in squishy, slowly widening circles around him.

"What have we here?" Sherlock held a muddy object.

"A hoof pick." Prufrock answered the question, though distracted by sad thoughts.

"Grandpapa..." Sherlock raised his eyebrows.

"What is it?"

"Oh nothing," his grandson replied. "I just thought...for a moment...oh it's nothing, really.

Lady Penelope did not see her husband and youngest grandson for dinner that evening. A police cart dropped them at Beaufort Manor much later that night. Lady Penelope was not amused.

V

The death of Harry Horbury circulated around Oxford as quickly and fiercely as an autumn rainstorm beats upon

Beaufort Manor's conservatory windows. Prufrock retired to his study to sit in his armchair, and stare into the fireplace at the ravenous flames. Three knocks on the door brought Prufrock back to the present. "Yes?"

Tressilian bowed, and deftly presented a small round silver tray on the tips of his white-gloved fingers. "A visitor calls upon my lord."

Prufrock removed the single card from the tray. "Let him in."

Within minutes, Tressilian returned with the guest. Prufrock stood up and shook the guest's hand. "Welcome, Monsieur de Chavannes. To what do I owe this pleasure?"

***

Maddock Holmes was on the next train from Paddington Station, and arrived the day after Harry's death. Prufrock filled his son in with as much information as he had gathered. The coroner had pronounced Harry's death a suicide, the result of a self-inflicted wound.

Maddock visited grief-stricken Drake Barclay later that afternoon. In the evening, Maddock sat on a settee across from Prufrock's armchair in the study. A roaring fire took the dampness out of the air, but did nothing to raise the low spirits of father and son.

Prufrock handed his son a box of cigars and a tumbler of single malt Scotch. "Lagavulin is the best medicine, in my opinion."

Maddock accepted the tumbler and took a sip. "He swears he did not kill Pippa, and insists that Horbury would take his own life."

"And what of this note Horbury kept locked away?"

"Barclay has no idea where Horbury would have hidden the envelope and feels nothing really matters any longer. His sweetheart is dead. His best friend was dead. Barclay has no will to live. He claims that without evidence or an alibi, no one will believe his story."

"And what would his story be?" Prufrock asked.

"Barclay claims he was being threatened to end his courtship with Pippa. He shared all of the information with Pippa, who insisted they not acquiesce to foolish demands. Individual letters from newspapers were clipped and pasted on foolscap in order to avoid a handwriting analysis. The anonymous notes, left at the University College Porter's Lodge, arrived more frequently until the day before Pippa's murder. Then the notes stopped."

"When Horbury told me about the envelope, he said no one would be able to find it except the devil himself. I wonder what that meant?"

"We shall never know, Papa."

"Dreadful business," Prufrock said. "Did anyone else know about the threats?"

Maddock shook his head. "Barclay seems to think not."

"Why weren't the authorities notified?"

"Pippa insisted they ignore the threats, convinced the culprit would give up. How wrong she was, and paid dearly with her life. Imagine how Barclay feels. Despite his objections, I filed a motion to release Barclay forthwith, given that he was incarcerated at the time of Horbury's murder. Regrettably, my motion was denied. Chief Inspector Morris's theory is that Horbury was an accomplice."

"That is rather bad news," Prufrock said.

"Indeed. I have sent an urgent telegram to my contact at Scotland Yard."

"Your refer to Chief Inspector Smythe? A brilliant detective," said Prufrock. "Any theories, Maddock?"

"None at the moment. But I am working on it, Papa. I reviewed Constable Spencer's interview notes and all statements. Smythe will of course examine the crime scene thoroughly."

"You might wish to interview Dundas, University College's Porter."

Maddock retired for the night. Prufrock sipped the last drops of his Scotch and watched the embers fade in the fireplace until he could barely keep his eyes open. He closed the study door and carried a small gas lamp into the dark foyer.

A stair creaked. "Who's there?" Prufrock squinted his eyes. "Sherlock?"

"Good evening, Grandpapa," Sherlock said.

Prufrock approached the stairway. "Whatever are you doing in the dark?"

"I...well...well...I was thirsty."

"Mmmm. I see." Prufrock moved the lamp closer to Sherlock. He noticed that his grandson carried a small leather-bound notebook.

VI

St. Mary's Hall was situated on fifty acres, with lush gardens leading down to the River Thames. Oxford's boathouse was an equal distance between University College and St. Mary's Hall.

Miss Hilda Holdhurst greeted Maddock, Prufrock, and Chief Inspector Smythe. "Welcome to St. Mary's Hall. How can I be of assistance?"

"We wish to interview your students, Headmistress," Smythe said.

Miss Holdhurst raised her soft voice. "Whatever for? Chief Inspector Morris and Constable Spencer have already done so, following...following..."

Smythe backed off. "There there, Headmistress, I can only imagine the difficulty..."

Miss Holdhurst pulled a handkerchief from her pocket and sobbed. "Imagine? Can you? Have you any idea how my girls have been affected by these deaths...murder...of... of...and suicide?" She struggled to regain her composure. "I do not wish to upset the girls any further. I trust you understand my position. They barely sleep a wink at night, afraid one of them may be next."

Prufrock cleared his throat. "Miss Holdhurst, in light of the most recent death, it might be prudent to set aside your grave concern for your girls' fragile emotional state, and consider the danger they may face unless the culprit is caught."

Miss Holdhurst dabbed her nose and composed herself. "I thought the culprit was in jail. And that Horbury was a likely accomplice, overcome by guilt and so taking his own life?"

"Possibly, and yet...just to be on the safe side..." Smythe trailed off.

"Headmistress, my name is Maddock Holmes. I shall be representing Drake Barclay. He professes his innocence."

"Well, I suppose, if it is for the girls' well-being," replied Miss Holdhurst. "I assume you wish to speak with Jane Forbes, Kathryn Maplethorpe, Sybil Lloyd, and Sophia Cavendish?"

Chief Inspector Smythe nodded.

Miss Holdhurst indicated their direction with a wave. "Just behind the Hall you shall find a set of playing fields, tennis courts, stables, and a punt house. You will find the girls there."

Smythe tipped his bowler and headed toward the tall hedgerows that hid the playing fields from view.

Prufrock observed that the four girls could not have been more different from one another. Jane was tall, a fair-headed athletic girl dressed in white tennis attire. Kathryn, impeccably dressed in a wispy cream frock of *mousseline de soie*, carried an off-white cotton lace umbrella. Sophia, quiet and mouse-like, adjusted her burgundy blazer, the school's crest displayed prominently on the breast pocket. Sybil's attire marked her as an equestrian, and, as the late Horbury had noted, she could pass for Pippa's twin sister. The girls assembled on comfortable seating near the tennis courts and sipped tea.

"We all made statements to Chief Inspector Morris," Jane Forbes said.

"We simply wish to confirm your statements, and then we shall be on our way," assured Smythe.

Jane glared at Smythe and Maddock. "Why are a Scotland Yard Chief Inspector and a London Barrister working on cases in Oxford? Has the crime rate in London diminished? Bow Street cells empty?"

"I'm afraid that's none of your business, Miss," replied Smythe.

"I am afraid it *is* my business, Chief Inspector. I should like to know why you're wasting time going over statements when you should be firming up the case against Drake."

Kathryn spoke up at last. "Listen to them, Jane! Drake might be exonerated..."

Prufrock was certain Jane mouthed the words *Be quiet* to Kathryn.

"The entire investigation must be revisited in light of Mr Horbury's death," explained Maddock.

Jane crossed her arms. "This conversation is over."

"For now, Miss Forbes," Smythe replied.

***

"Well, that was a total waste of time," Smythe said.

"Perhaps not," Maddock said. "Those girls are hiding something."

"I quite agree," Prufrock said. "Shall we walk the grounds for a bit? There may be more information we can glean from others."

"Maddock and I shall visit the stables," Smythe said.

"I shall explore the Hall," Prufrock said.

Prufrock entered the library and nodded politely to the elderly librarian. A girl in pigtails sat alone at one of the study tables. Prufrock approached her and sat across the table.

"Hello. Mind if I join you?"

"Not at all, but you mustn't speak or else *she* will ask you to leave forthwith." The freckle-faced girl inclined her head to the librarian's desk, and pushed up the bridge of her wire-framed spectacles.

Prufrock smiled. "I am certain *she* will not mind. My name is Professor Holmes and I..."

"Oh! Lady Penelope's spouse! No wonder you are not afraid of her." She grinned and lowered her voice even more. "I wouldn't even *be* here if Lady Penelope hadn't donated the grounds and the original building to St. Mary's." The girl extended her hand. "My name is Elspeth Moriarity. I'm pleased to meet you."

"Might I ask you a few questions regarding the recent tragic events?"

"No one *ever* asks me anything, even though I know *so* much. I have no friends here, and thus am quite invisible. That's why I *see* things, Professor, when others think no one is watching."

Prufrock raised his eyebrows. "For instance?"

"Well..." Elspeth drew out the word, placed one index finger at the corner of her mouth, and tapped her fingertip.

"Hmmmm...let me see. Where to begin? Jane Forbes fought with Drake Barclay a few days before Pippa's murder. Drake raised his voice. Jane tugged on his coat. I sat over there," she pointed, "in that window seat. I could hear their voices through the glass, but couldn't make out what they said. I really *must* learn to read lips."

"Interesting. Pray, continue, Elspeth."

"I spoke with Pippa in the Main Common Room on the night she was killed. Pippa was ever so nice to me. I asked Pippa if she'd enjoyed her afternoon bicycle ride. Pippa was puzzled. 'Bicycle ride?' she asked me, 'what bicycle ride?' I swear I'd seen her leave the Hall grounds. She wore her favourite red pea coat and black hat." Prufrock remained silent. "Pippa said she helped Sophia with her sums all afternoon. Sophia's hopeless at sums. And Pippa was ever so smart. Besides, Sophia hurt her hand in a fall. She's not very coordinated. Pippa wrote Sophia's homework."

Prufrock broke his silence. "Anything else, Elspeth?"

"The stable boy, Hunter, fancies Sybil. Sometimes I walk to the barns, though I am hopeless at riding. Hunter follows Sybil this way and that—'Bucephalus is groomed for you, Miss Sybil,' and 'do you need a leg up?' 'I can't find your cotton lead,' and so on. Hunter even shined her field boots. Imagine! 'Got all the mud off, Miss Sybil, though I can't think where you could have got your boots so filthy, the bridle paths are bone dry.'"

"Most intriguing," Prufrock said.

"Professor?"

"Yes, Elspeth?"

Elspeth sighed. "I am so grateful for Lady Penelope's generosity. I only wish...I mean to say...my older brother, James, will be able to attend Oxford and I cannot. I hope one day girls will be admitted."

"One can only hope. Good day, Elspeth."

"Good day, Professor."

When Prufrock reconvened with Maddock and Smythe, he recounted his conversation with Elspeth. "I believe a visit to Dundas at Porter's Lodge is in order."

***

Later than night, Prufrock retired to his study. Tressilian prepared a fire and filled his master's gold snuff box adorned with an amethyst on the lid. Prufrock opted for his Calabash and Lagavulin, stretched out his legs, and reclined in his armchair with one hand behind his head, the other holding his pipe—his usual pose. A knock on the door startled him.

Sherlock peered into the study. "Come, come, Sherlock! Sit here by the fire." Prufrock patted the armchair next to his. Sherlock stretched his legs, reclined, and placed one hand behind his head. He was dressed in pajamas and dressing gown. "Grandpapa, I realize it is late, but I must tell you what I found today." Sherlock reached inside his dressing gown and pulled out an envelope. "I believe you have been looking for this?"

Prufrock nearly dropped his pipe. "But when, how..."

Sherlock withdrew his small leather-bound notebook from his dressing gown pocket, and began to read his notes to Prufrock. He continued to read until the logs in the fireplace were mere embers.

<h1 style="text-align:center">VII</h1>

The group assembled in the Main Common Room of St. Mary's Hall eyed one another nervously. "Thank you for attending on such short notice," said Smythe. "As you know, two tragedies have befallen Oxford: the murder of Philippa Percevel, and death of Harry Horbury. Drake

Barclay awaits trial for Miss Percevel's murder, and very recently, certain facts have come to light—facts that cast doubt upon Mr Barclay's guilt, and may shed new light upon both tragic incidents." The crowd stirred. Smythe raised his hand. "After a thorough investigation, Scotland Yard, in cooperation with Chief Inspector Morris, are prepared to bring charges for both murders." Gasps filled the air. "Yes, you heard correctly. Murders. Both Pippa and Harry were murdered."

Smythe turned to Prufrock. "Given his immeasurable contribution to solving both crimes, I shall invite Professor Holmes to elaborate on the investigation."

Prufrock stood. "What we have here," he said, "are two tragedies, each the result of jealousy and desire. Jealousy of a happy couple's love for one another, and desire, due to irrepressible yearning. Jealousy, desire, and unrequited love." Prufrock paused. "Drake Barclay was in love with Pippa Percevel, a pure love that triggered jealousy in a person who could not have what she wanted." Prufrock pointed to Jane Forbes. "You were jealous of that pure love, were you not?"

Jane stood up. "Rubbish! I shall not stay and listen to this farce a moment longer!"

Constable Spencer blocked the door. "Sit down, Miss Forbes."

Prufrock continued. "Ah, yes, this is a modern version of Uriah and Bathsheba, wouldn't you agree? We all know the old story of King David's desire for Bathsheba. So intense was his longing that he conspired to send Bathsheba's warrior husband, Uriah, to the front lines of battle. You are King David in this case, for you desired not Drake, but his precious Pippa! And when she did not return your advances, you decided that no one could have her, isn't that so?

179

You sent threatening notes to Drake, notes in our posses-sion. There is a witness to a heated argument you had with Drake."

Elspeth waved to Prufrock.

"You wretched girl," hissed Jane. Elspeth grinned.

Prufrock looked directly at Jane. "You tugged on Drake's coat. What did you retrieve from that coat? A button, perhaps? But I shall come back to that later."

Jane sprang from her chair and leaped at Prufrock, but Chief Inspector Morris held her back.

"Next," Prufrock said, looking directly at Kathryn, "there is the tale of Narcissus, doomed to see his own face for eternity. Narcissism is a curse, is it not, Miss Maple-thorpe? Drake will never love you, now he knows you conspired with Miss Forbes."

Kathryn stood up. "No! We only wanted to drug Pippa, and frighten her!"

Jane screamed. "Shut it, Kathryn!"

"You only meant to drug her, drag her to the boathouse, and plant the button from Drake's coat in her hand," Prufrock frowned. "Drake would be framed, and Pippa would end the courtship."

"He was supposed to love *me*," Kathryn sobbed.

Prufrock searched the faces in the room till his eyes met Thierry's. "Nor would Monsieur de Chavannes ever have Pippa's heart whilst she lived, and her death provided Thierry an opportunity to hurt the only person who had once stood in the way of his beloved.

Thierry stood up. "*Oui, c'est ça, Professeur*. It is as we discussed in your study. Monsieur Barclay I did see return from the *rendezvous* with Mademoiselle Percevel. But to the *gendarmes* of Oxford I told of Drake's soiled clothing. It was I who stole Drake's clothes, threw them in the mud, and deposited them in the rubbish bin behind the King's Arms. My *affaire du cœur* was dishonourable."

"You must apologize to Mr Barclay upon his release from incarceration," he said. "That brings me to Miss Sophia Cavendish, who has confessed to the part she played."

"Idiot!" Jane yelled, but Prufrock ignored her.

"Miss Forbes, did you not exploit Miss Cavendish's weakness in mathematics by stealing a test paper?" Sophia nodded. "Sophia passed her examination, but Miss Forbes held that over her head. She forced Sophia to help carry out her wicked plan. Sophia didn't injure her hand, but Pippa didn't know that. She offered Sophia assistance with her homework, which served to keep Pippa out of sight. She extracted from Pippa a note in Pippa's own hand." Prufrock held up the note and read, "'Boathouse. Tonight. Ten o'clock'. Sophia pretended the note was meant for an unknown suitor, but the note was instead delivered to Drake."

Prufrock continued. "Miss Lloyd enters the scheme at this point." He turned to stare directly at Sybil, who placed shaking hands over her eyes. "Horbury referred to you as Pippa's twin. Of course! You could easily pass for Pippa. Whilst you distracted Pippa, Sybil dressed in Pippa's red pea coat and black hat and rode to town where she dropped the note at the University College's Porter Lodge. As I suspected, Dundas, the Porter, was at the betting shop nearby. 'The pink 'un' gave away his fondness for the ponies on the day I spoke with him about the note. Dundas saw someone who *looked* like Pippa stop at the chemist's and ride away on her bicycle while he was at the betting shop. But did he see Pippa? I think not."

Sybil uncovered her eyes. "I never meant for her to die!"

Prufrock raised one eyebrow. "My disguise theory was inspired by my grandson, Sherlock," he said, and invited the young sleuth to join him. "Sherlock reminded me of the time his parents hosted a masquerade at their home."

"You're barking mad," Jane shouted, but it was as if Prufrock hadn't heard her.

"Sybil purchased laudanum at the chemist's. A large dose of this opium tincture would cause a deep sleep. Once Kathryn signalled that Drake had given up on Pippa's making the promised rendezvous, Jane and Sybil carried Pippa's now-unconscious body to the boathouse.

"Oh, the plan was unfolding brilliantly, was it not? Until the laudanum wore off earlier than expected, and Pippa woke up. Panic set in. Pippa's hands had been bound with a cotton lead stolen from the stables. Sybil grabbed the lead and wrapped it around Pippa's neck. Jane retrieved a paddle from the boathouse and hit Pippa on the head."

Sybil pleaded with Prufrock. "I was only supposed to deliver the note, that was all!"

"Ah, but you did more. Hunter confirmed that he had cleaned your field boots. My youngest grandson Sherlock has a fondness for the study of footprints and soils. He noticed four sets of foot patterns at the crime scene, two fresh sets overlapping two older ones. Both an older and a newer set matched Sybil's field boots. "You see," Prufrock explained, "Hunter did a fine job, cleaning those boots, but there was a bit of soil left in one of the heels—soil that was not from the barn or the bridle path. That, along with the presence of a hoof pick, puts you, Sibyl, at both crime scenes. However, we have yet to determing just who stabbed Horbury."

Sybil sobbed piteously. "I had no choice! Jane threatened to expose my family's secret."

Jane jeered. "All your pretty clothes bought with dirty money from trading in slaves." Jane's sneer contorted her features almost beyond recognition. She turned back to Prufrock. "Your entire case begins with a tale of blackmail notes. Where are these alleged notes?"

Prufrock smiled. "Sherlock, would you like to tell how you found the notes?"

Sherlock cleared his throat. "I overheard Grandpapa discussing the case with Papa. Horbury had told Grandpapa that only the devil would know where to find the envelope the notes were in. I recalled the gargoyles in the Quadrangle at University College. Without my Grandmama's knowledge, I rode my bicycle to University College. There, directly beneath the devil gargoyle, I found the envelope tucked behind a loosened brick near the bottom of the wall, where only the devil himself knew it was hidden."

As the four accomplices were escorted out of the Common Room, only Jane required bracelets. Miss Holdhurst was carried away, having fainted from the knowledge that murderous plots had been hatched behind the hallowed walls of St. Mary's Hall.

VIII

Prufrock and Sherlock sat in the study, reading newspaper accounts of both cases. Sherlock didn't mind that his name wasn't mentioned. He was happy in the knowledge that he had participated in solving not just one crime, but two.

"What will happen to the girls, Grandpapa?"

"I am afraid, Sherlock, that determination is out of our hands. Leniency may be given to Kathryn and Sophia; however, I fear Jane and Sybil shall meet their fate at the gallows."

"But what I most want to know, Grandpapa, is how you

unraveled this complicated tangle of events. How did you reach your conclusions?"

"It is really rather simple, Sherlock. In solving any crime, one must eliminate the impossible, and then see what remains. Which, however implausible, is likely the truth."

Prufrock paused for a moment and turned to his grandson. "Elementary, I dare say."

"Elementary," Sherlock repeated. "Yes, I see."

Prufrock and young Sherlock sat together in the study for hours, each reclining in an armchair with his feet extended toward the warmth of the fireplace. In the wee hours, when the fire logs had turned to embers, Prufrock gathered the sleeping boy in his arms and carried him up to bed.

———

A flâneur *at heart, P. M. Pevato constantly seeks new experiences whilst strolling down the boulevards of life. Along this journey, the author earned degrees from Dalhousie Law School and the London School of Economics. For more, visit:* http://www.pmpevato.com *and her tumblr page* http://www.pmpevato.tumblr.com.

SILENT NIGHT, STILLE NACHT

Maria Elizabeth McVoy

The wolf also shall dwell with the lamb,
And the leopard shall lie down with the kid,
The calf and the young lion and the fatling together;
And a little child shall lead them.

— Isaiah 11:6

Mrs. Margaret Holmes
Oxfordshire, England

12 May 2008

Dear Madam:

I am writing to cordially invite you to a very joyous celebration. On eleventh of November 2008, the first official Christmas Truce Memorial will be unveiled in Frelinghien, France. As your father, Private Frank Richards, and uncle, Private Nathaniel Hawkins, served under my father, Captain Clifton Inglis Stockwell, in Frelinghien on the 25th of December, 1914, I would be most honoured if you would accompany me to the ceremony.

The planned events are a Mass in the village church, followed by a football game — not unlike the one played all those Christmases ago — and, of course, the unveiling of the memorial.

I look forward to your response, and your company on

the journey.

Your servant,
Major Miles Stockwell (retired)

* * *

Mr. and Mrs. Hawkins
   and Miss Alice Hawkins
Oxfordshire, England

Dearest Mother, and Father, and my beloved Alice,

I trust that this letter finds you well. I think of you all often: father in his spectacles grading term-end papers and writing up new articles to send to American journals; Mother knitting warm jumpers and baking sugar-topped scones; and my little Alice painting Wonderland, always with a dab of paint on her nose. These are happy memories that I carry with me, always.

It has been very quiet in our section of the field and I do not anticipate that I will meet my fate here, so far from you. But should it be God's will, know that I will not swerve from my duty. I joined the colours with a full heart, ready to assail the foes of our great nation with all the righteous fury of Britain. We are assured that any man who falls in the service of the King will be granted glory everlasting.

I will acquit myself with honour and will ever be
Your loving son,
Nathanial Hawkins

* * *

He carried the letter with him always, in his breast pocket, close to his heart. Most of the lads carried similar letters: undated missives penned carefully with gallant words that would comfort their families were they to perish on the field of battle. Nathaniel had penned his on the ship as they'd crossed the channel, months ago now. The son of a Professor of Medieval History at Oxford, he'd never imagined how much war had changed from the texts his father referenced. He'd never conceived how much time he would have to write letters and sketch scenes in the leather-bound journal Alice had given him before he left. Complacency, he knew, was the enemy that claimed the most victims. But standing by the railing, looking out over the water toward France, where they would push the enemy host back beyond their own borders, he had known nothing. He had penned the letter carefully, imagining glorious battles, like those of the Hundred Years War, on which his father lectured at Oxford.

Much to the amusement of his fellows, he'd thrown his head back, when he was finished writing, and dramatically shouted the famous speech from Shakespeare's *Henry V*:

"If we are mark'd to die, we are enow
To do our country loss; and if to live,
The fewer men, the greater share of honour.
God's will! I pray thee, wish not one man more.
By Jove, I am not covetous for gold,
Nor care I who doth feed upon my cost;
It yearns me not if men my garments wear;
Such outward things dwell not in my desires.
But if it be a sin to covet honour,
I am the most offending soul alive."

One by one the listeners were drawn in and stood as if under a magical spell, transfixed by an inflexible vision of future glory on the field of battle. As line upon line of Elizabethan poetry fell from his lips, they awoke slowly from their enchanted stillness and began to poke and jab one another, as discordant harmony to Nathanial's clear

187

descant; they each nodded with certainty at the glorious tales to be told, of exploits not yet transpired.

When he finished, his fist raised to the sky, his voice almost hoarse from shouting those perfect words for the eve of battle. The lads applauded loud as any audience at the Globe, as he bent knee into a flourishing bow. They were local lads, most of them, but some too who had come to study at Oxford and been swept away to the war on the continent, filled with noble prose and dramatic poetry. Not to be outdone, Frank Richards, his oldest mate, who had accompanied him and Alice on their childhood adventures in the pockets of Oxfordshire, recited Tennyson's *The Charge of the Light Brigade* and read excerpts from Homer's *Iliad.* Clarence Liddel, whom he had met only a week into Michaelmas term just before the lot of them joined the colours together, sang some heroic ballads in his rich Scots tenor. They disembarked in high spirits, prepared to face the wicked German Hun, to merit honour and imperishable glory, to inspire their own epic poems and songs.

What awaited them in France was not the grand field of battle they'd expected, but rather the stalemate of war in the trenches. After too many lives, on both sides of the field, had been lost in the first five months of the war, each army had burrowed into the ground, creating long slashes in the earth that ran for miles and miles. And the war was at an impasse.

Nathanial lay nearly flat in the trench, his booted feet propped up on his rucksack to avoid soaking in the ice-crusted water that lined the bottom of the trench. His sketchbook lay across his stomach, propped up slightly by the buckle of his belt, as he sketched with a sharpened bit of charcoal. Liddel was sitting nearly still, playing chess with Richards (whom Nathanial had given up asking to sit still while he sketched). Liddel was the better to sketch anyhow. Although Richards was a handsome fellow with the fair skin, dark hair, and sooty green eyes of a black Celt, there was something about the way Liddel's too-angular face reflected his every thought and emotion. It was perhaps the most animated face Nathanial had ever encountered, and he found himself constantly making quick sketches of his friend's moods.

Liddel's current mood was rather relaxed frustration as Richards avoided gambit after gambit on the checkered board. Nathanial's charcoal deftly sketched the slightly crooked smile, furrowed brow, and the almost lazily half-lidded eyes that probably meant Richards had finally made a mistake. And, with a triumphant smirk, Liddel moved his knight and, grinning wickedly, announced: "Checkmate."

Richards smiled good-naturedly and ran his fingers through his exactly regulation-length hair as he analyzed the maneuver that had finally won the match.

The sun was setting, and Nathanial could feel his eyes straining a bit to see the sketch before him. He scribbled the date in the lower right-hand corner of the page and closed the book for the night. Sometimes he sketched by candlelight, but they didn't have so many candles that he could indulge in that practice every evening.

He folded his hands behind his head and watched the clouds change from gold to red and to purple as the sun set over the horizon that he didn't dare stand up to see.

He thought of the letter he had received a few days previous, from his sister. Alice had written that Mother was recovering from a cold, but was well and had knitted him four pairs of woolen stockings for Christmas. The best gift he'd ever receive, he was quite certain. The stockings he had brought with him from England had long since worn holes and were currently more darn than stocking. He'd immediately slipped the soft, blue wool over his cold toes and was gratified to feel warmth return. When the stockings arrived, he'd offered two of the other pairs to his closest mates, who had sworn undying loyalty to Mrs. Hawkins.

Father, Alice had written, was loudly lamenting the fact that there was no one to attend his lectures in Oxford, except for "a bunch of silly lasses." But Nathanial knew that the man who had bought expensive oil paints for his daughter and made certain that she could read and write and do figures as well as her twin brother was rather pleased to have young women at Oxford. Father had sent along a copy of *Henry V*, one of Nathanial's favorite plays to read as a child (and a young man), and an American journal in which he'd recently published an article discussing the evolution of warfare in the Hundred Years War. Nathanial had found the article fascinating and had jotted down some points in the margin that he wanted to discuss with his father...someday.

Alice had sent her brother a slim case of charcoal pencils for sketching. She included also a small scrap of canvas, little more than the length of his hand. On it was a portrait in oils of their entire family: Mother and Father sitting together on the mission bench in the library, Alice standing behind with her hand on Mother's shoulder, red-gold curls pulled off her face with a sapphire-blue ribbon the very shade of her eyes, and Nathanial lounging on the floor at his parents' feet, hands behind his head, gazing out the window behind his sister. She had captured them all: Father's sternness, Mother's gentleness, Nathanial's prewar restlessness, and her own calmness in the face of what was to come. It was a miniature copy of the large portrait she had painted as a gift for Mother and Father the previous Christmas.

From discarded stubs of pencil and a small watercolour paint box they'd found in the cellar as small children (a relic left from their father's childhood), Nathanial and Alice discovered a passion for creating images on paper. But though Nathanial always preferred the soft black and white of charcoal, Alice had fallen in love with colour. Her earliest paintings were fanciful interpretations of her favourite book: *Alice's Adventures in Wonderland.*

Father had a volume from the original 1865 print run of Lewis Carroll's novel of literary nonsense, which had been sold to the American publishing house of Appleton. They had an 1866 Macmillan *Alice* also, but Father had always been more proud of his Appleton *Alice,* and always read to his children from that tome. He often supplemented the reading with a 'small' lecture on the War of the Roses which, he would tell them, was symbolized in *Alice* by the cards painting the white roses (representing the House of York) with red paint (representing the House of Lancaster). Most of their childhood reading with their father resulted in a 'small' lecture on the Middle Ages.

Nathanial and Alice had asked their father many times if he had named his daughter after the little girl in Carroll's novel, but he had never given them a completely straight answer. Nonetheless, Alice herself felt a deep kinship with the story and painted her images of Wonderland, first from the book itself and later from her own imagination. Nearly all her fantastic, and often absurd, paintings were entitled 'Wonderland.'

But in the months previous to the war, Nathanial would come into the parlour (with its long row of windows, it was the best room in the house for painting) to find Alice intent upon very different images: the sun burned white hot in skies that were angry and wore terribly wrong shades of red and yellow; great gashes in the earth tore across landscapes; trees and men and creatures tumbled into deep crevices jagged as the edge of a knife or a predator's teeth; the bodies of men and animals twisted in writhing pain; the horizon was obscured by green and yellow fog; and impossibly great explosions blackened the heavens. Image after horrible image bled from her brush onto the canvas. Tears burned her eyes, and smears of paint on her nose (which she always rubbed absently when she was concentrating) made her face seem ever bruised and lacerated. The day he told her he had enlisted in Britain's volunteer army her face became grey as death, and for an entire fortnight she had painted nothing.

The sun had set entirely as he reminisced, and snow was swirling slowly down from the heavens, obscuring the moon. A soft glow burned from the direction of the enemy trenches. Recklessly, Liddel was on his feet, poking his awkwardly long nose over the top of their trench.

"There are lights all along the German trenches."

Nathaniel frowned. He thought of the weapons of war about which his father lectured: fire arrows, trebuchets hurling flaming pots of tar, and the Byzantine Empire's secret weapon: pressurized siphons projecting Greek fire. By God, what horrible new weapon of war had the Hun devised?

But no flaming projectile was flung across No Man's Land and some of the other lads were darting up to take a peek at the German trenches.

Over the murmur of excited and curious voices in their own trench, came almost-unintelligible words raised in song, carried forth on the freezing wind:

"Stille Nacht, heilige Nacht,
Alles schläft; einsam wacht
Nur das traute hochheilige Paar.
Holder Knabe im lockigen Haar,
Schlaf in himmlischer Ruh!
Schlaf in himmlischer Ruh!"

For a moment, he did not quite believe his ears, but the song continued, and slowly all of the lads fell silent listening.

"Stille Nacht, heilige Nacht,
Hirten erst kundgemacht
Durch der Engel Halleluja,
Tönt es laut von fern und nah:
Christ, der Retter ist da!
Christ, der Retter ist da!"

As the third verse began some of the lads began to hum and some of them to sing along softly in both German and English.

"Stille Nacht, heilige Nacht,
Gottes Sohn, o wie lacht
Lieb' aus deinem göttlichen Mund,
Da uns schlägt die rettende Stund'.
Christ, in deiner Geburt!
Christ, in deiner Geburt!"

Christmas Eve night fell silent, as if waiting for a response or a sign from God. It was Liddel who stood tall, with his head thrown back, and projected his voice against the wind:

> "Hark! The herald angels sing,
> Glory to the newborn King!
> Peace on earth, and mercy mild,
> God and sinners reconciled.
> Joyful, all ye nations, rise,
> Join the triumph of the skies;
> With th' angelic host proclaim,
> Christ is born in Bethlehem.
> Hark! The herald angels sing,
> Glory to the newborn King!"

The other lads took up the carol, and Nathanial found himself standing shoulder to shoulder with Liddel and Richards, bellowing at the top of his lungs. When they too had fallen silent, nearly everyone, including Captain Stockwell, had their heads over the top of the trench watching the enemy line glowing with festive candlelight.

No shots were fired that Christmas Eve night. The only sounds were those of voices raised in song, to celebrate Christ's birth. Nathaniel drifted into dreams pacified by the Germans' singing, as if it were his mother sending him to sleep with a lullaby when he was very young.

Come morning, a face stared back at them, across No Man's Land and shouted across to them: "Don't shoot," his voice called, in a thick Saxon accent. "We don't want to fight you today; we will send you some beer."

Captain Stockwell climbed out of their trench and strode into No Man's Land, shoulders straight, every inch a British officer. The German company commander met him half-way between their armies. For a moment they stood and stared at one another. Nathanial thought, watching from the trench, that they were perhaps speaking, but he couldn't quite make out if their lips were moving. Then they formally saluted one another, and both trenches erupted with cheers.

True to their word, the Germans rolled over a barrel of beer. Lads on both sides clambered out and stretched their legs as the sun burned off the fog. Nathanial brought his sketchbook and cradled it in one hand as the other drew quick sketches of soldiers meeting and shaking hands, trading smokes and stories, jams and chocolates and photographs of family at home, laughing and wishing each other Happy Christmas or *Fröhliches Weihnachten*. He flipped pages quickly, trying to capture the impossible magic of the moment: sworn foes meeting as fellows.

Richards gathered some of their lads together and they played a game of football against some of the German lads. Nathanial propped himself against his rucksack, on the sidelines, and sketched as the figures ran up and down the makeshift football field, laughing and tumbling over one another like boys at interval. Richards took a fall against the frozen earth and one of the German lads paused to give him a hand up. They laughed and clasped hands before rejoining the game.

Mid-morning, they gathered somberly, British and Germans together, over an open grave. With snipers on both sides watching diligently for any fool to so much as raise a finger over the top of the trench, formal burials were generally next to impossible. But today, with a cease-fire acknowledged on both sides, they could honour the fallen. Reverend Southerland (perhaps too old to be serving in the trenches, but he was stubborn, not afraid of mud or wet feet, and going to bloody well stay as long as the lads needed him) led the service. His thin, reedy voice held a strength and compassion that evangelical men with booming voices and fiery sermons often lacked.

He opened his well-thumbed Bible and read: "'In those days shall men seek death, and shall not find it, and shall desire to die, and death shall flee from them.' Revelations chapter 9, verse 6."

Silence followed those dismal words, as each faced his worst memories of the war. Nathanial saw Alice's horrible pre-war paintings in his mind, with their brutal and almost clairvoyant kinship to the France that had awaited them when they disembarked, and felt dread creep into his heart for the first time that Christmas Day.

But Reverend Southerland continued: "This passage describes the end of the world, as it was foretold to John by the Angel of God. I say to you now: Armageddon is not upon us! War is not a new evil that has befallen us; it has ever been the purveyor of death and sorrow. Now that modern weapons of war have surpassed our traditional military tactics, there is no longer even an illusion of glory.

"But today we stand together: fellows in our celebration of the birth of Christ, comrades in our grief for the fallen. Illuminated in the great light of Christ's love, and in the candles of our neighbor's Christmas trees, I cannot believe that this is the end. The end of the world would not hold such love and fellowship within it.

"Remember this day, my fellows, for today the lamb and the lion broke their fast together and took rest in one another's company, unafraid. Remember this day, my brothers, for this day you have been given a glimpse of paradise."

He turned the page, and read from the very last leaf of his old Bible: "'And the city had no need of the sun, neither of the moon to shine in it: for the glory of God did lighten it, and the Lamb is the light thereof. And the nations of them which are saved, shall walk in the light of it: and the kings of the earth do bring their glory and honour into it. And the gates of it shall not be shut at all by day: for there shall be no night there. And they shall bring the glory and the honour of the nations into it. And there shall in no wise enter into it any thing that defileth, neither whatsoever worketh abomination or maketh a lie: but they which are written in the Lamb's Book of Life.' Revelations, chapter 21, verses 23 to 27." He closed his Bible and bowed his head, and each man followed his example.

After a few moments, Reverend Southerland raised his head and nodded at Liddel, who stepped forward. A young German soldier stood at his side, with night-dark hair, a deep tan complexion and a hawk-like nose. He barely looked old enough to bear arms.

Liddel began reciting Psalm 23 in his clear Glasgow tenor: "The Lord is my shepherd, I shall not want."

And the young German continued, his almost-soprano voice barely wavering: "*Er weidet mich auf einer grünen Aue und führet mich zum frischen Wasser.*"

"He restoreth my soul: he leadeth me in the paths of righteousness, for his name's sake."

"*Und ob ich schon wanderte im finstern Tal, fürchte ich kein Unglück; denn du bist bei mir, dein Stecken und Stab trösten mich.*"

"Thou preparest a table before me, in the presence of mine enemies: Thou anointest my head with oil, my cup runneth over."

"*Gutes und Barmherzigkeit werden mir folgen mein Leben lang, und ich werde bleiben im Hause des Herrn immerdar.*"

They had no flowers to place in the grave, but each shoveled a handful of soil over the canvas-wrapped figures, and made his last farewell.

They filed silently back to the British trench and were greeted with the rich, enticing scent of bacon sizzling for their Christmas feast.

They gathered 'round the fire pit, drank down drafts of the German beer, and feasted on bacon and dip bread together. The young German soldier who had recited the psalm with Liddel, was introduced as David Levi; he did not speak English, although he seemed to comprehend much of what was said to him. He shyly shook his head as he was offered bacon but consumed the bread with great appetite, and his eyes lit up as he saw Richards approaching with a Christmas pudding dowsed in brandy. With a dramatic flourish, Richards set the brandy alight and all cheered.

Nathanial grinned like a child as the pudding was carefully divided and passed around. Christmas pudding was, in his opinion, the best of all seasonal traditions. His mother's recipe for Christmas pudding had been passed down through many generations of her family. Although some families had begun to prepare their Christmas puddings in basins, Claire Hawkins still insisted upon boiling the special dessert in a pudding cloth, as her mother and grandmother had before her. The dark sugars, black treacle and heavy spices gave the Christmas pudding an almost black hue, like a hard, round cannon ball. She made the pudding each year on Stir-up Sunday, as did pretty much every other family they knew (even the ones who had conformed to the modern idea of steaming in basins). He wondered if rationing had allowed her the not-so-inexpensive ingredients to make the Christmas pudding that year. He wondered if Alice had taken a turn to stir the mixture and make a wish, as they had each year as children. It was always served after Christmas dinner, dowsed in ignited brandy, with a sprig of fresh holly garnishing.

He bit into his piece of pudding carefully, just in case they had included the tokens that were a traditional part of any Christmas pudding. And yes, his teeth met something unyielding, which was not a piece of dried fruit. He licked the item clean and held up a tiny silver anchor, meant to symbolize safe harbor. Liddel triumphantly held up a silver sixpence, considered the choicest token, believed to bring wealth to the bearer. Richards held up a tiny wishbone, bestowing good luck. And young Levi stared bemused at the silver thimble on which he had nearly broken a tooth. The three of them laughed and stumbled through an explanation; how did one describe the concept of thrift to someone who didn't quite speak English? Nathanial's German tutoring hadn't quite included the Saxon synonym for that word. Finally Levi's furrowed brow cleared, and his young face broke into a grin. Nathanial offered Levi the last sliver of his pudding, which the young lad accepted with gusto.

After Christmas pudding, they sang carols around the fire and smoked cigars that Captain Stockwell handed around. Nathanial tore out several pages of his sketchbook, which he signed and presented to his mates. He gave Liddel a sketch of him singing carols at the top of his lungs Christmas Eve night. To Richards he proffered a likeness of the football match as he clasped hands with the German soldier who had helped him to his feet. And to Levi he offered a picture of him and Liddel reciting the psalm. In that image he had added light illuminating the heavens, like the star over Bethlehem proclaiming Christ's birth. Levi smiled, delighted with the picture, and used his pocketknife to cut a brass button from the bottom hole of his uniform coat to gift in return. They all four clasped hands in fellowship, before the three British officers waved Levi off to his own trench, across No Man's Land.

The morning after Christmas dawned clear and cool. At eight-thirty, after they'd all finished breakfast, Captain Stockwell stood, head and shoulders up out of the British trench, and fired his revolver three times into the air. Liddel and Nathanial held up a sheet printed with the words: *Merry Christmas!*

The German commanding officer appeared on the opposing parapet, bowed low in their direction, and saluted. Behind him, two of the German soldiers raised a sheet of their own bearing the words: *Thank you.* He fired his own side arm twice in the air.

And the war reclaimed them.

As they all ducked down into the trench, and the sound of guns resumed, Nathanial felt a great sense of loss, as if he had for a short time experienced grace and would not find it again. In the valley of the shadow of death, he had shared a table with his enemy and found fellowship. This war, he knew, would last a very long time. It would not, he understood, be a question of weaponry or tactics. This would be a war of aggression, and too many men would die before it could come to an end. This Christmas Day was the end of an era of civilized warfare. To win this war they would eventually be forced to be ruthless and dogged. But someday, perhaps years hence, they would reach the other side of this terrible war. On the other side men like Liddel, Richards, Levi, Captain Stockwell, Reverend Southerland and all the lads with whom he had celebrated Christmas would meet in fellowship, and together make peace for all men, under God. And they would dwell in the house of the Lord, forever.

* * *

Miss Alice Hawkins
Oxfordshire, England

26 December 1914
My dearest Alice,

To you I can write these words that would only bring sorrow to Mother and Father. Let them believe that their son fights a war like those about which Father lectures, a war that makes sense. But to you who saw the truth through your paintings, to you I can open my heart.

We live in mud. The latrines are simply open pits of waste too close to avoid the stench. Corpses lie unburied (consumed by rats if we do not defend them with the butts of our rifles), for if one raises so much as a finger over the top of the trench it is shot off by the precise German snipers. We dream nightly of dry stockings, of wooden bedsteads with linen sheets and feather pillows. And everyone shares the nightmare of being buried alive in bloody mud. But we've grown used to all that.

The war is all terribly civilized. We neither shoot awfully much, nor are shot at all that much. Captain Stockwell has orders to send so many rounds across the lines each day, but they are not very specific about how or when. So we do not shoot at breakfast or dinnertime or tea. We try to fire at portions of the enemy trench that do not seem so enormously busy. And they do the same for us. Some have died, most of those were fools who stuck their heads out over the top of the trench, or crawled out into No Man's Land. But a few were caught by shrapnel. We could really use war helmets like those suits of armor in the British museum, to which Father was forever planning outings for us. Nonetheless, if we keep our heads down, we'll most likely live to fight another day, as will they.

We never really get used to the sound of the guns. It's like eternal thunder disturbing our sleep and giving us dreams of giants crushing the world under their heels.

But two evenings ago, the guns stopped. We crawled out of the mud and the stench. Captain Stockwell shook hands with the German commanding officer, and we ceased all hostilities to celebrate Christmas together. The Germans lit candles in trees and sent over a barrel of beer. We prayed together at a burial service for fallen comrades on both sides. The high point of Richards' day was a football match between them and us. We exchanged trifles: jams, chocolates, whatever the lads had saved from home or that one-week leave in Paris. I'm sending you a button one of the German lads, Levi, gave me off his uniform, for one of my sketches and an extra sliver of my Christmas pudding. It wasn't Mother's pudding, but it tasted like heaven nonetheless. My piece contained an anchor. I'm sending you that also, Alice, for you are my safe harbor.

They're good lads, Alice, the German soldiers. Don't believe what they tell you, in the papers, about the evil German Hun. Together, we celebrated our Saviour's birth with song and flaming candles. I shall never look down my sights again and think of the German soldier only as my enemy. They are just men like us, caught up in events that none of us really understands. Someday, when this war is over (and I pray that day comes soon), we could meet again as fellows. If not we, then our children, or our children's children.

I miss you every day, Alice: your solemn smile and the smudge of paint on your nose. I look forward to seeing the paintings you have done these past months. I understand your need to paint the evil you see around you—I have sketched it myself, to keep from descending into madness. But do not forsake Wonderland, Alice. Before this war is over, we will both need sanctuary from the evil that has poisoned our world. Your sanctuary has always been Wonderland; and mine shall be the truce shared with my enemy upon Christmas Day.

Take care of Mother and Father. They will need your fortitude and your love.

I am, forever,

Your beloved brother,

Nathaniel Hawkins

* * *

Major Miles Stockwell (retired)
Oxfordshire, England

25 December 2008

My dear Sir,

I wanted to write and thank you, again, for inviting me to attend the ceremony in Frelinghien, France, last month honouring the Christmas Truce of so many years previous that your grandfather and my father and uncle shared with their enemy.

The Mass in the village church, where our English voices intertwined harmoniously with our German brethren as we sang "Stille Nacht," brought tears to my eyes, as I remembered my mother singing me that song with her eyes so sad, but her face shining with love. Tales of the Christmas Truce of 1914 were my bedtime favourite throughout my childhood and my mother would always end the story by reading from Isaiah chapter eleven—you know the passage

I mean—and singing "Stille Nacht."

It was very moving to watch you present Oberstleutnant Joachim Freiherr Von Sinner, grandson of Hauptmann Maximilian Freiherr Von Sinner, with a cigar and a plum pudding — so like the gifts my uncle spoke of exchanging that Christmas when he wrote home to my mother. My uncle spoke also of barrels of beer and I was pleased to see that our German friends remembered their famous, and delicious, Christmas gift.

Like you, I think my favourite event of the day was the football match. As I told you that day, I have a sketch (drawn by my uncle) of my father getting a hand up at that Christmas football match in 1914. I was a bit disappointed to see the Germans take the field 2-1, but if we only ever face each other upon that ground as football adversaries, and not as enemies, I am content.

I have thought very carefully of your offer to send my uncle's wartime sketchbook and letters to be displayed with the signed football from our Christmas truce memorial match at the Militärhistorisches Museum der Bundeswehr in Dresden, Germany. I have decided that you are right; although cherished family heirlooms, they are a beautiful reminder of the goodness in all men—even in the midst of a terrible war.

So you will find within this parcel the letters and sketchbook belonging to my uncle, Nathanial Hawkins, whom I never met. Although three pages were originally torn out of the sketchbook, they have been recovered and with each a story of its owner:

My youngest brother, Clarence, was an attaché to our Ambassador to Germany some few years before the outset of the Second World War. He was dining at the home of a minor Nazi government official and came upon a sketch in our uncle's unmistakable style hanging framed over the fireplace in the private library. When he questioned his host at length, the man became nervous and embarrassed and offered the sketch to my brother as a gift. Clarence knew that at that time many Jews were fleeing Germany through the charity of German friends, and others were simply disappearing with vague promises and dire rumours left in their wake. We did not know then of the crowded cattle cars, the camps in Poland, and the graves that had no markers. I do not know the fate of David Levi. He would not have been the first Jewish-German soldier to be a victim of Nazi racial cleansing. Nor would he be the first Jewish refugee to present a treasured heirloom to the benefactor who helped him and his family escape. The Nazi who gave the sketch to my brother committed suicide in his cell before he could be tried at Nuremburg. I will never know if that sketch was a trophy or a gift, nor the fate of the enemy my uncle feasted with upon Christmas day.

My father wrote to my mother that Liddel fell during the first advance at Festubert on 16 May 1915. Some years after the end of the war, a young man with the same unhandsome angular features sat in the third row at my grandfather's lectures in Oxford. His name was Gerick, Clarence Liddel's younger brother. At the end of term he presented my grandfather with the sketch that my uncle had presented to his brother on Christmas day 1914.

My father, Frank Richards, survived the war without serious injury, although his health was never what it was before the war. He returned to Oxfordshire and married his best friend's twin sister, and childhood playmate, Alice. Father proposed to mother while on leave in 1916. Instead of the bands of gold that are so popular nowadays for courting couples, he gave her the sketch her brother had given him on Christmas day, so that she would have an image of him by her bedside while he was at war. She kept the sketch beside her bed, until the hostilities were ended and her beloved returned to marry her. Mother passed away in her sleep in the winter of 1972 and Father the following summer. They were thankful every day for the life they shared together. They are buried side by side with the epitaph: *The wolf shall dwell with the lamb — and a little child shall lead them.*

My uncle was killed within days of the Christmas Truce — I have often wondered if he met the man whose bullet killed him, if he shook his hand, and if he forgave him. As you will see in his final letter to my mother — penned the day after Christmas — my uncle believed that he and his fellows had been given a glimpse of paradise that Christmas day in 1914.

You and I, Major, have stood on the same ground and seen a truce of one day flower into fellowship. I thank you for inviting me to share in the first memorial for those men brave enough to lay down their arms and celebrate the birth of Christ as one.

Happy Christmas and God bless you!

Sincerely,
Mrs. Margaret Holmes

* * *

Author's Note: This is a work of fiction. Although names and events have been drawn from the pages of history, this story neither claims to represent real persons living or dead, nor does it claim to be a factual account of what took place in December of 1914. This story is, rather, an author's fantasy of the men in the trenches (and their progeny): where they came from, how they died, and the glimpse of paradise they experienced for one brief Christmas.

———

Maria Elizabeth McVoy was a Special Investigator retained by the federal government for nine years and has been an author since the publication of her first book, Thirteen Years of Christmas. *She lives in Virginia with her husband and their two children, Michael and Rosina.*

BEST FRIENDS FOREVER

Terry Korth Fischer

At nine in the morning Bea knelt over her flowerbed toiling with a cheery vigor. The flowers were laid out, evenly spaced, shed of their plastic nursery pots, though moist potting soil and Styrofoam bits still clung to the feathery roots. The sky was cloudless, and Bea wanted to get the plants into the ground before they wilted.

"Fine day to garden." An unfamiliar voice jolted her from her task.

The small spade flew out of Bea's hand. "Poop," she said and grabbed for the tool before it bruised the delicate pansies. Looking up, she found a slender stranger at the edge of the driveway.

"I didn't mean to startle you, Ms. Westcott."

He cast a shadow over the flowers and Bea's tilled soil. Bea closed an eye to scrutinize the man. She found him backlit by the sun and glowing like an angel.

"I believe in Jesus and right now, I don't have time to pray," she said, dismissing him with the intention of returning to her pansies.

"Oh," he said, "I'm not here to witness. I wondered. Well, I was hoping at least." He fumbled with the sentence and Bea watched him reach inside his suit jacket. At least, she thought it was a suit jacket. Her glance moved beyond his shoulder to the wooden plaque that hung from the eaves with a burnt "Stan & Bea Westcott" scrolled across its face. The plaque was weather worn, and she left it hanging even though Stanley was no longer with her. Her eyes moved back to see the man extract a leather wallet and flip it open.

"Special Agent in Charge, Derek Plank."

"In charge of what?"

"Just a title ma'am," he said and held the badge and ID card down so she could see them.

He need not have bothered, Bea was quite blind without her eyeglasses, which right then, hung on a beaded chain around her neck and were spotted with potting soil and this morning's hair spray.

"It's come to our attention that you and a friend, Millicent Groves, pretty much know everyone in town."

"We're breaking a federal law?" she asked, squinting at Plank, trying to make out his face.

"No, ma'am." He chuckled and put his identification away. "We need your help."

***

"That's what he said, Millie. Honest."

"What help, would that be?" Millie asked. They sat at the table in Bea's sunny yellow kitchen, where curtains embroidered with daisies flapped before an open window. "We'd look like two old women, and not convincing old women at that."

"What do you mean? I'm convinced I'm an old woman."

"You know what I mean—desperate, or foolish, or extremely idiotic."

"We can do it in disguise. You know, go undercover. Oh, come on! I've always wanted to be a spy."

Bea wondered why Millie seemed hesitant. They'd been best friends going all the way back to Grover Elementary School. Hadn't she distinguished herself as a baton twirler and served as president of the 1946 Dubbin Heights senior class? Millie always followed along.

Millie slowly bobbed her head. "Well, if you say so," she said. "But, I'm not going as a hooker."

Bea smiled, crossed to the enameled steel cabinet, and pulled open a drawer. She took out a pencil and a pink, five-by-seven inch lined tablet, and handed them to Millie. "Good. Now let's make a list."

***

Derek Plank leaned back in his chair and stared at the ceiling. Fifteen months. He'd been working on this case for exactly four-hundred and fifty-six days. That worked out to be 10,944 hours devoted to what he hoped would be its successful conclusion. He tried to calculate the minutes in his head. His door swung open, and Boyd Jackson's sumo-sized body stood in the doorway, a scowl tucked into the folds of his plump face.

"You remember that mother who donated her son's body in Detroit?" he asked. "His legs showed up in Phoenix. This morning his head and shoulders are in Chicago."

"You sure?" asked Plank.

"Not a single doubt. I just got word from the Chicago office."

Plank wrinkled his nose. "This doesn't make any sense," he said. "There has to be a connection between the illegal body parts and the funeral home."

"Plank, if the Body Finders Fellowship is connected to the local undertaker, it's news to me. And I've been on this case as long as you have. We can't tie the BFF to any of the illegal operations. Their records are clean, and they seem to run an organized system of finding and pairing up persons of need."

Shuffling a stack of papers, Plank said, "I don't know. There's something funny. If The Undertaker isn't actually peddling the bodies or the parts, he may be selling the names of clients who show up to inquire about donating."

"Uh-huh. I see what you're saying." Boyd sat down in the chair across the desk from Plank. "You got a plan?"

"Just a tiny one. It involves espionage."

"You mean spies?"

"You want espionage, you have to have spies. The way I figure it, The Undertaker is too savvy for any of our tricks. So I got to thinking, what if we brought in a couple of ringers? People he wouldn't necessarily associate with the FBI, a pair so ordinary they are beyond suspicion. We send them in to snoop around. All innocent, of course. They might pick up something useful."

"You're talking civilians?" Boyd shook his head vigorously. His eyes were swallowed up by his chubby cheeks and furrowed brow.

"Just to start, Jackson. No risk, no danger, no complications."

"I don't know."

"We could follow the paperwork, and see if the body or the parts end up at the BFF."

Boyd Jackson frowned. He hesitated long enough for Plank to calculate that, not counting today, they had spent more than 656,640 minutes on the illegal body parts case. Plank figured Boyd was calculating the minutes, too. He hoped they came up with the same answer.

***

Millie pulled the 1984 Buick Concorde to the curb and turned to face Bea. "You don't think we need to take our notes in, do you?"

"No. But just to be sure, why don't you drive around the block one more time and I'll read them aloud. Just to refresh our memories."

Millie pulled the car away from the curb and slowly maneuvered it down the street, turned the corner, and drove it, lumbering, past the undertaker's house. It was a rambling one-story brick affair with a beige awning that connected it to the funeral parlor, which faced the street behind. Great columns of white alabaster accented the front door and held a miniature portico in place. The house appeared foolish, its simple boxy shape accentuated by the pillars. A fifty-gallon cement pot sat on either side of the door, each holding a recycled funeral spray. A wooden stake, centered prominently in the front yard, held a hand-painted sign that read, "Garage Sale Today."

"Oh look, Bea!" Millie exclaimed.

"Not now," Bea said firmly, consulting the list in her hand. "One, Look him in the eye. Two, Be pleasant. Don't act aggressively. Three, Listen to what he isn't saying." She flipped the pink sheet of paper over and continued, "Four, Consult your third mind."

"Third mind?"

"You remember, conscious, subconscious, and gut: one, two, three."

"Oh. Eenie, meenie, and Moe."

"Precisely," said Bea.

They rounded the final corner, confirmed that no funeral service was in progress, and parked in the lot adjacent to the funeral home. Millie was still distracted by the activity at the garage sale, but Bea took her firmly by the upper arm and escorted her into the building.

A lean, rigid-faced man led them into an office in the back. "Mr. Metzger," Bea said, "I hope you don't mind us just dropping in." She'd always thought the man would make a perfect stand-in for Ichabod Crane, but unfortunately, the opportunity had never presented itself. She was

212

content, for now, to leave him in his role of coroner/funeral director.

"Always time for an old friend," Metzger said. "How have you been?"

Bea watched his face for suspicious ticks, but Metzger appeared sincere. He didn't look gleeful, or any more sinister than normal, so maybe he just meant what he said and there wasn't anything between the lines to read.

As she and Bea settled into the visitor chairs, Millie clicked the shutter of the hidden Instamatic in her over-sized handbag. Bea heard the film advance, and was thankful that Metzger, who wore a hearing aid, didn't appear to notice. It had taken them an hour to sew the camera into the lining so the lens would not slip from the new cutout. It took longer to disable the flash, and even longer to find the film.

Bea thought it might be better if they'd located a minia-ture tape recorder, but then again their resources were limited. They had scrounged through the Goodwill thrift store and purchased every box of Cracker Jacks in town. They had kept giggling to a minimum and operated in a covert fashion so as not to draw unwarranted attention. For their efforts, they were rewarded with one decoder ring and no real spy equipment whatsoever. Millie said it was unnecessary, but Bea insisted on wearing the ring, just in case.

"You certainly look, hum...stylish," Metzger said, taking his place behind the desk. He smoothed the length of his somber black tie and smiled tightly.

Good, stout Missouri Synod Lutherans, Millie and Bea, had foregone their usual polyester pantsuits and sturdy footwear for flouncy organza dresses and wide-brimmed hats that usually adorned First Baptist ladies. It wasn't exactly a disguise, but Millie and Bea had reasoned it out and decided to dress up like they were playing a part. That way, if they had to lie or act outside the bounds of their normal Christian demeanor, well, it wouldn't be *their* untruth or *their* personal bad manners. They agreed spying was a dubious business.

Millie spread her flounces. Bea sat stiffly on the edge of the chair with her feet firmly on the floor, hands resting on a Bible in her lap. One by one, she released her fingers from the prissy white gloves, taking a quick breath as she realized she'd exposed the decoder ring. Hoping Metzger hadn't noticed, she used her thumb to discreetly rotate the dial while keeping her face hidden beneath her hat's wide brim and steadying her nerves. She smiled sweetly at Metzger, and in her best Mata Hari voice said, "Charlie, it's about the second plot."

***

Meanwhile, at FBI headquarters, Jackson set his cup of thick coffee down on Plank's desk, flared his nostrils and shuddered. "Isn't it against the law to serve something this bad?"

"Not federal," said Plank taking a gulp from his mug.

"Tell me again, how exactly are these civilians going to help?"

"We checked the Metzger Funeral Home records. Right? Deaths, burials, cremations, and they seem to be in order. Right? In fact, they are almost too well organized. When I mentioned that to Charles Metzger, he said his wife does the books. Meticulous. I think that's the word he used."

Plank watched Jackson lift his right foot. He used both hands to help raise and place it on his beefy left knee. With his extended stomach and beer keg thighs, the position looked awkward, and leaned him away from the conversation. "It still strikes me as odd that he's also the county coroner," Jackson said.

Plank agreed. "Me, too. Too convenient. Of course, there's no indication that Metzger is working with the BFF, no evidence of funny business on either side. But to my mind, bodies are just too accessible."

"So we bring in the spies?"

"Yup, someone we know. Someone *he* knows." Plank leaned back, tapping his fingertips together while he explained the setup. "I asked Ms. Westcott to go to the funeral parlor and talk to Metzger about a change to her prepaid burial option. She's going to forego interment alongside her husband so she can donate her body to science. We'll wait and see what transpires."

The men sat a moment in silence while Plank studied the overhead lights and Jackson inspected the bottom of his shoe.

Jackson scratched his head. "Uh, according to my logic, she'd have to die."

"Yeah, I just thought of that." Plank rose swiftly and grabbed his coat. "Let's take a ride over to Dubbin Heights."

***

"That went rather well," said Bea. She and Millie were making their way over to the garage sale, leaving their car in the funeral home lot to avoid parking complications.

"He really didn't like your change of mind," said Millie.

"No, but I didn't ask for my money back, so what could he say? I have every right to donate my body if I see fit. Did you grab any of the casket brochures? We'll check them later for hidden messages and microdots."

"It's going to be weird not having a body in the ground next to Stanley. You are going to leave your name on the headstone, aren't you?"

"Millie, I'm not really going through with it. That was just spy tactics." Bea gave an impatient huff, and came to a decision. "Well, maybe I will. A person's life has to be meaningful. Giving my kidneys or my ears to an unfortunate child, that would be worthwhile. I'm so glad I never got my ears pierced."

"Good gravy!" said Millie waiting for Bea to catch up. They fell in step, advancing on the crowd perusing the sale. "Bea, you didn't read the papers very well. It's probably your eyesight. It said whole body. Whole body as in cadaver: classroom dissection, frozen-slash-refrigerated, wheeled out on a slab, naked with dozens of young med students looking on, not even real doctors yet."

Millie didn't finish because they approached the garage sale tables where a display of paperbacks caught her attention. "Look! Let's see if we can find any good westerns. Maybe we'll find Zane Grey or Louis L'Amour. I'm so tired of those Patterson books." And, she rushed forward, shouldering the other shoppers out of the way.

There weren't any good westerns among the dog-eared books. Millie was sure that if they had stopped before the visit to Metzger's, they might have snagged a few. Bea said they had done their civic duty, they had plenty of books at home, and there was always the public library. They skipped the children's clothing and the canned goods, zeroing in on the merchandise under the back awning.

"What in tarnation?" asked Millie, "Where do you think they got all these?" Against the back of the funeral parlor, a dozen full-sized freezers were lined up on the lawn. The freezers sat with their lids raised and their cavernous innards exposed. "Not from Metzger's, I hope."

"Millie! Bea!" Ollie Metzger shouted to them. Wide, low,

and dressed in a Capri outfit that would flatter a smaller-sized woman, she rushed from a cluster of shoppers inspecting Mason jars on a card table by the back door. Out of breath, she said, "I didn't recognize the two of you."

Bea and Millie exchanged a satisfied glance. "Remodeling?" Bea asked.

Ollie's face flushed, perhaps, from the exertion of waddling over, but more likely, Bea thought from being caught unprepared for the question. Ollie stuffed her hands in her pants pockets, which tugged the elastic waistband down, inadvertently exposing her flabby stomach. Her mouth moved in fish-out-of-water fashion without reply.

"Or is this a neighborhood sale?" Bea persisted, though she thought it unlikely the entire neighborhood had decided to replace their freezers at the same moment.

"Of course not," Ollie answered. "Charles has a business associate who is going out of business." Bea and Millie looked at her with skepticism. "If you must know," she rushed on, "they're dissolving the partnership with Metzger's. We agreed to sell the appliances, and there are other things Charles will no longer need. He is always looking for ways to be helpful. One with the community, you know, one for all, all for one? There are these freezers and, of course, our own things. We put the excess in the garage."

Millie, who was still thinking along the lines of suitable reading material, followed Bea, who followed Ollie, who led the way to the garage.

Grasping the handle with both hands, Ollie struggled to roll the door up. The wobbly rollers and rusty hinges resisted her efforts, but she succeeded in raising the obstinate door. Overhead, the torsion springs snapped into place and an overpowering scent of bleach rushed out of the building. The women gasped, and faltered.

Inside the garage sat a mountain of personal-sized coolers. White tops pointed out, more than a dozen high, and a dozen wide. Stacked on their blue and red sides, the wall of Igloo coolers dominated the floor.

Bea stepped in. "They've got to be four deep."

The Playmate coolers were piled between the lawn mower and the power tools, stacked in front of dangling rakes and winter shovels. Each cooler was adorned with a pre-printed $10 sticker. Moving closer, Bea and Millie could see an embossed "BFF" and the bio-hazard symbol prominent on every lid.

"Look!" exclaimed Millie. "Best Friends Forever!"

***

It was late morning, the sun blazing overhead. The agents, in their black SUV, sunglasses, and severe suits, were anxious. Jackson drove seven miles over the speed limit, and Plank, usually cautious, urged him to step it up. "I hope we're not too late," he said.

They rounded the corner and approached Metzger's Funeral Home just in time to see two First Baptist ladies crossing the parking lot.

"Are those our spies?" asked Jackson.

"Yup," said Plank.

Bea and Millie were juggling an armload of Playmate coolers between them. Spotting the SUV, Bea stopped and beamed broadly from beneath her hat brim. Millie stumbled, although she didn't lose her hold, and followed Bea's line of sight toward the car with its tinted windows and the FBI agents inside.

"It looks like we're in time," said Jackson.

Plank looked at his watch. It was day four-hundred and fifty-seven, and they were about to bust the illegal body part case wide open.

———

Terry Korth Fischer lives in Houston, Texas. Retired from a career in IT, she uses her time to read, write, and relax. Her work recently appeared in The Write Place at the Write Time, *and* Clear Lake Area Writers Selections — Fall 2015. *Terry is a member of Sisters in Crime International, Clear Lake Area Writers, and Pennwriters Inc.*

ALL DOORS OPEN TO A BARD

Michelle Markey Butler

823 AD Ciannachta territory

Fial had never been in a king's hall before. It was not as grand as he had expected.

But then the only ideas he had of kings' halls came from the bards. To live up to such songs, the hall would have needed gold-plated walls, chairs too encrusted with gems to sit on, and a hearth so large the hall was warm as summer. King Fintan's hall did not, alas, have walls covered with gold or chairs studded with jewels. It did have a fine long hearth, and the hall was warm, if not like the heat of summer. Which was itself a harper's exaggeration, come to think of it. Ireland was not hot, even in summer.

"Thank you for coming," King Fintan said.

Fial recognized that for the courtesy it was. His king had summoned him. He had no option but to come. "Of course, Lord. How may I be of service?"

King Fintan flicked a finger and the servant who had brought Fial departed. When the door closed, the king said, "I hear congratulations are in order."

"Lord?"

"Did your wife not present you with a daughter?"

"Oh! Yes. Thank you for your good wishes, Lord." Evgren was the sunlight and soft wind of his and Berrin's lives. But another birth in the kingdom did not warrant a royal summons. The king smoothed minute wrinkles from his *leine*. "The child is well?"

"Yes, Lord. A hearty eater, and she's growing. Likely to live, I think." Whatever the king was about, he wanted to get there by a side route. Very well. Shepherds learned patience. Fial tucked one hand inside the other and waited.

"Good, good," King Fintan said. "How has the weather been by the abbey? Did you get that storm two nights ago?"

"Generally, Lord, the weather has been fine, particularly for early April. We did have rain, yes, but it was not so much as to keep the sowers out of the fields." Fial was a tenant of Linn Duachaill, a nearby monastery at the juncture of two rivers. The abbey administered its own holdings, but King Fintan's adjoined theirs. Fial supposed that was the source of his interest.

The king crossed his legs at the ankles. "The abbey's herds?"

"Good, Lord. Indeed—" Fial broke off as the hall door opened. Another man entered. He did not wait for the king's leave to stride across the hall and stand at his elbow.

"My brother, Coman," King Fintan said, flashing the newcomer a smile of genuine affection.

Fial was not surprised; he had guessed the man must be close to the king to behave so in his presence. They did not resemble one another, though. King Fintan was red-haired, with a beard worn longer than was strictly fashionable. He was young, but his bulk was already beginning to slide towards paunch. His brother was taller and sleek as an eel, with black hair and beard trimmed short.

Fial bowed. "Lord."

"This is Fial. The shepherd at Linn Duachaill. I mentioned him."

Ice shivered down Fial's back. It was never good to come

221

to the attention of your king. It was *certainly* never good to be noticed enough to be discussed.

"Ah, yes." Coman's gaze riveted upon him. Fial's gut tensed. He had misunderstood the king's earlier chatter. King Fintan had not been working his way around to what he wanted. He had been waiting for his brother. "Do you know the countryside well?"

"Yes, Lord. My parents were tenant farmers for the abbey. Caring for the herds, I walk most of the land thereabouts." One of his hands shook. He squeezed it tight with the other. They wanted something; that was clear. He would know soon enough what it was. Sweet Saint Columba, but he wished King Fintan and his brother Coman had never heard of him. Powerful men saw people as tools to keep or enhance their power.

"So people are used to seeing you walking and do not wonder overmuch where you go?" Coman stroked his trim beard as if thoughtfully, but Fial doubted it was a real question. Coman already knew the answer. The point was in the asking, and in Fial's reaction.

"I would assume so, Lord. None of the monks stop me and ask my business, not for years."

Coman shared a look with his brother. Right answer, Fial guessed. Was that good or bad? *Most likely bad.*

"I also hear," King Fintan said, pushing casually at the cuticle of his thumbnail, "you once aspired to apprentice to a bard."

Fial tried to hide his surprise. Very few people knew that. His wife. His brother. He could not think of anyone else. Had one of them mentioned it? It was not a secret, exactly, but neither was it something he discussed. No man waves the tattered rags of a dream before his neighbors. "Yes, Lord. I suppose everyone has boyish ideas they put aside."

"What if you need not put it aside?" King Fintan moved on to the cuticle of his next finger.

"Lord, I know my place and am content in it."

Coman smiled. It was the smile of a wolf when it spots a rabbit. Another icy touch ran down Fial's back.

"Then the stories of the *sidhe* are real." Coman caught his brother's glance, as if sharing a moment of private amusement. "How else to explain harp music wisping across the fields of Linn Duachaill?"

The heat of a blush burned Fial's face. Not even his wife or brother knew of the make-shift harp he kept in the far pasture. He'd thought the hills swallowed the sound. If he *had* known his music—such as it was, self-taught on a cobbled-together harp—would be heard, could he have kept himself from it? "I meant no harm, Lord," Fial bowed his head. "I beg pardon if someone was bothered."

"Bothered?" King Fintan snorted. "Did we say anyone was bothered? You are not here because of a complaint."

"No," Coman said. "We have something else in mind." Fial practically heard a wolfish howl of delight in the hunt.

Fial knotted one hand inside the other. "Please tell me how I may be of service to my king."

King Fintan leaned forward, both hands on his knees. "We want you to become a bard."

"So did I," Fial said, more bitterly than he intended. "None would have me as apprentice." He touched the pouch hanging from his belt. "Bards favor apprentices capable of giving rich gifts in thanks for being chosen. Shepherds are not."

"We have secured a willing harper," King Fintan said.

"What?" Fial said. "How?" After a heartbeat, "Why?"

The king laughed. His laugh was not that of a predator,

like his brother's. It was almost a real laugh. *Almost.* "Which should we answer first?" He ticked off his fingers. "Yes, a harper has agreed to teach you. How? Because his king asked it of him. Why?" He looked at his brother as if handing him the reins of the conversation.

"All doors open to a bard," Coman said. "They cannot be denied the hospitality of any house. They travel a great deal yet their comings and goings raise no eyebrows." He tucked one thumb into his belt nonchalantly. "The king my brother has found that useful."

"You have persuaded a bard to spy for you," Fial whispered. "If I become his apprentice, he will teach me to spy as well."

King Fintan pursed his lips. "Not 'spy,' exactly. Listen actively. Sometimes in places he—in time, you—might not have gone otherwise.

"That sounds a lot like spying, Lord," Fial said.

King Fintan flipped a hand. "Call it what you like."

"Why would any bard agree? It is a betrayal of his calling, his training. A harper belongs to no man so that he can speak truth to all."

"Being a bard does not protect a man from loving drink too much and making bad bets. Calling and training do not pay debts." Coman spoke lightly but his nostrils quivered, which Fial understood as contempt for those with so little self-control.

"Brother, why not show him our gift?" The king gestured to a closed chest.

Slowly, deliberately slowly, Fial was certain of it, Coman went to the chest and opened the lid. He lifted a bulky object out. It was covered by a cloth, linen and, by the look of it, of a quality Fial had never touched. The covering did not conceal, and was probably not meant to conceal, what it was—a harp. A real harp.

Coman let the linen slide away like a lover slipping off a robe.

Later, Fial wondered if he might have resisted, had they not brought out the harp. It was dangerous to refuse a request from your king; such requests were not really requests, after all. He liked to think he might have done, despite the danger, had the polished willow-wood not gleamed like the sun on the sea. The *com* was carved with interlacing which was stained a darker color than the rest of the soundbox, while the neck bore a sequence of triskeles, each triple spiral larger than the last.

Coman ran his finger across the brass strings. Not correctly; a harp should be played with the fingernails. Fial suspected Coman knew this, that he rang the strings wrong on purpose to goad Fial.

It worked. Sweet Saint Columba. He *let* it work. He should never have touched the harp. But Fial was Irish, blood, bone, and soul, and there was a reason they spoke of heart-strings.

"Give her to me," he said.

***

828 AD. Tenant holdings of Linn Duachaill.

A firm shake of his shoulder woke Fial. He cracked his eyes open and smiled at his wife.

"I am sorry, love, but it's dawn." Berrin's hand was on his shoulder. Her other arm held their daughter perched on her hip. At five years old Evgren was too big to be carried by her mother, but the two babies since had died. Fial knew his wife was loathe to admit her lone surviving child was no longer a baby. As if obliging her mother, Evgren had a thumb in her mouth.

"Thank you." Fial ran a hand through his hair. "Lord Coman will be here soon. Have you been awake long?"

Berrin touched Evgren's nose. The little girl giggled. "Not long. This one woke up hungry a bit ago." His wife turned her gaze on him. "You must have been weary, to sleep through her complaints."

Fial got to his feet, tossing his head to clear it. He *had* been tired. *Was* tired. Between his herdsman's duties during the day (other men guarded the sheep and cattle at night) and learning from the bard at night, he slept less than he liked.

He glanced towards the magnificent harp, which he kept covered with its original linen cloth when not in use. He had named her Sile, the Irish form of Cecelia, the patron saint of music. He was so tired he sometimes stumbled when he walked, but Sile was worth any amount of fatigue. The other daytime shepherd, Tadhg, might be annoyed when he was unable to stay awake on occasion, but he couldn't do anything about it. After all, the king sponsored his apprenticeship. If the king wanted a bard from his own territory, the king would have a bard from his own territory. That was the story Coman told, and it was true, if not the whole truth.

He had worried he would have trouble accepting instruction from a harper willing to compromise his position. It turned out he liked Odhran. It would have been disingenuous to scorn the bard for agreeing to the same bargain he had. The harper also proved easy to like. Odhran was everything he'd imagined a bard would be. Long-bearded, blue-robed, deep-voiced. Long, supple fingers. Odhran, of course, had his own harp and did not touch his, of which Fial was glad; he would have been jealous to see Odhran's fingers on Sile. For five years, he had learned from Odhran.

Soon, he hoped, he would be ready to be examined for the first rank of bard.

He had also learned from Odhran the subtle skills of gathering information without seeming to. Asking friendly questions with his own hidden purpose. Listening while seeming to sleep. Playing Sile with his eyes closed and softly enough to overhear a whispered conversation. He was equal parts pleased and chagrined to find he was good at it. He also traveled with Odhran from Armagh to Clonmacnois, and he could wholeheartedly admit to himself that he loved seeing more of the countryside than he had ever dreamed.

The sound of horse's hooves approached the woven-wattle house, cutting through the usual background murmur of the neighbors' morning activities.

"That must be him," Berrin said, shoving a piece of bread wrapped around a slab of cheese into his hand. "You'll have to eat as you go."

"Thank you." He kissed his wife, then his daughter, and headed out. Coman did not like to be kept waiting.

***

Fial stepped from the house. None too soon. Coman stood by his horse, fingertips drumming his saddle.

"Finally. Let's go." Coman began walking, leading his horse.

Fial had to jog to catch up. Coman used to come once a month to hear what Fial had learned and instruct him what to listen for. Now he came once a week. Always on Wednesdays. Fial suspected he knew why, and he did not like it. On Wednesdays, Tadhg's sister walked her brother to the fields.

"Any rumor of raiding from Brega?" Coman said as Fial reached him.

"No, Lord. It's early in the year, though. They usually hit when we've more to steal."

"Except when they've had a bad winter and wish to feed themselves on our cattle." Coman squinted across the landscape as they walked, as if he could see to Brega and know if they were mounting a raid.

To their left, the joined rivers spilled into Dundalk Bay. They swung right, taking the long way to the ford. Going straight would mean passing near the monastery, and Coman did not care to be seen by the monks. The farmers would see him, of course, but they would not know who he was. Horses being costly, they might note the horse with interest. But it was widely known Fial had apprenticed with a bard and he traveled by horse. Casual questioning had told Fial that his neighbors assumed his regular morning visitor was the harper. They did not know Odhran by sight; his real visits were at night.

"What of the sea-wolves?" Coman asked.

"I have heard no stories of Viking attacks near." Fial waggled his hand noncommittally. "Lots of rumors about attacks elsewhere, mind." He gave a short laugh. "If the stories are true, half the coast of Ireland is in ruins."

"Don't laugh," Coman snapped. "More are true than you credit. There have been raids. Many of them. That's not what I'm asking." Scorn filled his voice. "If the Vikings had attacked in my brother's territory, we would know. What I'm interested in are signs they've been here without attacking. *Yet.* Scouting, planning, deciding where a raid would be most profitable. Evidence of a fire on a rarely used coastline. Rubbish left where farmers don't go. Strange footmarks, or unfamiliar gouges in the sand from landing their boats."

"I see, Lord." Fial would have liked to stroke the horse's

glossy neck, but he had learned on Coman's earlier visits to keep his hands to himself. The king's brother let no one touch his horse but himself. "I have not heard of such things, but I will listen more closely."

"And watch," Coman growled. "Don't rely on other people's eyes. Use your own."

"Of course, Lord." Their steps slowed as they moved down the bank towards the ford. The tide was high. The ford stones were visible but not by much. Fial suppressed a sigh. He hated getting wet. He let Coman go ahead with his horse, waiting until they were halfway across before he started. Not from kindness, or courtesy to his king's brother. He wanted to avoid getting splashed.

Still mostly dry, Fial scrambled up the opposite bank.

"What of strangers in the area?" Coman asked.

Fial tried to shake one boot surreptitiously, hoping to get the water out before his sock was soaked through. Sweet Saint Columba, he *really* hated wet feet. "There is a new monk at the abbey. They say he is visiting from Dun Leire."

"They say? Is there any reason to suppose they're lying? He might be here from elsewhere?"

Fial shrugged. "Not that I can tell." He trotted as Coman pushed the pace faster, following the river to the place where the abbey's pasturelands met the forest.

"Hmm. Very well. But watch him. Try to find out why he's — " Coman broke off.

They had crested the small hill. Tadhg stood there, talking to his sister.

Coman's head raised like a hunting dog catching a scent. Even as a happily married man, Fial understood. Tadhg's sister Aine was not merely beautiful. She was heart-stopping, once in a lifetime perfection that made him half-believe the *sidhe* were real and had bred with her ancestors.

Her hair was sunlight gold, her eyes blue like a midsummer sky, and her skin was creamy with a faint dusting of freckles. She was the wonder of the territory, like a soft-eyed heifer springing from a herd of goats.

But she was a farmer's daughter, not a girl a king would allow his brother to wed. Nothing good could come of Coman's pursuit. But Aine did not know this man was the king's brother, and Coman had been clear that he wanted it that way. Fial had threshed his brain like grain, trying to think of a way to hint that this was *not* a good man to become involved with. No ideas had come to him. He was enough older than Aine to know vague warnings would only make her more interested, youth being what it was.

"Oh," Coman said in what seemed to Fial a passable imitation of surprise. "Hello there, Tadhg. Aine."

The width of Aine's smile matched the depth of Tadhg's scowl. "Good morning." She patted her brother's arm. "I should get home."

"So you've been saying for a quarter-hour," her brother grumbled. "Can't imagine why you're hanging about, if you need to go."

Aine narrowed her eyes at him before turning her smile back to Coman.

"Are you headed to the ford?" Coman asked.

"Why yes," she said. A breeze caught strands of her gold hair and pushed them over her shoulder. She brushed them back.

"Will you allow me to walk with you?" Coman stepped closer. "Better yet, would you like to ride?" He waggled the ends of the reins at her.

"I've never ridden a horse," she said, blue eyes sparking.

"Nothing to it. Really. This is a gentle beast." Coman took her hand and laid it on the horse's neck. "See?"

She giggled. "He's warm. Silky." She frowned slightly. "And large. I don't see why he would go where I wish."

"Surely all creatures do as Aine bids," Coman smiled. "But if you would rather, I will lead him."

Aine considered. "All right."

"Let me help you up," Coman said.

That was too much for Tadhg. "If you must, let me, sister." He glowered as he helped her into the saddle. "Don't dawdle."

"You're not my keeper," she hissed, not quite softly enough for only Tadhg to hear. "I'll go where I please, with whom I please, thank you very much."

"Please," Tadhg hissed back. "Take heed."

She tossed her head. Coman gave Tadhg a haughty look until he stepped away.

"What's your bard playing at?" Tadhg snarled when Coman and Aine were out of sight.

Fial looked after them. "Everyone bandies words. It's a flirtation. Nothing more."

"It had better be," Tadhg said.

Fial hoped so. But he worried Coman meant to have more, and his hope was not equal to his worry.

***

Three days later, Fial pretended a need to speak with the monastery's steward about the cattle. It was an excuse to do Coman's bidding and check on the visiting monk.

His brother Breasal accompanied him. "I hardly see you nowadays," he said. "Let me walk with you and catch up as we go." Fial did see much less of his brother now he was learning the harp (not to mention spying, his inward voice added), but he suspected there was more at work. In the last year, Breasal had taken every opportunity, real or plausible, to visit the monastery. His brother, whether he knew it or not, was thinking of becoming a monk.

A woven-wand fence, meant to keep animals out of their garden and orchard, surrounded the abbey. Fial thought about the northern raiders Coman had spoken of—that *everyone* was speaking of—and worried about the monastery. If the Vikings came, the fence would do nothing to keep them out. Rumor had it they stole *people* as well as goods. He shuddered. God knew there was plenty of raiding between their own kingdoms. The Irish revered saints, but they did not emulate them. But such raiding was for property—cattle, sheep, stored crops. They did not enslave one another.

"Did you see the gardens?" Breasal was all but burbling as they left. Fial had successfully garnered that the visiting monk was there about a rumor that had reached the abbot of Dun Leire. Someone had told him the monks of Linn Duachaill still wore the Irish tonsure instead of the Roman the Irish church had agreed to adopt more than a century before. The misunderstanding corrected, the monk would return to Dun Leire later that day.

"And the orchards?" Breasal spilled on. "Have you ever seen such tidy, well-kept trees? And—"

Fial nodded but he wasn't really listening. His brother waxed on about the beauties of the abbey the way a young man praised his beloved. A month at most, he wagered, before Breasal approached the abbot about joining the brethren. At last his brother had found a way he wished to live that both cheered his soul and was possible. Breasal had wandered fields, pastures, fishing, hunting, not to mention beginning and abandoning apprentice work in least three trades, and found nothing that pleased both his hands and heart. The abbey was a good landlord; anyone else would have assigned him a place years ago and made him stay put. The abbot had, perhaps, recognized Breasal's inability to settle down as a longing for something else. If so, that faith was soon to be rewarded.

"I felt such peace in the church—" Breasal grabbed his arm, pulling him to a stop. "Quietude, Fial. Like I have never known." His eyes widened. "I think—I think I may want—"

Fial waited. Breasal needed to find this path himself.

"A monk," Breasal breathed. "I want to join the brothers." Both his hands gripped Fial's arms. "Can you believe it? Me, a monk? I would never have. But when I think it—when I say it—it feels like—like all the pieces in my head are in the right place at last." His mouth was open and he stared, but Fial knew he was not seeing him. What was he seeing? The glory of God? Choirs of angels? Saints in heaven? Breasal's face glowed.

Fial turned his hands, squeezing his brother's forearms in return. "I am so happy for you, brother. Brother Breasal."

"Don't tease," Breasal said, looking down as if embarrassed.

"I wasn't." Fial pulled back. "You will be a wonderful monk."

Breasal looked over his shoulder, back toward the abbey. "I need to go. I need to see the abbot."

"Of course." Fial made shooing motions. "Go."

Breasal flung his arms around him and pulled him into a quick, tight hug. "Thank you."

Fial whistled as he crossed the ford. The tide was out, his feet would stay dry, his brother had finally found his place in the world, he was learning to play a beautiful harp, and being King Fintan's spy was not as bad as he had feared.

His good cheer lasted until he crested the hill.

Aine was there, about halfway across the pasture, and

she was not alone. A man stood by her, closer than was polite. She clasped her hands before her, managing to seem both modest and coy. The man had one hand on his hip, and as Fial watched, he flung his head back to laugh at something she said. The man took half a step closer and shook his finger at her in what appeared to be mock-reproach. Even at this distance, Fial could see her simper.

Sweet Saint Columba, why was she here? Where was Tadhg? It wasn't Wednesday, and it wasn't morning. Why was she here? His thoughts having circled back on themselves, Fial decided there was nothing for it but to make his presence known and try to get control of the situation.

He came to a dead halt before he'd taken ten steps.

The man with Aine was not Coman. It was King Fintan.

Fial thought, but managed not to say, an oath that would have shocked his soon-to-be-monk brother. What was King Fintan doing here? His lips twisted. Foolish. It was obvious what King Fintan was doing here. He had learned of Aine's beauty and come to try for her himself. It was even less likely a king would give Aine a proper marriage than a king's brother would. They were simply in competition to be her ruin. Struggling to get control of his mounting fury, Fial strode across.

"Oh, hello," Aine smiled. "I brought Tadhg's dinner," she gestured at the basket near her feet, "but I can't find him."

Fial glanced at the basket, then back at Aine's oh-so-innocent face. A plausible excuse, but not the true reason. Aine never brought Tadhg's mid-day meal. Tadhg brought his own dinner. It would be foolhardy to bring dinner to a herdsman; he might be in the farthest pastures with the animals. "He's out with the flocks." Fial gazed inland. "See? You can just make out the cattle on the far hill."

Aine shaded her eyes prettily. "Oh, yes. How silly of me not to have realized." She returned her gaze to King Fintan. Who was, of course, her real reason for being there. Fial wondered how they had made the arrangements. How many times they already met. "This is Faolan."

Faolan. *Wolf.* Appropriate. From his clothing, it was clear the king was not there as himself. He was dressed well, but not as a nobleman. A prosperous farmer, certainly no king of a *tuath*. Sheep's clothing, as it were, tricking the poor girl into thinking him an ambitious but attainable match.

King Fintan's eyes blazed a warning Fial did not need. "Faolan. Nice to meet you. I am Fial, a herdsman like Aine's brother. Aine," he turned, an idea coming to him, "since Tadhg's not here, do you think he would mind if I ate his dinner? I hate to think of your work going to waste, and truth be told, since I had to go to the abbey to speak with the steward, there's been no dinner for me today." All true, although not quite as he meant her to take it. He had been too busy to eat the scant dinner Berrin had sent, currently tucked into his belt pouch. He meant for Aine to believe he had forgotten to bring anything because of anxiety about reporting to the abbey. Flirtatious, credulous, and eager to marry well she might be, but she was good-hearted.

Aine looked at the basket, then at 'Faolan.' "But we — no, of course," she interrupted herself. She picked up the basket and held it out to Fial. "Please do."

"Thank you." His words were breathy with relief. He had not been sure there was food in the basket. She might have brought it as a ploy, but empty, knowing she would not find Tadhg. But Fial had thought it likely she would have packed something that could pass as Tadhg's dinner if caught, but was really meant for a romantic sit-down with

"Faolan."

Fial sat cross-legged and proceeded to eat with as little courtesy as he could. Never had apple been crunched as loudly. Never had bread been chewed so long, so well, and with so many wide-mouthed praises of its excellence. He twirled chunks of cheese on his fingertips before tossing them into the air and catching them in his mouth.

Aine, sweet dainty Aine, watched. Fial sweated, wondering whether her food or her patience would run out first.

"I should go," she said at last.

Fial smiled broadly, knowing full well he had bits of cheese in his teeth. "Oh?"

Aine looked as if she were trying not to shudder. "Yes. I will be needed at home."

"Faolan" caught her hand as she stepped away.

"Later," she said before he could speak.

"As you wish, lady." He kissed her hand. Her silver bell giggles rang as she walked away.

King Fintan kept his temper until she was out of sight. "You ungrateful, interfering—"

Fial scrambled up. The king's arm stopped before it could descend. Or rather, *was* stopped. He looked over the king's shoulder to see whose hand had caught it.

Coman.

Sweet Saint Columba.

"How strange to see you here, brother," Coman said.

King Fintan wrenched his arm away. "Not at all. When a fair flower blossoms..." he raised one shoulder. "People talk."

"I most certainly did not," Coman said. "I am well aware of your eye for the ladies."

"Which you share," his brother countered.

236

"Go home," Coman said.

"Why?" King Fintan's voice was mocking. "Because you saw her first? She's not the last piece of bread on the platter."

"I have advanced my wooing over months," Coman said.

"Why should I give way because you move slowly?"

Coman's hands were in tight fists. "Do you refuse to yield?"

"Of course," King Fintan said evenly, obviously enjoying overturning their usual roles — the king was a notorious hothead, whereas his brother was normally unflappable.

Which meant, Fial realized, the king did not really want Aine as much as he wanted to take something his brother wanted.

"You—"

"Do either of you intend to offer the girl marriage?" someone said. Fial realized a heartbeat later the voice was his.

King Fintan blinked.

"What?" Coman said.

"Marriage. Do you mean to marry her?"

Coman laughed. "A farmer's daughter?"

King Fintan made a weighing moue. "If I were already married, I might take her as a second wife. Unofficially, of course, since the church no longer approves. As my acknowledged wife...? No." He gave a smile that was, now, like his brother's — predatory. "I might want to pick a splendid hedge rose. But it is still a hedge rose."

Fial thought of Sile and pressed his teeth together until they hurt.

"So confident, hm?" Coman said.

"Oh, yes," King Fintan breathed. He stepped closer to

his brother. Barely a handspan separated their noses.

"Care to wager?"

"Why not?"

"You've a fine foal from your bay mare."

"And you have quite a handsome new cloak. Fur-lined."

They shook hands.

Sweet Saint Columba and all the saints in heaven, they were betting—literally betting—on which of them could talk poor silly Aine out of her *leine* first. Fial clamped his jaws tighter.

The saints bestowed a minor gift. King Fintan and Coman each turned on his heel and stalked away in opposite directions.

***

Another month passed, and calving season was upon him. Fial was glad. It was the busiest time of year, not his favorite, and less so since he began studying with Odhran. Coman's interviews were briefer than usual, which helped, although Fial suspected that was for Coman's own reasons, not out of kindness. He did not see King Fintan again. He thanked Saint Columba for this mercy and prayed to be less of a coward. Also, since he could do nothing about it, he was glad not to observe any further pursuit of Aine, though that did not mean it had stopped.

Then one day, Coman arrived with a bay colt tied to his saddle. Fial tried to school his features into stillness but his revulsion must have shown.

Coman laughed, leaning in his saddle to tousle the colt's ears. "Quite a beauty, yes?" His gaze rolled skyward. "Such a splendid creature. What stamina. New to the paces, of course, but taking to them eagerly."

"A king's brother should keep himself to a fitting mount, not a green country pony," Fial snapped.

Coman's laugh redoubled. "It is fortunate for you I find your disapproval amusing." He sat up straight in his saddle, shifting his hips. "Crossbreeding improves the herd, as everyone knows. Now," he went on before Fial could decide if he were rash enough to reply, "Tell me what you have learned since we last spoke. Quickly. I have no time to walk with you to the pastures today."

"Rumors of Vikings to the north, on Strongford Lough," Fial said, cravenly glad of the change of subject. "But a company coming up from the south spoke of them further down the coast." He spread his hands. "I have no way of knowing if either, both, or none are true. There have been so many attacks. Folks are frightened, and seeing forms in shadows."

Coman tapped his chin with a knuckle, apparently considering. "I will go south, towards Dun Leire. Other ears have heard of sightings that way." He untied the colt's lead. "Take him to the pastures until I return. I will use more speed than he can give."

"Alone, Lord?" Fial asked.

The king's brother shook his head. "I have men waiting at the abbey. Only a few. We mean to scout, not give battle." His arrogant smile returned. "I am touched by your concern."

The colt tossed his head, giving a shrill whinny. "Shush now," Fial crooned, stroking his neck. "He'll be fine, Lord."

Coman turned his horse. "If I'm not back in a day, send word to my brother. He's waiting at the abbey with more men."

Fial's hands tightened on the lead. "You think an attack is coming. Soon."

"Perhaps. Or perhaps, as you say, people are worried and starting at shadows." Coman hesitated. "If so, many have seen those shadows in the south. I have to check it out."

"Take care, Lord." Fial watched until Coman galloped away, then stuck his head inside the house. "Berrin, there may be trouble. Can you come to pastures with me?"

His wife turned from her loom, weaving sword in her hand. Evgren was nearby, pushing the swinging churn. "Are you sure? The cream would sour if I leave and I really must work on this cloth." She swatted Evgren's back gently. "This one is growing faster than dunghill weeds. Her *leine*'s split at the shoulders."

Fial debated arguing with her. It would be a lengthy discussion given the set of her chin, and since he did not *know* there was danger, it might well be a discussion he would not win. "Very well. But be ready. If I hear trouble *is* coming, you must be able to leave at once."

"I will." Berrin turned back to her loom, working the threads down into a tight cloth with the weaving sword. "Evgren, get the basket. I'll tell you what to put in it. Fial," she said without looking at him, concentrating on the loom. "You must go. I'm sure Tadhg is wondering where you are."

Fial stood in the doorway, hesitating. Outside, the colt tugged on the lead.

"I know you're still there," Berrin said, a smile in her voice. "Go. We'll be fine."

Fial turned, leading the dancing colt to the ford.

***

Fial sat on a slight rise in the pasture. Tadhg was settled under a tree across the way. Close-shorn sheep lay between them like so many hillocks, while at the far edge of the pasture, cattle lay in the shade of the forest, Coman's bay colt with them.

Was a Viking raid coming? Were the sea-wolves even now rowing into Dundalk Bay? Or were they in the south, as rumor said? What, if anything, had Coman found? What exactly had the king heard that made him suspect an attack was coming?

At least, Fial thought wryly, his terror and worry would keep him from nodding off today, no matter how deep his weariness.

***

Fial woke to someone screaming. He was on his feet nearly before his eyes were open.

"I saw them!" His nephew Ruarc, all of seven years old, ran towards him, towing his younger brother Meallan. The smaller boy, only three, stumbled. Clearly terrified, Ruarc did not stop but dragged his brother until the little one could get his feet back under him and run again.

Tadhg was there the next instant. "Who, child?"

"Boats." Ruarc gulped mouthfuls of air. "Big boats. With heads. With *teeth*."

Meallan wailed. Fial picked him up, patting his back, soothing him as he'd soothed the colt. "It's all right. Shush now. Where?" he looked at the older boy over Meallan's shoulder.

"The tide had. Gone out." Ruarc's words came in heaving bursts. "We were. Picking up. Pretty rocks. At Dunany point. Ships passed—"

Sweet Saint Columba, thank you for low tide. That was surely why they had gone further south. The tidal pull of Dundalk Bay was strong; the river mouth and a wide slice of the bay's coastal bottom went dry during low tide. Vikings could not sail into the river and strike. Landing in the tidal-bare bay, having to run so far and drag their prey back–that was not how Viking raids worked.

But they might return. Strike to the south and swing back towards Linn Duachaill as the tide turned —

"How many ships?" Tadhg asked.

The boy's mouth screwed up in concentration. "Three. I think. Three."

"Did you tell your parents?" Fial forced himself to not seize the child's arm. The poor boy was frightened enough. "The abbey? Berrin? Did you warn your aunt Berrin?"

"What about my sister? Did you tell Aine?" Tadhg said.

Ruarc's head swung back and forth. "Mam and Da are upriver. Fishing. I didn't see Aunt Berrin or Aine or," he gulped, "anyone. I ran straight here." He looked up at Fial, eyes brimming. "I couldn't think of anyone else. Did I do wrong, uncle?"

Fial patted the boy's shoulder. "You did perfectly." He joggled Meallan. "Especially taking care of your brother." He spoke reassuringly, but his mind was racing.

Coman. The King's brother was scouting to the south. He was looking for Vikings *in* the south. He would be caught unawares by ones approaching from the north.

Berrin. Evgren. Fial's chest squeezed until he could hardly breathe. He had to get them to safety.

King Fintan. In the abbey with a group of men. He needed to know about the Viking ships right away, so he could lead his men to the defense of his people.

Fial wished he could split himself into three parts, and each become a bird, that he might carry word to them all at once. He snorted an incongruous laugh. Maybe he would write a song like that for his bard testing. If he lived. If any of them lived.

Now, though —

"Ruarc, you've done a great job." Fial set Meallan down, ruffling his hair. "I need a little more help. Can you do it?"

The little boy's brow furrowed but he nodded.

"Good boy. I want you to take Meallan. Go that way," Fial jerked his head inland. "See where the cows are? The end of the pasture, where the forest starts? Hide among the trees but don't go too far. It's a thick, old forest and easy to get lost."

Ruarc gripped his brother's hand. "Yes, sir." He started walking.

Fial turned to the other herdsman. "Could you warn the farms? Especially my wife. Tell them all to go where I sent Ruarc. I'll warn the abbey."

"I'll go to Berrin as soon as I find Aine."

Fial hesitated. He wanted Tadhg to warn Berrin first. But how could he claim his wife and child were more important than Tadhg's sister? They were to Fial, of course, but not to Tadhg. "All right. But hurry. Get to Berrin as fast you can."

In answer, Tadhg set across the pasture at a run. A heartbeat later, Fial was behind him. They sprinted towards the ford.

***

"Where is the abbot? Where is King Fintan?" Fial shouted as he ran through the gap in the woven-wand fence.

"How did you know the king was here?"

Recognizing the voice, Fial swung round. "Breasal. What are you doing here?" He shook his head, remembering his brother was now living among the monks to learn if he was truly called to be one of them. "Go to the far pasture. Now."

"Why?" Breasal leaned his hoe against a tree.

"Vikings. Go. Please. I'll tell the king and abbot."

After a shocked stare, Breasal set off at a trot, stopping only long enough to warn monks he passed.

Fial whirled, shouting again. "Where is the king? I bring news for the king!"

King Fintan stepped from one of the buildings. "What are you doing?" He pincered Fial's elbow. "Do you want your secret known?"

"Vikings!" Fial hissed back. "They sailed past because of low tide. Heading south. Where your brother is. With only a few men." He turned a wild circle. "A horse? I can warn him in time." Sweet Saint Columba, why had he said that? He needed to get to Berrin and Evgren. He didn't even *like* Coman. Why risk his family for him?

King Fintan gave a low chuckle. The sound sent ice across Fial's shoulders. "Surely you saw my brother with my bay colt. Best foal my herd has dropped in ten years. Not to mention he got the hedge rose. Warn him?" The king looked down his nose. "I think not. I think I shall let the foreigners rid me of an increasingly irksome brother."

"Lord—" Fial whispered, appalled. "You are angry. You have cause to be," he said, although privately he was not convinced, "but he is your brother. The right hand of your rule."

The king's face hardened. "I have two hands of my own. They are strong enough to hold power." He turned, snapping his fingers as he strode away. "My horse. I wish to depart at once."

***

Fial could not have told how he galloped south, how he managed to find Coman. He did, and in time, though he got no thanks for his efforts. Coman cursed and turned his horse with an impatient wave for his men to follow. Where he planned to go, what he meant to do, he did not say.

Fial had taken a horse from the abbey's stables without asking, grabbing a monk on his way and bellowing, "Tell the abbot. Vikings are coming. Run to the far pastures." He had not waited for an answer. *Coman, then Berrin*, the horse's hooves seemed to say. He could not accept the king's casual treachery, but he would not sacrifice his family for Coman. He had warned him; his conscience was clear. *Berrin. Evgren.*

The horse was lathered and blowing and could gallop no longer, no matter how much he urged her. Her canter gave way to a trot, and the trot to a walk. Fial swung down, putting the reins around her neck and slapping her rump. She would find her way back. He would go faster on his own feet now.

Faster. But not fast enough.

Vikings swarmed over the hill as he burst through his door. To his horror, Berrin and Evgren were still there. What had happened to Tadhg? But he had no time to worry about Tadhg. He had hoped—he had persuaded himself—he would check, and if he died in the effort that was fine if they were safe.

They were not safe.

"We have to go. NOW." Fial swung Evgren up. Berrin grabbed the basket and they ran from the house. All around, their neighbors streamed out of the half-dozen houses in the farmstead, crying and shouting. Fial ran, following his wife. His legs burned, and his breath came in choking heaves. Berrin drew ahead, not realizing how tired he was, too tired to keep up. One of the houses was burning. Fial heard the laughter of flames, and of men, behind him.

Suddenly a man stood before Berrin, a sword in his hand. Where had he come from? Fial couldn't tell. It didn't matter. The man reached for Berrin's arm.

"Drop the basket," Fial screamed. "Run, Berrin. Run!"

The basket fell. But Berrin did not run. She couldn't. The Viking had seized her arm and was pulling her towards the river. The tide had turned enough for them to land.

Fial set Evgren down. "I have to help your mam. Run, fast as you can, to the pastures. Hide in the trees. Ruarc and Meallan are there. Stay with them."

"Da—" her little hands clung to his sleeve.

"Go. Run. It's your only chance." He swatted her back gently, as Berrin had done not long before, but Sweet Saint Columba, how long ago it seemed.

Evgren ran. Fial ran the other way. The Viking turned, his sword raised. Fial launched himself, aiming to duck beneath the sword and take the man to the ground.

It must not have worked. There was a biting slap against his throat and his vision blackened.

***

Fial woke, and wished he hadn't. His neck ached and burned. Something was terribly wrong, but he couldn't remember what.

"Ssh. Ssh. Don't try to talk. You're still healing." Breasal's voice. "Lucky it was the flat and not the edge. Here."

A spoon touched his lips. Fial tried to swallow and coughed instead. "Berrin?" Sweet Saint Columba, was that *his* voice? That croak? "Evgren?" He made himself speak, but the sound of his voice hurt more than his throat. That was no bard's voice.

"Ssh. It will keep." The spoon returned.

Fial turned his head. "Now."

Breasal sighed. He set the spoon down. "Evgren's fine. She's with family. Berrin..." he hesitated.

Fial grabbed his sleeve. "Tell me."

"She's...gone."

"Dead?" Fial's fingers loosened as if all his will had left him.

His brother's hands clasped tighter. "They took her."

Fial closed his eyes. Berrin. Captured by Vikings. His imagination supplied a hundred hideous things that might be happening to her. Or she might be dead. He did not know.

He would *never* know.

Curse the heathen bastard who had stolen her, and curse him twice for letting his hand wobble when he struck Fial. The edge would have been better.

"Your daughter lives. She needs you," Breasal said.

Fial turned onto his side. His eye caught Sile. How had the harp escaped the Vikings? There she was, covered with her kingly linen. Safe. His child was motherless. His clever, beautiful wife was a slave or dead. But his harp was safe.

Judas had sold his lord for silver. *He* had lost his family for a harp and the chance to have the status of bard.

Judas had been a better bargainer.

His fingers clutched his brother's sleeve again. "Sell it."

Breasal gasped. "Do nothing in haste, I beg you. You will regret it later."

"There is no song left in me." Fial shifted his grasp to his brother's wrist. "I do not deserve the angels' music. Sell it. Or I will burn it as soon as I can stand."

Breasal bowed his head. Fial turned his face to the wall.

———

Michelle Markey Butler teaches at the University of Maryland, usually Tolkien or medieval literature and history. Her novel, Homegoing *came out in December 2014. A co-authored novel,* The Last Abbot of Linn Duachaill, *is with S&H Publishing, Inc. Learn more from michellemarkeybutler.com.*

LONGEVITY UNDER COVER

Margaret Pearce

I bumped into Doctor Bill Smith when I worked as an undercover cop. My Chief, who has a sensitive nose, was interested in him.

There had been some queries about a young homeless man who had died on Dr. Smith's premises. The autopsy revealed a heart attack and a soon-to-be-fatal cancer. A similar death had taken place in the same place twelve months earlier, the victim a young homeless man whose autopsy showed a heart attack.

'Big coincidence, two homeless young men with no families both having weak hearts,' my Chief decided. 'Doc Smith doesn't deal, so what's happening to all those drugs he buys?'

'He's a retired doctor, and does research,' I reminded him.

'Why does he use connections for stuff that he can buy legitimately?'

'Because he doesn't want a record of what he's buying?' I suggested.

'So he's up to something! You're delivering his next lot.'

'I haven't got a weak heart,' I protested.

'Syd Robinson has no family or friends, and he's the next candidate for a heart attack,' the Chief decided.

'So why don't I get a bonus for living dangerously?'

'Syd Robinson, the great hero,' my Chief jeered. 'Stop whinging and start earning the over-inflated amount you do get paid.'

I hung around the usual places for three weeks before I was ordered to deliver a package to Bill Smith.

'Midnight exactly,' ordered my bad-tempered contact. 'And clean yourself up a bit. You give couriers a bad name! If it wasn't for the fact that Jerry got himself booked, I wouldn't use you.'

Jerry was in jail because I needed his courier job.

'I'm reliable,' I protested. 'What about an advance?'

'On your return, as usual,' my contact said. 'You can piss it against the wall then. Use the downstairs bathroom to clean up. Find some clothes out of the boxes down there.'

My contact was a big wheel in some charity organization. He often fed, dressed and housed homeless men in his downstairs flat. The Chief had decided he was such a treasure trove of information that he was left to run his lucrative courier business.

I tied my hair back into a pigtail with my sneaker lace. My tattoos were sufficient to place me in the pecking order of small time crims. I collected my package.

'Take the bike,' my contact ordered.

I put on a helmet and rode up to the mansion on the hill. I arrived at midnight. The gates opened just as I rode up. They closed behind me. There was a long winding drive.

I got off the bike, took off my helmet, and held the package up to the ornate doorknocker on the closed-in porch as per the instructions. The door opened. Dr. Smith was a grey-haired fit-looking sixty, wearing heavy glasses, well-cut slacks, and an expensive polo jumper.

'You're the new courier?' he asked.

'Jerry's busy for a while,' I explained.

'Sorry to ask you to come at this time of night, but I'm a bad sleeper. Come in and have some coffee,' he invited.

I followed him down the carpeted passage. There were original paintings on the wall. Whatever the retired doctor was up to was profitable! The mahogany furniture looked original heritage. He noticed me looking.

'Inherited a lot of it,' he explained.

'Bit old-fashioned but nice,' I said in my current identity.

He opened a door. Inside was a library plus study. There were comfortable armchairs around the big room. He dropped the package on the cluttered desk and moved across to a bench where a coffee machine bubbled away.

'Would you prefer hot chocolate?'

'Black coffee's okay.' It's harder to disguise stuff in black coffee.

'You do much work for my friend?' he asked as soon as I sat down.

'Some,' I said. I looked around at the shelves and shelves of books. 'Gee, you got a wonderful lot of books here.'

'You like reading?'

'Some,' I admitted. 'Always liked books.'

'It's nice to hear of a family that encourages kids to read,' he said.

'Hard to do much reading where I come from.'

'And where do you come from?'

'An orphanage.'

Behind the heavy glasses his eyes lit up. 'You're an orphan? How sad.'

'It was okay. We all came through healthy.'

'You do look healthy. Another cup of coffee?'

'No thanks. I'd better head off.'

'It's pretty late. Would you like to stay? Plenty of bedrooms in this place.'

Interesting thought. 'Nah — gotta go collect my pay.'

'Ah, yes,' said my host. 'Perhaps, as you like to read, come back some time and borrow a few books.'

'Gee thanks,' I said. 'Should I ring you first to let me in?'

'Just press the button on the gate. Any time between ten at night and four in the morning.'

'You're a real night owl,' I said.

'I'm busy during the day,' he explained.

'Love to know doing what,' my Chief grumbled when I reported back. 'We got hold of some original plans. That place has an enormous cellar underneath it. Must be his laboratory. He keeps his booze in the study. Keep snooping.'

His library had first editions that a museum would envy. Syd Robinson never moved beyond children's classics. I stayed longer and longer talking to Dr. Smith. I drank only black coffee and takeaway food I had bought myself.

'Call me Bill,' he suggested.

Bill Smith insisted on giving me a thorough medical check over. He was very impressed with my good physical health, especially my good eyesight.

'What a pity you haven't got any family to check if it's a genetic thing.'

'No family,' I said sadly. 'I've been doing a bit of regular work for Mr. X and can afford a room, but if I go through a bad stage I live on the street.'

'No friends to take you in?' Bill asked.

'Not too good at making friends.'

'That's so sad,' Bill said happily. 'I need someone to keep the grounds clear and maybe do a bit of cleaning. You would have to live in. Would you be interested?'

'I dunno,' I said hesitantly.

Should I be interested? It had taken him four solid weeks of poking and prying before he made that offer. He named a salary that had my eyes widening.

'Also I'll throw in your food for free. Cooking is one of my hobbies.'

'I'll take it,' I said.

'You can sleep in the old chauffeur's cottage. Work on the grounds during the day and don't come in to clean before ten at night. I don't like people in the house during the day as I am busy. I'll leave your lunch at the cottage.'

'You're on,' I promised. 'Shift in as soon as it suits you.'

'So he will have plenty of opportunities to have you ingesting foreign substances. We'll do blood tests daily,' the Chief mused. 'Leave your blood donation out with the milk bottles.'

'How am I going to find the entrance to the cellar if he's there all the time?' I grouched.

'We'll arrange for him to go somewhere at some stage.' the Chief soothed. 'Also the place is like Fort Knox. Arrange an easy entry for us.'

Jerry was out of jail and back to delivering. I collected the drug package from him every midnight once a month. He refused any invitation to enter.

'Bit silly of you to get so matey with the old guy,' he sneered and roared off on his bike.

I was there for a pleasant two months before anything happened. I worked keeping the lawns and gardens under control. At night I borrowed books, vacuumed and cleaned. I ate like a king. I sent off my blood tests daily.

'How good is the antidote?' I nagged the Chief across the cheeses section of the supermarket one morning.

I'd been taking it daily as well, but I was getting a bit nervous about what I was actually supposed to be taking it for.

'The lab seemed to think that what you're ingesting is

something to slow down your thinking. Just act more stupid than usual.'

'Gee!' I said.

'Shouldn't be hard,' the Chief scoffed. 'That's why you're so successful as an undercover.'

'The antidote?'

'The lab said it's working,' reassured the Chief.

Doctor Bill Smith was the most highly educated scientist I'd ever met. I was more and more impressed. I couldn't understand why he'd been so content just to have been an ordinary family doctor. Not that Syd Robinson would understand the implications of the pile of advanced scientific papers.

'Dunno why you like staying here all the time. Pretty dull sort of a life,' I said.

'I like a simple life,' he explained. 'I enjoy my life and pottering around with my experiments.'

'What sort of experiments?' I asked.

'Just the usual,' he said, staring at me suspiciously.

So I said, 'Gee!' and the wary look vanished from his eyes.

Bill had to visit the Tax Department in person as there was some question about his tax. That gave me two full days to search. I found no entrance to the cellar.

'Syd!' Bill called after he returned. 'I want to talk to you.'

I walked into the study and sat in my usual armchair and waited.

'You know, Syd,' Bill explained. 'I have no kith nor kin, and I won't get much older. Weak heart, you know. My wife died years ago and I have no children. You're the only person I have actually got close to since my retirement.' He paused. 'Syd, I am changing my will. It was going to a charity, but I guess you are a more worthwhile charity.'

'Gee!' I said. I wasn't using my usual four-letter word as he had taken exception to it, so I substituted 'Gee' all the time.

'Is Sydney Robinson your full name?'

'Gee!' I stammered. 'On the birth certificate it's Augustus Lionel Robinson, but everyone called me Syd.'

'The only thing that I ask is that you legally change your name to Bill Smith.'

'You really think I should do it?' I asked the Chief in the frozen section of the supermarket. 'The wife's a bit funny about it.'

'You can change back legally when the job is finished,' the Chief said. 'He inherited the mansion and his wealth from some old geezer who had taken him into the house and adopted him on the understanding he change his name to Bill Smith.'

'Still haven't found out where the cellar entrance is,' I admitted.

I went through the process and changed my name. After that, a solicitor and a doctor came in to witness the will and that I was the beneficiary.

On a Friday afternoon about a fortnight later, I was mowing the lawn when Bill came out of the house.

'Come in for a cuppa,' he called.

I followed him into the study and sat with my usual black coffee. It was a cold day. I wrapped my hands around the mug to warm them.

'This is really a celebration,' Bill said happily. 'I have at last finished what I have been experimenting with.'

'Gee!' I said.

'I have found a way to remove drug addiction but still give a lift! Just think of it, the drug problem solved overnight!'

254

'Gee!' I said again.

I didn't think that Mr. X would be too happy about drug problems being solved, but that was none of my affair.

'So you can come down to my lab and try it out,' Bill said.

'I ain't been on the heavy stuff since I moved in here,' I almost wept.

'But you would be happy not to have to fight the addiction day after day?' Bill said.

'I dunno. I'm doin' all right,' I said.

Bill got up and walked across to the bookshelf. He pulled out a book. The bookshelf swung back. Behind it were steps.

'Gee!' I said.

No wonder I hadn't found the cellar entrance. I followed him down stairs into the cellar. It was a very well-equipped laboratory. There was an open fireplace in the corner of the room. Bill Smith must have used it for burning notes by the amount of fresh ash piled in it. There were two big glassed-in boxes linked by wires and tubes. I looked at them nervously.

'Now Syd,' Bill said. 'You have to trust me.'

'Gee!' I gulped and nodded.

'This can swap the addiction to an animal in this other box. It is quite painless. The animal can then be slaughtered and sold as good quality meat. All they have to do is destroy the liver that could retain some of the addiction.'

'Gee!' I said.

There was no animal in the other box. I started to wonder about getting a regular job, like bus driving or something that didn't have some of the disadvantages of my current work.

'Syd!' Bill said earnestly. 'You know I have a weak heart.

I'll be the guinea pig to transfer the addiction into. I only have a few more weeks to live anyway so what's the harm? If it works as it should, I'll be addicted for a few weeks, and if it doesn't work, it's still a painless death for me. If that happens, open the gate, take my body up to the study and ring my doctor to say I collapsed.'

'Gee!' I said. 'I dunno.'

'You will inherit my house and wealth and be without any trace of your previous addiction,' Bill coaxed.

'Gee!' I said again. I scratched my hair, activating the panic button. I had disarmed all the gates and traps as I did every day.

'Syd! You must trust me!' Bill sounded very sincere and his eyes glistened with the intensity of his sincerity. 'This is successful. I have already tried it out on other guinea pigs.'

Two young men had already died, and I was on track to be the third guinea pig with a heart attack. Unless, of course, he was telling the truth. How likely was that? I shuffled nervously. I didn't like the odds.

'I trust you, Bill,' I said. 'But I dunno.'

'Come on, Syd,' Bill urged. 'Just this little favour for me. I get a painless death and you get everything I own. Just step into that glass box and I will get into the other one. Everything will go smoothly.'

'I dunno,' I said again. What was keeping my rescue team?

'I love you like a son, Syd.' Bill climbed into one of the glass boxes. 'Trust me.'

I shrugged. Either I was all right or I wasn't! I stepped into the box.

'Don't I have to connect something?' I asked.

'No! It is special conducting glass.'

He grinned. It was a nasty grin. The hair on the back of

my neck lifted. What with being undercover for so long I had a very strong instinct for survival. I grabbed the knob. I was too late!

It felt like an electric shock, only ten times worse. The blinding pain was blotting out my mind. For a few seconds it almost felt as if there was another mind in my head as well. A nasty cold merciless sort of mind. I screamed! Then it was gone and I had this dreadful headache.

My heart thudded like mad. I opened the box and staggered out. Bill was huddled in the other box. I opened it and checked for a pulse. Nothing. I dragged him upstairs and rang his doctor.

'If he's dead there's no hurry,' the doctor grumbled. 'I've got a bad birth to get through. Leave the gate open for me.'

I went back down to the laboratory. I checked out the only desk in the laboratory. There were bank statements, cheque stubs and receipts. There were neat lists of chemicals, with dates and prices beside them. The writing was an elegant copperplate that isn't taught in schools these days.

I fanned through the letters. There were apologies about the difficulties in finding some chemicals. There were requests for information about missing men and boys.

I sat and studied them. Nothing proved anything. Was it because I had nearly been electrocuted that the hair on the back of my neck was still standing up? If the doctor knew he had a weak heart, why had he deliberately killed himself. Why had he deliberately killed the other young men with weak hearts? What were his experiments designed to do?

I went back to scan through the list of drugs and chemicals he had been experimenting with. Some of the drugs had been to slow and dull the mind, as my Chief suspected, but for what purpose?

I went back upstairs and opened the bookcase. The Chief sat in the library smoking, gazing at Bill Smith's body slumped in the big armchair. He looked up as I swung the bookcase open.

'Very neat,' he approved. 'No wonder it was hard to find. I'll arrange an autopsy of our Bill Smith.'

'I rang for his doctor. He seemed to think that it was his heart,' I said.

'The team is around dismantling all the booby traps. Untrusting soul wasn't he?'

'What did my antidote actually do?' I asked.

'Disposed of the drug as fast as it was being fed in. You could've ended up a mindless vegetable else.'

'Pretty uncomfortable few months I've had,' I grumbled.

'So what happened? What was he doing with the drugs? Marketing them?''

'Using them for experiments.'

'Did he leave any notes?' the Chief prompted.

'All carefully burned.'

The Chief was a bit miffed at how legally waterproof the will was and at me resigning from my job as undercover cop. The autopsy confirmed that it was his heart, although the coroner did want to know if he had received a shock or something.

'Nothing,' I lied. 'He was just sitting there when he sort of collapsed.'

My wife, despite her grumbling about the changed name, was contented enough and we went travelling. So our four 'Smith' kids have been born all over the world, which is very educational.

I donated the laboratory to the police science mob and turned the big house into a rehab centre.

I still wake with nightmares and the memory of the presence of that cold, merciless analytical mind nudging mine. Bill Smith was so very logical and not at all altruistic. Which is why I break out in a cold sweat when I remember how interested he was in my good health and my good eyesight.

Still I must say I appreciate being left all that money. I reckon I earned it.

———

Margaret took to writing (mostly fantasy) instead of drink when raising children. She has had children's and teenage novels published, three romances released with Robert Hale, and several more published as ebooks. She lives in Australia, and currently lurks in an underground flat in the Dandenongs – still writing.

SPYING ISN'T EASY

George G. Moore

From under the hoop, Nick watched Alan take a jump shot over Zack at the foul line. On any other day, it would've been good, and they would've won the game. Today, the ball floated to the hoop and bounced off with a clang. Charlie grabbed the rebound away from Nick's fingertips and passed it to Zack, who was already beyond the key. He squared up and took the jumper over Alan.

The ball swished through the hoop. Charlie ran to Zack and high-fived him. After the all-around "good game" from everyone, Charlie and Zack went to the locker room.

Nick turned to Alan. "What's up? You never miss those shots."

"It's Britt." Alan sounded agitated as he picked up the ball. "She says she has a parent conference at five tomorrow."

"A conference? In December? Does she have a problem student?"

Alan tossed the ball to, Nick and sighed. "No. And this is the third one in as many weeks. It's nearly Christmas. You know parents've already checked out."

As much as he wanted, Nick couldn't argue. He'd seen the same thing for the six years he'd been teaching. Unless a kid had serious problems, parents were as scarce as a vegan at a barbecue once October rolled around. "What's going on with her?"

"I don't know." Alan hung his head, his shoulders slumping. "I think she's cheating on me."

"I can't believe that. Have you talked with her?"

"What if I'm wrong? I'm basically telling her I don't trust her."

Nick refrained from saying they wouldn't be having this conversation if he trusted her. "What are you gonna do?"

"I need you to follow her tomorrow after school. Find out where she's going. Who's she seeing."

"What? Are you nuts?" Nick couldn't believe his ears. Britt had always struck him as down-to-earth and genuine, not the type of person who'd cheat. Alan was jumping to conclusions.

"Nick, I can't live like this. Not knowing. And I can't strap Jimmy into a car seat and follow his mom around. Moves like that get you on the Terry Faller Show. And before you suggest it, no, you can't babysit him. *I'd* have to lie when she asked where I was after Jimmy announced, 'Nick was so much fun tonight!'"

"What can I say, I have a knack with kids." Nick chuckled, but Alan only stared at him, his face emotionless. Alan needed his help, and as much as he hated the idea of spying on Britt, he had to help Alan out. "I'll see what I can find out. And don't worry—however it turns out, I have your back."

* * *

Parked across the street and down the block from Broad Ridge High School, Nick turned off his Explorer. Britt's white Camry sat in the teachers' parking lot. He breathed easily. It was 4:30, and classes had ended at 3:15. If she were having an affair, she would've left already.

Probably.

Part of him wished her car hadn't been there. He could've forgotten about the folly of following his best friend's wife and gone home. But that would've only delayed the inevitable. Her next parent/teacher conference would put him back in this spot.

Nick rubbed his hands together and blew into them. Without the engine running, the frigid December air was taking its toll. Turning on the car for a few minutes would do the trick. However, that'd draw attention, a lone guy, hanging out by a school. Someone might call the cops.

He considered going inside to talk with Britt while getting a first-hand look at what was going on. And the building would be warm, too. He only needed an excuse. Maybe he could ask for her advice on some subtle bullying in his classroom.

As he reached for the door handle, Britt strolled from the main entrance with her leather briefcase and purse hanging from her shoulder and got in her car, acting as if she didn't have a care in the world. It was 4:41. There was no parent/teacher conference. Everything still might be okay, though—maybe it'd been canceled.

She pulled out of the parking lot and headed away from him. She wasn't going home. So much for his canceled theory.

"You're gonna kill Alan," Nick muttered to her tail lights in the rear view mirror. He started his car, made a U-turn, and followed. The radio was playing *I Want To Know What Love Is,* a song his parents had played when he was young. He glared at the radio and slapped the power button.

Traffic was moderate, which posed a problem. He didn't want to get too close and let Britt spot him. But he didn't want to lag so far behind that he lost her, especially if she made a light and he didn't.

Britt headed toward Harrison Highway where the intersection was controlled by a stoplight, which was red. He let off the gas a bit. One car passed, pulling in front of him, followed by a second. Nick regained speed to keep pace with traffic, satisfied he had enough of a buffer.

Just before the turn lane on to Harrison Highway, Britt flashed her right turn signal and drifted over. The car immediately behind her continued forward. The lone car that remained between didn't signal but slowed.

Were they turning? If not, he'd end up directly behind Britt, and she'd surely see him. He'd have to smile and wave, and give up following her. It'd only postpone the inevitable. Alan would ask him to do a better job of following her the next time.

The car between them drifted into the right turn lane behind Britt. He smiled. For the first time ever, he was glad a driver changed lanes without signaling. He joined the line waiting on the red light, happy for the lucky break. Tailing people wasn't as easy as Rockford and Magnum made it look on those old TV shows.

The light changed, and they headed east on Harrison Highway. The car between them pulled into the left lane, accelerating past Britt's Camry. Nick drove the speed limit, and Britt pulled away.

He turned on his headlights. From her perspective, the glare from the setting sun and his headlights should obscure the car's details, especially who was driving. At least, he hoped so. He needed to look like a run-of-the-mill commuter heading home after a long day's work.

For ten minutes, he paced her from a distance, until they approached the Richwood intersection. Britt signaled and took the exit lane. Nick followed, leaving plenty of space between them as they drove into a neighborhood past homes on the left and a strip mall on the right.

In the strip mall's parking lot, a car approached, not slowing. Nick let off the gas, and, a second later, slammed on the brakes when it turned on to the road in front of him.

He expected the driver to take off like a scared rabbit, but no, the car went on at a steady twenty miles per hour. At first, he suspected the driver was drunk, and considered calling the cops, but looking closer, he saw the driver had his hand to his ear, surely holding a cell phone. "Idiot!"

Far ahead, a car turned left into a neighborhood. It could be Britt, or not. He'd lost track of her while trying to prevent a nasty crash.

He passed the oblivious idiot and hoped the car ahead was her. He'd already lost her if it wasn't. And depending on the car's turns in the neighborhood, he might lose her yet.

When he reached the street, he also turned. Half a block ahead in a driveway on the right, a car's headlights turned off. Britt was already exiting her car as he drove by. He didn't slow, but noted "214" above the door of the single-family house.

He exhaled. He'd caught another lucky break.

At the next cross street, he made a right, parked by the curb, and turned off the lights and engine. He speed dialed Alan on his cell. "She's in Richwood."

"Richwood?" Alan paused for a moment. "Where?"

Nick looked up at the street signs on the corner. "214 Elm Street."

A few more seconds passed. "That's my sister's house."

Nick exhaled with relief. "Okay, then. I told you have nothing to worry about. I'm going home."

Alan harrumphed. "You're kidding. It's worse than I thought. I never figured Britt would mess around with her brother-in-law."

The idea of an affair was hard to swallow, but Britt messing around with her brother-in-law was beyond ridiculous. "Britt wouldn't do that."

"This'll tear the entire family apart, and you know my folks'll figure out a way to blame me."

"You're jumping to conclusions." Nick rubbed his eyes. Alan wasn't hearing him.

"We're gonna be an entire episode of the Terry Faller Show."

"Listen, Alan, there has to be another explanation."

"Maybe, but she still lied about where she'd be and what she'd be doing." Alan's tone was dead serious. "You need to find out what's going on."

Nick shook his head. "You're asking me to peep in windows."

"I know. I'll owe you a big one."

"I'm not keeping score. Do you understand what you're asking me to do?"

"Believe me, nothing's ever been clearer," Alan said, adding a sigh.

Alan needed to know what was going on. If he were in Alan's shoes, he'd be going out of his mind, too. "I'll call you back."

Nick shoved his phone into his jacket pocket and walked the deserted sidewalk toward Rick and Sue's house. As he passed their house, he glanced over to the bay window, finding the drapes drawn. Of course, they were. Nothing was ever easy.

He glanced around and saw no one. He muttered, "Act natural, like you belong here," and cut between houses, crunching brown, shriveled leaves along the way. At the side window, he leaned over a rose bush, peered inside, and couldn't believe his eyes.

He crouched down and speed dialed Alan.

After the second ring, Alan picked up. "That was quick."

Nick whispered, "You won't believe this. Your sister and wife are on the couch, drinking wine and talking."

"You're sure it's Sue, not Rick?"

"C'mon, I can tell the difference between your sister and brother-in-law."

"Okay, okay. Are they arguing? You know what happens when two queen bees get together."

Yeah, Alan had mentioned some of their arguments. Sue might have a first-class education and be a practicing doctor, but Britt was smart in her own right and street smart besides. Britt had held her own. This was completely different, though. They looked like old friends catching up. "Nope. Just chatting."

"You sure? I don't wanna get a Terry Faller Special."

"Yeah, just talking. Alan, listen, Britt's not cheating on you. It's good news. You can rest easy."

"Why'd she lie? Why's she hanging out with my sister? You can call it good news, but it's damn odd."

"Take a breath, Alan. Maybe she's asking for medical advice." It was a shot in the dark, but if it got him out of there, he'd go with it.

"Nope. Can't be that. Sue was clear as soon as she got her license that she couldn't treat family, so we weren't to ask."

"Okay." Figuring out what was going on would be easier if Alan would think things through instead of insisting his suspicion was true. Nick pushed back his irritation. "Is there anything going on with Sue or your parents? Something new."

"No, just the usual. Well, my parents have started talking about another overseas vacation. To India or China, I didn't pay much attention."

"It's been over a year since their last one, so they're on schedule." Nick tried to think of another plausible scenario, but nothing came to mind.

"It's useless guessing. You have to find out what's going on."

For a second, Nick looked at the phone, not believing what he'd heard come from it. "How am I gonna do that? Put my ear to the window."

"I don't know. Read lips. Try something."

"Hang tight. I'll see what I can do." Nick hung up and stood, looking for the least painful way past the rose bush's thorns to reach the window. Perhaps he could hear something, a risky move, but this needed to end tonight.

Someone tapped his shoulder. He jerked and turned only to be blinded by a flashlight shining in his eyes. Off to his left, a hand holding mace came into view.

"Okay, Nick, what's the deal?" The voice came from the mace-holder and was unmistakably Britt's.

"You're damn lucky Britt recognized you because I was ready to call the police on a perv peeping in windows." And that was Sue, standing beside Britt, holding the flashlight. "I still might."

They'd busted him. Everyone was gonna be pissed, but one good thing could come of it. He could find out exactly what was going on and maybe save Alan's marriage. "Okay, okay. Let's go easy on the perv talk. It's not what you think."

"What I think is that I don't want to give my neighbors a free show." Sue turned off the flashlight. "Get inside."

* * *

With his jacket in his lap, Nick sunk into the most comfortable armchair ever. Regardless, the living room was more like a museum than a home. It might be how rich doctors lived, but he'd rather live where he didn't have to worry about dropping crumbs on the carpet.

Off to his left, Sue and Britt sat on the couch. Sue's cheeks were red, and the fingers of her right hand tapped the cushion. Britt's eyebrows were drawn together, and wrinkles were etched into her forehead.

While Sue's gazed never wavered from him, Britt never looked at him. She was worried.

"We're waiting," Sue said.

Nick said as calmly as possible, "Alan asked me to follow Britt."

"Damn." Without looking up, Britt asked in a monotone, "Why?"

"Umm..."

"'Umm' isn't an answer." Sue crossed her arms. "Just spit it out."

"Fine." Nick struggled to voice the words he'd never have imagined speaking. He looked to Britt. "He knows you're lying. He wants me to find out what you're doing."

Britt's eyes filled with tears. "He doesn't think I'm..."

Nick couldn't finish her sentence — he could only nod.

Sue reached over and patted Britt's hand. "You're not messing around. We'll just tell Alan what's going on like I wanted to from the beginning. He'll have to grow up and deal with it sooner or later. Might as well be sooner."

"What is going on? Why all the secrecy?"

"Mom and Dad are adopting a little girl from Nepal."

Nick couldn't believe his ears. "How on earth did that happen?"

"One of Dad's colleagues is volunteering to treat survivors from the series of earthquakes there. The kid's an orphan. Her parents died in a quake."

He pictured Sue and Alan's parents raising another kid but couldn't get past the age difference. That wasn't the issue, though. "Britt, why're you lying to Alan about this."

"You know he has issues with the family—"

Sue, dismissively waving her hand, interrupted, "Wah, wah, wah. He had to go to Mason instead of William and Mary. I'll be laying in my coffin, and he'll still be complaining. Just once, I wish he'd acknowledge our parents' investments took a downturn, and they did their best to keep me in school and get him started."

"It wasn't just William and Mary, and you know it," Nick said, tired of Sue's compassionless attitude toward her brother. Their parents had arranged for her to volunteer at all the right places and to get all the right letters or recommendation to get into the best schools. Yet, they'd never found a few hours to attend Alan's basketball games, even after she'd left for college.

"Sue, ignoring Alan's feelings doesn't help." Britt glared at her. "Alan made great strides with his business this year, and he can't even get a 'well done' from your dad. He's ready to turn his back on all of you. I barely got him to attend Thanksgiving dinner as is. So, I consulted with a counselor because I really want Jimmy to know his aunt and grandparents. And now they're climbing a mountain of red tape to get that little girl. Alan's going to think they care for a stranger more than him. It'll be the last straw."

For a moment, Nick thought Sue would jump in with a helpful suggestion or even an argument, but she simply sat with her hands folded in her lap. After all of these years, he should've known better. He shifted his gaze to Britt, who was losing the battle to maintain a relationship with her in-laws. "Britt, I get it. You're trying to do the right thing, but you caught a bad break. You have to talk to Alan. Tonight, whether you're ready or not."

Determination set into Britt's eyes as they met his. She grabbed her cell phone from her purse, touched the screen a few times, and placed it to her ear. "Hi, Hon. I'm not at school, and there's no parent/teacher conference." She paused. Alan's voice sounded from the phone, but it was too muffled to understand. "I'm at Sue's, and Nick's with us." She paused again for Alan to speak. "Of course, we caught him. He has no future as spy—that's for certain." She gave Nick a thin smile while Alan spoke. "I'll explain everything when I get home. I'll see you soon."

She slipped the phone in her purse, and stood. "Sue, thank you for your thoughts."

"Anytime." Sue drained her wine glass.

"Nick, walk me out. I'd like your thoughts, too." Britt donned her winter coat, lying on an armchair facing him as Nick followed, putting on his jacket. Once outside, Britt said, "I could really use your advice. Sue's was useless."

"No surprise. I hope she's better with her patients."

At her car, Britt said, "You know you're an idiot for following me."

"Not my idea." Nick shoved his hands into his jacket pockets. "I even tried to talk Alan out of it. But he saw through your lies like they were glass. You need better lies."

Britt chuckled. "I'm not making a habit out of lying to my husband."

"Good. Now, you need to make things right."

"I know. You're closer to him than anyone. I'll listen to any advice you have."

Nick pursed his lips. Britt had a tough evening ahead of her. "Just admit to lying. Don't make excuses. Alan'll bitch and moan, but he'll respect you for coming clean. Then, tell him about his new little sister. He'll complain about that too. Try to convince him that his parents ignoring him was their problem, a blindspot that had little to do him. Tell him that adopting her has nothing to do with him."

"I tried that before, and he didn't buy it. I'll try again, but it still doesn't solve my original issue with Jimmy knowing his family."

"His parents will never be able to make up for what they did to him. What they did for Sue or will do for the little girl doesn't matter. The question is, will he do better with Jimmy? Ask him if he's willing to deprive Jimmy of the opportunity of knowing his family. Alan loves that little guy. If you can focus his thoughts on what's best for Jimmy, he'll move past everything else."

* * *

Nick dribbled the basketball as he slid two steps to his right. Each bounce echoed throughout the gym. He jumped and shot toward the glass backboard. The ball bounced off and into the basket, not touching the rim. He had the stuff today.

"Nice shot."

"Alan, you made it."

Alan grabbed the ball on the first bounce and passed it back to Nick. "I almost didn't. Britt and I had a late night talking. I'm dragging, but I didn't want to miss our game."

"Everything okay?" At the foul line, Nick shot a jumper.

After the ball slipped through the net, Alan caught it and put in a lay up off the backboard. He grabbed the ball and joined Nick. "Yeah. I can't believe my parents."

"Their hearts are in the right place to adopt the little girl."

"I guess." Alan glanced at the floor and shook his head. "Are they gonna treat her like me if she doesn't go into medicine?"

That insight was new. Of all the times they'd talked about Alan's parents, he'd never mentioned anything like that. "Do you think that's their problem?"

"While Britt and I were talking, it kinda hit me. And you know what Britt said?"

Nick shook his head.

"'Then she's going to need a big brother who understands what she's going through and can help her.'"

Britt played that well. In the end, Alan could be a very positive force in his new little sister's life. "Either way, she can use a big brother."

"I know. It's kinda cool." Alan smiled. "And I'm sure 'Uncle' Nick would be welcome."

"You know it." Nick returned his smile.

Alan leaned in closer. "I have to tell you — Britt and I decided that my parents'll either see my success and be happy for me or not. It's their loss if they miss it. Britt, Jimmy, and I are gonna be happy regardless."

Things were working out better than Nick imagined possible a day earlier. "I have to tell you I hated spying on Britt, but I couldn't be happier that you're in a good place now."

"Me, too." Alan gestured to the locker room door. "Hey, here comes Charlie and Zack."

"Today's our day. It's butt-kicking time."

They bumped fists, each opening his hand as he pulled it past his face. In unison, they said, "Boom."

———

George lives in northern Virginia. He tends to write science fiction and speculative fiction, and has had several short stories published. He likes golfing, swing dancing, and reading in addition to a day job managing a group of software engineers. Learn more from georgegmoore.com.

DANCING DUTCH COMES HOME

Olympia George

A small wind blew into White Horse Meadows, setting bright marigolds and long-legged marguerites dancing with stiff-necked geraniums in window boxes out front of the Model Home Office. It circled a sign declaring in pleasant, homey script—geranium red on white — "Come Right In!" It was a quiet wind, but not without some strength—the kind that, to a person who knew anything at all about the weather, signified change.

Harvey Sussman, his dark green polyester tie loosened and the first button of his matching short-sleeved shirt undone, stood outside the office enjoying the breeze. If he squinted just right, he could screen out the piles of dirt and cement rubble, could imagine what White Horse Meadows would be in just a few months' time.

On the north side of the third house from the end of what Sussman thought of as the "good" side of Appaloosa Lane, he could see narrow Martin Hoodenpyle on an aluminum stepladder putting a third coat of white paint on the trim of his new yellow Victorian-style farmhouse, which had twelve-paned windows in front and an old-fashioned veranda wrapped around three sides.

Sussman chuckled to himself, thinking how Hoodenpyle, his pretty, chubby wife Marion and their two bored kids had made pests of themselves poring over the plans for their new home, haunting the building site, demanding changes at every turn, and finally moving in before the paint was dry. How each morning, now they were in residence, Hoodenpyle was out prowling the perimeter of his newly-acquired turf, kicking fenceposts as if each were a suspect tire, checking each stake and side of string encompassing his sparse, vivid green lawn, just now sprouting like a bald man's hope of hair.

Proprietary. That was the word for Martin Hoodenpyle. Sussman grinned, hitched his white belt around his bulging real estate salesman's waistline, and turned back into the hot office, toward his room in back, equipped with his bed, his color TV, his refrigerator full of beer.

The sun, orange as a marigold, prepared to sink over the western rim of Martin Hoodenpyle's tidy world—and as it did so, the wind picked up.

Harv Sussman, thinking of Vanna White and Mr. Weinhardt's Private Reserve, closed his door.

***

Martin Hoodenpyle afforded himself a moment's pure thrill in the ownership of this seventy-five- by one hundred ten-foot piece of land, the trim yellow and white house he had caused to be built upon it, the flat and springing new green lawn he had planted around it, his son's red BMX bike with chrome trimmings neatly kick-standed in the drive, his daughter's pink Smurfette Big Wheel parked next to it, the pink, blue and white streamers on its handlebars rising and rustling in the wind, which lifted to bring him the smell of salmon grilling on his patio, the clean smell of white paint rising from the bucket just under his nose.

Martin sighed his satisfaction, adjusted his glasses, and once more picked up his brush. He dipped it, making a fine point of the bristles loaded with thick white paint, and applied it lovingly over the second coat, which he'd put on only the day before.

***

Dinner was, of course, wonderful. The grilled salmon steaks, fettucini with fresh basil and cream, chilled asparagus à la vinaigrette followed by a splendid peach sorbet. Marion was as superb a cook as she was mother and housekeeper. He beamed at her plump, aproned form bustling in and out of the kitchen.

The children, already bathed and fed, watched the Bill Cosby Show in their Superman and Smurfette pajamas while their parents dined. The polished teak table was set with white linen, fresh flowers, good china, and goblets filled with a wine as sparkling as the prismed Austrian crystal chandelier. Rosy sunset light coming through the twelve-paned bay windows touched a flame to the couple's matching blond heads so that nine-year-old Michael, coming into the room for another roll during a commercial break, laughed.

"You look just like that picture of Grandpa Dutch," he giggled, pointing to Martin's temporarily fiery head. The giggles stopped abruptly at his father's fierce glare, his finger pointing to the dreaded Bench. No words were needed.

Outside, a dust devil formed on one of the Morgan Lane construction sites two streets over. It whirled cross-lots to fling gray grit at the Hoodenpyle's front windows and onto Martin Hoodenpyle's new front lawn.

An hour later, the dust had settled inside as well as out, and Michael, released from Bench Time in his red, white and blue Superman motif bedroom, joined four-year-old Melody in her Smurfy pink and white nest for a bedtime read. Melody's choice was "The Three Billy Goats Gruff," which never failed to scare her silly, giving her an excuse to stay up at least another half hour, thereby getting one up on Michael, who had the bigger bike. "Not fair," Michael grumbled.

By ten o'clock the house was quiet, the blonde kiddies snoring gently in their beds, the kitchen once more immaculate. The happy householders, Marion and Martin, in their matching blue and white terry robes and scuffs, were watching the evening news.

"Mind explaining what all that was about?" Marion inquired drily, her pink-nailed hands wrapped around a cold glass of seltzer and orange juice.

Martin grunted, his usual reply to questions centering on his father.

Marion, watching her truculent husband from under thick yellow lashes, finished her seltzer and went quietly to bed.

It was a long time before Martin joined her.

***

Out on the main highway several miles distant from Appaloosa Lane, an old man stumbled along the moonlit shoulder, thumb held at arm's length and down, as if to condemn to the junkyard all passing cars for their drivers' refusal to abandon set destinations in favor of his, which was far less clear.

A green Ford convertible with the top down roared past full of screaming girls, their waving arms and hair whipping like so many flags. Next, a Mack truck whose driver pulled a short blast on his air horn in salute or warning — the old man wasn't sure which. Then a Greyhound bus deadheading for the barn, followed by nothing for a very long while.

The old man staggered out into the middle of the highway, stood on the white line waving his overcoat, his brown-paper-sack-swaddled bottle. "I have a son, damn you all, you can't do this to me," he shouted down the empty road.

He took off his hat, revealing skimps of hair that might once have been red, searched with dirty fingers inside the hatband for a slip of paper he seemed to remember putting there for safekeeping some while ago, just how long he could not recall.

Absorbed with the hatband, the old man was startled into a scream by the rapid advancement of what looked like the twin headlights of a very big car with no intention of slowing down for anything, least of all for him. He clapped the hat on his head, both hands over it, ducked, and began to run.

The car revealed itself to be a pair of huge, shiny motorcycles, their headlamps separating as the cycles roared around the ancient drunk, their drivers' blatting laughter carried back to him over their shoulders as they continued down the road.

"Damn you, I have a son," he yelled again, more to himself than to any part, wheeled or otherwise, of a world that was moving far too fast for him, and in the wrong direction.

***

Three days later, the sun was once more on the westward slope of Martin Hoodenpyle's roof, gliding down the ridgepole as it had done these many summer nights in a marigold blaze. This time it was steaks, the best New York cuts, grilling on the patio, sending up their exotic steam.

The grass was now a soft green fur, the shutters pristine in their fourth coat of white paint. Hoodenpyle had moved his folding aluminum ladder to the back yard, where he was at work fixing a bird house, a yellow and white replica of his own, to the top of a meticulously white-painted pole.

Melody splashed happily in a Smurf-colored wading pool closely watched by her fond parents, one on the ladder, one at the grill. "Look at me," she squealed. "Watch this!" She jumped up and down in the shallow water, causing the ruffles on her blue Smurfsuit to bounce.

At that moment, Michael, who had been skidding up and down the gravel lane on his red BMX bike, practicing Evel Knievel-style leaps over chunks of firewood, his sister's pink Smurfmobile, and the cat, caught the whiff of steak grilling and turned back toward home. He hauled to a stop outside the Model Home Office, arrested by the distant sight of a strange man stooped outside his house, clearly trying to see inside. An old guy whose baggy pants hung from knotted suspenders slung over a plaid flannel shirt, black overcoat over one arm, brown hat flopped on his head like something a flying cow might have deposited there.

Drop-jawed at the vision of this particular old man who, Michael noted instantly, had the remains of what might once have been red hair sticking out from under that awful hat, he suddenly became aware of his heart thudding mightily under his tank top. Looking down, he could see its movement under the orange cloth.

The boy startled painfully when the real estate salesman touched him on the arm. "Says he's your grandpa," Sussman offered in his froggy voice. He nodded down the hill, toward Michael's house. Together, Michael and Sussman stood surveying the scene with intense interest.

Below them, the old man bobbed and wove like the prizefighter he once had been—slower, of course, and less sure on his feet—as he worked his way along the sidewalk first in one direction, then the other, angling for the best view inside or around back of his son's house, where he figured all the action was.

Finding the perfect vantage point, Michael's own secret watching place at the north corner of the lot behind a clump of vine maples left to redden decoratively on a small hummock near the road, the old man began inching forward, nudging, as he did so, the string that cordoned off Michael's father's new lawn.

In the back yard, on his ladder, Martin Hoodenpyle turned quickly, testing the air for wind. At that moment, there was none. But like a ranger spider hurrying to check any small vibration to its web, Hoodenpyle rappelled down the rungs, tense and ready to deal with... what? His too-rambunctious son crashing his BMX into his newly-laid lawn?

Michael leaned toward lumpy Sussman, a kind of comforting hill, and together they watched his father round the northeast corner of his new home, ready to defend his territory—ready for anything—and come face to face with his own father peering at him through screens of alcohol and vine maple with glad and needy eyes.

"Marty?" Dutch ventured.

"Oh Jesus. Oh shit," Martin replied.

Michael watched his father stop, advance, turn around at the very edge of that much-protected patch of grass, tramp down a small circle, then retreat toward the back yard.

"Marion!" Dutch Hoodenpyle's only grandson heard the boy's father yell for his mother, not so much his usual order as a plea for help even a ten-year-old could recognize, though Michael was not yet ten years old. He saw his mother come out on the front porch, still armed with the barbecue mitt and fork, saw her hover tentatively near the rail waiting to hear what was needed, heard his father bark, and his mother, flanked by soggy, shivering Melody, turn back into the living room and abruptly close the door.

The thud of the door's closing, solid and heavy as half a heart-beat, came to him on the wind, which had again begun to rise. It brought to him the smell of steak burning. Michael watched the old man who might actually be his grandfather untangle himself from the vine maple and his father's string fence, watched him cross the lane, clamber up a pile of dirt, and sit down on top.

From the pinnacle of his new roost, Dutch Hoodenpyle, never taking his eyes off the neat yellow and white house, pulled a brown paper-wrapped bottle from an overcoat pocket and took a long, shaky drink.

Michael, remembering his father's impassioned response to the suggestion of a resemblance to the old man on the rubble heap, was tempted to avoid further trouble by sneaking home the back way, unseen. But some kind of fellow feeling for the shambling old man overcame him. Bidding Sussman good night, he wheeled bravely down the lane and into the drive. He parked his bike neatly where his father had told him to always park, and marched up to the house as if he too were a visitor to his father's door.

The door was locked.

Michael rang for his mother, and as he waited for her to open, he turned for another look at the old guy across the street. The red plaid flannel arm, cuff turned back a jaunty turn and a half, waved, bottle in hand, a kind of paper-bagged salute.

Michael grinned. His own arm was lifted as the door opened. His father grabbed him by the orange shirtfront and dragged him inside.

***

It was a long, troubled evening inside the Hoodenpyle

281

house on Appaloosa Lane. The sunset, more a slice of dead daffodil than marigold, winked out under cover of lowering clouds. And the wind, such a merry, prankish breeze these last few days, gathered strength enough to topple Michael's red bike off its kickstand, bang the white shutters against the house, and loosen vine maple leaves prematurely gold, plastering them against the sidewalk and front porch—a chorus of pleading hands.

Shifting quarters, the wind blew fistfuls of gray subsoil from the rubble heaps across the way against the Hoodenpyles' west windows, and threw apart the rough plywood shelter the old man had built for himself. Then the rain began—fat, warm drops spotting the dust, pooling into rivulets that formed tributaries and islands as it ran down into the coat-lined nest where the old man slept off his booze. Later, it chilled to a downpour that leaked off his hat and into Michael's red, white and blue Superman bedroom where a defect in the roof flashing, somehow undetected by his father, let in the rain.

More resourceful than he ever would have imagined, Michael tiptoed down the hall for one of the yellow plastic sand buckets he knew were stacked on the back porch. He would set it under the leak, then take his sleeping bag to Melody's room for the night.

As he crossed the hallway, the boy heard above the drone of the TV news his mother's calm voice and his father's, wrathful and petulant. Quietly, he slid open the patio door, padded out for the bucket, surprised by the strength of rain and aware of his grandfather sitting on top of the trash heap across the street. Too far away for lamplight, still he could see the outline of the old man's sodden hat and black overcoat. He could see the miniature marigold fire of a cigarette, and smell its slightly acrid smoke.

"Hi, Grandpa," he whispered. He grabbed the bucket, slipped back into the house, and closed the door.

Marion, in her own way as sensitive as her husband to minute changes in the uneasy atmosphere of their perfect home, felt her son abroad and went to check. Finding a puddle, she began pulling fresh pajamas from Michael's drawer, moving quietly so Martin would not hear—he was so angered by Michael's faults—and took the sheets off the bed.

When Michael returned, she was surprised to find his shoulders were damp, but his pants were dry. Together, Michael and his mother moved the bed, set the bucket, replaced the sheets. As she tucked him in again, he asked, "Mom, why does Dad hate Grandpa?"

Marion sighed. "I don't know that he does, Michael. Go to sleep now. Life will be good again in the morning." She turned toward the door.

"Grandpa was a fighter, wasn't he?" Michael whispered after her. "Mr. Sussman says he was famous, a real barnstormer." His voice sounded eager and proud. Marion wondered if a punchdrunk former fighter might not prove a better hero for her son than Evel Knievel, who seemed bent on a different, more contagious kind of self-destruction.

Perhaps even better, she thought disloyally, than a father so closed in on his own past, so closed off from the world that he could not abide burned steak, imperfectly washed dishes, birds snatching seed from his new lawn, his son's occasional youthful incontinence, his daughter's childish clumsiness, the suspicion that his wife might sometimes think differently than he...never mind the untidy arrival of a father he'd never forgiven for some grave fault he wouldn't, or couldn't, seem to name.

"Good night, Michael. I love you," she whispered, then closed the door.

***

In his bedroom at the back of the Model Home Office, Harvey Sussman found himself unable to fall asleep, thinking about Martin Hoodenpyle and his once-famous old man, Dancing Dutch.

All evening he'd paced between the beer-stocked refrigerator, the recliner in front of the TV, his bed, and the window he kept looking through, knowing perfectly well it was too dark to see anything but needing to look anyway.

It boggled Sussman's mind, thinking one was the son of the other—the father, the grandfather. What could have happened that they should greet one another so? And what the hell could that old man be doing down there on that rubbish heap? What did he want, anyway?

Sussman's feet were cold. Catching a flash of light in the corner of one eye, he sat up one more time in the ruin of his twisted bed, heaved his feet over the side, and in the dark planted one set of toes square in the tinfoil tray left from his TV dinner. There was hot sauce left in it. Kicking and cussing, Sussmann wiped his foot on the rug, hitched up his pajama pants, and sidled up to the uncurtained window. Sure enough, the Hoodenpyles' porch light was on. Was somebody going to let that wet old man in after all?

That would be a relief!

As he turned away from the window, Sussman saw Michael come out onto the porch, snag the yellow bucket and accidentally topple the other one into the yard, where it rolled around mashing his mother's marigolds. The boy went back inside. But before the door closed, did the kid wave? Harv ducked back, afraid he'd be seen. It was then he spied the old man's cigarette glowing in the dark like a single bright eye.

"Aw, Jesus and Mary," he muttered, and began pulling on his clothes.

***

Across the street from his son's new home, Dancing Dutch Hoodenpyle hunkered down among the dirt, rocks, bits of wood, nails, and concrete ends that accumulate on a construction site and with Harv Sussman and a new case of Weinhardt's squatting beside him fell to brooding over his life, his many triumphs in the ring.

Triumphs that others, he told Sussman, including most notably his own wife and only son, had seen as failures. He thought on the filial impiety of that son. "Honor thy father. That's what the Good Book says."

"A man should be proud of his family," Sussman returned, thinking of his own war hero father, his long–dead wife and her wealthy brothers with their no-good sons. Sleeping Jesus, the things you didn't see in this business!

Dutch settled into the rush of the booze. His own father had been an itinerant preacher and sometime Watkins products salesman. Taking young Dutch with him, he made his rounds in a battered Chrysler up and down dirt country roads, stopping in at the primitive homes of housewives who had, at best, like his own mother, linoleum floors and running water, at worst no electricity, no running water, and cracks in the floor wide enough that swept dirt never reached the door.

Out of Dutch's mouth into Sussman's sympathetic ear, the years peeled back easily until, toward the end of the second bottle the old fighter had hidden away in his coat pocket for a rainy day like this one, he began to think once more how his son, then the age of that spindle-shanked kid on the red bike — what was his name? Mike? Michael? — had turned away from him a little more each time he returned home bearing gifts. An autographed glove, a signed bout poster, clippings in which sports columnists spoke of his legendary roundhouse swing, his near misses, his reputation outside the ring.

The boy's mother, he complained to Sussman, was a stiff, unforgiving woman, a devout Methodist. Somewhere along the foggy path of years she died, and the boy went to live with her old-maid aunt in a place it had taken him, Dutch, a long time to find.

What had the boy's life been like, with that old woman? Sussman wondered.

"Books, that's what," Dutch snorted. "Lots of books. But never no sports, sure as hell no boxing or wrestling." That was Fern's wish, he explained, passed on thin-lipped and glaring to her Aunt Heather, he was sure. "But the boy fooled 'em," Dutch hooted, tipping down another beer. "He took up numbers and computers instead of the lawyer's outfit that united female front served up to him with every hard cookie or plate of thin stew."

Grade school, high school, then college — Dutch told how the boy had climbed carefully, soberly, up each rung, never once asking him, his own near-famous father, for advice or the favor of an autograph for his friends.

Sussman listened as Dancing Dutch talked on, telling how gradually, over the years, the road home looped back less often as he saw his son turn from him first in what now seemed as if it might have been shame, then in anger, and finally with contempt. "And now what is he? A goddamned accountant!"

The night wore on, the rain came down, and together on the rubbish heap, the two old men got colder and wetter.

"Come on back to my place," Sussman said for perhaps

the fiftieth time, as together they struggled to replace the plywood shelter, anchor and shore it up. "I got stuff to eat, and dry clothes. And you can have the bed."

But Dutch wouldn't budge.

"What the hell you waiting for?" Sussman demanded, his patience frayed. "That kid of yours'll have you arrested before he'll let you in."

Dutch stuck out his chin and stared over it belligerently, fixing the real estate salesman with a haughty glare, as without looking he opened his third pint, this one the Old Granddad he had given himself when he stumbled across Marty's grown-up path at last.

"I don't recall inviting you to share my shack here," he growled. "You want to go home, go home. No skin off my back."

Old Granddad. Those kids, that skinny boy and his sister, the little blonde dumpling with the high-pitched squeal, they might be calling him that right now, if Marty's wife hadn't shooed them inside like so many chickens and locked the door.

He might even be sitting inside that house with them, he thought, eating a piece of the pie he'd seen his son's wife — what's her name, Mary? — take out of the oven, maybe even topped with a scoop of real ice cream and sided with hot coffee and a tot of good brandy to warm him up, untie the knots. That boy, so much like Marty was, he'd love the stories his Grandpa Dutch could tell.

Still, he reflected, "I can't blame the woman. It appears she's a good mother to those children. A good wife to Marty, too."

In the time he'd been sitting there, watching his son's family, he told Sussman, she'd never been still, always moving about with that fine, firm way she had, picking things up, putting them away, baking, cooking, washing up, speaking quietly with the kids. And they listened. They allowed. She even had a calming influence on Marty.

"A good woman knows how to be useful," Sussman observed.

"If nothing else in the world is right, a person at least ought to be of some use." Dutch raised his voice and hands, moving into a harangue. "People ought to take care of each other, help each other out when they need it."

Like he'd helped his buddy Jim "Socker" Wilson stay out of the hands of those guys from the hospital, he told Sussman. They'd wanted to pin Socker's hands up around him in a white jacket just because he'd busted up a bar that time in Portland.

A man can't be of use when he's locked up in a hospital, he'd told Jim then, feeling the righteousness course through his veins. Socker was just little bit punch-drunk, that was all. He hadn't meant to hurt anyone. Dutch's mind slid away from the fact that his friend Socker had busted up several bars, not just one, the bartenders too. That he had eventually died in a fall from a hotel balcony.

"My head. There's something wrong with my head, Dutchy." He could still hear the Socker's words, still see the way his friend's face had twisted with the effort to figure it all out.

"You going to come home with me or not?" Sussman demanded. Soaked and chilled far beyond his small endurance, he wanted his warm room, his bed, the comforting society of his TV, which required no conversation or agreement, and which did not argue back.

"You want to go home? Go home!" Dutch Hoodenpyle roared at him.

Sussman went.

***

Some time later, the old man woke with a start. The wind had changed, and the rain had stopped. A small light shone a welcoming, perhaps forgiving, gleam somewhere deep inside his son's cozy home.

Such a nightmare, he thought, accusing him of being the real thief of his only son's childhood. Dreams of his son's eyes, now set in his grandson's face, turned sadly, wistfully, toward his father's retreating back. Dreams of his father's face—his own, so many years younger—turned gaily, eagerly, toward the road, the ring, success, freedom.

But freedom from what? Certainly not from bruises, broken bones—his own and others'—cauliflower ears, a booze-soaked brain he was sure moved separately inside his skull each time he shook his head. Had the Socker's been like that?

And the road. It was one of those Mobius strips, where you started out in one place and ended back there again, thinking all the time you'd been headed somewhere else. When he was young, setting out to make his fortune, it had been exciting, driving cars till they broke down, then catching a bus or train, hitching rides, or walking from one ring to another, each scheduled bout a fresh chance at fame.

Mornings, especially, were wonderful on the road. When you passed through a place in the daytime, all you saw were people rushing back and forth, scurrying like so many ants. At night you saw nothing but the mystery of lighted railway stations, crossing lights, the blinking neon Vacancy signs in front of fleabag motels, each room holding a single bed, a stained mattress, a dangling lightbulb, maybe a Gideon bible, if someone hadn't already taken it.

But early mornings, when you were traveling, the world was new. The houses and buildings were there, all right, but somehow you didn't see them. It was the land itself that made itself felt in the first light of day — the land, huge and permanent and somehow tolerant of all this human foolishness.

Once, on the way to a fight in California when he still had a manager, a good car and good clothes — a satin jacket, red with white lapels, and his name, *Dancing Dutch Hoodenpyle*, embroidered on the back — he had stayed the night in a fancy Portland hotel. He'd closed the bar. Then, back in his room, watched old TV movies — one starring Jimmy Cagney, his favorite actor.

Next morning, while it was still quiet and dark, he'd heard a sort of tapping in the bathroom, and he'd known it was Cagney, telling him in some kind of crazy Morse code to stop dancing, stop fighting, give up the ring and the road. Go home.

But he just couldn't do it.

He'd closed himself in that bathroom for hours, practicing Cagney's steps, loving the way the tiled walls and high ceiling sent back the sound, exhilarated nearly out of his mind by his own movement.

He'd gone on to California. It was his one big chance. So were they all.

How could he, true knight of the road, have given life to Marty, this stick-in the-mud son?

But then, there was Socker. After Socker, the road leaned downhill, the Mobius strip came unglued, or twisted, so he never got where he was going, never got back to where he was from either, and finally ended up here on this rubbish heap, useful to no one, not even himself.

Water he was sure was not rain tapdanced down his face, and full of self-pity, Dancing Dutch Hoodenpyle bowed his head on his huddled knees.

Let the damned sky leak down the back of his neck! Let him die of pneumonia! They would, too, damn them all. "My son," he said to himself, the words bitter in his mouth as the taste of dead leaves.

The rain drummed on his plywood roof (dead Cagney signaling him again?) and after a while the old man lifted his head toward the marigold glow of the night light in his son's kitchen.

"Those kids need a granddad," he told himself. It was a revelation!

Then, showered with applause, Dancing Dutch Hoodenpyle rose from his corner, grandly shucked his red satin dressing gown, bowed to Sussman (now sound asleep) and the rest of his audience, lumbered across the street through the strings surrounding his son's new lawn — spread like a green apron in front of his son's magnificent new house — and up the steps to the porch. He lifted the knocker and let it fall once, twice, three times, before Michael opened the door.

"Grandpa Dutch!" the boy shouted, his blue eyes wide. "It's you, isn't it?"

Marion appeared, put her hands on the boy's shoulders, and tried to steer him indoors. "Michael, ssssh!" she said. "It's past your bedtime."

"But Mom," Michael pleaded, "it's Grandpa! He's come home, and he's wet! We *have* to let him come in!"

"Sssssh!" Marion said. "Your father will hear."

"I'll hear what?" Martin demanded. Then he saw his father standing in the door.

What a scene! In rapid succession, Martin orders his wife and children into the house, orders Dutch out, orders him not to darken his (Martin's) door again. Michael shouts "No! No! He's my grandpa!" Melodie claps her hands over her ears and climbs under the table, but Marion refuses to budge. Their mingled shouts and cries escalate in range and volume, and while all that's going on, Michael leads Dutch by the grimy hand into his parents' clean, well-appointed bathroom, supplies him with washcloth, soap, and his dad's biggest, fluffiest towel. "I'll get you some dry clothes," he tells Dutch, and produces a pair of his father's sweats — too long in the leg and much too small around the middle.

Sensing his father's sudden absence, Martin strides toward the bathroom door loudly threatening to eject his father in the altogether, but Michael and Marion bar the way.

"Don't you dare!" Marion blazes. "If you do, I'll...I'll...I'll stop cooking!" Marty stops mid-stride and stares at his wife.

"It's okay, Grandpa," Michael says through the bathroom door, "You're home now. You can sleep in my bed. I'll sleep on the floor. I do it all the time."

***

Snug in his red plaid pajamas, Sussman couldn't resist another look through the window that looked down Appaloosa Lane. The rain had stopped and the moon was up, round and white, surrounded by clouds wispy as pill bottle cotton. The lane was still, bathed in silver light that rendered even the Hoodenpyle residence peaceful.

Through the dining room window, he saw Marion's broad beam bent over the table as she cleared it for dessert. He could almost smell the coffee, the heady scent of fresh peach pie. Beautiful, he thought, how the calm after a storm works to smooth the passions and the passionate.

And the little tykes? Michael stood straight and tall beside his father, his adorable little sister bouncing with excitement in the presence at their family table of Grandpa Dutch. And his mother? She was fairly beaming as she piled the whipped cream high on Dutch's piece of pie.

"Ha!" Sussman guffawed, slapping his flannel knee. Who'd have thought it? The ornery old duffer actually managed to wheedle his way through the door. Yep, Dancing Dutch Hoodenpyle had one more dance in him— not back in the ring, but in the circle of family.

———

Olympia George grew up in a small town, now a sizeable city, where she still lives. She was fortunate to spend part of her childhood in her grandparents' multi-national immigrant farming community. A newspaper reporter/editor for many years, she taught at Pacific Lutheran University, where she earned her MFA in 2007.

FORGET ME NOT

S. M. Kraftchak

Corynn slid to the edge of the hundred-foot cliff on her antique Buzbee 250 hover-cycle, allowed it to settle onto its stand, and grabbed her e-noculars. She swung her leg over the handlebars to scan the valley and distant ridge, knowing the glare of the setting sun behind her would allow the few minutes she needed to verify the landmarks without being seen. She double-checked the note scribbled on her palm and continued to survey the valley end to end before lowering the e-nocs to trust her own eyes. This was obviously the right place, but something felt wrong.

Glancing over her shoulder — some habits let you live long enough for them to become old habits — she lifted the e-nocs and closely examined the quaint little white house, surrounded by neatly trimmed, thick green grass. A solitary hammock chair twisted slowly in an old willow tree at the corner of the empty front porch where two narrow sheets, two pair of panties, a single bra and a calico print dress rippled gently in the evening breeze between the support posts. The front screen door barely hid the foyer, which appeared as still as the yard.

The whole scene was a vivid oasis in the middle of a terracotta-colored, rock-strewn valley with no paths leading to or from the house. Something definitely wasn't right, but this was the first bit of intel on Erik in the two years since he had just up and disappeared within minutes of capture. She trusted her source, but not the intel.

Putting her e-nocs back in the pouch attached to the middle of the handlebars, she ran her fingers through her close-cut hair, stretched, and guided her hover-cycle away from the cliff. Whatever was wrong would have to wait until she could get some sleep and think it through.

***

It hadn't taken long to scramble down the fractured cliff in the gray light of early morning. At that hour, even against the monochrome landscape, deep in shadow occasionally punctuated by a spiny gray-green cactus or ashen tumbleweed, her heather-gray flight suit was less visible to anyone who might be in the oasis. Not that she thought there was anyone there, but why take unnecessary chances?

She had argued with herself half the night about how best to investigate this lead. Stealth would take time she really didn't want to spend on this God-forsaken terra-moon, but boldly walking up to the front door and knocking seemed foolhardy; time or foolhardy, time or foolhardy. As she stepped off the gravel that crunched loudly underfoot onto the soft, silent green grass, she stopped. Everything was as she had seen it from the top of the hill, serene, welcoming, and wrong. Corynn reached to unsnap the peace-tie on the two laser pistols that clung, one to each hip, before calling out.

"Hello? Anyone here?" She watched the hammock chair slowly spin as though someone were turning their back to her, but got no answer. She took two silent steps on the soft grass, glanced behind her and took three more until she stood in the shade of the willow tree.

"I'm Corynn Haslo. I'm a private investigator." This wasn't exactly true, but announcing herself as an agent for the Galactic Research, Intelligence, and Development Agency didn't usually get a very warm welcome. As she

295

waited, breathing through her mouth to be able to hear even the faintest sound, she took four slow rolling steps that brought her to the foot of three white stairs. Her heart leapt when she spotted tiny clusters of bright blue forget-me-nots tucked carefully into the neatly tended garden. Over the years, Erik had left them, like a calling card, whenever he'd finished a job and managed to slip away. Was this a calling card, or a coincidence? With her left hand, she lifted her pistol from her hip and released the safety as she eased it behind her. Carefully, she placed her right foot on the first step.

"Hello? Anyone here? I'm Corynn Haslo, private investigator. I just have a few questions to ask." Four more calculated steps brought her to the screen door. Her eyes traced the outline of the door looking for any of Erik's special gifts before she reached out to ease the door open and stepped in.

The foyer was barely ten-feet square. The hall tree had one Irish driving cap, identical to the one Erik always wore, a closet, a hall heading to the back of the house, and the braided oval rug that protected the shining wooden floor from her dusty boots. Her eyes checked all the corners, knobs, and doorways for cameras or traps and finally examined the floor for any surprises. Nothing.

"Hello. I'm Corynn Haslo, private investigator. Anyone home?" The only sound was a steady tick-tock from the room to her left. She decided to investigate there first.

The parlor, as they would have called it nearly two centuries earlier, was dim, not because the lace sheers obstructed light from the picture window, but because the morning sun came from the back of the house. The room was sparsely furnished. On a five-foot square, worn burgundy rug sat one dark blue upholstered chair across from an identical chair upholstered in white. The seat cushion of the white chair had soft dents from many hours of use. The chairs faced each other, as if having a silent conversation, ignoring the nearby fireplace that held a pile of white ash behind closed glass doors. Next to each chair sat a small table set with a doily and a tea cup. On the table next to the white chair, Corynn spotted pale yellow stains on the doily and lifted the teacup from its saucer to sniff the dried tan remnants. She pulled it away quickly, wrinkling her nose at the bitter smell, most likely a sedative.

She walked over to peek into the teacup next to the blue chair and found it perfectly clean, then turned and scanned the mantel. It should have been full of picture frames with family photos to make this scene more perfect, but held only two electronic picture frames in sleep mode and an old brown wooden clock, the source of the tick-tock.

With a glance over her shoulder that encompassed the rest of the bare room and the closed six-paned glass doors that led into a library, she lifted one frame and pressed the On button. Within moments, a headshot of a blonde-haired girl, with vaguely familiar blue eyes and round cheeks appeared. At the bottom a title appeared, Dryn 6. The next was the same girl, Dryn 9, except her hair was shoulder length, and her face was slightly older and thinner, but her eyes were missing the sparkle of the first. In the next picture, Dryn 12, her hair was nearly to her elbows.

Corynn gasped when the last picture loaded, Dryn 15. The girl's hair had been cut short like a man's, her face was gaunt with dark circles under her eyes and her lips pressed tightly together. Corynn rotated back to the first picture and set the frame back on the mantel, where had she seen those eyes before?

Turning on the second frame, she glanced quickly

around the room, pressing her lips together. It was Erik Lancer, the way she had first seen him in his dossier. His toothy smile was wide, and eyes as blue as the girl's stared out at Corynn. She forwarded to the next photo. This man she had seen many times. Clean cut with a blond swirling front cowlick and an expression that meant business. The third photo, though he still had a smile and that familiar look in his eyes, showed a tinge of gray at his temples, and the slack set of his jaw revealed how tired he had become. Advancing to the next picture, she nearly dropped the frame. Erik sat stiff and tall on a stool with his hands on his knees, the corners of his mouth turned slightly down, his eyes brimming with tears, and a hand emerging from out-of-frame pressing a laser pistol to his head. Corynn forwarded to the next photo, half expecting it to be a picture of a dead man, but instead there was a message. 'Everything I do...Forget me not.'

The clock's second hand ticked off the seconds as Corynn clicked through details in her mind. Who was the message to, and who was it from? What did it mean? Why were these pictures here? She guessed by the likeness, that Dryn was Erik's daughter. Corynn's mind swirled with details she tried to connect.

She knew Erik's first mission. She'd never forget, much less forgive him. She'd understood every mission since, and even had gotten ahead of him before he disappeared. And then there was the eerie feeling of some connection when, time after time as she hunted him mercilessly, he had never once tried to kill her. It wasn't for lack of opportunity. He always waited just long enough to make eye contact with her from a distance, offer up a bouquet of forget-me-nots, and then, having accomplished his mission, he escaped with a smile. Not even the two times she managed to foil his plans did he try to harm her, although his smile had been smudged with anger, and he'd slammed the bouquet to the ground.

Corynn placed the frame with the message on it back on the mantel. There had to be something more here. She glanced at the library and shook her head. She'd come back to the library if necessary, but since she was sure now that Erik wanted her to find him through his connection with his daughter, she'd check out Dryn's room first. She paused to consider the girl's picture. If this is where his daughter had been kept, where was she now?

Returning to the foyer, Corynn followed the hall to the stairs at the back of the house. She peered into the kitchen, which was perfectly neat, except for two plates in the dish drainer next to the sink. Turning her attention overhead, she cautiously peered up the stairs and then ascended. On the second floor, ceilings seemed lower, almost squeezed under the roof. The front bedroom door was open, and it was easy to see how the front wall sloped steeply, interrupted only by a dormer window with neat lace curtains. The same sparse tidiness she'd found downstairs continued upstairs. A simple blue bedspread covered a single bed. A round metal alarm clock with two bells waiting to ring sat motionless atop a single chest of drawers. Corynn wasn't sure whose room this was, but knew it wasn't the room she was looking for, so she followed the railing around the stairwell to a door that was barely ajar with a simple paper sign written in crayon and thumbtacked to the door, 'Keep Out'.

Out of habit, Corynn scanned the doorframe and peered inside as much as possible before shoving the door open with one finger. She paused and then entered. It was everything she expected from a girl's room: pink walls with one or two idol posters; a frilly pink-flowered single canopy and bedspread; an assortment of large and small stuffed animals neatly arranged on the bed; shelves of knick-knacks; a desk with an assortment of textbooks, an oil lamp and a pencil cup. Behind the door was a double-wide dresser with a small flowered jewelry box centered in front of a full-width mirror surrounded by an assortment of perfumes and lotions.

Corynn went to the knick-knacks first, trinkets from around the galaxy. Cataloging them in her mind, she wasn't sure how she felt when she realized there was one from each place she had encountered Erik, except the last one, when he disappeared. She wandered over to the desk and scanned the stand of books sandwiched between two bronze dragon bookends. With raised eyebrows, she gently pushed each book to be sure it was real: geometry, literature, galactic history, astrophysics, and a cookbook. Unsure what she was looking for, but going on instinct, Corynn moved to the dresser.

The Battenberg lace dresser scarf, pale yellow with age, showed one or two white half-moons and a narrow sliver where the bottles and the jewelry box had prevented discoloration. Before Corynn pushed the door closed to look behind the dresser, she noticed the small carpet in the center of the room was puckered where the dresser legs might have pushed against it when pulled out. Peering into the narrow space between the mirror and the wall, she saw nothing obvious, but noticed the attachments to the uprights holding the mirror above the dresser were worn enough to make the connection slightly loose. With reasonable care, Corynn transferred the bottles and jewelry box to the desk, pulled the dresser to the edge of the rug and flipped the mirror. The smooth dull gray back of the mirror stymied her. She humphed, stepped back to get a wider perspective, and then sat on the end of the bed.

As soon as she settled, a heads-up display winked to life. A map of the Khyrreon galaxy appeared in front of the gray mirror back. Corynn leaned forward to examine the several dozen news snippets scattered over the map, noting dates and places. A red line stringing each square like a bead on a looping necklace draped across the galaxy's shoulders. When the line finally pierced the tiny terra-moon she was currently on, she stood with surprise, and the heads up display disappeared. She immediately sat, re-activating the display, and her eyes jumped back to the beginning.

Dating back nearly nine years, the first headline was about overcrowding on Galaxy Prime and how it had led to an unfortunate mass suicide. Corynn growled at the News Service's twisted truth. She remembered this tragedy. It had taken her sister, Adryann. Next to the article was a small blue dot. Corynn tapped the dot and a handwritten note with two distinct styles appeared. The top one said, "My hands are soiled. My soul is robbed to pay my heart," and below it in a more childish hand, "There had to be another way!" As she read each successive news clip and accompanying note, she recognized the missions she had tried to prevent Erik from completing. Her mouth grew wide with dismay at the apparently strained conversation between father and daughter. Finally, after reading the last snippet from two years ago, she read the comment. The upper message read "SCROLL" and the lower hand she'd come to assume was Dryn's read "I will not forget." Corynn paused to consider the change in tone, then allowed her eye to follow the line past the tiny terra-moon she was on, where there was no snippet or comment, back to Galactic Prime, completing the circuitous route at the first snippet.

Corynn scowled as she looked between the last message and the first snippet that listed the victims. Why did the line come back to the beginning? She glanced back at the last message, SCROLL, and then looked at the first snippet and flicked her finger to scroll through the list. She paused partway through to notice her sister's name wasn't in its alphabetical place and then finished scrolling to the bottom. There at the end of the list was her sister's name with a flashing blue dot next to it. When she tapped the dot, a tiny square appeared, which she pinched to expand, and was unable to suppress a yelp of dismay. She knew the face, but was baffled by the writing in red below, across the bottom of the scanned photograph: 'Mom'.

She stared at her deceased sister's face and her eyes welled with tears. Did this mean Erik's daughter was—? No, it couldn't be. Why would he have killed her if she...? How could she have not known Adryann had been pregnant? Corynn buried her face in her hands to hide from the memory of that horrible argument over auralink. Corynn had begged Adryann to turn on the video so she could see her because she had sounded so strange and kept avoiding questions. Finally Corynn had lost her temper and refused to talk anymore unless her sister turned on the video. Adryann begged her to understand, but when she got nothing but silence, she'd shouted good-bye and disconnected. Corynn tried reconnecting, but the signal wouldn't go through. It was nearly four years before she heard from Adryann again, and then she sounded more desperate, and twice as cryptic: something about trouble, and needing to keep something safe. Two days later, she'd read her sister's obituary on a mission report and agreed to hunt down the maniac who had killed so many people.

Corynn wiped her eyes and was about to stand when she noticed something strange about the data code in the bottom right hand corner of the picture. GD22120704GPI12108. The date was yesterday, followed by a string of letters and numbers that didn't belong there. With a finger, she hid the date and suddenly recognized the rest as a location. Corynn stood to close the display. She wasn't sure who she would find at the end of the red line, but whoever it was, she'd make sure she got some answers.

***

Corynn entered the elevator and reached to slide her card into the security slot, when a man called out, trotted to the door, and extended his arm to prevent the doors from closing. The doors re-opened and he stood in the threshold. Corynn assumed parade rest but remained tense, ready for anything.

"Commander Haslo, we weren't expecting you for another six days."

Corynn maintained a stoic expression and bobbed her head as a greeting to the man. "Director Pacquin, good to see you, too."

"Did you have any luck?"

"With what, Sir?" Corynn's brow creased momentarily.

"I heard you had an excursion to the outer edge?"

Corynn watched the man's pupils dilate and contract. She almost smiled at the telltale sign of lying, but maintained her measured expression.

"Oh, you know the trail has been cold for two years. It was a re-hash of everything — just an abandoned squat."

"Sorry to hear that. What brings you here so early?"

Corynn spotted a drop of sweat meandering down from behind his ear. It's sixty-five degrees in here. He shouldn't be sweating. He's stalling. Why? What does he know? "Oh, just a personal matter I wanted to see Dr. Sita about."

"Nothing serious, I hope? Can't have our top agent—"

"Oh, please, Sir, nothing earth-shattering, but if you don't mind, I'm going to be late for my appointment," Corynn snapped to attention and bobbed her head in lieu of a salute, which kept her hands near her weapons. Her smile was pleasant but held secret satisfaction at making the man squirm.

"Very well, report to my office immediately after your appointment," he said stepping back.

"Of course, Sir," she said and pushed the Close Door button. She slipped her security card into the slot. Every floor above six at the Galactic Prime Infirmary required clearance. She nearly pressed twelve, but first pressed eight, then ten, and finally twelve. She was pretty sure from his demeanor that Pacquin would be watching to see which floor she chose. Tapping her card against her thumb, she watched the numbers slowly climb. Different scenarios had mingled in her mind, and multiplied when she added into the mix the Director's apparent surprise at her presence. She contemplated getting off at eight and walking up but decided that would take too long, so she pressed the Door Close button on floors eight and ten as soon as the doors opened. When the doors finally opened on twelve, she paused, looked out each side of the doors, and quickly exited. Finding room 108 immediately to her left, she slipped into the room.

The privacy curtain was drawn, and a heart monitor beeped slow and steady somewhere behind it. Corynn squatted to peek under the curtain—no feet—then eased around it to find Erik's daughter in the bed, hooked to an IV and heart monitor. A bouquet of forget-me-nots sat on her side table. Checking the IV and the other smaller bag feeding into it, she found Dryn was being sedated. With a sigh of exasperation, Corynn tipped her head to examine the teenager's face and was surprised by how much she looked like her sister, Adryann.

"Tell me who you are right now or I'll call security," the girl whispered as she slowly opened her eyes.

Corynn stepped back and half drew her weapon as her eyes darted around the room.

"Last chance," Dryn said.

"I'm looking for your father, Erik."

"Lots of people are looking for my father. Who are you and what do you want with him?"

"I'm...someone who has been looking for him for a long time. I'm not here to hurt you. I'm here for answers. Why aren't you asleep?"

"I've folded the IV line to slow the drip. I can't stop it, but I can almost keep my wits about me."

Corynn reached up, pulled the small bag connection from the IV and let it drip onto the floor. "There, that should help."

"Thank you. Now would you mind telling me who you are?"

Corynn pressed her lips together and then pointed to the small bouquet of forget-me-nots. "They were my sister's favorites."

"My mother's too...you know it wasn't his fault." With an audible sigh of relief, Dryn brought both hands out from under the covers, laid a pistol on her stomach, then rearranged the IV line so it unfolded. "My father said you would come."

"Your father was here? How did he know I'd come here?"

"Yeah. I escaped Terra-moon 327 and found him here.

You can find out almost anything when you're a hack genius."

"Then why are you still here?"

"We have a plan."

"To what, get rid of me so I quit following him?"

Dryn shook her head. "You don't think you're here by accident, do you?"

"I followed a lead."

"A lead my father left for you on Terra-moon 327, how do you think you got there?"

"I had a lead from a reliable source..."

"Dad is good at planting signposts. He says it wasn't too hard to get information into the right hands. You know we don't have much time until they figure out you're here."

"My boss already knows. He saw me enter the elevator."

Dryn groaned. "Then you need to get out of here, immediately. Go to the far end of the hall—"

"Wait a minute, how do I know you're not setting me up?"

"You won't, until you meet my father, and then he can explain everything. Now are you ready to put an end to all this and avenge your sister?"

Corynn nodded.

"Good, put the sedative back in my IV and listen closely."

***

Corynn stood outside the stairwell door at the far end of the hall, pushed the door open a crack, and listened. A team of soldiers was coming up, maybe two floors below. Quietly, she entered the stairwell staying close to the wall and took two stairs at a time until she reached the fourteenth floor. There she exited and eased into the laundry next door, grabbed a pair of scrub pants to slide over her jumpsuit, and slipped on a white coat, unzipping her collar and laying it back underneath the buttoned-up coat. She paused to listen at the door, then slid a surgical cap over her hair and draped a mask around her neck before hurrying down the hall. When she heard the elevator ding, she ducked into a room, grabbed the nearest patient chart, and continued on down the hall, examining the chart all the way into the elevator. A two-man team stepped out. "Be careful not to shoot the patients," she said to them just before the door closed.

Corynn was impressed with the instructions Erik had left with Dryn, all carefully thought out. It was highly likely they'd be looking for her on the secure floors, so she got off on the third, the public maternity, and walked halfway down the hall and caught the laundry elevator the rest of the way down to the basement. From there she walked through the sky-tube, a busy clear glass walkway that connected the new and old GPI wings, and then up and out the old wing's unsecured front doors. She snatched her hat and mask off, pocketed them as she scanned the busy plaza, and began walking to her right.

Several minutes later a man behind her asked, "Do you like hibiscus flowers?"

Out of habit, she slowed a half step and without looking around said, "I prefer forget-me-nots."

"Forget-me-nots are very special, but Yen Cho's makes a lovely cup of hibiscus tea and is a quiet place for conversation. Ask for Aura Lee. She'll take good care of you."

When she paused at a crosswalk, she expected to find Erik at her elbow but turned to find a pair of school girls.

Ten minutes later, Corynn entered the establishment called Yen Cho's. A slender, dark–skinned woman dressed in a kimono greeted her with a smile. "Good afternoon, and welcome. How may I help you?"

"I was told to ask for Aura Lee?"

"Ah, yes, this way please."

Corynn surveyed the room as she followed the young woman. The pale spotlights bathed each table in the replica ancient twentieth century Japanese restaurant. She scrutinized the two couples seated at one small grill, waiting for their food to be prepared the old-fashioned way, and figured they were just what they seemed. "Here you are," the woman said holding her hand out to a very private booth with a small sprig of forget-me-nots sitting in the spotlight on the table. "Would you like a cup of hibiscus tea?"

Corynn gave one last look around and nodded to the woman. "Yes, thank you," she said, sliding into the booth far enough so she could see the entrance. She picked up the flowers, twirled them through her fingers and sniffed their delicate scent, remembering when she and her sister had filled each other's hair with forget-me-nots.

"It wasn't my fault, you know." A man's quiet voice interrupted Corynn's reminiscing.

When she looked up, she was face to face with her nemesis of the past seven years. He slid two delicate tea cups filled with steaming liquid onto the table before joining her in the booth. Corynn narrowed her eyes at the man who had killed her sister. "I'm here. What is stopping me from shooting you this time?"

"Your need to know the truth." The light above the table reflected in just the right way, so she could see Erik's blue eyes staring at her, unflinching.

"So what lies do you have this time?"

"I'd never have hurt Adryann. She was the love of my

life and the mother of my daughter."

"Like you didn't mean to kill the 233 other innocents? Poison is rather deliberate. I should shoot you where you sit for everything you've done."

"I didn't do it." Erik placed his hands flat on the table on either side of the teacup.

"Like hell you didn't. It had the same signature of every single job you've ever pulled and then some. I read all the gruesome details."

"I said I didn't do it." Erik's fingers curled slightly as if he was trying to dig his fingertips into the table.

"Why? Why didn't you at least get Adryann out first? Did you enjoy using a slow, painful poison?"

"It wasn't me," he whispered as tears rolled down his cheeks.

"They found your DNA at the scene on the bottle of poison!" Corynn's voice was a harsh whisper, barely escaping her clenched teeth.

Erik's jaw jutted out just before he spoke. "And who handed you that pack of lies in a dossier folder? A man you trust so completely that you're sitting here with me instead of turning me over to him?"

Corynn bit her lower lip.

"What? No more self-righteous comebacks? No more threats to shoot me? Are you ready for the truth?"

Corynn swiped at her own cheek and then nodded as the corners of her mouth pulled down.

"Interstellar Common Rights needed someone with my expertise to do their dirty work and my name appeared at the top of their list. Sure I met with ICR. The money was good. It would have set us up for the rest of our lives and gotten me out of the game...given me time with my daughter. But when they told me what the job was, I told them to go to hell and walked out."

"Just like that."

"Yes, just like that. They needed a whole bushel of martyrs and I wasn't willing to make them. I went home to tell Adryann we needed to leave, and found her in tears. While I was at the interview, they had taken our daughter and told Adryann that if I didn't take the job, they'd kill Dryn."

"So you took the job."

"No! While I was demanding my daughter, they poisoned my whole residential block and told me I should be more careful, or I'd find myself turned over to the authorities for domestic abuse and terrorism. And I'd never see my daughter again. What choice did I have?"

Corynn watched Erik lower his head. Only his gasps for air betrayed his sobs. She waited patiently until his breathing eased and then asked, "How long did she live at the white house on Terra-moon 327?"

"Most of the past eight years, she told me. I spent five or more hours every night searching the galactic net for any remote clue of her. I'd receive a video of her talking to me each time I completed a job, but I was never permitted to keep it. I only got the still photos you saw on the mantel. Once I thought she was old enough to know the truth, I managed to get a secret message to her through a soft-hearted administrative assistant. They found out about the message, the man disappeared, and I was brought in for a special photo, the one I'm sure you saw of me. Life changed for both of us after that."

Erik picked up the forget-me-nots and twirled them between his fingers. "Dryn began planning to escape in earnest. They underestimated her from the start. They had assigned her simple caretakers who never thought to question what she was studying on the galactic net besides her assigned lessons. She finally got a message to me two years ago. I managed to disappear and finally followed it to find her. I brought her here under an assumed identity. But when it became apparent that to be free, we needed to take down the real motivator behind ICR's targets, I knew we had to have your help."

"What do you expect me to do, join your little family reunion and forget about everything you've done?"

"I'm not asking your forgiveness for anything. I know why I did it and would gladly pay twice the price to keep my daughter safe, but you have a chance to help me stop this and face the man who gave the word to kill your sister. I know who my handler is."

"So why not kill him and be done with it?"

"He's the only one who can prove I didn't kill those 233 people and that all the other jobs I've done, which you have documented so nicely, were done under duress to keep my daughter alive."

Corynn watched Erik's bloodshot, blue eyes, stare into hers without flinching. "And who is this monster?"

***

Corynn turned toward the graffiti-covered wall in an alley ten minutes' walk from the GPI as she activated her auralink. She'd received her assignments numerous times in that discreet location.

"Galactic Prime Intelligence, Research and Development Agency, how may I direct your call?"

"Director Pacquin, please."

"One moment please. I'll see if he's available, Commander Haslo."

Pacquin was absurdly cheery. "Commander Haslo. How was your appointment? I thought you were instructed to come to my office when you were done?"

"Director, I'm sorry for the inconvenience, but I came across an unexpected lead. I finally captured Lancer, but given his proclivity for slipping away, I don't want to risk transport in single custody. Can you arrange for a collection team?"

"Excellent work, Haslo. Stay put and keep your eye on that bastard. I'll personally bring a team to you in ten minutes."

"Thank you, Sir. I look forward to seeing you. Haslo, out," Corynn grabbed the comm-orb out of the air in front of her before turning to face Erik. "He's on his way. What are you going to do if he brings a team?"

Erik smiled. "You aren't really that naïve, are you?"

***

The click of Pacquin's boots in the smooth cement alley slowed as he approached the end. When he tossed a small square over his shoulder, a blue wall of light winked across the alley and then disappeared. He took two more steps and stopped. "Commander Haslo?"

Corynn stepped out from behind a stack of abandoned metal shipping crates. "Director. I'm so glad you've come. Where's the team?"

Pacquin tossed his head backward, gave a great belly laugh, and stood with his hands behind his back. "So you've finally captured Lancer? How long have you been following him?"

Corynn's brow creased as she answered. "Seven years, Sir, not including the two years he went to ground."

"Frankly I was surprised at how persistent you were." Pacquin smiled and surreptitiously glanced around the alley.

"I had a reason to be, Sir."

"Oh, because he kept bruising your professional pride by slipping away at the last minute?"

"No, Sir. When he murdered those 233 people and made it look like a suicide, he killed my sister."

Pacquin's smile faded. "Wow! That was a bit of an oversight."

"According to evidence, it wasn't Lancer at all, Sir."

"Who gave you that load of malarkey?"

"Actually, Sir, you inadvertently gave it to me. I found quite a bit of evidence on Terra-moon 327. There was a nice neat trail from the outer edge right back here to the GPI. I didn't think too much about it until you got the sweats when you saw me back early. And then — imagine that — I found Lancer's daughter, who was kidnapped nine years ago, just before the supposed suicide deaths, right where I'd never find her. Once I pulled her sedative, she actually had quite a lot to say, which will be easy to corroborate with my case files and prove that you, Sir, are Erik Lancer's handler."

"That's preposterous! She'd say anything to get time with her father. The man works for Interstellar Common Rights."

"Huh, that's strange," Corynn pulled her weapon and pointed it at Pacquin. "Neither Dryn's existence nor Erik's employer are mentioned anywhere in his dossier or my case reports. Furthermore, Erik doesn't even appear by name in their data, but you do."

"Don't be ridiculous, Haslo. You and I both work for Galactic Intelligence and Research here on Prime. I've got all the evidence we need to put this troublemaker and his daughter to rest once and for all. After we turn him over to the collector team, I'll debrief you and show you your oversight."

"Not a chance," Erik said and stepped out from behind a shipping crate, his weapon leveled at Pacquin. "I'm not going to give you the opportunity to cover up your dirty business like a cat and walk away. I've got the proof and with Commander Haslo here corroborating everything, I'll finally be free of the ICR. And now that my daughter is safe, I'll make you pay for killing my wife."

Pacquin smiled and tilted his head. "What makes you think your daughter is safe? I *let* Haslo here visit her in GPI-12-108. How else could I get her to finally meet with you and end your infernal investigation of my office? If I don't report back to GPI in thirty minutes, they'll give your daughter the same cocktail I personally gave your wife. So, now do you shoot me and sacrifice your daughter or turn yourself in and trust yourself to my mercy?"

Erik took a step forward and activated the laser sight on his pistol. "You don't think I'm dumb enough to leave Dryn alone with you around? While you were busy hunting Haslo, I slipped her out the front door."

Dryn, wrapped in a blanket, stepped out from behind the shipping crate.

Pacquin held his hands out to his sides, staring at the girl with a pinched frown. "What do you want? I can give you anything...a new ID...credits to go anywhere in the universe."

"I don't want anything from you. I want you dead." Erik's pistol and Corynn's pistols flared at the same time, and Pacquin fell backward. His body shimmied in the electrical current that slowly smoldered his hair and clothes.

"So what do we do with him?" Corynn asked as she deactivated the shield wall square, allowing Pacquin's body to fall to the ground.

Dryn looked down at the smoldering corpse. "Leave him here. I've sent a copy of his files to the Inspector Central — after clarifying them, of course. I've cleared both your records, and expunged all the evidence he was twisting to keep you two playing cat and mouse while doing his dirty work. I also updated all the back pay that was withheld for the past nine years, calculated lost pay from my mother, and calculated a salary for myself."

Dryn rocked between her heels and toes, and grinned at her father and aunt. "I'm pretty sure we can afford a family vacation. I know this cozy little out of the way place...known to very few. It will need some renovation if we're all going to stay there very long, but it feels like home."

———

S. M. Kraftchak spends most of her time with dragons, elves, and aliens, yet still enjoys sunrise on the beach, sunset in the mountains and portraying Elizabeth Tudor. She has three awesome daughters, two dogs, and one cat. Her husband is her best friend, harshest critic and most fervent supporter. Writing is her passion.

YOU ARE A GARDEN

Jane Buchan

She was a small woman, maybe five one in her dress pumps, good shoes, Clarks or Air Steps, the heels sturdy and eerily silent on the school's terrazzo floors. Tiny of proportion, she wore tailored clothes small enough to come from any teen department although the crisp white blouses with the Peter Pan collars and the reversible skirts, knee-length and meticulously pressed, more likely came from Windsor's Scotch Wool Shop.

The guys in our class called her The Body, once so loud she crimsoned to the roots of her dark, meticulously styled hair. She looked a perennial forty when she taught us, but she was likely older. Before she died of cancer a few years after our graduation, she'd taught English to hundreds of post-war, anxiety-ridden adolescents ground down in the crucible of fifties dichotomies. Without her unfailing belief in the healing qualities of poetry and drama and prose, of Bradstreet and Dickinson, Keats and Shelley, of Shakespeare, Milton, and George Eliot, we would have perished spiritually, but this is a recent insight.

After having a gym teacher teach us English in grades nine and ten, we were unprepared for her passion for literature in third year. When she discovered Danny Wassily asleep after she'd played the second of four thirty-threes that crackled out Michael Redgrave's reading of *Silas Marner*, she removed the needle and her glasses, pausing to rub the bridge of her nose while the student behind Danny, it might have been Meredith Truro or maybe Darlene Ackermann, subtly prodded him awake. He sat up, his face sheepish. Collectively we cast off the torpor of Great Lakes' May humidity and sat forward, anticipating what was to come.

She turned off the record player as she had turned off the overhead lights before playing the recording, with an intention that made us feel the electricity generated by Niagara Falls was now free to flow elsewhere. She shared with us a perpetual connection to the larger world so that when we were in her classroom, we were always many other places simultaneously. Her favourite questions required that we imagine what historical events informed the play or novel or poem or essay currently under study. Her questions made us fall in love with her, for they pulled from deep inside us information we didn't know we possessed. She made us feel like orphaned royalty marking time until the absolute truth of our nobility manifested. She was brilliant, homely, and, despite her blushes, indifferent to our opinions of her.

The day Danny fell asleep in class, she personalized her message to us. Without rancour or disparagement, she turned her full attention upon our sleepy classmate and began her benediction. 'Although you don't know it, Mr. Wassily, you are a garden,' she began. 'Just now you are doubtful that George Eliot's story might become fertilizer for the life you yearn for beyond these walls. Don't be fooled by the appearance of your healthy body or the agility of your restless mind. One day, despite your strengths, you, like Silas, may be cast out from your community, not because of any personal flaw, but because life is not and never has been fair. After such tragedy, it may happen that you too will lose whatever gold you substituted for lost love and trust and become sorrowful beyond enduring. And when your sorrow has sufficiently prepared you, your true heart's desire may come to fill your emptiness. If this happens, Mr. Wassily, you will be one of the truly blessed, for you will live out your days in contentment, no matter what else may befall you."

During her quiet speech, the room gathered itself around us in a shadowy dampness that worked on our minds and bodies simultaneously. The shock of hearing this small patient woman's belief in one of our own touched us as nothing had up to that moment. We sat silent, alert, on the cusp of some great knowing.

Danny Wassily wasn't my best friend, but we liked each other after we were jilted in quick succession by Maria Tobias earlier that year. I knew he worked two jobs, one after school and one on the weekends. His after-school job at a machine shop required him to unload and shelve parts and haul scrap. On weekends at the local roller rink, he was the Nureyev of cement, giving private and group lessons when he wasn't rescuing the faltering during social skating. He played football for the school, as I did, and his football prowess fed a certain swaggering obnoxiousness that was evident everywhere except in our English classroom. As she spoke to Danny, he tilted his head toward his battered classics edition. I don't think I was the only one who thought he might cry.

I didn't know it then, but I know now that Danny Wassily awoke that day for me, for all of us. Back then most of us couldn't articulate the damning nature of our everyday lives. We were told we were lucky to be alive, that all of life was before us, that we could earn whatever we wanted in life, cars, homes, boats, any plaything we could imagine. We weren't using the word then, but we were urged by television and advertising generally to consume every new and shiny thing. Sandwiched in between these urgings were images of bodies in pits, of mushroom clouds, of empty-eyed, sunburned soldiers coming back from far-off jungles and tainting every gleaming car and appliance with the stench of falsity.

No one I knew was talking about this stench. Perhaps we weren't capable of recognizing it because it had always been there. We had been born into carnage and its aftermath. Whatever good had come to us as a people had come to us because of this carnage. As we jived into the sixties and that decade's openly rebellious attitude to the old order, religious fanatics likened our times to Sodom and Gomorrah, predicting the second coming and the end of the world. But at home, drugged by thoughts of more and more money, our parents pretended educating us would bring us good jobs and the ability to buy everything that would make the awful stench worthwhile.

On the day of Danny's awakening, our lives were broken open by our teacher's simple words. We all smelled the carnage those new cars depended on. That day, although we couldn't see it yet, the worst we human beings were capable of circled our dusky classroom but was held at bay by her image of Danny as a garden. She said it clearly. Danny Wassily had the ability to find meaning in *life*, that green wild force that took back parking lots when they weren't meticulously tended by the cement mixers.

When she finished delivering her quiet promise, she turned on the old record player and placed the needle on the third record. Michael Redgrave resumed George Eliot's story. Our eyes found the place in the narrative in our battered texts. And Danny Wassily remained awake for the rest of the period, perhaps for the rest of his life. It wasn't a long one.

It's been decades since I first recalled Danny's encounter with truth, at the Top Hat Tavern after leaving his graveside at Heavenly Rest. After the priest's few comfortless words, his mother and father thanked me far too effusively for coming. Their desperate gratitude drove me to my favourite bar stool, my confessional. I was the only one at the funeral from our high-school graduating class.

I didn't tell his parents that he'd stopped me for speeding just three weeks before he shot himself. I wish I had, but I somehow couldn't bring myself to say that he'd asked after my wife and kids and told me how he read my column in the *Star*. I didn't tell them that we both remembered what she'd said to him that day, how he'd looked away when he repeated her words, toward the north, as if he might be able to see the river through the apartment building that squatted on the street where he'd pulled me over.

Danny Wassily wasn't teaching skating anymore. I know because I asked him what he did when he wasn't being a cop. He told me, without any prompting, that he'd shot and killed his first suspect a few months after he'd hit the streets, a young black kid who'd allegedly robbed a jewellery store and was fleeing the scene of the crime. The boy was fourteen. Danny told me about his first murder as he was bending over my car, looking into my back window at the baseball gloves and skates littering the back seat, his ticket book in his hands, a stubby bouquet.

I asked him why he decided to be a cop, because I couldn't think of anything else I could ask that would help him hold back his emotions. He laughed and said he had the body for it. I knew what he meant. He was tall, strong, big-shouldered. He was a line-backer with amazing skater's legs. I told him about the Eric Nesterenko film I'd seen, an NFB doc about the hockey player's passion for skating. He said, 'Oh, yeah, Nesterenko. He was a drunk for a while, too.'

I have two sons. At the time I am remembering, in-lines were the new thing and both boys loved to skate with me on the trails that run from the park to the bridge. We skated in the early mornings, before the joggers and tai chi groups crowded the river front. Usually Michael stopped to talk to the Vietnamese man who gave him his first lure. It was a prize he wore in his Detroit Tiger's baseball cap. He had his mother stitch the lure in after he'd given the cap its final trampling. My younger son, Marcel, didn't talk to anyone at the river. His eyes were on the water, on the gulls, while his heart was tuned to the vibrations the sirens made on the other side of the river as they coursed up and down the John Lodge or Woodward Avenue. Unlike Michael, Marcel was born knowing he was a garden. Danny Wassily would have understood this difference between my sons.

That afternoon at the bar, after Danny's funeral, the Top Hat filled with men and women who'd settled for money instead of meaning. I remember thinking that if I had another beer or two I would be drunk enough to tell Danny's story to anyone brave enough to sit next to me at the bar. From the moment I sat down, Edwin, the barkeep, declined to meet my eyes. He was uncannily aware of sorrow and determined to keep it at arm's length. I'd noticed this on the many occasions he kept his distance from certain customers. The slant of their shoulders and the fierceness of their smiles said everything he needed to know.

About then I began to think of the column I was to

deliver to my editor by eleven that night. I had written drunk in the past. I'm not bragging about this, but I still accept it as an occupational hazard, the way I did then. I think Danny would like my pragmatism. Or at least understand it. I called home, told Eva I was going to go in to work to write. She put the boys on. Michael asked if I was all right. He'd taken down my yearbook to muse over the pictures of Danny Wassily just before I left for the funeral that afternoon. Marcel didn't want to see the photos of the young football player but when I called, asked if the casket had been open, if I'd seen the place where the bullet pierced Danny's temple. I told him no and received his sigh of relief as the gift it was meant to be.

At the *Star*, the night editor was talking on the phone and shut her door when she saw me come in. She was a good writer and better editor, but she panicked when she thought she was about to be scooped. My column distressed her. I sometimes thought I knew why but was frequently wrong about her motivations and over the years of our association suppressed my urges to speculate about her. We are both the better for this act of kindness. That night I sat in the smoky newsroom imagining tears on Danny Wassily's *Silas Marner* pages. I wished I could talk with my editor about Danny.

A friend died, I began that column, by his own hand. It's happening to too many of us these days.

I ripped the paper from my typewriter and placed it face down on my desk.

A friend died, I began again, a friend who learned in third form that he was a garden. The person who told him this was a small woman, perennially forty, and devoted to our spiritual lives.

I read this sentence, suddenly moved by its truth. A

small plain woman told us who we were and predicted, thanks to George Eliot, the possibility of a future worth living. Perhaps Danny Wassily shot himself because he felt this possibility slipping away.

I cried for a while, as drunks do, and then thought of Eva. She'd planted flowers and shrubs where the front lawn used to be, a radical move in those times. To drive the more upwardly mobile of our neighbours mad, she'd sown in a few beefsteak tomatoes and stalks of corn. She hated tidiness, hung bird feeders everywhere, refused to use pesticides, and was one of the first to campaign for others to abandon all poisons and go natural. She was a teacher of high school English. Like our younger son, Marcel, she was born knowing she was a garden.

That night, I called home a second time. When she answered, I could only cry. She didn't say anything except my name. At the end of my long lament she said, 'Come home, Jack. Put it all into words and come home.'

I began again. "I had a teacher who loved *Silas Marner*. She once told Danny Wassily, 'You are a garden. Just now you are asleep in the sun and George Eliot's story seems unlikely fertilizer. But one day you may be cast out unfairly and laid low, because life is not fair. And afterward, you may lose your gold, just as Silas loses his. You may, after all these losses, become deeply sorrowful. And when your sorrow has sufficiently prepared you, the true thing, your heart's desire, may come to fill your emptiness. If this happens, you will be one of the truly blessed, for you will live out your days in contentment, no matter what else happens to you. This possibility of deep joy exists for you because George Eliot's story will, if you open to it, nurture this seed in you.'"

Many years have passed since Danny's death. A long

time ago, I had a friend. He was a man who went to a place of deep sorrow, but whose heart's desire didn't come to fill his emptiness. It's happening to too many of us these days. I think of the boys across the river still signing up for Iraq.

Marcel was the first to read that column the morning following Danny's funeral. His grave eyes filled and he went out to the back garden to sit with Pooch, his best friend at the time. Pooch knew everything, as all black labs did and do. Pooch was losing his battle with cancer and hobbled about on three legs when he wasn't sitting or lying in Eva's violets. Marcel never said, as Michael frequently did, that life is not fair. Marcel was born with his knowledge of loss already fully developed.

The night my younger son was born, Eva and I fought so bitterly that I broke her jaw and she called 911 to prevent me from throwing myself off our balcony. Michael was staying with his grandparents across town. Up to that point, everyone in the family had been pretending that I wasn't a drunk and that Eva's scrapes and bruises happened because she was clumsy, unlucky, or both. When Marcel was born prematurely, I held him in my arms and felt my destructiveness in a new way. I vowed, maudlin as it sounds, to never touch anyone in anger again. I couldn't vow sobriety.

About a year later, my shrink told me I'd learned to 'manage' my liquor, as I'd learned to 'manage' my rage. He facilitated a men's group at the mental health centre. Although I didn't let on to anyone on the outside, I was deeply moved by the men in that group. When we were together I saw myself as a garden bordering many other gardens. Together, we made a kind of skewed, all-male paradise.

Three weeks before his suicide, the day Danny Wassily

stopped me for speeding, I mentioned the group to him. I told him it was a closed group, but that members could bring guests for an evening. If the fit felt good on both sides, the new men were welcomed. I can still see how Danny put up his hands, as if to shield himself from the starkness of my knowing. He said he'd think about it, looked at his ticket book, and then put it away. I'd had four beers at lunch. I shouldn't have been driving. He should have given me a ticket, made me take a breathalyzer test, booked me, but he didn't. We aid and abet one another in our bouts of madness. Our small teacher knew this. During her day our madness may not have been so obvious, but it was there.

She spoke often in our classes of Hitler and the many other tyrants declaimed by our history books. I remember her telling us that dictators and despots appropriated art for their ends and that it would behoove us to get involved in politics while keeping the classics close to our hearts. After we left her classroom, we laughed at her idealistic view of literature. She was "the body" after all, someone we could keep distant, with our ridicule and diminishment, from our feeling life.

The day after Danny's funeral, I sat with Marcel on the back step. Together we looked out at the sun and shadow playing in the back garden. 'I'm glad you're not a cop,' he said. 'They must see terrible stuff.' We leaned into each other. I recall the sound my shirt made as I slid my arm around his small frame. It was the most natural act in the world. From the circle of my arm, he looked up at me. 'It's all right to cry, Dad,' he said. 'Rosie Grier says so.' He was quoting the record his aunt had given him for his birthday, Marlo Thomas and Friends, *Free to Be*.

When I was young, my father pushed me away when I

tried to hug him. He had been a member of the Essex & Kent Scottish Regiment, a World War II vet traumatized by what he'd seen on the beach at Dieppe, but no one was using the word trauma back then. He went away the way I went away when I drank, but he traveled on wisps of memory that violently intruded on his strange afterlife as an insurance salesman. My mother told my brother and me to let him be if we ever forgot ourselves and asked for the commonplace, a trip to the river to fish, a baseball game in the garden.

My brother died of a heroin overdose when we were at Western together. He was supposed to be the doctor in the family. I was supposed to be the guy who wrote about his medical breakthroughs. My father cried and cried at his funeral. I was dry-eyed, drunk, and entirely vicious in my thoughts about the old man. My mother was too, and told me so. 'A whole family,' she said afterward, choking with rage, 'a whole family sacrificed to pretending.' We didn't talk about what we had been pretending. My father died before I understood that I might have talked to him about the things he'd seen, that I might have been his life-line away from that terrible August day in nineteen forty-two and the following years as a prisoner of war if I'd only had the courage to speak of his terrible wounding, to acknowledge his pain and his fear.

The morning after Danny's funeral Eva beckoned to me with the family-room phone and coaxed Marcel into the kitchen to check his lunch box. Mr. Wassily, Danny's father, was on the line. My face grew hot with a shame I didn't understand at the time. 'You said you were his friend,' he shouted. 'His good friend.' I listened, repulsed by his screaming voice and unnerved by my lack of charity. He'd lost a son, after all. 'We were going to ask you for dinner,' he cried. 'We were going to ask you to tell us about Danny when he was young. He wasn't a homo. Just because he wasn't married, that don't make him a homo. You make him sound like a homo. You were his friend. How could you make him sound like that?'

The line went dead before I could speak. I became aware of the way I was clenching the receiver. I had no spit in my mouth. I wanted to put on boxing gloves and beat the living shit out of anyone foolish enough to step into the ring with me. I put my head down. The madness I have felt all of my boy-man's life rubbed up against me like a promiscuous tomcat but instead of lashing out, I stayed put and felt the pain beneath the rage. My heart quieted. My thoughts settled. I am a *garden*, I reminded myself.

Into that place of shadow and light, on the tomcat's silent paws, came my heart's desire. I wished with all my might that Danny Wassily had not shot himself, that he would be waiting for me at the Top Hat, that we could grow old together talking about Maria Tobias, about *Silas Marner*, about skating and writing, about love. As I felt that sorrow, that terrible grief, I understood I was in the presence of another of our teacher's gifts.

Danny Wassily has been dead more than twenty years and my sons are living in Toronto, a little farther away from the shadows cast by the giant both north and south of us because of our unique geographical position. Since retiring from teaching Eva has been fighting with others for legislation banning pesticides for cosmetic use. Her groups are close, very close, to victory. The paper's circulation has increased by forty thousand since the days of my men's column. I am an editor now and must stick to hard news. I write about war, which is also, for the most part, a men's column. It is very hard news indeed.

At unpredictable times, often with my hands on the keyboard in my smoke-free office, I find myself wondering what my perennially forty-year-old teacher would make of the life I am living. I no longer drink or smoke, and I swim three times a week in the university pool. I've been out of therapy for ten years and haven't had the urge to hit anyone for at least that long. Eva and I are steadfast guardians of goodwill toward one another, and Michael and Marcel are people I am proud to know.

Mark waves to me from across the newsroom just as 'Anthem' begins to play on my iPod. Despite her passion for earlier centuries' literature, I believe our teacher would approve of Leonard Cohen. If she were teaching now, she would recognize his rightness for these times and finely tune us to his background stories.

I drop my head. The room beyond my editor's window is abuzz with the current hurly burly. Contentment is such an odd animal with its ragged coat and eviscerated bowels. Mark stops at the threshold of my small office, throws copy on my desk from the open door. He is gone before I can ask him why I might be remembering Danny Wassily today.

———

Jane Buchan, a transplanted Canadian, has lived in Vermont's North East King/Queendom since 2002. She is the author of Under the Moon, *a novel exploring the limiting attitudes to aging. You can learn more about Jane by visiting her website* http://www.winterblooms.net.

DID YOU ENJOY THE BOOK?

MAKE THE AUTHORS HAPPY

LEAVE A REVIEW!

S & H Publishing, Inc. is proud to publish this and other books by many of these very talented authors. Visit us at http://sandhpublishing.com